About the Author

Michelle Vernal is the author of the three other novels. She lives with her hubby Paul and their two boys in the gorgeous wee South Island town of Oxford in New Zealand. It is a place where the cheese scones are superb, and there is always loads more going on than meets the eye.

If you enjoyed *The Traveller's Daughter* then taking the time to say so by leaving a review would be so very much appreciated. I would like to invite you to pop by my Facebook and website too.

www.michellevernalbooks.com
www.facebook.com/michellevernalnovelist

The Traveller's Daughter

MICHELLE VERNAL

A division of HarperCollins*Publishers*
www.harpercollins.co.uk

Harper*Impulse* an imprint of
HarperCollins*Publishers*
1 London Bridge Street
London SE1 9GF

www.harpercollins.co.uk

This paperback edition 2017

First published in Great Britain in ebook format by
Harper*Impulse* 2017

Copyright © Michelle Vernal 2017

Michelle Vernal asserts the moral right to
be identified as the author of this work

A catalogue record for this book
is available from the British Library

ISBN: 9780008226527

For my sister Rachel, for being so brave

PART ONE

Chapter 1

The older the fiddle, the sweeter the tune - Irish Proverb
Rosa's Journal

Kitty, if you are reading this, my darling girl, then we have come full circle. Oh, I've sat down so many times and picked up a pen sure that this time I will write my story down for you. The problem was that I could never find a place in which to start. The thought of writing down all those words, well it would overwhelm me. So then I would think perhaps it would be better if I just got on a train and came to see you instead.

Yes, Rosa old girl, that's what you should do, I'd tell myself. I'd sit you down with a nice, strong cup of tea and give it to you straight. Face to face before it was too late. But then I'd come back to what stopped me writing it all down in the first place. Where should I begin? I think perhaps, at last, I have realized that therein lies the answer, but I'm not ready, not just yet, and so I'll digress.

My past was my Pandora's Box, and while I kept the lid firmly shut on it, I found that I could keep moving forward. Perhaps I shouldn't have done so, but I had my reasons, or at least I thought I did. It's strange the way we humans can twist and turn our actions until they fit inside that box just the way we want them to. I am learning though that this getting older is a funny business and not in a laughing sort of a way either. Its finiteness puts a different perspective on the things we've done, and the choices made when one finally stops and looks back at the complicated pattern they've weaved throughout life.

I imagine that writing this and getting it off my chest will be cathartic for me. There's a nice lady, Sandy something or other who, works at the hospice I will go to when it's time, who told me she thought it was a grand idea. She makes a cup of tea the way it should be made, so I trust her judgment. Life is like a cup of tea; it's all in how you make it.

It was over tea and one of those chocolate biscuits – you know the ones you always loved as a child? – that I told her I wasn't ready to let go. The time wasn't right, not when I still had things sitting so heavy on my heart. She patted my hand and told me that some people find it easier to write down what needs to be said. It's easier to be honest with the written word.

She's a woman of good sense, so that's what I have decided to do because this time I shall just have to get on with it. I don't have the luxury of procrastination any longer. Sandy's a kind soul and a brave one too, volunteering the way she does at the hospice, and the next time I popped my head in the door to see her she had this book for me. She knows I love roses, so she chose the cover of it well. I think it makes it look a bit more special, like something you might want to keep hold of. She told me I had no excuses to leave anything left unsaid now. That's another thing about Sandy; she doesn't mince her words, and she tells you it like it is. I like that about her because what's the point in someone dressing things up and saying, 'sure, it will all be fine' when you know full well it won't be.

Yes, she's a fine woman, and I am glad she will be there holding my hand when my time comes. She's promised me that, and I know you will feel it should have been you there with me. I hope when you've read all that I have to say though you'll understand why I couldn't do that to you. Know this though Kitty: while Sandy will have been of great comfort to me at the end, my thoughts will have been with you. Mothers hold their children's hands for just a little while and their hearts forever.

I think it will be the cleansing of a troubled soul that lost its faith a long time ago, this business of sitting here putting my story down on paper. I'm hoping that in doing so, I will finally be able to let go of the past that has never been very far behind me. For you though my lovely girl, hearing what I have to say might be similar to a child finding out they are adopted years after the event. It might seem like a betrayal of sorts, and perhaps, as I now wonder, you might think that it was an unnecessary secret to have kept from you. I couldn't go back, though, and I knew if I told you where I came from, you would want us both to do just that.

Chapter 2

A nod is as good as a wink to a blind horse – Irish Proverb
Kitty

"Oh, Mum, who were you?" Kitty Sorenson whispered out loud to the empty room as she stared at the Facebook message blinking back at her from her phone. Only a moment before she had been thinking that she would have to get around to changing her profile picture. The selfie had been posted, as all good selfies too often are, after a few wines one evening. She'd taken it last year before the proverbial shit had hit the fan. Her grin was huge. She had been happy that day; she thought with a pang conjuring up the carefree feeling of warming up to dance the night away.

It felt like a lifetime ago now. If anyone had told her as she'd twirled to the music that night what lay ahead for her and Damien, she would have told them they were bonkers. Nor would she have believed that she would be sitting here at her mother's house at 66 Edgewater Lane on this gloomy afternoon. She was waiting to hear from the Estate Agent handling the property's sale, and the shadows were beginning to stretch long.

The message had pinged its arrival and startled her from her thoughts. She had been wondering how Yasmin was getting on without her at the market. She had assumed the message would be from the agent, Mr Baintree because a quick glance at the time confirmed that the auction should be just about done and dusted by now. She had contacted the firm when her mother's estate had been wound up. The oily proprietor, the one and the same Mr Baintree had rubbed his hands together at her listing. He had assured her that with its stone's throw location from the café lifestyle of Wigan Pier, the house would fetch a pretty penny. She had raised an eyebrow at that. A stone's throw if you had an arm on you like a champion discus thrower perhaps, but still, if that was how he chose to market the property then who was she to interfere?

The two-up two-down where her mother had lived up until her death five months ago was quite at home in the sea of red brick that made up the old part of the town of Wigan in the north of England. Rosa had mumbled something about the house being low-maintenance and close to the town centre when she'd bought it. Kitty could tell from her tone that she knew full well her daughter wouldn't like it. Still, it wasn't her that had to live in it, she'd told herself when she'd come to visit. It was the third house in four years her mother had moved into since Kitty's father had died. She hadn't been seeking her daughter's approval of it, though, and she didn't get it because Kitty had thought this latest house with its modern renovations, characterless.

It hadn't felt like a house her mother should be in. It didn't suit her or her ways. Rosa needed a house that was quirky and full of character. A house like Rose Cottage stuffed with books and treasures that made it a home. Okay, so Kitty got that with her illness, her mother had wanted something low-maintenance and close to the shops. Of course, when she'd been busy passing judgment on Edgewater Lane she hadn't known how ill her mum was. Sitting here now, though, she couldn't conjure up any real sense of Rosa ever having lived here. It wasn't just because her mother, ever mindful of not making Kitty's life harder, had packed up all her belongings in anticipation of this. She'd sent all her worldly goods except for a box of treasured photographs and her engagement and wedding rings to charity before she'd moved into a local hospice. There, it transpired later, she was on good terms with a woman called Sandy, who was by her side instead of her only child when she slipped away.

Kitty twisted the rings she now wore on the middle finger of her left hand, an understated gold band and the solitaire diamond engagement ring that shone blue in certain lights. She knew Rosa had done things the way she'd done them because she hadn't wanted to burden her by telling her she was nearing the end. Not when Kitty had been so desperately trying to pick up the pieces of her life and soldier on down in London. Still, it wasn't fair leaving her like that without giving her the chance to say goodbye and to tell Rosa that she loved her.

Rosa hadn't even had a funeral service – choosing instead to be cremated like one of those people with no known family or money. Kitty had collected the ashes after the event; stored in a sealed, nondescript urn from the hospice where she had died. She had met with Sandy, who, as much as she hadn't wanted to admit it to herself, had been very nice. She'd made her a cup of tea and opened a packet of chocolate biscuits. Then, resting her hand on Kitty's, she told her that her mother's death had been a good one. She had slipped away peacefully and free of pain.

Kitty had wanted to scream at her that it couldn't possibly be a good death because her mother was only sixty-five years old. It was an unfair death; that's what it bloody well was. She hadn't said a word though because there was something so calming and dignified about Sandy with her soft and soothing voice. She could see why her mother had wanted a woman like her by her bedside.

Sandy informed her that just as she'd promised Rosa she would, she had held her mother's hand until the end. But it should have been me, Kitty said silently removing her hand from beneath this stranger's. As if reading her thoughts, the older woman had said in that same calming tone that sometimes people didn't want their loved ones' last memory to be of them dying. By not asking her to be with her in her final hours, it didn't mean her mother loved her any less. Kitty had felt uncomfortable then thinking about her mother confiding in this woman and had put the biscuit back on the plate. She had picked up the urn and clasping it to her chest made her excuses to leave.

It wasn't fair that her mother kept her impending death from her, not when there was so much unsaid between them, but then she shouldn't have been surprised. Rosa had spent Kitty's whole life keeping things from her; she thought, her eyes sweeping the room. It was a soulless space; there was no essence of her mother etched into its walls as there had been at Rose Cottage.

This house lacked the warm, homely feel of the semi-rural property in which she had grown up on the outskirts of Preston. It's headily-scented rose garden a riot of colour in summertime had given the cottage its name and Kitty been heartbroken when her mother decided to sell it shortly after her father's death. She hadn't sought her daughter's approval then either. It still rankled, she realized, feeling simultaneously guilty for the anger that surged even now with her mother gone because if Rosa had held onto the cottage, then she wouldn't feel so alone. Rose Cottage had been her home too. She knew that were she sitting in its cosy, familiar living room instead of this bland space, then she would still feel she had a part of her mother and father with her.

She had just wanted Mr Baintree to call and tell her the deal was done. To her mind once the proceeds of the sale were sitting in her bank account this final phase of winding up her mother's affairs would be complete. Then she could begin to figure out how she was going to move forward now that she was officially orphaned. She'd heard it said somewhere at some time that when you lost both your parents, you truly knew what it was to feel grown up. Kitty sighed for the umpteenth time that afternoon; she didn't feel grown up, just awfully alone.

Now she squeezed her eyes shut hoping that when she opened them, she'd find that she had just suffered a bizarre hallucinatory episode. One brought on by her early morning start. She would find that the message was in fact just a nice, normal chatty one from Yasmin.

She had been desperate to know how Yas's morning had gone at the Broadway Market. Had she sold out of cakes like Kitty did most Saturdays? Had the sweet Justin Bieber look-a-like with the bit of fluff on his chin managed to win his girlfriend back with her favourite Vanilla Kisses cupcake that he had bought for her last week? He'd promised he would come back and tell her how he had gotten on as she had placed the cake in one of the pretty pink boxes she'd picked up for a steal from the Pound Shop. What about the lovely old dear who always bought two of Kitty's favourite Chocolate Dream cupcakes? One for her and one for her older sister who was riddled with arthritis. It was their Saturday afternoon treat. How was she doing? She would have liked to have known because the damp weather they'd had these last few mornings wouldn't be doing the sister's bones any good. Had she been there she would have given the old dear her cakes on the house this week.

Instead, she had gotten this, a message from someone claiming to be a French photographer called Christian Beauvau. What he was asking of her just didn't make sense, she thought, reading through his message once more. She ignored the paper clip attachment at the bottom of it tossing her phone to one side as though it had scalded her. She didn't know how many minutes passed as she sat in the ever increasing murk of the room. There were no sounds other than the rain hitting the glass and the swish of tyres through puddles on the slick road outside.

Oh stop being ridiculous Kitty, she told herself mustering up the courage to read through the message one more time. She picked up her phone and scrolled down not knowing why she was surprised that the words were still the same as they had been the first and second times she'd skimmed over them. It still didn't make any sense, and she wondered if perhaps it were some elaborate hoax. Was this Christian person a fraudster who, instead of being from Paris as he'd stated in his message, was really from some obscure African country? Perhaps he was trying to wheedle confidential information out of her in a very roundabout way so he could raid her bank account? If that were the case, he'd be best to wait until tomorrow when there'd hopefully be some money in it; she thought chewing her thumbnail.

Tiny flakes of the Coral Sunrise polish she had pinched off Yasmin settled on her tongue, and she thought of how her friend had told her off for this bad habit just the other day. She'd threatened to buy some of that awful smelly stuff to paint her nails like you did to stop children sucking their thumbs. Wiping the orange flakes on the back of her hand she was glad neither of her flatmates was present to tell her off. Mind you Piggy Paula with her unsavoury habits was hardly in a position to judge. Yasmin, however, would know what she should do about this strange request. She'd ring her, she decided, feeling pleased she was taking some affirmative action as she hit speed dial.

"Kitty? I am at the gym, what do you want?" A strained voice yelled upon answering after a few short rings.

In the background, Kitty could hear the fast beat of an old nineties song. She recognized the dance hit, *What is Love?* The lyrics ran through her mind as she shouted, "Yas, you need to stop doing squats or rolling around on a Swiss ball or whatever it is you are doing. Pay attention to what I am going to tell you, okay?" Only Yas would have a pocket for her phone in amongst all her Lycra sports gear she thought. Mind you, only Yasmin was enough of a gym bunny to go and do a workout after the crazy time she'd risen that morning.

"Okay chill out, Kitty." Her breath was coming in short, rapid bursts. "I know it must be weird being at your mum's old house for the last time, but do you remember those yoga poses I showed you? Well, you need to go and salute the sun or get into the downward dog pose or something because it will calm you down."

"There is no bloody sun; it's drizzling and it's not that—"

Yasmin was on a roll, though. "Well, you don't need to stress about things here because the morning sped by and yes, your regulars did miss you. A young lad bought two Vanilla Kisses and said to tell you he's back on with his girl. He reckons whatever your secret ingredient is it's better than oysters. He had a right swagger in his step."

Kitty frowned; she hoped her cakes weren't encouraging underage shenanigans – he only looked to be sixteen. "Good, that's great, but Yas listen—"

"And I'd sold out completely by midday, so I packed up and came to the gym. I needed to after all that icing I licked off the spoon this morning. I knew if I went back to the flat I'd go straight to sleep and not wake up until the wee hours of Sunday morning. That's if Paula didn't decide to draw her blinds and shut the bedroom door for another of her Saturday afternoon sessions with that slimy little git, Steve, she's been seeing." There was a gagging sound down the phone. "Yuck, the thought of it."

"Yas, would you shut up for a minute and let me talk!"

"Alright, alright hang on, one, two, three, clench and release."

Kitty rolled her eyes; she didn't want to know what kind of exercise her friend was doing.

"One, two, three, clench and release – all done, thank God. I won't be able to walk tomorrow after that last lot. Hang on while I grab a drink."

Kitty held the phone away from her ear but could still hear the glug, glugging noise that followed.

"That's better. It's important to keep hydrated with good old H20 you know. Give me one more sec and I'm all yours."

When she came back on the phone, Kitty couldn't hear the pounding beat in the background anymore just the sound of running water.

"I'm in the changing room. So come on then, spill."

"I have just gotten the most out there Facebook message."

"Delete it; there're all sorts of weirdo's in cyberspace. I once had a complete random, some chicken farmer from Devon sent me a friend request. I mean it's not as though Facebook is a dating app and more to the point I don't even like eggs."

Kitty shook her head.

"No, not weird like that. Just listen, this French photographer called Christian something or other French-sounding says that he took a photograph that became quite famous of my mother with her boyfriend. Who, by the way, was not my dad but some guy called Michael, in a French town back in 1965. He reckons *Tres Belle*, you know the fashion magazine—"

There was a loud squeal, and Kitty held the phone away from her ear. "Oh, I love *Tres Belle*! Watch this space because one day my designs are going to be all through its pages."

"I don't doubt it, but for now the magazine has commissioned this Christian fella to recreate the same scene in the photo he took back in 1965. It was called *Midsummer Lovers* which is kind of a gross title for a photograph with my mum in it. He wants me to pose for it along with the nephew of mum's old boyfriend to mark the fiftieth anniversary of the original being taken."

"What? Repeat all that and slower this time? Much slower."

Kitty repeated what she had just said, and there was a moment's silence as Yasmin processed what she'd been told. "Okay, so firstly I'm thinking how did this French guy find you and secondly, what was your mum doing in France in 1965? I thought she was Irish."

"She was, though she'd spent the best part of her life here so in a way she was more English than Irish. She never lost her accent, though, and she was always saying these mad Irish things like it's no use boiling your cabbage twice. I have no idea what she was doing in France or who this Michael was either." Kitty did a quick mental calculation. "She'd have only been about sixteen in 1965. Christ, if I'd swanned off to the Continent with a boyfriend at that age she would have killed me! She never mentioned anything about having spent time in France; my parents were Majorca package holiday devotees." Kitty frowned, picking a bit of carpet fluff off the dark denim of her jeans. "I've told you how Mum's life prior to meeting Dad was a closed book. Anything before the age of nineteen was a no-go zone that she refused to talk about, no matter how many times I asked her to. She'd just tell me her childhood was uneventful so therefore it was not worth talking about."

"Yeah you've told me, it's well weird that." Yasmin's voice was muffled, and Kitty pictured her cradling the phone between her chin and shoulder as she undid her laces.

"You didn't know my mum, she wasn't weird, just as stubborn as they come and if she made her mind up about something, then that was it, end of story."

"Still, you don't believe all that crap about her childhood being uneventful, do you because otherwise why all the secrecy?" Kitty could hear Yasmin unlocking her locker. Probably fishing her bag out of it with her spare hand. Kitty's mother had been an enigma, unlike Yasmin's mum with her hard face and dodgy back that got noticeably worse whenever she'd dragged her brood into the local benefits office to sign on for the sickness.

Yasmin's childhood had been so very different to Kitty's quiet and civilised upbringing. She'd grown up in a council flat fit to burst with half-brothers and sisters in Hatfield. There hadn't been much in the way of money, but there was plenty in the way of noise. Their reasons for coming to London were so very different too. Yasmin's had been to escape that noise for a while. She wanted to make her way in the world far away from the council estate existence she'd always known. Kitty's had been to put as much distance as she could between herself and her ex, Damien, who lived in a posh Manchester apartment.

14

Both women had their dreams, though, and this was the common denominator that brought them together and sealed their friendship. Kitty's was to open her cupcake café, and Yasmin's was working towards designing her clothing label. One day, she would often say, the High Street stores she loved to browse, fingering the newest fabrics and imagining how she would improve the latest looks, would be stocking her brand. The models would be wearing her signature twist on the rockabilly look as they showed off her designs at London Fashion Week. They would strut their stuff down the catwalk to the tune of her all-time favourite performer, Elvis, after which they would spend their morning tea breaks at Kitty's gorgeous little café. Slamming the locker door shut before sitting down on the bench, Yasmin asked, "Have you seen it, this photograph I mean?"

"No."

"Didn't he attach it?"

"He did, I just haven't opened it yet."

"Why the hell not?"

Kitty cringed. "Don't shout, Yas and I haven't opened it because I am scared. This is the first real clue to my mother's past I have ever had."

"All the more reason you need to open it!"

"I know, I want to, I just can't seem to make myself do it. I wish you were here with me, and I wish I could bake. Baking always calms me down."

"Right, Kitty Sorenson, listen to me! Now is not the time to be thinking about cakes." Yasmin adopted the tone she used with her little brothers and sisters when they were awkward little toads. "You, my girl, are going to hang up this call, and then you are going to count to three, and when you get to number three you are going to open that attachment. Got it?"

"But—"

"No buts. I said got it?"

"Got it."

"And then when you have done that you are going to forward the picture to me for a sticky beak. Right?"

"Right."

"Right then, hit the red button."

Kitty disconnected the call and counted to three.

Chapter 3

A Turkey never voted for an early Christmas – Irish Proverb

Kitty chewed her bottom lip as she stared at the black and white photograph filling the small screen. Her eyes alighted instantly on the young girl pictured, and she barely registered the man next to her. It was like looking at a picture of herself as a teenager and at a stranger both at the same time. The difference being that her go-to outfit at sixteen had been a black T-shirt, denim mini and leggings, her hair had been straightened with almost religious regularity to resemble Jennifer Aniston's do of the day. This girl in the photo, her mother, albeit a much younger and softer version than any she'd ever known, was dressed in a demure, feminine style.

Her look was that of Audrey Hepburn. Rosa was wearing a white, boat necked dress with puffed sleeves, cinched waist and a full skirt; her shoes were flat sandals. Her blonde hair was pulled up into a high ponytail, and she was sporting a blunt fringe that was sitting just above startlingly thick and dark eyebrows at odds with her fair hair. They were Kitty's eyebrows, except her mother's were obviously unfamiliar with tweezers back then, and as for that fringe, she cringed. It suited the times, but the length was one that would have seen her suing Tamsin at *'Your Style'* who cut her hair whenever it got to the driving her bonkers length.

She continued to soak in the photograph absorbing not the background scene with its hazy stone archway and buildings but rather the look on her mother's face. She was gazing up at the man next to her with a broad smile on her face obviously laughing at something he had just said. It was the naked longing in her eyes that shocked Kitty, though. His brooding, good looks were half hidden beneath a head full of thick, slightly too long dark curls as he looked down at Rosa. He was dressed in a plain shirt, half tucked into a pair of loose fitting, dark trousers. His sleeves were rolled up and on his feet he had a pair of boots that looked like they had seen better days. Strong worker's hands gripped the wide, handlebars of an old-fashioned bike, its big wheels denoting its era.

The light surrounding the couple in the picture was dappled by sunshine peeping through the leafy arbour they were wandering beneath. This, their obviously private moment had been captured forever in a photograph that had the title *Midsummer Lovers* scrawled across the bottom left-hand corner of it. Her mother's face was positively luminous Kitty realized, unable to tear her eyes away from the picture. "Oh, Mum," she whispered aloud to the empty room for the second time that afternoon. It struck her then that she had never seen her mother look at her father the way she was looking at this stranger in the photo. Was that kind of blatant adoration the sole domain of the very young, she wondered, knowing that nobody who had ever been hurt or let down would ever be able to love with such an obvious unguardedness. It had been a long time since she had looked at anyone with that kind of heart on your sleeve openness and after Damien, she doubted she ever would again.

"What's your story, Rosa?" Kitty closed her eyes. It was too much to take in. All these years of not knowing and now this photograph. It was a clue to her mother's past, and yet at the same time, it told her absolutely nothing. All she knew now, was that at sixteen, she had been so bold as to be in some small town in France with a bloke with whom she was clearly besotted. Did she even want to know the story behind this picture? Her mother obviously had her reasons for never talking about the first nineteen years of her life.

As a child, Kitty had been curious but not bothered about what her mother had done before she'd married and before she had entered her life. For one thing, she simply could not imagine any other existence of importance for Rosa than that of being her mother and her father's wife. That had changed though when the hormones had come home to roost, and she had begun to resent the secrecy behind Rosa's past. As a teenager, she'd desperately wanted to know her maternal history. She'd imagined the worst, no matter how many times her mother assured her there were no skeletons hidden away in her closet. Mean Nuns hadn't reared her in a cold stone convent or anything like that; it was just a past that was not worth revisiting. This vague, hand sweeping reply had not satisfied Kitty in the slightest, but her mother would not be swayed to confide in her nor would her father whom she could normally twist around her little finger. Eventually, she ran out of steam and had to let it go, exhausted from her years of pent-up teenage frustration.

Now as a woman in her early thirties, Kitty's romantic notions of where her mother had come from had faded to give way to thoughts that perhaps she had been abused as a child. For all Rosa's vague hand sweeping and bravado when the topic of her childhood was raised, she couldn't help but think perhaps she had been the daughter of a poor Magdalene girl. Despite what she said, maybe she'd spent her early years slaving in the laundry of an Irish convent. It had happened to others after all. Perhaps this was why she wouldn't speak of her childhood. She simply did not know, and so she had come to nurture a quiet acceptance that her mother hadn't just been her mother, she had been a person with a right to privacy. She couldn't help but think, though, that with Rosa having passed away the rules must now have changed.

A conversation she'd held with Rosa as a child began to run through her head as though she had just pushed play on an old video recorder. The image of them both in the kitchen of Rose Cottage was vivid. She could see in her mind's eye that the bay window, a focal point of the room, was fogged up with steam from the sink full of dishes before which her mother stood. It blocked her view out to their sprawling garden that as a child had seemed to go on forever. This illusion she knew was due to the low stone wall that encased the bottom of their garden. On the other side of the wall were fields that in summer glowed gold with rapeseed and in winter wore a snowy eiderdown. For the most part, their home with its front garden full of vibrant blooms in the summer and twiggy branches that would tap at the window in winter had been a happy one.

"Tracey at school said that her mum was an air hostess before she met Mr Hennessy. Her plane used to stop in places like Disneyland," Kitty said this from where she was sitting up at the table; school bag abandoned at her feet while she waited for the toaster to pop. Her mother was dressed casually; her glasses pushed up on the top of her head which meant she had been studying, *again*. She was always doing some course; textbooks would be strewn across the kitchen table and swept away as Kitty flung the back door open home from school.

"It's a gift to be able to learn, Kitty," she'd say, stacking the thick tomes on the sideboard.

Kitty thought that was a dumb thing to say because the last thing she would do when she was finally old enough to leave school was more homework. And besides, her mum never actually did anything with all that stuff she was learning about.

"That's nice for Mrs Hennessy I bet she enjoyed meeting Mickey and Minnie." Rosa's tongue in cheek reply came as she plunged her hands into the hot water and began to scrub at the dishes left over from breakfast and lunch. She had meant to tackle them well before Kitty got home. She'd gotten side-tracked again by picking up the book she was in the middle of and before she'd known it she'd heard the familiar sound of the front door banging shut. It announced her daughter's arrival home for the day. Her answer sailed right over the top of nine-year-old Kitty's head. She was intent on retrieving the freshly browned bread from the toaster and slathering it in butter. "You know madam if you ate properly at lunchtime you wouldn't be so hungry when you get home. It's no wonder you pick at your dinner when you're stuffing yourself full of toast at this time of the day."

"But I'm hungry after school not at school." Kitty had replied perfectly logically in her opinion, her chest puffing up self-right-eously as she added, "And Tracey doesn't have to sit at the table until she's cleaned her plate up. If she doesn't like something, her mummy says she can give it to the dog. I'd rather play with my friends than eat a yucky old school dinner any day." Her bottom lip jutted out; the conversation was not going the way she'd planned. She had thought that by telling her mother what Mrs Hennessy used to do her mum might have decided to tell her what it was she had done before she married her dad. She did not want to be reminded of the stinky stuff that had been plopped on her plate at lunch time. Or the unfair way in which she was never allowed to leave anything on her dinner plate, not even peas, and she hated peas, thank you very much.

Sitting there staring at her mother's back as she bit into her toast, butter dribbling down her chin, her eyes widened as a thought popped into her head. Maybe she had been a princess once upon a time. She was pretty enough to have been one when she took her glasses off and brushed her hair properly.

Maybe, her evil stepmother the Queen had been mean to her, but then daddy had rescued her, and the stepmother had been so angry that she waved her wand and cast a spell. Just like in

Sleeping Beauty, and if her mother ever spoke of having once been a princess she'd fall asleep for a hundred years! Her mother dried her hands and left the dishes to drain. She sat down at the table with the cup of tea she'd abandoned on hearing her daughter come in. Kitty wondered if it was normal behaviour for princesses to dunk biscuits in their tea.

"Your friends aren't going anywhere Kitty, and you need to eat the meal provided at school if you're to be able to pay attention in your afternoon lessons. Sure, how can you expect that poor brain of yours to concentrate on learning when it's being distracted by your rumbling tummy? As the old cock crows, the young cock learns."

Kitty frowned; she hated it when her mum spoke in riddles. She looked at the soggy biscuit she was about to pop in her mouth, it was only a plain old digestive, not the chocolate ones she liked. Still, she wondered what her chances of both toast and a biscuit before dinner were. "It was only boring old maths this afternoon," she answered, deciding the odds probably weren't very good. She wished, as she finished her toast, that next time her mother did the shopping she would buy some of that yummy chocolate spread stuff. Tracey said she got to have that on her toast every single morning. As she chewed, she began to ponder how she could swing the conversation back round to where she wanted it to be when her mother interrupted her plotting.

"It's not boring old maths and boring is a word that only boring people use. Maths is very interesting when you pay attention because we use it for all sorts of everyday reasons."

Kitty had raised a sceptical eyebrow at her the way she had seen Tracey do to Mrs Chalmers this morning when the teacher had informed her class that dolphins sleep with one eye open. It had been such a cool thing to do but then that was because Tracey was so cool. She paused in her chewing to send up a silent prayer that she would be invited to the social event of the school year, Tracey's tenth birthday. She'd given Tracey her best Strawberry

Shortcake rubber, so she was confident that guaranteed her an invite.

"Don't give me that look, young lady, you're not a teenager yet, and it's true you know, you need maths for all sorts of things like telling the time and handling money. A penny gets another penny. Sure, when you work out how much of your pocket money you are going to save and how much you are going to put aside for sweets you're doing maths."

Kitty scowled. "I knew you would mention saving." Her mother was big on drumming the importance of saving into her. It was right up there with the importance of paying attention in class because both, she told her daughter regularly, would allow her to be independent when she was older.

"Alright then here's another example, you need maths to be able to bake."

"No you don't, you just use that measuring thingy for the sugar and an egg. Oh and usually you add some flour too."

"Okay, Little Miss I Know Everything, when you have finished your toast how about you and I make some of those cupcakes your daddy is so fond of? Then you will see what I am talking about."

"Can I lick the bowl?"

"I suppose so, though you'll never eat your dinner."

"I will if it's something yummy."

Having washed her hands, Kitty donned an oversized pinny that her mother wrapped around her waist twice before standing on tiptoes to stare at the open cookbook. That was the afternoon she learnt how to read a recipe as she made her first batch of cupcakes. Her mother oversaw the proceedings watching as she followed the instructions to cream the carefully measured butter, sugar and vanilla until it was light and fluffy before cracking an egg into the mix. She'd turned the handle on the old fashioned beater until her arm felt like it was going to drop off and was relieved when her mother said it was time to measure the flour and baking powder out. Sifting was much easier than beating, she'd decided, tapping the side of the sieve until it was empty and a mountain of white sat on top of the wet mix. Tired of standing on tippy-toes, she'd pulled a chair in from the dining table and kneeled up on it. She'd watched with her chin resting on her clasped hands, elbows on the bench as her mother demonstrated how to fold the dry ingredients into the batter adding a bit of milk as she went.

"See it needs to be a dropping consistency like this."

Kitty was transfixed as the mixture plopped back into the bowl. She was hoping there would be plenty left in it for her to scrape up with her finger once the cakes were in the oven. It was time her mother said to spoon the mixture into the paper cases lining the patty tin.

"Too much in that one Kitty, three-quarters full. Aha!" she clapped her hands. "There do you see what I mean? That was a fraction right there."

At nine years of age, Kitty was not too old to concede that her mother was right, and she decided tomorrow she would try not to drift off when Mrs Chalmers made them chant their times tables. Fifteen minutes later when she donned the oven gloves and pulled the plump cakes from the oven, she puffed up with pride. She couldn't wait until her daddy got home from work so she could tell him she had baked the cakes all by herself. "Can I taste test one, please?"

"I suppose so, sure as a rule of thumb a good cook should always taste what she makes. Food is a good workhorse."

Kitty couldn't believe her luck. She peeled the paper off a little hot cake and leaving half the mix stuck to the wrapper, popped it in her mouth. That was the moment that her life-long love of baking had been born.

The thing with baking was that at the fundamental core of a good batch of anything there was the need for a reliable recipe. Despite this, and no matter how measured and precise her ingredients were, now and then something would go wrong with the mix, and her cakes wouldn't rise. It was the same with life Kitty thought as her eyes refocused on the photograph this Christian Beauvau person had attached to his message. For the most part, each day ticked along much like the one before but now and then something would be tossed into the mix and it would test her ability to rise to the occasion.

She shivered, the house had that unlived in temperature that seeps through to your bones she thought as her phone beeped another text's arrival. Closing the photograph, a quick glance revealed the message to be from Mr Baintree, her stomach flip-flopped and despite her nerves at what he might have to tell her, she was glad of the distraction. Crossing her fingers and hoping it was good news she scrolled down and breathed a sigh of relief, the auction had closed four thousand pounds above reserve! He finished his message by saying he would meet her back at his office in an hour. Kitty's face broke into a grin; it had not been a wasted journey. She was buoyed by the news and decided she'd rather wait in the agency's warm reception area than sitting here freezing.

Quickly flicking back to Christian Beauvau's message, she forwarded it through to Yasmin adding the good news regarding the house's sale. Let Yas mull it over, she decided. She'd talk to her later about what she should do. Stuffing her phone back in her bag, she got to her feet. As she picked up her wheelie case and walked down the hallway, she realized she had never managed to swing that long ago conversation with her mother back around to what it was she used to do.

Chapter 4

A trout in the pot is better than a salmon in the sea – Irish Proverb

Kitty shut the front door of the house that no longer belonged to her mother, locking it before stuffing the key in her jacket pocket. She glanced up at the grey sky with a frown. She wished she'd packed a waterproof jacket instead of the lightweight belted one she was wearing. Stealing herself against the steady drizzle, she didn't look back as she set off down the road toward the offices of Baintree & Co.

Her feet were clad in her usual choice of thoroughly unsuitable heels, and she stepped around the freshly formed puddles. She momentarily wished she had a bit more sense when it came to footwear but ever since she'd had a say in the matter, she'd always opted for pretty over practical. Still, she comforted herself, at least she didn't have far to walk, and as she tottered down the empty footpath, her mind drifted back over how she'd come to be here.

The letter had arrived from the firm of solicitors, whom her mother had been with for as long as Kitty could remember, four weeks ago. In her opinion, Rosa had single-handedly kept them in business these last few years with her conveyancing, not to mention her final bit of business, dying. It held no surprises, apart from what she thought was an odd request on her mother's part, that Kitty keep her ashes for at least six months before scattering them. Apart from that, her affairs had all been in order.

Rosa's will was quite straightforward with no beneficiaries other than Kitty, and so the house at Edgewater Lane was hers to do with as she wished. She hadn't bothered to glance at the statement attached, knowing the firm's bill had been paid from her mother's bank account. The account was now closed, and the balance was to be transferred to her account. It was the formality and finality of the letter that made her eyes burn with threatened tears. She'd sat there for an age in the dip of the old couch in the London flat she shared with Yasmin and Paula feeling utterly lost.

She and Yasmin had only let the room to Paula for two reasons. Number one, being that the third bedroom was a box room so small that no one else had been keen to take it upon viewing it. The second reason was the smell; not everybody could stomach the permanent smell of curry that hovered in the air thanks to the flat's upstairs location over a Bangladeshi takeaway.

Their flat was located in the East End near the old Spitalfields Market and Brick Lane, which was known these days as London's Curry Capital and had long been nicknamed Bangla Town. Kitty loved the little pocket of East London she had run away to just on a year ago, determined to put as much distance between herself and Damien as she could manage. You could almost smell the history seeping from the bricks; that's if you managed to block the smell of curry!

She liked to imagine the drama that had been played out on the streets as she wandered around them and to know she was now part of that thread work made her feel special. Sometimes she'd pause down bustling Brick Lane and imagine she could hear the call of the Costermongers' selling their fruit and veg. Once she had gotten herself in a right stew hot footing it home as she conjured up the darker side of the East End's infamous past, Jack the Ripper. She could sense a shadow lurking behind her and had picked up her pace so that she'd been puffing by the time she burst in through the front door of her flat.

"What's up with you? You look like you've seen a ghost." Yasmin had stated as Kitty locked the door behind her before swinging round to face her friend, wild-eyed.

"Nothing, I've got an overactive imagination that's all, my mum always said so, but I think I might need a drink." She filled Yasmin in on her journey home, deciding not to add that she genuinely had sensed a darkness that had spooked her. She got these little feelings from time to time, like when things had come to a head with Damien. She had felt something coming. When she sat back night after night over the following weeks torturing herself by examining every tiny detail of their breakup, there had been no warning signs, though. Nothing apart from the strangest sense of darkness and impending trouble. It had been there during her mother's final days too, although at the time she hadn't known she was dying. She'd found out after the event. A fat lot of good it was having a sixth sense when she had no idea what it meant.

There were other feelings too, such as knowing instinctively who was on the other end of the phone, or sensing who was at the door without answering it. Silly stuff really, and she had asked Rosa about it once. Kitty had thought at the time that her reaction had been most peculiar but like a lot of things her mother had chosen not to elaborate.

As for the encroaching darkness, these days it didn't frighten her because it had already brought the worst that could happen with it. She had broken up with Damien and lost her mother all within a year. For the here and now, she was trying so hard just to focus on the positives. So it was lucky that her passion in life was food. Most days the smell of spices wafting up the stairwell was enough to make your eyes water!

She shared waitressing shifts with Yasmin at Bruno's, a trendy little Italian Eatery on nearby Ashwin Street. Its main claim to fame was that a café just a few doors up had been tipped by Vogue magazine as the coolest place in Britain to dine. Bruno's was determined to bask in its glory. Kitty didn't mind. The busier work was, the better, in her opinion because it kept not just her body but her mind busy and she needed all the distraction she could get.

Of course, she didn't plan on waitressing forever. Once the money from the sale of Edgewater Lane was in her bank account, there would be nothing stopping her from pursuing her dream of opening her very own cupcake café. Nothing stopping her, except for a chronic fear of failure that was.

Kitty wasn't a trained baker or chef nor did she want to be. She had been there and tried that. It had seen her spend a year living on minimum wage in exchange for being shouted at by a Gordon Ramsey lookalike. The experience had well and truly put her off the idea. She had packed in her apprenticeship in Edinburgh and hot-footed it down to a secretarial job in Manchester, instead deciding it was high time she had a bit of money in her pockets and fun to boot. The decision to move in with her girlfriends in the North's big smoke and take a position typing in an architect's firm had been one that her mother had not approved of. Kitty had told her in no uncertain terms though that it was her life, and she would do with it what she wanted.

She was the first to hold her hand up and say that she found it hard to follow instructions, especially if they were barked at her. She found it hard to stick at things too because her feet got itchy, and she felt the need to move on, but despite her change of course she had never stopped loving baking. She had known though that, if she'd seen her apprenticeship through to the end, bit by bit her love for it would have been snuffed out.

Now in a round about way, until she opened her café she had come back to her first love by selling her cakes at the market on Saturday mornings. There was something so intrinsically comforting in the measuring of ingredients, the amounts of which never changed. As for the sweet and tempting result, well that was pure satisfaction. That was why she didn't mind the early starts on those cold Saturday mornings. Bundled up in her coat with her woolly hat pulled down well over her ears, she would sell her cakes at the Broadway Market in Hackney. All of her cakes were made with love, and Kitty liked to think it was this that made them that little bit extra special.

The unsociable hours she waitressed along with her early Saturday starts suited her just fine. She had Yas for company, and after the disaster that was Damien, well the less time she had on her hands for repeating that epic catastrophe, the better. She was quite happy to whip up her sweet treats at the ungodly time of three o'clock in the morning in readiness for sale at her popular stall. Or at least she was after she'd had a strong cup of coffee. It filled her with a certain pride as she bantered with the punters to know that she was standing in the shadow of the East End's famous Barrow boys. They had plied their trade with their unique salesman patter.

Her takings supplemented her meagre earnings from Bruno's enabling her to scrape by, but it certainly wasn't the money that kept her baking her little cakes. She knew too that the latest fad was to frown upon sugar but hadn't those sugar free converts ever heard the phrase, 'everything in moderation'? That was her motto. She'd even heard mutterings that cupcakes were passé and that it was all about the sickly sweet macaron these days, but Kitty wasn't swayed. In her opinion there was something so marvellous about the look of pleasure on a customer's face when they bit into one of her cakes, swirled high with a piped frosting finish. It reaffirmed her belief. Sugar might be bad for the waist-line, but it was oh-so-good for the soul!

Now, Kitty yawned as she spied the row of shops at the end of the road she had just turned onto. Baintree & Co.'s office sat in the middle of them with a Cancer Research Shop somewhat aptly, given the reason for her selling her mother's house, on one side of it. There was a travel agents on the other. Her eyes watered, and her body ached with weariness as she tottered along dragging her case behind her. The couple of hours' sleep she'd grabbed before her usual ungodly Saturday morning start had been fractured. The temptation to ignore her alarm when it shrilled had been strong. She knew, though, that if she was going to get her cakes baked and iced as well as catch the first train up to Wigan, then she needed to get up and get moving.

It was a nuisance having to go all that way just to sign off the last of the paperwork for the house and to hand the key over but needs must. It was simpler than trying to arrange it all by proxy. So, she'd switched the alarm off and grudgingly thrown on the closest thing to hand, a T-shirt and her jeans before padding through to the bathroom. She washed up and tied her hair back in a tight ponytail. A stray hair in a red velvet Pink Lady cupcake would be a recipe for disaster.

She had only got as far as cracking the eggs into the kitchen aid, her one splurge since she'd begun selling her wares at the market, when Yasmin had appeared in the kitchen doorway.

"You're mad, Kitty do you know that?" she'd said rubbing her eyes and moving across the tired old lino floor in a swish of pyjama satin. Her practised hand picked up the cup of flour resting on the bench, and she began to tip it slowly into the mixer as Kitty had demonstrated time and time again.

"Three teaspoons of baking powder," Kitty mumbled, measuring out the first and adding it to the mix before looking up at her friend; Yasmin was as tall as she was short. "I know, but you don't need to be. Go on back to bed; you're going to have a busy enough day as it is." Yas would never cope with the pace of the market if she were on anything other than top form, she thought, turning the speed up on the mixer a fraction.

The first time Kitty had shared a shift with Yasmin she had thought her like an exotic flower with her penchant for 1950s style frocks. She was studying fashion design at a local college and used her wages and tips from Bruno's to supplement her meagre student allowance. She was willowy with olive-hued skin and bobbed ebony hair that played up her flashing brown eyes. For her part, Yasmin had confided when they knew each better, she'd thought Kitty was like a dainty pixie. She had felt gangly and ginormous next to the petite blonde with the dancing blue eyes offset by unusually dark eyebrows and a big smile.

Opposites attract, though, and once Kitty had gotten used to Yas's way of going on, it hadn't taken many snatched coffee breaks for the two women to establish common ground. They were both new arrivals to the city in need of permanent accommodation. Adrift in Britain's capital, they'd been grateful to find one another, and they had been firm friends ever since.

"Thanks for doing this Yas, I'm sorry to land it on you."

"It's no biggie, all I ask is that when you open your café, you let me design the uniform. I think it should be something that's short and sweet, now should I add the melted butter?"

Kitty startled back to the present as a car horn tooted at another driver's indiscretion, and she realized she was there. As she pushed open the door of Baintree & Co., a bell jangled announcing her arrival. She stepped inside and shut the door quickly behind her not wanting to let in a blast of cold air. A girl of no more than eighteen shoved something in the drawer of the front desk she was sitting behind. Her phone Kitty was guessing, not caring if that was how she wanted to pass a quiet day at work; Mr Baintree might not be so easy going about it, though. She looked up at Kitty guiltily before affecting what she must have thought was her professional face. How she could get her facial muscles to move underneath the layers of powdery foundation slathered on her face was a wonder.

"I love your shoes – oh my God are they Alexander McQueen's?" she asked, standing up to peer over the top of her desk and at the same time waving Kitty over to the two-seater couch against the wall. A stack of realty magazines was on the table beside it, and she sat down to await Mr Baintree's imminent return.

Kitty crossed her jeans-clad legs lifting the top one up to allow the girl a closer inspection of her shoe. "I wish, they're a Spitalfields special."

The girl looked at her blankly.

"Knockoffs."

"Oh right." Disappointed, she sat back down and decided this client didn't look the type to dob her into her boss, so she fished her phone back out of the drawer and resumed her frantic texting.

Kitty's phone went at that moment, and she answered it knowing it was Yasmin even before she said hello. She was grateful she was not going to have to while away the minutes flicking through the magazines on offer.

"Okay, so you have to go to France, Kitty. I don't even know why you are thinking about it. That picture was incredible. I Googled it and apparently it is quite famous. How could you have not known that you had a famous model mother? It's called *Midsummer Lovers* and has been reprinted thousands of time. Gosh, she was beautiful. I can see where you get your looks from and as for the stud muffin she was gawping up at, well I don't blame her for having such a daft look on her face." Yasmin paused then huffed. "My God, Piggy Paula and Slimy Steve are going at it today. It's disgusting. It's put me right off my Mars bar."

Kitty doubted this was true; she could tell Yasmin was talking with her mouth full. "Why don't you bang on the door and tell them to keep the noise down. Or, better still run in there with a water pistol, all guns a blazing, that should dampen their ardour."

Yasmin laughed. "Not a bad idea, but it could also put me off sex for life. Maybe that's it, maybe I am just jealous. It's been so long." She sighed and then brightened. "Did I tell you about the guy who came into Bruno's for lunch on Thursday? Talk about tall, dark and handsome. Honestly, Kitty he was gorgeous – I just about dropped his Spaghetti Amatriciana in his lap I was so busy gawping at him. My luck though, he was dining with an equally stunning female companion, but he did leave me a nice big tip, so I suppose that's something. Where are you now the Estate Agent's?"

Yas talked a million miles an hour, Kitty thought with a fond smile. "Yep, I am waiting to hand the key for Edgewater Lane over to the Agent, who should be back in the office any minute and then my work in Wigan is done. I reckon I will make the six o'clock train back to London."

"No, you won't, Kitty because you are going to do what this Mr Booba has asked you to do."

Kitty frowned looking up at one of the many framed sales and marketing certificates adorning the agencies walls. They didn't hide the fact the place could do with a paint job and with the daylight robbery commission Baintree & Co commanded on their house sales you'd think they could afford to liven up the office bit. "It's Beauvau, and I can't go, Yas, I have responsibilities."

Yasmin made a snorting sound and Kitty held the phone away from her ear knowing she was about to be on the receiving end of a rant; she was right.

"You are making piss-poor excuses, Kitty Sorenson. You've told me that you have spent your whole life wondering who your mum used to be, and now you've been given a golden opportunity to begin unravelling the mystery. Not to mention an all expenses trip to this Uzés place in the south of France no less. Abandon ship, go! I can cover your shifts at Bruno's, and you'll be back well before next Saturday."

Kitty chewed her bottom lip; she was running out of excuses and it was making her squirm. This Monsieur Beauvau person had said his P.A. would arrange everything. All she had to do was say yes, and the tickets would be there for her to collect at the airport, whichever airport she decided to fly from. A car would pick her up at Marseille Provence Airport to take her on the two hour trip to Uzés. The nephew of the man in the photo had agreed to be there for this anniversary photo shoot *Tres Belle* magazine was so keen to commission, so it was down to her as to whether it went ahead. She was curious, of course, she was curious as this was a chance to hear about a side of her mother she never imagined existed. She massaged her temples as she wondered why it was her life was never straightforward.

At times, she felt like she was driving down a long and never ending road filled with unexpected potholes to send her veering off course. Sometimes it would be nice not to feel like the rug had just been pulled out from under her. It was a feeling she'd first encountered when her father passed away, and her mother had sold Rose Cottage. It hadn't lessened each and every time her mother had announced she was selling up and moving again either. Then, just when things had settled down, Rosa had rung her up one afternoon at the apartment she shared with Damien. She'd told her the reason she'd lost so much weight of late was that she had pancreatic cancer. The prognosis was not good. The circling shadows Kitty had felt over those last few weeks had suddenly made sense.

Her first reaction had been to begin frantically Googling all the different treatments for the disease that had her mother in its grip. Her hope was that she would spot some miracle cure that the doctors treating her had somehow missed. Even as she did so, she knew she was kidding herself. Realizing it was futile, she chose instead to cling on to the fact that at least Rosa had had the chance to meet Damien, the man she was going to marry. She could slip away knowing her daughter would be loved and looked after. Then he had gone and done what he did. Three months later Rosa had died with a stranger holding her hand because, knowing her daughter's heart was shattered, she had not wanted to add to her woes.

These last few months, she'd felt like she was getting her act together. It was still early days in the grieving process, but she had found a modicum of happiness in her new London life. Did she want to delve into the past she knew nothing of? And would the answers as to where her mother came from be answers she needed to know? Her mother hadn't thought so, and perhaps she'd had very good reasons.

"Kitty?"

"I'm still here."

"If you don't go to France, I will, and I will pretend that I am you, and I will get to the bottom of the mystery of who Rosa Sorenson once was."

"You can't do that, Nancy Drew because for one thing you look nothing like my mother; Monsieur Beauvau would know you weren't me straight away."

"You underestimate my powers of sneakiness. I've already thought of how I'll get round the fact that you are five foot two, blonde, fair-skinned and petite, and I am five foot nine, brunette, olive-skinned and big boned. I will tell Mr Boobo that Rosa had it off with a Lebanese man and that he buggered off back to Lebanon never to be seen or heard from again as my dad did. The elements of truth will give my cover an air of authenticity. And, my friend, I will get to have a lovely little break in France all expenses paid while getting to the bottom of whether your mother has been in witness protection all these years. Or, whether she has a second secret family or if she is a member of the Royal family who abdicated for the love of a common man. Or maybe her family were notorious gangsters, and for your protection she kept you hidden from them all these years, or—"

"Enough, Yas! He's already seen my picture on Facebook, duh." Nothing she was saying wasn't anything Kitty herself hadn't wondered about over the years. "It's far more likely she fell out with her parents over this man in the photo and being a teenage rebel she took off to France with him. End of story."

"Oh but it's not the end of the story, is it? Rosa's story hasn't even begun, Kitty, and I mean it if you don't go, then I will. You've got a chance to put some of the pieces of your family history together, something I'll never have, so don't you dare let this opportunity pass you by because you're scared. Not knowing and wondering is a lot scarier, my friend."

Kitty knew Yas's past rankled, but until that moment she hadn't realized just how much. Her mother, Gina had always been so blasé about her daughter's background telling her an abbreviated version of events roughly along the lines of her having met Yas's dad at the local markets. He'd been selling shoes, nice sparkly ones, she said and as he handed her her change he'd asked her out. They'd gone out a couple of times to the local pub, and he was a bit of a sweet-talker, so one thing led to another. To cut a long story short, she'd gotten pregnant, announced this to him, and his response had been to pack his bags and hotfoot it back to his pregnant wife in Lebanon. It was unfortunate, but men can be assholes, was how she'd usually finish her story with a shrug of her careworn shoulders. Gina had thought the name Yasmin was a nod to her eldest child's Middle Eastern birthright. Plus, she had been a huge fan of Duran Duran in her younger days and that Simon Le Bon, who she'd always thought was a bit of alright, was married to a Yasmin. Yas had once confided in Kitty that Gina thought she was cultural when she ordered a kebab at the local takeaway.

Gina wasn't put off by one bad experience, though. She went on to move in with a salt of the earth truck driver called Barry with whom she had the rest of her brood in quick succession. Sadly, Barry found the chaos of having four children under six years old too much to come home to when he parked his truck up after his weeks of driving up and down the country. So, deciding he wanted a more peaceful life, he had headed off on his run one day and never bothered to come back. All further correspondence between Yas's mum and Barry had been through the Benefits Office. Both her father and Barry's treatment of her mother had left Yasmin with an understandable mistrust of the male species, and so she tended to be a bit of a three date wonder.

Kitty despaired at times because a couple of those dates had been worth going on a fourth. Then again, with her poor judgment of the male character, she was in no position to go on at her friend.

A mental picture of Damien popped up unbidden, and she gave him a good shove telling herself to concentrate her energies on problem present, not problem past. Strangely enough, though, she realized that thinking of Damien had just made her mind up for her. He had hedged his bets and kept a secret from her. A big, hurtful secret that had ended their four-year-long romance and left her feeling like a dog that had been kicked. He was the reason she'd packed in her job and packed her bags to scurry off to London with her tail between her legs. It was a time when she should have been with her mother, but she had needed to put physical miles between herself and the hurt.

Okay, so Rosa hadn't lied to her the way Damien had but still she had kept a secret. No matter that she'd done her best to be a mother who was present and loving, her past had always been the thing lying unsaid between them.

Kitty liked that term the Americans used, a milk and cookies mom, it summed Rosa up. She had been there after school with afternoon tea waiting ready to listen to her daughter talk about her day. She had helped with homework and watched all Kitty's ballet practices despite it being obvious fairly early on in the piece that with her two left feet she would not be the next Anna Pavlova. She'd taught her how to bake and by doing so instilled a passion in her daughter but still she had not shared her past with her.

Rosa could never show her the courtesy of confiding in her as to where she came from. She didn't trust her to be able to handle whatever it was she was refusing to speak of, not even when she was dying. Maybe, Kitty thought, if she had, she might not have been left on her own. Well, she was sick of it. This time she resolved as she sat in the pokey reception area, she wouldn't wait to find out the hard way. Not the way she had with Damien by ignoring the encroaching darkness until it could no longer be ignored. This time she would learn the truth her way. She would go.

"You win, Yas. I am not having you masquerading as my mother's half Lebanese love child. I'll go."

Chapter 5

It's easy to halve the potato where there is love – Irish Proverb

It had all been surprisingly easy once Kitty had made her mind up. Sitting in Baintree & Co.'s that afternoon she'd disconnected her call to Yasmin and rang the number Christian Beauvau had provided before she got cold feet. A woman called Simone Cazal had answered. Introducing herself as his P.A., she'd told Kitty that Monsieur Beauvau would be very pleased to hear she was coming. If she left matters in her hands, she would organize everything. She'd ended the call by telling her she would phone back within the hour to give Kitty her flight details and to discuss payment.

Payment? She hadn't even thought about that. As Kitty hung up, she caught Texting Queen's, who had finally put her phone down, curious gaze and the butterflies set in. Was she doing the right thing? What if she was opening a can of worms she had no business opening?

There had been no more time to dwell on it though because with a blast of cold air Mr Baintree himself opened the door. He stood in front of her in his greatcoat that, in Kitty's opinion, was a bit over the top given they were in April. She tried not to focus on his hair and concentrated instead on what he was saying, but her eyes had kept straying upwards. It was like a grey bird's nest she concluded. It even had a little hollow in the middle for the eggs. She managed to drag her eyes away from his hair as he informed her in his plummy tones that the finances would soon be on hand and that her solicitors would take care of his company's commission. Clapping his hands together, he added that all that was left for her to do to complete the sale was to give him the house keys.

She thanked him for a job well done and handed over the keys without ceremony, not feeling much of anything because she couldn't say that she was sad to see the house go. The thought of her impending trip to France was filling her mind, and there wasn't room for practical thoughts like the fact that she was now in a position financially to make her café a reality. She'd shelve all thoughts of running her own business until she was able to give them her full attention. She quashed the little voice that taunted, excuses, excuses at her. Shaking the hand Mr Baintree was proffering, she said goodbye to him and the Texting Queen, who was now industriously shifting papers around on her desk.

Kitty shivered as she left the warmth of the office, the temperature had dropped another degree in the time she had been sitting in the toasty reception area. She made her way the short distance to Wigan's town square, her wheelie case banging over the cobbles behind her. At least it had stopped drizzling, she thought, gazing at the late afternoon sky with its patches of blue trying to break through the omnipresent grey.

She'd told that Simone woman that she'd fly from Manchester in the morning, so she needed to find a place to stay for the night. She'd try her luck down past the train station at the bottom of the hill. It made sense to find somewhere near the station because she would be in for an early start to get to the airport in the morning.

The road she set off down was filling up with bag-laden

Saturday shoppers rushing to catch their train home. She picked up her pace so as not to feel left out, keeping a tight hold of her case, and that was when she saw him, well actually she felt him before she saw him. She just knew with a sudden sick lurch of her stomach that he was there and looking up she saw she was right. He was walking against the crowd in her direction a bit like Moses parting the red sea. "Shit, shit, shit," she muttered under her breath, oblivious to the pursed-lipped look a woman herding her teenage daughter who was toting a Dorothy Perkins bag shot her as they strode past. She thought about ducking into the Post Office but knew it was too late; he'd seen her. A split-second later he was standing in front of her with that smile of his that always made her knees go to jelly.

"I don't believe it. Kitty, wow! Is it you?"

"Hello, Damien." She paused knowing she should keep walking, but a lifetime of having good manners instilled in her prevented her from doing so. The throngs of people either side of them seemed to vanish as Damien lunged forward, his lips grazing her cheek and leaving her feeling like she'd just been branded.

"Whoa I can't believe this, it's so good to see you. What are you doing here? I've just had lunch with Sam and thought I'd race up to the WH Smith before they close. The latest Lee Child is out."

She'd forgotten his younger brother lived in Wigan, but she remembered how much of a Lee Child fan he was. Unbidden, a memory of them both on a wet Saturday afternoon curled up at opposite ends of the couch lost in their books sprang to mind. What had she been reading? She couldn't remember now and what did it matter? Gosh, he looked good she thought, wishing he had acquired a beer belly, gone bald and been afflicted by a case of adult acne in the last six months. If anything though he looked better than ever. He was dressed for the weekend, and she'd always liked him best when he was casually rumpled. His brown hair was shorter these days, and it suited him. She unconsciously raised a hand to her hair hoping the damp air hadn't caused the irreparable fringe curl.

"Hey," he said reaching out and touching her arm. "I was sorry to hear about Rosa. I mean I knew she was sick and everything, but it was very quick in the end wasn't it?"

She nodded, not meeting his eye and not trusting herself to reply. So he did know then, she had checked the post for a sympathy card from him every day after the hospice had rung to say her mother was gone, but one never came. In the end, she had given him the benefit of the doubt thinking that perhaps he hadn't heard the news or didn't know where to find her.

"I heard through one of the old gang, and I was going to send a card but, well to be honest, I wasn't sure you'd want to receive one from me." He shrugged. "You look well, I mean despite what's happened, er you know losing your mum and everything, you still look wonderful. I have to say London obviously suits you."

Speak Kitty, speak, she willed herself. "Uh yes, it does thank you. I've settled in."

"I heard you had a stall at one of the big markets down there selling your cupcakes. I guess it's a step in the right direction towards owning your café. Good for you."

Kitty frowned, he seemed to have heard a lot. "Yes it is thanks, and well, now I've got some money behind me thanks to mum there's no reason I can't make it a reality." Too much information, Kitty my girl, don't tell the bastard anything. She mentally kicked herself before deciding to turn the tables. "How's everything with you and er—" She realized she didn't know the name of the girl he had spent three months bonking behind her back. No doubt it had come up in the explosive row they'd had when she had caught him out. It was thanks to a stonker of a headache and the strangest feeling that something was amiss that she had left work early one afternoon. She'd come home and stumbled on them post-coital lying in *their* bed and had turned and walked straight back out of the flat. Wandering around the Manchester streets, she'd been in complete shock at the collapse of her world as she knew it. It was growing dark when the numbness gave way to anger, and common sense told her it wasn't a good idea to be walking around unfamiliar streets on her own, so she'd gone home. Damien had been sitting at the dining room table waiting for her, and all hell had let loose. It was hard to believe they were now standing opposite one another on the Wigan pavement exchanging banal pleasantries. She doubted since they were being nice to one another that he'd appreciate her asking how 'The Bitch' was as she'd come to think of *her* either.

"Leanne, her name was Leanne."

She watched him run his fingers through his hair.

"She was a mistake, Kitty. There's not a day gone by since you left that I haven't regretted what I did to you, to us. It just sounds so trite to say I am sorry, but truly I don't know what else to say because I am."

He rested his hand on her arm once more, as though frightened she would walk away. Fat chance of that though; her legs were rooted to the spot.

"We broke up a few weeks after you left. I wanted to call you so badly, but after the way I'd treated you I didn't think you would want to hear from me ever again."

He looked at her as though expecting her to contradict him. When she didn't, she could tell by the little boy lost look on his face that he was as thrown by her presence as she was by his.

"I went round to see your friend Gemma once not long after you left. I asked her not to say anything to you, but I needed to know how you were doing."

Kitty didn't know, but then she hadn't heard from Gemma for a few months. Mind you, it was a two-way thing; there was nothing stopping her from having contacted her old pal. How did he think she was doing? You didn't have to be Einstein to figure out that when your fiancé does the dirty on you it stands to reason you'll be left feeling like shite.

44

"She wasn't exactly pleased to see me and she didn't want to tell me whereabouts you had moved to. I can't say I blame her."

What was she supposed to say to that? She stared up into his familiar blue eyes. For a while after she had arrived in London she had kept seeing him everywhere she went, only for him to vanish when she reached out to touch him. She'd have given anything for him to turn up on her doorstep and tell her that he had made a mistake. She'd missed him so much that any shred of pride or self-respect she'd had left when she'd walked out of the apartment they had shared together for three years would have disintegrated. She didn't know if she could have forgiven him for what he'd done to her, but she did know she was a long way from being over him. Gemma might have thought she was being a good friend and protecting her, but she should have told her Damien had called round. She should have let her make her mind up as to whether she wanted to see him or not.

"Have you got time for a quick drink?" He raised an eyebrow, and his expression was hopeful.

Kitty became aware of the people rushing past them then. For a moment, there had been no one else on that busy street leading to the train station other than him and her. She knew a 'quick drink' was a bad idea, just as she knew it would be anything but. For some reason, even though the word 'no' had formed itself on the tip of her tongue, as she opened her traitorous mouth the words, "Okay, a quick one then," tumbled out unbidden instead and she followed his gaze to the pub across the road. A moment later, he steered her through a break in the traffic and as he opened the tavern's door a warm glow and the smell of ale greeted them. She followed him inside, barely registering the split-level layout and the low beams that lent the buzzing room an air of cosiness.

"A glass of Sauvignon?" He raised a questioning eyebrow remembering her tipple as he pushed his way through to the crowded bar.

"Hmm, yes please."

"How about I order while you grab a table?"

Kitty nodded and went to turn away, but he stopped her. She could feel the heat of his hand on her shoulder as with twinkling eyes he asked, "Are you still a prawn cocktail girl?"

Her mouth curled into a small smile at his reference to her favourite crisps. It had been one of those silly couple jokes between them, her love of the prawn cocktail crisp and the fact she'd never share her packet with him. "Of course," she replied, knowing that her churning stomach wouldn't let her touch them even if he were to buy a bag.

Leaving him waving a tenner trying to attract the barman, she weaved her way through the tables. There was a soccer match blaring from the television bracketed to the wall at the far end of the room. The pub was heaving, but she managed to spot a table near the loos, empty for obvious reasons. She didn't care, though; she needed to sit down because she was frightened that if she didn't her legs might give way.

Leaning her case against the wall, she pulled the chair out and sank gratefully down on the seat before resting her elbows on the table. Lowering her head she massaged her temples, in an attempt to still the throbbing. What are you doing, Kitty? She knew if Yasmin were to walk into the pub right now she'd drag her out by her hair. At the very least she'd tell her she was a bloody fool. She'd be right too. Raising her head, she tucked her hair behind her ears and inhaled slowly. She needed to get out of here before she did something she knew she'd regret and getting to her feet, she slung her handbag back over her shoulder. She had just grabbed the handle of her case intent on leaving when Damien materialized through the group of lads standing in a huddle staring up at the telly.

He stopped in front of her, a drink in each hand. "They sold out of prawn cocktail, but that's no reason to leave." He didn't smile despite his attempt at humour. "Please don't go, Kitty." His eyes pleaded. Eyes that were so familiar to her with their flecks of dark blue around the irises, and as she hesitated, she knew she was lost even as she tried to be strong.

"Damien, this isn't a good idea."

"I'm so sorry for everything." He put the drinks down on the table and pulled her chair back out for her. "Please just give me five minutes to talk to you. I miss you. I miss us."

With every fibre of her being telling her not to, she sat down again and watched warily as he sat down opposite her. "Thank you, I know you have every right to walk away. It's just that it's so good to see you. I've missed you so bloody much."

Don't say that! She picked up her glass taking a large swallow, not wanting to meet his gaze over its rim. To look anywhere other than at him, she put her glass down and fished around in her handbag for her phone. The French women had said she would confirm her travel arrangements within the hour and hoping for the distraction her call would bring, she placed her phone down on the table.

She caught Damien's raised eyebrow and launched into her reasons for being back in the North and why this time tomorrow she would be in the small Provencal town of Uzés.

When she'd finished, Damien stared at her, his pint glass paused halfway to his mouth.

"That's pretty much it in a nutshell." It sounded mental saying it all out loud, and it was all down to her mother and her bloody secrets.

"Life's never dull when you're around Kitty, that's for sure."

She bit back the retort that it wasn't exactly dull when he was around either, and for all the wrong reasons but he didn't miss the look that flashed across her face.

"Believe me, I have had plenty of time to think about what I did, how I ruined everything."

"Why did you do it?" she asked softly.

"I was scared." He shrugged.

"Of what? I thought we were doing okay?" She was clutching the stem of her glass so tightly she was surprised it didn't snap. It was a conversation she'd never expected to have.

"We were. We were better than okay; we were great. I wanted to marry you more than anything, and believe me I have thought about what went wrong. I've thought about nothing else, and the only explanation I can come up with is that I was frightened of making that final commitment and Leanne was my subconscious way of sabotaging our relationship."

Kitty drained her glass, in her opinion, there wasn't anything subconscious about shagging someone else, you either were or you weren't, simple. "So you were a commitment-phobe, is that what you are trying to say?"

He had the grace to look sheepish. "It sounds stupid I know, but that's what it boils down to. You know the crap Sam and I went through with our parents when they split up."

She nodded, she had known his parents' ugly divorce had left its scars, but then nobody got through life without accumulating baggage along the way, it was just the way of the world. She'd had to deal with her mother's past being a closed book all her life. The scenarios she had conjured up to fill in the blanks had been endless. On top of that, she'd found herself orphaned at thirty-one years of age. So yes, she knew better than most that life sucked sometimes, but that didn't mean you had to go around bonking someone behind your fiancée's back.

Her phone shrilled, and she was grateful for the interruption, but her hand hovered over the phone not wanting to be rude. Damien leaned back into his chair and waved his hand toward it. "You'd better take it."

The lads who were glued to the match let out a roar and Kitty frowned holding the phone up to her ear. "Can you wait just a moment, please?" she shouted into the mouthpiece before covering it and looking at Damien. "I'm just going to pop into the Ladies. I can't hear a thing with that lot carrying on."

Damien nodded, and she felt his eyes on her back like twin laser beams as she walked off. Closing the washroom door, she was grateful for a few moments to compose herself. "Sorry about that I'm in a pub, and it's very noisy." She peered into the smeared mirror at her flushed face and dishevelled hair and shook her head. God, she looked a mess.

"Bonjour, Mademoiselle Kitty, it is Simone Cazal, Monsieur Beauvau's assistant calling you."

"Hello, Miss Cazal."

"It is Simone, please."

"Er okay, then Simone." Kitty turned away from her reflection and leaned against the sink. She listened as the woman told her that her tickets for a ten a.m. flight would be waiting for her to collect at the Lufthansa desk at Manchester Airport in the morning. She would be there to meet her upon her arrival in Marseille. Her return flight would be booked at the end of the photo shoot. If Kitty was happy to sign the contract upon her arrival and provide her bank account details the sum of five thousand euros would be deposited into her account. It would be a one-off, full and final payment for her participation in the photo shoot.

Kitty just about dropped her phone "Er pardon me, Simone, did you just say five thousand euros?"

"Yes, this amount is not up for negotiation – you are happy with it, oui?"

"Oui, yes thanks."

Simone said goodbye, reiterating that she would meet Kitty at Marseille Airport in the morning. Kitty barely heard, she was reeling. All that money, just for posing for a picture! She wondered what this Christian Beauvau chap was being paid by *Tres Belle* if he could afford to pay her that amount. It was dawning on her ever so slowly that this print her mother had featured in all those years ago was indeed a big deal. She turned back to the mirror and smoothed her hair wishing she'd bought her handbag in with her so she could have at least run a comb through it and put a bit of lippy on. She sighed deeply, what an afternoon this was turning out to be. She needed another drink.

Making her way out of the bathroom, she saw that Damien, as though having read her mind, had purchased another glass of wine and a fresh beer sat in front of him. She sat down and took a big swig of her glass. "Oh, I needed that."

Damien looked at her concerned. "Kitty, listen I was thinking, are you sure this photo thing is all legit? You know you read about this kind of thing in the papers, young women being lured overseas. You might get there and find yourself part of some French slavery ring."

"I don't know what papers you read, but it's a very elaborate con if it isn't legit, look." She pulled the photo up on her phone, and Damien took it from her staring at the picture for a moment. "Gosh! Wow, that's Rosa? Seeing her young like that's so weird. She's just like you if you were in the same outfit with a different hairstyle. I wonder if the bloke's nephew looks anything like him."

"I don't know. I don't know a thing about him."

"It's a bit of a creepy idea if you ask me. Do you know anything about the backstory around the photograph?"

"No, and that's why I have to go. Simone, that's the photographer's assistant, just told me they are paying me a one-off fee of five thousand euros for agreeing to pose for the new photograph."

Damien spluttered into his beer. "How much?"

She repeated herself and Damien morphed before her very eyes into the business mode that befitted his job in the Share Market. "You should get your solicitor to look over any paperwork you are going to sign, you know. I mean, if they are prepared to fly you over to France and pay you that much it is obviously a pretty lucrative job for this Christian Beauvau fellow. There could be a lot more in it for you in the way of royalties. I'd be interested to know if your mother has received hers over the years too. Do you know how much they are paying the bloke's nephew?"

Kitty felt her back stiffen; there was no way she was giving a penny more to her mum's solicitors. "No! Stop. Damien, the money will be nice, but that is not what this is about. You know my mother never talked about where she came from, and this is my chance to find out about a side of her that I never knew."

Damien knew how Rosa's refusal to talk about her past had eaten away at her. "You're right. Sorry, it's the stockbroker in me, I can't help myself."

"It's okay." She relaxed and sat back in her chair drinking her wine a little too quickly.

"Watch it; you'll get tipsy." He smiled. "So where are you staying tonight?"

"I'm not sure. I was going to find a B&B."

"You can stay at mine; I can drop you at the airport in the morning."

Kitty's eyes widened.

"I'll behave myself I promise, but I can't leave you to wander around Wigan looking for a Bed and Breakfast. It will be getting dark soon out there. Besides, you'd have to get up at a ridiculous time to get your flight."

Kitty knew it wouldn't be dark for at least another hour. There was nothing to stop him offering to drive her around Manchester looking for a B&B if he was worried about the distance from the airport. For some reason, though, she couldn't summon either the strength or the willpower to contradict him.

Chapter 6

God is good but never dance in a small boat – Irish Proverb

Kitty lay on her side in Damien's bed with the sheets pulled up under her chin staring at the window. The sheets felt crisp and cool against her bare skin, Egyptian cotton, she guessed, because Damien had always been partial to the finer things in life. It had caused a few arguments between them during their time together with her having a thriftier nature. Opposites were supposed to attract, though, and she had reined him in and he had loosened her up so that they met somewhere in the middle. Egyptian cotton sheets hadn't featured in that middle ground though because she had won that particular battle. The sheets they'd once shared together had come from Tesco.

There was a gap where the blinds didn't quite meet the sill. She could tell by the greyish light seeping in under them and the faint shushing sound of cars far below that it was early morning. It must be some time just after five a.m. she guessed before shifting her hip slightly. It was going numb thanks to Damien's hideously uncomfortable futon. Another post break-up purchase he had said, although he hadn't worded it quite like that, to help with his back. He'd been in a minor car accident before she'd met him and had suffered from back pain for as long as Kitty had known him. It was beyond her, though, how sleeping on what equated to an oversized rectangular rock could benefit your back but when she'd questioned him on this Damien was adamant it was working wonders on his.

His leg strayed over to her side of the bed; he had obviously gotten used to starfishing, she thought, as he let rip with an ungentlemanly snort. She'd forgotten he always snored when he'd had a few drinks and they'd both had more than a few before they'd wound up skipping the light fandango on the Futon. She hadn't been complaining it was uncomfortable then, though, she thought ruefully. The sex had been good because they already knew each other's bodies intimately, so there were none of those embarrassing fumbling, clumsy moments. They were like a well-oiled machine in that respect. As Damien erupted once more, she felt her foot twitch under the sheets. Six months ago she'd have given him a swift kick to startle him into rolling over. Now that he was technically a one-night stand she didn't feel it appropriate to put the boot in, so to speak. Besides she knew she'd never get back to sleep now, snoring or no snoring.

God, she was hungry too she thought, wrapping her arms around her tummy in an attempt to stave off the pangs. Again, she realized that if this had been six months ago, she'd have been in their old apartment, and were she lying wide awake like this she'd have gotten up. She pictured herself tiptoeing into the kitchen the way she'd done hundreds of time when she'd woken up peckish to stuff her face with whatever leftovers she could find lurking in the fridge. This wasn't her apartment, though, and it didn't feel right to sneak into the kitchen for a rummage in Damien's fridge. What if he woke up and busted her sneaking about, he'd think she was snooping around the place or something. No, she'd just have to wait for his alarm to go off. The room got lighter and her tummy rumbled louder. She couldn't help but think as she rolled away from the window, how had it come to this? Where once she'd shared her life with the man lying flat on his back next to her, now she felt like a prisoner in his futon.

They'd had no dinner the night before, that was the problem. She hadn't been hungry when they left the pub, enjoying the warm slightly addled feeling from the three glasses of wine she'd ended up downing. It had been such a strange day. She didn't feel like being sensible, and of course, had she been sober then common sense might have won out. Damien, as though sensing this, had been in far too much of a hurry to get her back to his apartment. He wasn't going to risk suggesting they stop off for something to eat in case she changed her mind about staying.

She'd sat with her head leaning back on the plush headrest of his new black Audi as he drove them to his apartment. It was another post break-up splurge. He'd looked like a little boy as he told her that not only was it turbocharged – whatever that meant – but the roof was retractable too. She'd refrained from remarking on how useful that would be living in Manchester because not only could you get soaked through to the skin, you also got to breathe in traffic fumes. She shook her head, trying not to listen to him telling her again how much he'd missed her since she'd left, and how sorry he was for what he'd done. It was as though he thought the more he repeated these sentiments, the more chance there was of her saying all is forgiven I'll come back.

The Bitch, she registered him saying, although he hadn't used that terminology, had moved to Glasgow after they'd split. She had taken a new job there so Kitty wouldn't have to worry about ever bumping into her were she to come back. He'd do anything to get her back he stressed as the lights of Greater Manchester twinkled in the distance. Part of Kitty wanted to believe him even as she wondered idly if his version of anything stretched to selling the ridiculous sports car she currently found herself sitting in.

His hand had snaked over to rest on her leg. She could feel the heat of it through the denim fabric of her jeans as he steered them deftly around the achingly familiar streets of Manchester's trendy Northern Quarter. It was where they'd lived together, enjoying the regeneration it had undergone along with all the other twenty and thirty somethings' that had gravitated to the area. She'd stared out the window at all the restaurants they'd dined in. They passed by cafés they'd met friends for coffee in, pubs they'd drunk in and clubs they'd gone on to dance the night away in. The streets they were passing were streets they'd once strolled hand in hand down. It was all so comfortingly familiar when everything around her at the moment was so bewildering.

Damien had opted to stay in the Northern Quarter; he told her, driving into the underground car park of an apartment complex. He could have stayed on at their flat had he got someone else in to share, but he didn't want to do that. The memories were too painful, he said. For you and me both, she'd thought, recalling her mother having uttered the same sentiment when she sold Rose Cottage.

Her phone had rung once as they rode the lift up to his apartment on the fifth floor, and a quick glance at the screen told her that Yasmin was wanting a word. She'd flushed guiltily knowing full well what her friend would have to say to her if she knew what she was about to do. Switching off her phone, she stuffed it as far down in the depths of her handbag as she could manage.

His apartment, although small, was shiny and new, and Kitty had thought, with a glance around, rather impersonal. She'd stopped thinking altogether though when he'd put Adele on. It was their favourite CD, the one they'd always had sex to. She'd sunk into his open arms and raised her mouth to meet his as they began a slow, remembered dance.

The beeping alarm brought her back to the present, signalling it was at last time to rise and shine. Damien stirred for a moment before reaching over with a practised hand to bang the snooze button and snuggling back under the bedding, but Kitty sat up gratefully. Her hand went to her hair, and she sighed, it was mussed beyond redemption. She knew too that her mascara was probably down to her chin by now, and her mouth felt dry and stale. Had Damien been someone new that she had staggered home with last night then she'd have been desperate to get into the bathroom to tidy her act up before he got a good look at her. As it was, she knew the sight of her with her hair standing on end, and the remnants of the previous day's makeup was one he had been treated to on many occasions. He would not be fazed.

Sensing her eyes on him, he opened his and blinked a couple of times before his mouth curved into a slow, lazy smile. He reached up and stroked her cheek.

"Morning, gorgeous."

"Gorgeous is a stretch! I'm a fright."

He grinned. "Well the Robbie William's *Let Me Entertain You* eye makeup isn't your best look I agree, but other than that you look pretty darn tasty to me." He reared up to pull her back down beside him, but she broke free.

"No way, don't even think about it. I've got to get to the airport, and I need to have a shower and tidy myself up. I can't get off the plane looking like—"

"The wanton woman you are."

She leaned over and smacked him lightly before swinging her legs over the side of the bed vaguely self-conscious about being naked. She stood up and made her way quickly to the en-suite hearing a wolf whistle from the bed before he called out. "Towels are in the cupboard. Shall I join you?"

"No! Make yourself useful and get some breakfast organized. I am starving," she called back. Her casual banter belied the tumult of emotions vying to make themselves heard as she locked the door behind her, and leaned her head against it for a moment. She didn't trust him not to come in, remembering full well that he was a morning man.

A few moments later, she was standing under the jets of water enjoying the feel of the hot needles hitting her skin, sluicing away the morning-after fog. She picked up the bottle of shampoo from the ledge and peered at the label. It was a salon brand she didn't recognize and opening the lid, she sniffed its contents. Coconut, she thought, envisaging palm trees swaying in the breeze as she squeezed a dollop into the palm of her hand and began massaging it into her scalp. Damien had always been a bit of a metro man when it came to his grooming, and she used to find it amusing that he spent more on his hair products than she did.

Oh God, she thought, letting the water run over her head with her eyes squeezed shut so as not to get shampoo in them, what on earth was she doing here? Did she think she could go back and that they could just pick up as though The Bitch had never happened? Common sense told her that no; it would never work. The part of her that still loved Damien wanted to kick common sense right up the backside, though; forget all about this mad trip to France and unpack her bags.

By the time she emerged from the bathroom ten minutes later with her hair towel dried and a fresh layer of warpaint on her face, she was feeling more composed. She'd dressed once more in her jeans, having packed lightly under the assumption she'd be back in London by now. As she zipped up her case, she made a mental note to wash her smalls by hand when she got to Uzés or she'd be in a bother.

Ready to face the day, she straightened up and prepared to venture forth. Well almost ready, she thought, sniffing the air and catching a whiff of coffee mingling with frying bacon. Good, Damien had taken her literally. Walking through to the small living area, she found him stationed at the hob of the open-plan kitchen with the frying pan in hand. Her stomach did a little dance as he grinned at her, and she pinched her forearm to make sure this whole surreal scene was unfolding.

"Good shower?"

She glanced down at the red welt on her forearm. "Um yes, great shower thanks. Those power shower thingies are amazing. I feel human again, or I will do when you make me a cup of that coffee." She eyed the fancy looking machine taking up half the bench space. Back when they'd lived together, it had only ever been instant on offer because they'd preferred to go out for coffee. He had certainly gone to town since she'd left. "Do you need a licence to operate that thing?"

Damien left the sizzling pan and fetched a mug down from the shelf overhead. "It brews a mean espresso, and you won't be making snide remarks when you taste it."

He was right, she thought, taking a sip from the mug he'd slid down the countertop towards her a moment later. Licking the froth from her upper lip, she watched him from underneath her eyelashes as he dished up the bacon and eggs. A strong sensedéjà vu assailed her; they had played this scene out so many times before. Damien had loved his Sunday fry-ups. It was like they had hit the rewind button and everything was the way it had been. Then, as she glanced around and realized she was in an unfamiliar flat surrounded by things she didn't recognize, the hurt began to seep in around the edges again.

Damien pushed her plate towards her and came round to sit on the bar stool next to where she was perched at the breakfast bar. "I meant every word I said to you last night, Kitty. You know that, don't you?"

Kitty picked up her knife and fork not wanting to meet his gaze. "I know you did."

"Will you promise me you'll think about coming back? Please."

"I will." Her voice cracked. "I promise." As he laid his hand on hers and gave it a gentle squeeze, she wanted to cry. Thank goodness she was leaving today, she needed to put some distance between them so she could think clearly.

He let go of her hand. "Right, well tuck in, and then I suppose we'd better get you to the airport." He picked up a toast triangle and dunked it in his egg. "I have to say, though, Kitty, I don't feel entirely comfortable with this whole France scenario."

"It will be fine," she muttered, hearing her mother's voice

telling her not to talk with her mouth full but being too famished to care as she shovelled in a forkful of bacon. "Don't worry."

In record time she'd cleaned her plate and with caffeine coursing through her veins and a full belly she felt much improved. Damien announced he'd better go shower and so seeking distraction from dwelling on the night before, she began stacking the dishwasher as he disappeared back into his bedroom. Popping her mug in the rack, she remembered Yasmin's call last night and felt guilty at not only having ignored it but at switching her phone off too. Setting the dishwasher to run, she went and fished her mobile out of her bag and a moment later her inbox filled with missed calls and texts from her friend. She'd better ring her, she thought, flopping down on the couch with a heavy sigh. Staring out the window at the adjacent high-rise, she took a deep breath knowing she was in for a rightly deserved drilling. Yasmin answered after two rings.

"Thank God, Kitty! I was worried about you. I imagined all sorts of things and none of them were good." The relief in her voice flooded down the line.

"I'm fine, Yas. I am so sorry! I know I should have called you back and let you know where I was staying last night."

"Yeah you should have and what's with switching your phone off? What were you up to? I have hardly slept a wink. It didn't help that Piggy and Slimy were at it all night again. Honestly, I thought the headboard was going to come through the flipping wall at one point."

Kitty shuddered watching the morning light play on the glass panels of the building opposite. "Oh poor you, nobody deserves that."

"I know! It was horrific and it's quite possible that I might have been scarred for life. If I were religious last night's antics would have been enough to convince me to join a convent, but I am not and couldn't possibly be with Mr Amatriciana on the loose. I can't stop thinking about him by the way; it's a shame he's taken. Never mind all that, though, did you find yourself a nice B&B in the end?"

"Um no. I stayed at an old friend's place actually. I bumped into uh, her in Wigan, and she invited me back to her new flat for a bit of a catch-up. That's why I turned my phone off because we were so, um, busy chatting." Kitty studied a fingernail. She eyed its chipped polish with distaste. Her story sounded perfectly plausible, and it was almost true, she'd just swapped genders and left out all the juicy details.

Yasmin wasn't buying it, though. "Kitty, I don't need to be one of those FBI behavioural analyst's like off the telly to tell that you are lying. It's in the funny pitch of your voice."

Kitty had never been a very good liar. She reckoned it was the pressure of having been an only child because it was very hard not to tell the truth when it was always two big people against one little person.

"Whatever, now spill, what have you been up to?"

Kitty squirmed in the leather seat. "You're not going to like it."

Two minutes later she held the phone away from her ear as her friend launched into a tirade that mostly involved her repeatedly yelling, *"How could you be so stupid? After the way he hurt you!"*

It was pretty much what she'd expected Yasmin to say. She'd watched her mother get burnt time and time again. The experience meant she was of the firm belief that once a cheater always a cheater, so there wasn't very much Kitty could say to dissuade her from her point of view. There was no point adding fuel to her friend's fire either by telling her Damien wanted her back and that he had promised he would never stray again. Part of her wanted to believe him because part of her wanted desperately to return to this world that had once been hers. There was another voice whispering in the background of emotions, though, telling her that she couldn't go back. She was carving a new life of sorts for herself in London. She had her dreams to follow and they were within her grasp now thanks to the sale of Edgewater Lane. But would those dreams be hollow if she didn't have him by her side?

He had never been enthused about the idea of her opening her café. He'd felt she would be better sticking to the safe option of working nine to five for a guaranteed wage. It was ironic given the gamble of his stockbroking work. But then he used to say he was gambling other people's money not his own, so it was different. He had never understood that to her baking wasn't just a hobby and something she enjoyed doing at the weekend. It was her passion, and she wanted to turn that passion into a job. She wanted to spend her days doing what she loved, not tapping away at a computer. Perhaps he might feel differently now she had some money behind her. That same little voice whispered that it really shouldn't matter to her how he felt.

Oh, she thought, as she bit what was left of her thumbnail down to the quick, she was glad she would be sitting on a plane in just under two hours. She needed to get away from Damien and even Yasmin so she could think about what it was *she* wanted.

Damien appeared in the living room doorway looking decidedly delish in a fitted V-neck sweater and jeans with his hair still wet from the shower. At the sight of him, Kitty was almost tempted to hang up the phone and tell him that she wanted to start again, but something stopped her. Instead, she cut her friend off midsentence. "Listen, Yas, I have to get to the airport, my flight leaves at half-nine. I promise I will phone you when I get the chance from Uzés."

She hung up on her friend who was still in mid-rant.

Chapter 7

As you ramble through life, whatever be your goal; Keep your eye on the doughnut, and not upon the hole – Irish Proverb

Kitty scanned the arrivals hall of Marseille Airport and spotted a little girl jumping up and down holding onto a piece of cardboard with the words Mademoiselle Sorenson printed boldly in black across it. As she weaved her way through the crowd, wheelie-case trundling along behind her, she realized the little girl wasn't a child after all. Rather, she was a tiny woman who looked to be around her age too. She took a deep breath; she couldn't quite believe she was here on French soil. Her free hand strayed unconsciously to her stomach and rested there for a moment; it was a bundle of knots.

"Er hello, I'm Kitty," she ventured stepping into the woman's line of sight.

The petite figure lowered her cardboard, and her bold red-lipsticked mouth twitched into a tight smile. Her glossy brunette hair was slicked back into a bun, and she was wearing a white trouser suit with the kind of killer heels that would have some women stalking along like an ostrich. Kitty adored them instantly and felt a stab of kinship at the sight of them. She could also sense from the woman's stance that she meant business and would see an in-depth conversation as to where she had found such gorgeous footwear as a frivolous waste of her time. The hand she held out in greeting was dainty and smooth, free of rings, her nails perfect half-moons painted in a clear, shiny polish. Her whole demeanour oozed with an understated professionalism and Kitty realized she was one of those rare species of women that could wear all white and not get a mark on it.

"I'm Simone Cazal, Monsieur Beauvau's Assistant, we spoke on the phone. I am so pleased you have come, and I welcome you to France."

Jeez, for a little girl Simone sure had a grip and a half on her, Kitty thought, wishing she'd let go of her hand. Her English thankfully was much better than Kitty's non-existent French. As she released her hand, she was relieved to be able to cross the language barrier off her mental 'why this trip was madness' list.

"The car, it is outside." With that, she gave a come, come wave of her hand before turning and gliding in the direction of the nearest exit.

She was so elegant, so … what was the word she was looking for? So French! That was it, Kitty thought, watching her in awe before tottering along after her. Not even her beloved Alexander McQueen wannabes could stop her feeling like an unglamorous Heffalump clad in jeans in the presence of such effortless style. Not for the first time, she cursed the impromptu nature of this trip and wished she'd had the time to head back to London to pack a wardrobe suitable for a trip to France. Instead, she was stuck with the bare necessities she'd stuffed into her wheelie-case when she'd headed up to Wigan. Oh well, there was no point worrying about it now, she decided. As the glass doors slid open, she blinked at the bright blue sky that greeted her.

The car, a sleek Peugeot, pulled up with precision timing as Kitty nearly collided into the back of Simone who had come to a sudden kerbside halt. She barely had time to enjoy the balmy

Marseille breeze before a stocky man with a shock of silver hair, dressed in a dark suit got out of the car. With a nod in Simone's direction, he made his way around to the rear of the car to open the boot then turning his attention to Kitty, he muttered something guttural at her. She smiled blankly back at him in that *I haven't a clue what you just said, but I guess it was something along the lines of give me your bag* way as he retrieved her case from her. He placed it in the trunk and closing the boot made his way around to the passenger door. He opened it for Simone. She gave a brief nod of thanks before sliding into the seat and reaching for her seat belt. She was obviously used to being driven around, Kitty thought, as he opened the back door for her, and she ducked into the car mindful of not doing something dumb like bang her head. She smiled up at him. "Gracias."

A flicker of amusement flashed across his craggy, clean-shaven features before he closed the door, and she felt her cheeks flame. *He's French, Kitty, you idiot, not Spanish!* she told herself as she buckled in. Settling back in her seat, she decided that from now on her best course of action was not to speak unless spoken to. It was a shame because she had hundreds of questions she'd like to ask Simone about her mother and *Midsummer Lovers*, but she supposed they could wait until she got to Uzés.

The chauffeur got in and turning to Simone fired something off in French. It elicited both a tsking sound and an annoyed expression from her before he started the engine. He pulled away to navigate his way deftly out of the airport. Simone angled her head toward the back seat and Kitty leaned forward to hear what she had to say.

"We will have to take the scenic route because there has been an accident on the motorway and the traffic it is very bad. It is most annoying because it means I will have to ring Christian and tell him we will be delayed." She pursed her lips. "Our schedule is very tight. He won't be happy." As she turned away to make the call, Kitty heard her make more of the tut-tutting sounds.

She doubted the people involved in the accident were very happy either.

She kept her opinion to herself, though, offering up somewhat lamely. "Oh dear, that's a shame." Simone wasn't listening, and Kitty looked out the window. She was secretly pleased with the turn of events in so much as the scenic route around Provence's back roads sounded much more exciting than a featureless trip down a motorway.

She'd only ever been to France once before, and that was for a long weekend in Paris with Damien. It had not been long enough by far. She closed her eyes for a moment recalling how they had left their hotel room in the Latin Quarter to explore the famous area's winding, cobbled lanes. Damien had set a pace that was far too fast for her liking. She had thought, as she paused to press her nose to the window of a patisserie, that surely Paris was a city in which to meander? The patisserie had the most gorgeous array of glossy baby fruit tarts, macarons, éclairs of all colours and flavours as well as other delectable treats that she had ever had the good fortune to lay her eyes upon. How she had wished she could bypass the young girls serving behind the counter and head straight through to the kitchen to watch the artisan bakers' at work. Damien had pulled her away before she could get a foot in the door, though, eager to get to the Louvre and tick off another sight on his Paris in three days list.

She opened her eyes again; Simone had begun talking into her mobile, and as the car passed over a speed bump, Kitty felt an uncomfortable sensation. Oh bugger it, she should have gone to the loo while she had the chance. She glanced back over her shoulder at the airport terminal watching until it disappeared from view.

That would teach her for indulging in yet another cup of coffee followed up by a glass of pinot gris all before ten o'clock just because she could. It wasn't every day she found herself on a business class flight to France. As she'd sipped on the fruity wine and stretched her legs out, she'd told herself she deserved it. What had happened to her in the last twenty-four hours was enough to drive any girl to drink. And she didn't need much of a nudge when it came to a glass of vino at the best of times!

Now, she watched as the urban scenery of terracotta roof tiles gave way to leafy tree lined roads. The shades of green forming an arbour over the car were soft, almost as though they'd been brushed with silver. She sat forward in her seat eagerly as she spied the open fields beyond the trees. They were filled with sunflowers beginning to take a cautious peek at the world. The rolling hills in the background were smattered with medieval villages and she wished she had time to go and explore their charms. She wondered if her mother had passed down this road with her boyfriend all those years ago and looked out at the same views she was now soaking up. It was a scene that surely, apart from the tar sealing of the roads, would not have changed in the last few hundred years let alone fifty.

She glanced at Simone, toying with the idea of asking her for more information about the history of the photograph that had brought her here. Simone had put her phone away, but her head was now bent as she tapped away with urgent fingers at her iPad. Not wanting to interrupt her, Kitty settled back into her seat trying not to think about the fact that actually, she really did need to go to the loo. She crossed her legs. It was no small feat in the back of a Peugeot, and she jiggled her foot to distract herself, but as the car hit a pothole, she realized she had reached the point of no return.

"Um excuse me, Simone." She leaned forward and tapped her on her shoulder.

"Oui." Her tone was curt as she looked up from whatever it was she was doing and twisted round in her seat to see what Kitty wanted.

"Er, is there any chance we could stop at a restroom please?"

Simone's expression was blank.

"Um, loo er, you know, toilet?" A bog, a crapper she mentally added, desperation making her crass.

"Er oui, toilette?"

Yes, wee, wee, wee! Kitty nodded enthusiastically. "Yes, toilette please."

"Non, sorry." Simone turned back to her iPad and began swiping at the screen again.

Kitty was having none of it and she tapped her on the shoulder again. "The thing is Simone I really, really need to go."

She paused mid-swipe but didn't bother to look around this time. "In France, Mademoiselle Kitty we do many things well. Amour oui, cuisine oui, histoire oui, public toilettes non."

"But I won't make it to Uzés. I have to go now!"

The desperation in her tone must have gotten through to Simone because she leaned across and said something unintelligible to the chauffeur before turning her attention to Kitty.

"I have asked Pierre to stop up there." She waved her hand in front of her and Kitty peered through the gap in the seats. At the sight of the shops ahead, she found religion. "Thank you, Lord," she whispered silently.

Pierre indicated left and pulled into the car park coming to a halt in front of a patisserie. A quick sweep of the block confirmed to Kitty that this was her best shot for a loo. The hairdressers at the end of the block was shut, and she didn't rate her chances of the furniture shop having a public amenity. She flung the back door of the car open half expecting Simone to clap her hands and say. "Chop, chop we haven't got all day." She didn't say a word, though, as Kitty knock-kneed headed in the direction of the patisserie. Pushing open the door she saw that there were no other customers in there. Her mind automatically registered that the glass-fronted cabinet held a delicious array of baguettes stuffed full of savoury goodies and cream filled cakes. She wondered what would happen to all that gorgeous food at the close of business which going by the ghost town outside wouldn't be far off. Stop thinking about food, Kitty she admonished, arranging her features into a smile, and concentrate on the job at hand.

"Une toilette, merci?" she asked the woman behind the counter who was wielding a broom, hoping her pitiful attempt at French would soften her austere features. Her hair was stretched tightly back and knotted into an unflattering bun. Kitty knew she had read somewhere that the French appreciate tourists making an attempt at speaking their language.

"Non." She didn't stop in her sweeping shaking her head vigorously to emphasise her point.

Not one single hair on the woman's head had moved out of place during this exchange much to Kitty's fascination. Her panic, though, was making her feel nasty and she wanted to shout back at the women. "Oh go and eat some cake you skinny old cow." But she didn't fancy getting smacked with the broom, so instead, she bit back the retort and hobbled out of the shop.

Pierre was leaning against the car smoking, and Simone was still sitting in the passenger seat doing whatever it was she was doing on her iPad. It was no good, Kitty thought; she had to go. There was no way she could be bounced around in the back of that car for the duration of the trip to Uzés even if it were only half an hour up the road. Her eyes strayed over to the scrub filled lot beside the patisserie, and she made her mind up. There was nothing else for it; she'd just have to hope she could find a particularly leafy dandelion to hide behind.

Squatting down and knowing full well she was delusional if she thought she was hidden from view, the relief a split second later was immense. When she'd finally finished and done a little jiggle, she began the task of trying to pull her knickers and jeans back up without actually standing up. Her thigh muscles were getting the best workout of their lives. The job was almost done when she registered an intense burning sensation in the right cheek of her bottom. As her hand automatically flew around to pat the spot she almost lost her balance. "Calm down, Kitty," she muttered, steadying herself. The sight of her rolling around on the ground with both her undergarments and jeans sailing at half-mast would not be a good one. Twisting her head back over her shoulder, she was just in time to spy a self-satisfied wasp buzzing toward a little mound on the ground. It was only a short distance from where she was crouched. She realized with some dismay that she'd just squatted beside a wasp nest, been stung for her effort and that it bloody well hurt!

With one last herculean effort, Kitty eased her pants up over her stinging cheek. As she stood up and glanced back at the little mound, she saw a cluster of the wasp's humming little buddies emerging. The bastard had told them lunch was served she thought, charging back across the lot toward the car. She ignored the woman in the patisserie window who was busy wagging a finger at her and shouted at Pierre to get back in the car. She couldn't see his expression as he ground his cigarette out, so intent was she on reaching the sanctity of the back seat. It was with huge relief that a moment later she flung the door open and threw herself into the scat. She slammed the door shut before she could be swarmed.

Simone turned to look at her and raising one eyebrow asked. "Better?"

And so it was that thirty minutes later Kitty arrived in the beautiful, historic town of Uzés with a rapidly swelling derriere and a dwindling sense of pride.

Chapter 8

Marry a mountain girl and you marry the whole mountain – Irish Proverb

"I am Christian Beauvau," a man with an impressive head of silver hair swept back from his face and knotted at the nape of his neck in a low ponytail said. He pushed his chair away from the table and stood up. Dark glasses covered his eyes and he was sporting a dodgy tan. It made his teeth that were bared in a wolfish smile appear almost neon in their Hollywood whiteness. His suit, Kitty noticed, was white like Simone's, but unlike hers, his had a tell-tale red wine stain on the lapel. The stain's culprit was in the half drunk wine glass on the table he had gotten up from. It stood next to a little dish filled with olives and an empty bowl of mussel shells. To her surprise, he placed his beringed hands on either side of her face and studied her for a moment before exclaiming, "Tu es tres belle! You are beautiful just like your maman. It is such a treat for me to feast my eyes upon Rosa's daughter at last." His breath smelt garlicky, but it wasn't unpleasant she thought, as he released her face and waved for her to sit down in the empty seat opposite him.

Thanking him for the effusive compliments, she sat down

gingerly. She wished she'd had time to pick up some antihistamine cream. She'd spotted a pharmacy's green cross blinking amongst the other shops on the shaded main road as they'd driven through the busy town. She hadn't dared ask Simone to get Pierre to stop the car again, though, not after the wasp debacle and so had missed her chance. Instead, she'd sat with her nose pressed to the window and gazed at the crowded pavement cafés and pretty shop frontages sheltering beneath their red awnings. She'd tried to imagine her mother as a young girl wandering amongst them. All the while, she kept her hands tightly clasped as she resisted the urge to stick her hand down the back of her pants and scratch the sting. The sensation of which had recently moved from the burning pain phase into the intense itching stage.

Pierre had navigated his way expertly around the ring road surrounding the town before pulling in to park in the gravelled grounds of a Cathedral. Its spire, Kitty thought, resembled the Leaning Tower of Pisa rearing up lopsidedly against the bright blue sky. As she got out and pushed the car door shut behind her, she spied an old woman sat on a cushion in the shade of the Cathedral's grand entranceway. Kitty stared over at her with open curiosity. She was plump and swarthy with grey hair peeking out from under a headscarf. Her skirt was voluminous and black. It was bunched around a stout set of legs she'd crossed at the ankles. Kitty watched for a moment as a group clad in standard-issue cargo pants and comfortable walking shoes with cameras dangling from their necks – to reinforce the fact they were tourists – approached the entrance.

The Gypsy woman picked a bowl up from the ground next to where she was sitting and shook it at them. Kitty saw the spark of hope that had flared in her eyes at their approach die as they ignored her and disappeared inside the realms of the Cathedral. How very Christian of them, she thought, feeling a surge of anger. How dare they treat the poor woman as though she were invisible! She opened her handbag, rifling in it until she produced her purse. Unzipping it, she gazed at its contents in dismay. She'd not had time to change any money into Euro's, and pound coins would be of no use to the Romany woman. She felt a tap on her shoulder; Pierre had gotten out of the car. She watched as he thrust his hand into his pants pocket to produce a few shiny coins that he held out for her.

"Merci." Kitty grinned, getting it right this time.

He nodded and slid back behind the driver's wheel beside Simone, who was finishing a phone call. Kitty strode over to where the woman was sitting and dropped the coins into her bowl; she was rewarded with a toothless grin. She smiled back at her and was about to turn away when something in the old woman's nut brown eyes made her hesitate. She beckoned for Kitty to come down to her level. So, for the second time that day, Kitty found herself squatting down as she let her take hold of her hand.

She admired Rosa's rings and made a comment Kitty could not understand before her rough fingers stroked the back of her hand in a familiar manner. Then, after a moment she turned her hand over and stared intently at her palm before running her index finger down the different lines. All the while she was muttering softly and Kitty wished she knew what it was she was saying. She hoped from the gummy grin she got when the woman finally looked up at her that whatever words of wisdom had just been imparted they'd all been good. As she released her hand, Kitty stood up hearing Simone call out.

"Mademoiselle Kitty! Come, come." She clicked her fingers in the same manner she had used at the airport. Kitty knew that if she had an umbrella to hand she would have held it up like a tour guide as she stalked to the carpark entrance before striding across the road.

Kitty nodded goodbye to the old woman before scurrying after Simone. She was surprisingly fast for such a little lady, she thought, puffing as she followed her click-clacking heels down a cobbled street. She knew she had better be careful not to cause an ankle injury on her own too high heels. She moved into the shade afforded by the tall buildings. They were all joined to one another forming a sinuous, mellow stone arc. When they reached the end, she saw that it had bought them out into what had to be the town's main square.

She didn't have time to pause and admire the ambience of the shaded square, though or search for the spot where her mother had stood when *Midsummer Lovers* was taken because Simone had taken her by the elbow and was steering her toward a nearby café. She weaved her way expertly through the outside tables filled with lounging tourists and locals alike. She pushed past the harassed looking waiter with his pen and pad in hand as he stood in an effeminate stance, finally coming to a halt at the table where the man Kitty had just sat down opposite had been enjoying his tipple in the mid-day sun.

Now, she sat with her hands clasped in her lap. She felt like she was watching a friend board a plane to an unknown destination as Simone retraced her steps back from where they had just come leaving her alone with Christian Beauvau. She had told them she would meet them both back at la maison before saying au revoir. Somewhere at the back of her mind Kitty knew maison was the French word for house, and she was curious to see where they would be staying but first, "It's nice to meet you too, Monsieur Beauvau. Thank you for paying for my flight over here and for arranging to have me picked up."

"You are welcome and no more of this Monsieur Beauvau. It makes me feel old to have a young woman address me so. Call me Christian, oui?"

"Er oui, okay."

"So firstly I thank you for coming to la belle town of Uzés which holds very happy memories for me and did so for your maman too. I am so pleased you have agreed to make the recreation of *Midsummer Lovers* possible. I trust you are happy with the remuneration Simone discussed with you. Oui?"

Kitty nodded liking the way he pronounced Uzés, Oo-zez. It seemed to just roll off his tongue. "Um yes, thank you it's very generous. About the photograph Mr, er, Christian, the reason I decided to come and do the shoot was in the hope that you might be able to tell me the backstory behind *Midsummer Lovers*."

He lifted his sunglasses pushing them up onto his head, and Kitty was surprised at the intense green of his eyes against the leathery lines surrounding them. "Ah oui, your belle maman when I came to England to say my goodbyes to her and to ask how she felt about me contacting you regarding this anniversary photograph told me of this. She said you know nothing of her life before she met your father. She chose always to close the door on her past and only look to the future."

"But you contacted me despite this?"

"But you see, she did not say non. Your maman, she wanted you to come here to Uzés because she felt it was the right time. She had her reasons for this as you will find out in a little while."

It was like having a carrot dangled in front of her nose, Kitty thought, not wanting to interrupt in case she missed a vital clue in the puzzle.

"Rosa was such a wonderful woman. My commiserations for your loss, ma chérie. To lose your maman, it is a very hard thing." He reached over and touched her forearm. It was a warm and kind gesture befitting the inflection in his voice when he spoke of her mother.

Kitty stared hard at him, trying to comprehend that her mother had known a man such as this. He must have cared for her because he had come to see her one last time in the UK. Christian was so very different from her mother's friends that Kitty had known. There was the staid bunch of women from the book club that all fancied themselves intellectuals. As for their old neighbour Dorothy with the hyena laugh, it had seemed when Kitty was growing up that she was forever popping over for cups of tea and slices of cake. Rosa would sit quietly not able to get a word in edgewise while she babbled on about who had done what to whom. She was so busy pondering the differences between them and this flamboyant Frenchman with his deep tan and silver ponytail that she barely registered him clicking his fingers to grab the waiter's attention. It was a gesture she would have found embarrassing had anyone else done it. But Christian, for some reason could get away with it.

"You will drink the red wine, oui? It is very good."

She nodded dumbly. Red, white, she didn't care so long as it was made from a grape and had an alcohol base. She finally managed to form the words to ask the question that had sprung to the front of the forming queue in her mind. "So did my mother keep in touch with you in the years after you took the photograph, then? Because I never even knew that she had been to France let alone once posed for what became a famous print. The first I heard of *Midsummer Lovers* was when you contacted me. I have to say it came as a huge shock to find out my mother was in it and at such a young age too."

Christian ordered her drink and then looked at her pensively for a moment. "I am sorry for this shock you have suffered. I can see how hard it must be to learn of your maman having had a life with another man before your père. You must remember that one relationship does not detract from the value of the other, though, Kitty. What you need to understand is that the allure of *Midsummer Lovers* lies in the very fact that Rosa and Michael did not pose for the photograph."

"I don't follow, sorry."

"That day I had focussed my camera to take a picture of the café scene where we are sitting now – it has not changed in fifty years you know – but then I saw them. They were strolling along, Michael pushing that cursed bicycle with Rosa by his side, just over there." She followed the direction of his gesticulating hand almost expecting to see the girl her mother had once been, and her eyes fell on the sun-ripened, stone building that framed the right-hand side of the square. The bottom of the building had archways cut into the stone to provide a shaded walkway alongside the row of shops that were recessed back into the building. Above the arches loomed another two floors and with their wrought iron balconies and faded blue shutters, Kitty guessed they were apartments. How wonderful to fling open your windows each morning to gaze at the bustling square below, she thought.

"I have never again seen such naked adoration on a woman's face as I saw on Rosa's that day when she looked at Michael. I owe my career to their *amour*."

Kitty squirmed in her seat at this waxing lyrical talk of naked adoration and amour where her mother was concerned then wished she hadn't as she felt a painful throbbing start up.

"When I captured that moment between them it was real. The beauty and the magic of that is what reached out from the photograph to grab people here." He thumped his chest. "That split-second decision to point my camera at them and push the shutter changed the course of my life." He frowned. "Of course this for me now is where the challenge will lie in the photograph I will take of you and Jonny tomorrow. It will not be easy because the expressions Michael and Rosa had on their faces were, as I said, genuine." He shrugged. "Still, this is what I am getting paid a ridiculous sum of money for so we can but try."

Kitty hadn't thought about what was required of her for the shoot; she'd been too busy focussing on finding out about her mother. It seemed that knowledge was going to come at a cost. She'd never been very good at drama, and now here she was being paid handsomely to feign total adoration for someone she'd never even met. Oh well, she thought, helping herself to another sip of her wine – which combined with the hot sun was making her feel magnanimous – as Christian had just said, she could but try.

"And oui, to answer your question I have kept in touch with your maman over the many years that have passed since that day.

We have written to each other to keep track of one another's lives because after everything that happened we became good friends. Of course, too, there were the royalties from *Midsummer Lovers* I used to send her."

"Royalties?"

"Oui royalties. I made a lot of money from that photograph of your maman and Michael, so it was only right that I shared it with them although we never put anything in writing."

Kitty frowned; the solicitor hadn't pointed out any ongoing payments from anybody, let alone a French photographer, being paid into her mother's account when he had wound her estate up. As far as she had known Rosa had lived quietly off the savings she and Peter, who'd been an accountant and had earned a more than comfortable salary, had accumulated over the years. She'd had the proceeds of sale from Rose Cottage and her constant downsizing too.

Christian saw her frown and explained, "You are wondering where this money is now, eh?"

Amongst a million other things, Kitty thought, meeting his gaze, yes she was.

He smiled. "Don't worry I am not pulling a fast one on you."

His use of such an American phrase sounded odd, Kitty thought, finishing what was left in her glass as she listened to his explanation.

"When Rosa married, she no longer wanted this money and the memories it brought with it. Your père, Peter was her fresh start and so she asked me to forward any further monies to her sister, Kitty Rourke. The money, it goes to an address in Ireland."

Her mother had a sister? She had an aunt she was named after still living in Ireland! Her mind raced wondering whether she looked like Rosa and whether they both had that same stubborn streak that Kitty had railed against so many times. She was glad when Christian ordered her another glass of wine. She had the feeling she was going to need it to try and process what she had just learned and what exactly to do next with this information. Her mother obviously had fond memories of her sister or she wouldn't have named her daughter after her. This woman, Kitty Rourke, as far as she knew had never tried to track Rosa down, though. So would she appreciate a visit from her sister's daughter all these years later? And Kitty already knew that she would have to find this woman, her aunt.

Christian remained silent watching the myriad of thoughts skip across her features as he sipped his drink and waited for her to speak.

"I didn't know mum had a sister. I always thought – Well that's the thing, I don't know what I thought." Kitty took a deep breath. "Please, Christian, that's why I have come. Tell me everything you know about who my mother was before she met my father."

He nodded, not looking surprised by her request before piercing an olive with a toothpick and popping it into his mouth. Kitty watched him chew it in frustration waiting for him to finish; he took his time.

"I think your maman kept her secrets because she wanted to forget about the gypsy in her, oui? It was a part of her past she would always associate with her family and with Michael."

"What gypsy in her?" She stared at him blankly thinking about the old woman at the Cathedral. She was nothing like Rosa; her descent was Romany not Irish. Perhaps he meant that when she was younger, she had been a bit of a free spirit or something? Well, that was a given, Kitty thought, she had been cavorting around the French countryside with her boyfriend when she was barely out of nappies after all. Still, it had been the sixties so maybe she was into all of that peace and love stuff.

"Rosa and Michael, they were how you say? Travellers."

"Yes well, they must have been if they were in France together."

"Non." He shook his head and speared another olive. Kitty wanted to slap it out of his hand and tell him he wasn't allowed another until he'd bloody well gotten on with it and told her what she wanted to know. He studied the glossy, black fruit for a moment. "I mean Travellers who are from an erm, what is the word I am looking for? Ah, oui, that is it, er tribe or maybe clan."

The penny dropped as her wine was placed down on the table. "Merci," she said to the waiter. She took a sip of the red liquid trying to process what Christian was telling her but barely even tasted it as it slid down her throat.

Her mother came from a family of Travellers. He was talking about those people she'd see in a convoy on the M5 from time to time or taking over fields with their camps. They'd been on the news over the years too, up in arms about being moved on and claiming they were getting a rough deal. There were two sides to every story, though, and the farmers whose land had been taken over by them claimed the Travellers always left a ton of rubbish in their wake. Kitty shuddered; she didn't even want to think about that reality programme where the gypsy girls all tried to outdo one another with their ridiculously huge wedding dresses. The girls and their families came across on the screen as a coarse and uneducated people. The men all smoked, seemed to like a fight and used the 'f' word a lot and if that telly show had been anything to go by, then the girls all fancied themselves as Beyoncé. They were fond of orange spray tans too and had accents so thick she could hardly understand what they were on about.

Her mother didn't smoke; she'd never had a spray tan and there was absolutely nothing rough around the edges about Rosa Sorenson. The only time Kitty could remember her swearing was the day her car had been wheel clamped most unfairly. It was an event that would make the mildest mannered of persons use bad language and even then her mother had only used the 'b' word. She was well read too and loved a game of scrabble. It always brought out her competitive side. No, Kitty decided, this Christian Beauvau fellow must have his facts wrong. He'd spent too much time soaking up the Mediterranean sun over the years. Just look at his skin, for goodness sake! You could cover a settee with it. The sun must have cooked his brain; that was all there was to it.

"You are shocked? I can see that I have shocked you once more by telling you this, oui? Your maman, she made a new life for herself with your father. She became a different person. It was her way of dealing with her grief when Michael died so suddenly."

Kitty stared at Christian. She had not expected that. She had assumed Rosa and Michael's teenage romance had been like a firecracker that had fizzled brightly for a moment in time and then burned out as first love affairs often do. She swigged from her glass trying to calm her thoughts and put the pieces of the puzzle together. "Look, I'm sorry Christian, but I am finding it hard to follow what you are telling me. I mean are you sure there hasn't been a mix up somewhere along the way? You know what with the language barrier and all maybe you misunderstood them because my mum can't possibly have been one of those Traveller people. Yes, she could be a bit kooky at times but she used words like rambunctious for goodness sake, and she knew how to spell it too." Kitty knew she was grasping at straws and the thing that was niggling at her was that, despite her protestations, Christian obviously had a good grasp of the English language. He had no reason to embellish Rosa and Michael's story unlike Rosa herself who it was becoming clearer had obviously had her reasons for not talking about it.

Christian leaned forward and placed his hand on top of hers, making a tsking sound as he saw her chewed nails. They felt stumpy and strange, and she wanted to curl her fingers up and hide them away, but it was too late. She'd chomped them all off on the flight over and hadn't even known she was doing it until she'd felt the woman in the seat next to her eyeing her curiously. He gave her hand a squeeze and she felt the warmth of it as she studied his rings. Despite what he had just told her, she instinctively liked him, this link with her mother's past. He was flamboyant and a little egocentric, but she could sense that he was also genuine. She wondered idly how on earth he'd ever get those rings of his off. His knuckles were large and knobbly and looked to have expanded over the top of the gold bands with the passing of the years.

"Listen to me, ma chérie. I will tell you what I know from the beginning. I can see you need to know this." He removed his hand from hers and sitting back in his seat clasped his hands around his middle. "I had come to Uzés on an assignment to photograph the annual running of the bulls. Instead, I take the photograph of Rosa and Michael, and it made me famous." Christian clapped his hands then held them out palms up. "It is fate. If I hadn't decided to stay on for a few more days before returning to Paris, then I would never have taken *Midsummer Lovers*." His eyes twinkled. "Maybe not just down to fate because there was a certain waitress who had caught my eye. That was why I was sitting here that day just like I am today. Although sadly this maître d', he does not possess the same charms as the lovely Eva did." His gaze flicked toward a nearby table whose patrons had left an array of dirty dishes. The waiter was loading his tray with them, a scowl on his unshaven features. Kitty guessed he hadn't been left a tip.

"I was people watching that afternoon when I saw them. You know this is a photographer's favourite pastime because the ways of the human race are a fascinating thing to observe through the lens of a camera. Michael, he saw me take their picture and he was not happy. The gypsy people they are erm, hot-blooded," he paused and Kitty could tell he was enjoying the drama of his tale. He cleared his throat and took a sip of his wine before continuing, "But they are also a poetic people with artistic souls, and it is this side of Michael I appealed to."

Kitty frowned, the Travellers she'd seen on the telly had never struck her as poetic people, dodgy but not poetic.

"He liked the romance of what I tell him I have just frozen forever on film, and as I am by myself, I invited them to join me

81

for a glass of vino. They did, and this is when they tell me a little of their love story."

She was nervous Kitty realized, her sting momentarily forgotten as she leaned forward in her seat, determined not to miss a word of what she had waited so long to hear.

"Michael told me that he and Rosa had run away together to start a new life." He released her hand and shrugged. "I wondered as we sat here talking if perhaps this is because their families did not approve of their love affair. They were both so young to be married."

"Married?" Kitty's jaw dropped. She had not expected that. Her mother's marriage to her father was her second. She wondered if he had known.

"Oui. They probably had no choice, it was a different time, and the Irish were so much more uptight about affairs of the heart than we French."

Kitty sat there shocked as she tried to envisage her mother as the girl she had been at sixteen. A girl so much in love with a man that she had thrown caution to the wind and married him. Not only that but she had left her family behind for him and what a family they'd been, if what Christian were telling her was true. She couldn't visualize that kind of unbridled passion or rebellion in the gentle, quietly spoken mother she had known. Nor did she particularly want to but then she supposed most daughters struggled to imagine their mothers having had a life so separate from their own. When she thought of her mother, she didn't think of Rosa the woman, she thought of her mum, a wife in an apron, a homemaker. When she wasn't pottering about the house or garden, or listening over the fence to Dorothy's latest gossipy tidbit, she had her nose buried in a book.

Her life as a widow without her daughter at home had been a rather solitary one despite the numerous groups she had joined since Peter had passed away. Looking back, Kitty felt guilty at not having spent more time with her. She had been so caught up in her life with Damien that she had never stopped to think that perhaps her mother might have been lonely. Maybe if she had taken more time with her, Rosa might have felt she could confide in her. That was the problem when someone you loved died; there was no going back to try and do better by them because it was just too late.

Christian sat back in his chair. "I fear I am going to disappoint you, ma chérie because Michael and Rosa's story it does not, as you know with his death, have a happy ending. Then c'est la vie I think because if it did, then you would not be sitting here with me now."

He was right, Kitty realized, feeling a bit strange at the thought. "You said they'd run away together; I am assuming they ran away from Ireland? I know that's where my mother came from, but I don't know any more than that."

"Oui, this is so. There was a fight of some sort between their families I think, and Michael and Rosa felt they had no choice but to leave their old life and its traditional ways. I could see that it hurt them both deeply to leave the people they loved behind. They came to France to put some distance between their memories, and they were happy together picking grapes for a while in the small village of Gigondas. When the season finished, they hitched a ride and came here to Uzés with no plans as to what they would do next. That is when I met them, and sadly Michael died only a few weeks after I took their photograph."

Christian's eyes had misted over at the memory. Kitty paused for a moment unsure as to whether she should keep pushing, but she had come a long way and she had waited a long time to hear this story.

Chapter 9

A friend's eye is a good mirror – Irish Proverb

"How did Michael die, Christian?" The sun was still high in the sky and Kitty wished she had a hat with her because she could feel its heat penetrating her scalp. Christian sighed and laid his hands down flat on the table. They were mapped by bluish-green veins and she wondered fleetingly what the gypsy woman outside the Cathedral would read in his palms. Whatever it was, she was sure it would be colourful.

"It was a tragédie. It always is when one so young and so bright is taken too soon. A hit and run, the worst kind of cowardice, as he rode his bicycle back into Nîmes one night. It was dark, the driver he must not have seen Michael but still not to stop, it is incomprehensible."

"Oh my God!" The cry escaped unbidden from Kitty's mouth.

Christian reached over and took her hand in his. "Rosa and Michael had only been living in Nîmes for a few weeks. Michael, he had found work on a farm on the outskirts of the city. Rosa, she was waitressing in a café. They had rented a tiny apartment furnished with no more than a bed. Rosa told me later that the night he died she sat on that bed feeling the four walls close in on her as the hours passed and he did not come home to her. She told me that she felt it when he died. She knew he was gone, but she couldn't bring herself to get off that bed not even when the knock on the door eventually came."

Kitty felt a solitary tear roll down her cheek, her poor mother she had been widowed so very young.

"Ah, life it is precious and far too short, ma chérie. When we are young we think we will live forever, and it is the hardest lesson of all to learn that our time here is so finite." He squeezed Kitty's hand and did not let it go as he continued with his tale. "The door to their apartment it was unlocked and so the policeman let himself in and found Rosa there. She said he was a kind man. He made a hot, sweet drink for her and put a blanket around her shoulders before telling her that Michael's death was instant and that he would not have known anything about it. She tried to find comfort in knowing that he didn't linger, suffering. But still, my God she was devastated. She had given up the world she had known to be with him and made him her life. Rosa, she was lost. She did not know where to go, but she had my address and so when morning came, she packed her bags and came to me in Paris. She would not go back to Ireland because she feared Michael's family would blame her for what had happened. But it was an accident I told her; she mustn't blame herself. But non, she was adamant; she could not go back."

"So she came to England instead where she met my father," Kitty finished for him.

"Oui, and when your maman wrote to tell me she was getting married, I was so happy for her. She deserved to smile again, and your père helped her to do this. I never met him, but I think he must have been a very good man."

Kitty felt the familiar twinge of sadness she always did when she thought of her dad. He had always been there for her and then one day he simply wasn't anymore. "Yes, he was. She didn't meet him until she was nineteen, though, did she stay with you in Paris all that time?"

"Non, Rosa she only stayed with me for a year. She got by cleaning apartments in the building we lived in. She was not the same girl I met that day in Uzés though, because with Michael gone her heart was shattered." He shook his head. "She was so thin and she had no appetite for food or life. Then this crazy thing happens, and *Midsummer Lovers* began to storm the photography world and no longer am I a poor and struggling artist. Suddenly I am in demand and everybody wants to know me. They want to know who the couple in the photograph are too, but Rosa was not interested in sharing her story with the world. For me, the work and the commissions they roll in. I think perhaps the mystery of who the couple in the photograph are only adds to its appeal. It is like the enigmatic Mona Lisa, oui?

Kitty nodded, spellbound.

"When I told Rosa I must share this fortune with her she asked me to do two things. She wanted me to write and tell Michael's family he was dead and to send his share of the royalties to his younger brother, Tyson. It is Tyson who is Jonny's father."

Jonny was the man she would be photographed with tomorrow, Kitty realized, and she tilted her head to one side as she listened to the story unfold.

"She felt it was the right thing to do. It would give him the chance for a new life if that were what he wanted. The money I gave your maman, while it did not bring her any happiness, it did bring her choices, and she decided to go to England. I was very sad when she told me she was leaving, but I understood it was time. Rosa, she was like a sister to me, you understand?" His voice cracked and he took a sip of his drink, savouring the wine in his mouth a moment.

"She wrote to me now and again to tell me that she was well. But I sensed reading her words that she was still a wandering, lost soul. She was always moving and never staying in one place long enough to make a life for herself. Then one day a letter arrives and her tone, it was different. Lighter, happier because she had met a man, Peter. He is kind she told me, and he would look after her. I love him, she said, and my heart sang for her when I read they were to be married. Little ceremony, no fuss, she told me. I know it was her way of telling me that I would not be invited." He shrugged. "This was okay with me because I understood that I was her link to Michael. Then she wrote to say she no longer had need of the royalties. Peter, he didn't want the connection with her old life to taint their new one so, as I told you before, she asked me to send the money to your aunt."

Kitty rubbed her temples; there was so much to take in.

"An olive, ma chérie?" Christian offered her the little dish in an attempt to lighten the sombre atmosphere that had settled over their table.

She shook her head. "No thank you." She had never been a fan of the stone fruit ever since she had shovelled several in her mouth as a child thinking they were grapes.

Christian put the dish down. "I didn't hear from Rosa again for many years until she was pregnant with you. Your maman she wrote to tell me she had her happy ending at last and that, ma belle, is where my story ends – well almost."

Kitty's eyes prickled with the pain of losing her mother. It smacked into her afresh the fact she was gone, taking her unawares. Blinking back the tears, she realized Christian had said his story wasn't quite finished, and she looked at him expectantly.

"Rosa has given me something to pass on to you. When I went to see her that last time she told me she had a gift she wanted to leave for you."

"What is it?" Kitty was astounded at her mother's absolute certainty that she would agree to come to Uzés for the photo shoot with this Jonny whose history was, in a way, tangled up with her own and Christian's. At the same time, she couldn't help but wonder why her mother hadn't just left whatever it was with her solicitors to give to her like she had her rings.

"It is a journal, ma chérie and the reason she asked me to give it to you here is that she felt it right that I am the one to pass it on to you. I was both her friend and her tie to the past you see."

Kitty's heart began to beat faster. "Where is it? Do you have it with you now?" She needed to see it with her own eyes, to touch it before she would believe it existed.

"It is at la maison where we are staying. I will give it to you when we get back there because I think you will need privacy in which to read it, oui?"

She nodded, that made sense but it didn't stop her wanting to hold it in her hands right this minute, and when her phone announced the arrival of a text she was grateful for the distraction. Retrieving it from her bag, a quick glance revealed it was from Yasmin. She chewed her bottom lip; she owed her friend a reply after hanging up on her the way she did earlier. Christian still had half a glass of his wine to finish before they'd head back to the house, wherever it was. "I'm sorry Christian I need to reply to this. Would you excuse me a moment?"

"Oui, of course. More wine?"

"No!" She didn't mean to snap, but she was desperate to get hold of the journal and did not want to while away another hour sitting here sipping wine, as lovely as it was. All that aside the painful throbbing in her nether regions was getting worse. If she had to take an antihistamine later to take the swelling down, she was probably best not to overdo the alcohol or she wouldn't be able to give the journal the attention it deserved. "Sorry, I mean no thank you. I didn't mean to snap."

"I understand you want to see this book of Rosa's. It is fine; I will finish this." He tapped the side of his glass. "And then we will walk back to the house together."

She smiled her thanks and began tapping out a message to Yasmin. She told her she had arrived in Uzés safe and sound, adding that she would phone her once she got to wherever it was she was staying. She'd fill her in on all that she had learned so far. Pushing send she grimaced, she had an itch she most definitely couldn't scratch in a public square!

"You look uncomfortable, ma chérie, are you alright?" Christian's craggy features creased with concern.

Kitty didn't fancy launching into an explanation as to how she'd come to get a wasp sting on her bum so she said, "It's just been a huge day, Christian that's all."

"Oui, I forget you have had an early start and then all this information, it is a lot for you to take in, I think." He waved up at the sky that to Kitty's surprise was beginning to darken. She had been so lost in what Christian had been saying she hadn't noticed the dark clouds rolling in or that the air had gotten heavy with the promise of rain.

"It is a spring storm brewing. Still, it does not matter because the forecast is good for tomorrow when we will take the photograph. We will have the midday sun shining down on you and Jonny, the way it did on Rosa and Michael. Un moment." He lifted his glass to his mouth.

The way the pairing of their names rolled off Christian's tongue made the little hairs on Kitty's arm stand on end, and once more her gaze swept the square half expecting to see, what exactly? She was getting fanciful she told herself, watching as Christian downed what was left of his wine and smiled at her. His teeth, she noticed, weren't quite so neon white after all those glasses of red wine.

"Shall we go, ma chérie?" he asked with one eyebrow raised.

"Yes please." She was already up and out of her seat, glad not only to get moving but to take the pressure off her backside. As much as she wanted to head straight back to the house, she knew she was going to have to get something for the sting. She'd obviously had an allergic reaction. "Do you mind if we call in at a pharmacy first? I think I saw one up on the main road; it's through there isn't it?" She pointed to the opposite end of the square where a woman dragging a child behind her along the path under the arched walkway disappeared from their line of sight.

"Oui no problem, you have a headache? Too much wine, too much sun maybe?"

"Mm, something like that." Butt ache more like she mentally added, slinging her bag over her shoulder.

Christian stood and she was surprised at how tall he was in his rumpled white suit. He held out his crooked arm, and as she linked hers through his, she understood why her mother had chosen to stay with this man after Michael died. There was something innately kind about him that made her feel safe in his company.

Her eyes flitted over to the beautifully dressed windows of the shops they meandered past and she slowed her pace to match Christian's. She got the feeling that these days he didn't rush anywhere for anyone. She told herself to be patient as she wondered how old he was; she guessed somewhere in his early seventies so at his age why shouldn't he take his time? Her eyes alighted on a rather gorgeous looking sweet shop. Under ordinary circumstances it would have urged her to come inside and fill a paper bag with its barrels of brightly coloured sweets, she made a mental note to pop in before she left. If she took a stash of sugary treats home for Yasmin, she might finally let the Mars bar incident go.

They left the peace of the square behind them as they rounded the corner and took a left onto the tree-lined, main road. The green cross she'd spied from the car earlier was a beacon of hope. Yes! Thank goodness relief was nearly at hand she thought, clenching her fist to resist the primal urge to scratch. That would not be the look in this part of the world where the women all seemed to have been blessed with a natural born sense of style and grace. She sniffed the air as a yeasty waft of freshly baked bread tickled her nostrils and she scanned the shopfronts ahead for the culprit. Ah there it was, she spotted the requisite patisserie a few doors down. A young, suit-clad man strode out, cell phone in one hand, baguette in a brown paper bag in the other. He paused to bite into the crusty loaf then carried on, and Kitty realized her stomach was rumbling.

"You go ahead, oui? I will go in here to buy some cigars." Christian gave a phlegmy cough as though to prove his intention as he paused outside a Tobacconist. Kitty nodded and disengaged her arm glad that he was not going to follow her into the pharmacy.

She averted her eyes as she walked past the array of glazed and glossy looking treats in the patisserie's glass fronted cabinets and pushed open the door to the pharmacy next door. The shop area was mercifully empty as she stepped inside and made her way down the narrow middle. It was flanked either side by overstocked shelves she noticed, heading toward the counter at the far end. As she approached, a young girl who looked like she must be bunking school appeared from somewhere out the back of the shop. It must be the dispensary area Kitty thought, watching her wipe her mouth with the back of her hand before she smiled. Oops, I interrupted her lunch, she realized. The girl said, "Bonjour." Then looked at her expectantly in an invitation for Kitty to tell her what it was she wanted.

"Er bonjour, um hi." She wished she didn't feel so silly every time she dropped a French word. She was well aware that it was arrogance on her part to assume French people would speak English too, but well, needs must. "I'd like some antihistamine tablets for a wasp's sting, please."

The girl looked at her with a blank expression. "English?" To Kitty's ear, this sounded like Einglash but it was close enough, and she nodded gratefully.

"Oui."

"Non-English." She smiled apologetically holding her hand up. "Un moment."

Oh, come on Kitty thought, furtively glancing back toward the door while the girl disappeared out the back once more. She scanned the shelves herself while she waited but couldn't see anything that looked remotely like what she was after. A sticking plaster would not suffice she thought, with a disdainful glance at a box of Band-Aids.

She heard someone clear their throat and looked back at the counter where a woman, the pharmacist she assumed in her white coat, had appeared. She was older with hair like steel wool, and she did not look amused at having just had her lunch interrupted.

"Hi er, bonjour, um could I have some antihistamine tablets for a wasp sting, please?" Kitty repeated.

The pharmacist looked at her blankly. "I do not understand."

"Um." Oh bugger it, Kitty thought, casting a quick glance over her shoulder to check that the coast was still clear. "Bzzzz, Bzzzz, Bzzzz." She flapped her hands for a moment and then pointed toward her bottom before pinching it. "Ow!" she yelped for effect.

The woman looked at her as though she were mad for a moment, and then as enlightenment dawned Kitty sighed with relief. It was the bloody worse game of charades ever, but at least she'd got a result. The pharmacist said something to her that went completely over her head as she came out from behind the counter. Scanning the shelves, her hand settled on a tube of ointment that she handed over to her with the self-satisfied smile of a job well done. Kitty snatched it from her gratefully; she'd wanted tablets but at this point she'd take what she could get – then spying the label she frowned. It was for the treatment of haemorrhoids. Oh for goodness sake she thought, I don't believe this. How could the silly woman have mistaken her impersonation of a bee for that of straining? "I don't have piles." She enunciated slowly and rather loudly as though raising her voice would help the woman understand what it was she wanted. "I have a wasp sting. I would like something to take down the swelling and stop the itching, please."

She was met with a blank stare once more and she saw that the little girl who'd served her initially had reappeared to see what all the noise was about. Great, she had an audience. Well, she'd better put on a performance then, she decided, unzipping her jeans and dropping her pants low enough to show them the angry red area. "Look! See a wasp sting. Itchy!" She scratched at it angrily.

"Ah oui, oui ze bee sting!" The pharmacist clapped her hands and Kitty thought about taking a bow but decided she would settle for the packet of bloody pills the woman had grabbed off the shelf behind her and was now proffering. At last, she thought, so engrossed in checking the label to see that this time she had what she was after that she never heard the shop door open until it was too late. She swung round, pills in one hand, jeans held up in the other, piles ointment in pride of place on the counter. Christian, who had once more pushed his glasses up on his head, stared at the scene with a perplexed expression. She caught a fleeting glimpse of a dark-haired man behind him looking equally bemused.

"Erm, Kitty ma belle, you are alright?

"Yes I am perfectly fine thank you, Christian. I won't be a moment." She knew her face was the same colour as her right buttock as she zipped herself back up quick smart, and went through the motions of paying for the tablets. Stuffing her credit card back in her purse, she snatched the paper bag off the Pharmacist, broke open the box inside and shovelled two pills down swallowing them dry. Then, with as much dignity as she could muster she walked from the shop leaving the two women to shake their heads and mutter on about 'ze rude English woman'.

Christian, sensing her mortification, had the good grace to wait outside for her, and she spied him sitting on a nearby bench seat. He was in conversation with the same dark-haired man she'd seen fleetingly in the pharmacy. Oh great, she thought, another witness to her humiliation. As she approached, she took the opportunity to do a quick inventory. Hmm, his thick black hair was worn just a tad too long, swarthy skin, dark Celtic features, yes she had a fairly good idea as to who this man was. He had to be Michael's nephew she concluded, assailed with a strong sense of already knowing this man. It was like an impossible déjà vu.

As though he had sensed her eyes on him, the man swung his gaze toward her and stared back unflinchingly. Kitty's step faltered as she registered his scowl and Christian seeing her standing there did not pick up on her reticence as he did the introductions. "Ah, Kitty, look who I have found exploring this belle town. Kitty Sorenson may I introduce Jonny Donohue."

"Er hi." She held out her hand and then dropped it, taken aback by the naked dislike on his face as she realized he wasn't going to accept it.

She barely registered his broad Irish accent only the words he spoke. "So you are the daughter of the woman who killed my uncle then."

Chapter 10

Broken Irish is better than clever English – Irish Proverb

Kitty took a step backwards at Jonny's words feeling as though she had just been slapped. Christian got to his feet as hastily as a man of his age could. His expression beneath his tan was aghast. "Jonny non! That is unfair. What happened it was an accident, you know this. The past is as they say histoire and ma chérie, Kitty, she is not responsible for it. Pardon, Kitty, I apologise for this." He reached his hand out to rest on her arm in a gesture of comfort, and Kitty could feel the trembling of his fingers on her forearm as he looked to Jonny expectantly.

"Don't apologise on my behalf," he snarled, and Kitty took in the flashing glints of amber in his eyes. He was filled with a simmering fury, but then she realized if he blamed her mother for his uncle's death he'd had his whole life with which to fuel it.

Taken aback by this stranger's vehemence toward her, her gaze swung between the two men. Jonny glared back at her. His hands, Kitty saw were shoved into the pockets of his jeans, and his belligerent stance suggested he was not in the slightest bit repentant over what he had just said. His build was on the lean side but still he was intimidating. Christian was slowly shaking his head unsure how to diffuse the situation. It was at that moment a screech of burning rubber distracted all three of them as a small, bright yellow car swerved to a halt at the kerbside next to where they were standing.

It crossed Kitty's mind that with the speed in which it had just veered into park alongside them it could have easily mounted the pavement and bowled all three of them over. Her mouth began to form the words 'bloody French drivers' just as the passenger window was wound down. To her complete shock, a familiar voice called out her name in an English accent.

Her eyes widened, surely not? It couldn't be, could it? She took a step toward the car before bending down to peer in the window knowing who it was even before she saw him. "Damien, what on earth are you doing here?" He grinned over at her looking very pleased with himself.

"I had to come, Kitty. It didn't sit right leaving you to come to a foreign country on your own to meet up with a bunch of complete strangers." He pointed at the two flummoxed men staring at the car from the sidewalk. "I mean this whole photograph thing could have been a crock. I wanted to make sure everything was kosher because if anything ever happened to you, I'd never forgive myself. I love you; you know that." He fixed her with a look that made her insides go wobbly in a way she didn't need. What she needed at this moment in time was to be strong.

"I got halfway home after I'd dropped you off this morning, but I couldn't stop thinking about what you were doing and imagining every worst case scenario. I knew going home was pointless because I'd just be climbing the walls wondering what was going on, so I turned around and went back to the airport. I managed to get a cancellation seat on the next flight to Marseille and then I hired this car." He tapped the sides of the steering wheel with both hands. "She's not what I am used to driving, that's for sure, but it was all I could get at such short notice. The GPS is great, though, and she got me here, so I can't complain.

Good things come in small packages." He winked at her in a way that left no room for wondering whether or not he was talking about her.

Kitty did not crack a smile; she was still reeling from Jonny's frosty reception and the fact that Damien was here. Part of her was relieved and grateful to see his familiar face when everything around her was so unfamiliar. The other part of her was angry that he had shown up here now when she had asked him just hours ago to give her some space. That was Damien all over, though, if he wanted to do something he simply went ahead and did it, he'd never talked things through with her beforehand. She wished her body wouldn't automatically react to his physical presence the way it did, though. It would be much easier to deal with him if she hadn't been feeling the tug of the good times they had shared together ever since their random meeting in Wigan yesterday.

For the moment, though, her attention was drawn to the tiny Citroën he was squashed inside. It wasn't his style she thought, noticing that his head nearly touched the ceiling. Her feet were beginning to ache in her heels, and she crouched down grateful to take the weight off them for a moment. Resting her hands on the car's windowsill, she glanced over at the backseat where a large overnight bag was perched. He obviously planned on staying then, she realized.

"This was my third circuit of the town and I was beginning to worry because I hadn't thought what I'd do when I got here if I couldn't find you." He flicked her a slightly accusatory look. "You've changed your mobile number and un-friended me on Facebook, so I had no way of contacting you to tell you that I was here."

The wobbly insides dissipated. She did not feel bad about the un-friending bit; she'd had to do that to stop herself from cyber stalking his account to see what he was up to every five minutes. She'd known the first time she'd typed in his name to eye his relationship status and to see if he had posted any loved-up photos with The Bitch that it was not a healthy thing to do. She knew too that if she continued to check in on him like that, she would make herself sick. So she had hit the button that would mean she'd no longer have access to his page with some degree of satisfaction and tried to put him out of her mind.

As for her cell phone, well she'd biffed it at the bedroom wall the day she'd walked in on his tryst. She had decided a new number might help with her new life. Of course, it hadn't made the slightest difference. All that aside, she didn't know why he looked dejected, he had more than bloody deserved being erased from her life at the time. He had no right to look so wounded now. She was the one to whom the damage had been done, not him.

A spark of anger flared at his audacity in coming here and expecting her to look pleased about it. "Look, Damien, you have had a wasted journey because as you can see, I am fine. Christian—" she gestured behind her, "is a lovely man and I am in safe hands." She wasn't so sure she was, not after the way Jonny had just spoken to her. He didn't need to know that, though. "I mean what did you think would happen when you got here, behaving like a bloody Knight roaring up in his bumblebee version of a car? It doesn't change what I said to you this morning about needing space to think, and what exactly are you planning on doing now that you know I am okay?" She promptly burst into tears.

"Aw, Kitty you're obviously not fine. Come on, hop in and you can tell me what's been going on." He patted the passenger seat.

"I can't." She sniffed. "I'm on my way to the house where Christian is putting us up." She glanced over to where the older man was standing looking perplexed. Spying Jonny's glowering face, she was almost tempted to do what Damien was asking and ride off into the sunset with him.

He drummed the steering wheel in that impatient way of his

she remembered only too well, and she took a deep breath. "Look its a long story but I have spent the last couple of hours talking to Christian about my mum, and he's told me so much about her that I didn't know. It's all been a bit overwhelming, and then you go and show up like this, but I am okay. Truly I am," she said in response to his raised eyebrow deciding not to drop the sting she'd received to her bottom into the mix. "The thing is, Mum gave Christian a journal she wrote for me just before she passed away. I'm hoping it's about her life before my dad and for some reason she wanted Christian to be the one to give it to me here. So you see she wanted me to come and do this photo. I don't know why it was important to her but unless I stay and do it, I never will."

"Even still I think—"

"I'm staying Damien. You of all people know how long I have waited to find out who my mum once was, and I need to be on my own to do it. Can you understand?"

Damien nodded slowly. "I get it, of course I do. I'm just not happy about you going off with some strange old man who looks more like a pimp than a photographer, and what's with all the rings?" As his eyes looked beyond Christian, Kitty flushed and hoped he hadn't overheard the conversation. "And what's with the other chap? He looks like he'd like to throw me into a boxing ring for a few rounds."

She knew who would come off worst in that scenario. "Keep your voice down." She lowered her voice. "That's Jonny; he's the nephew of Mum's old boyfriend, he's going to be in the recreation photo with me tomorrow. Like I said it is a long story, but from what Christian has told me I think he's probably finding it hard being here in Uzes." She heard Christian clear his throat eager to move on. "Look, why don't I give you the address of the house I am staying in and my mobile number, will that make you feel better?"

Damien shook his head. "No, I'll come with you, and once

I've checked it all out, I promise I will leave you in peace." She didn't believe him, but she recognized the look on his face. She knew it meant that he wasn't going to discuss it any further with her. A car horn sounded startling them both and irritation flickered over Damien's smooth features. "Wait here for me until I can find a bloody parking space and I'll walk with you to wherever it is you're staying so somebody other than those two there knows where you are."

Kitty didn't know what to do. All she wanted was to go somewhere where she could be alone with her mother's journal. She didn't want Damien here distracting her and yes alright his intentions had been good, but now she was torn as to what she should do. "Kitty?" She felt Christian's hand on her shoulder and sensed the question behind the gesture.

She straightened, smacking her head on the car frame, and hot tears prickled again. She rubbed at the sore spot before turning to face him. "I'm okay, Christian; it's just been a huge day that's all. He's um…" Who exactly was Damien to her these days? Her ex-boyfriend who had cheated on her and had now decided he wanted them to put all that behind them and get back together. "Uh his name's Damien, he's a friend of mine from England. Do you mind waiting for a few minutes while he parks the car because he'd like to walk with us to see where it is we'll be staying if that's okay?"

He shrugged as if to say he was mad. "Oui, of course."

"Wait there, I'll be back as soon as I can," Damien said giving a two-fingered salute to the car behind him as the driver sat on his horn once more before driving off.

"And what is he doing here, this friend of yours?"

Kitty watched the yellow car disappear up a side street and turning her attention back to Christian, she caught his quizzical look. "To tell you the truth I don't know why he's here. He's overprotective when it's not his place to be so any more." Swiping her cheeks with the backs of her hand, she hoped she hadn't just smeared mascara all over her face.

She registered Jonny's impatient muttering that he was off, but she didn't give him the satisfaction of looking at him before he turned and walked off.

"Don't worry about him; a walk will cool him down. He is hot-headed, it is in his blood. He will find his way to la maison when he is ready." Christian led her over to the seat he had been sitting on with Jonny before Damien's unexpected arrival, and they sat down to wait for him to come back. She was glad to take the weight off her feet for a few moments, and she wished she could take her shoes off and give herself a foot rub. One day she vowed, she would wear sensible shoes but not until she was at least ninety and only if she grew another foot.

Christian looked relaxed as he crossed his legs and rested his arm on the back of the wooden bench, settling back to watch the world go by. A comfortable silence stretched between them, and Kitty was grateful to him for not probing further where Damien was concerned because it was the last thing she felt like talking about. The air had cooled rapidly, and she shivered wishing she had her jacket with her, but it would be at the house now waiting for her in her room or so Simone had promised. Her eyes were drawn to the patisserie window mesmerized by the bright, yellow, greens, pinks and purples of the gooey looking macarons displayed there. Should she find out what all the fuss was about them? She was spared from having to decide by the reappearance of Damien.

He stood over them both holding his hand out to Christian as he introduced himself as her friend but with an air of propriety about him that suggested they were so much more. Kitty didn't have time to feel irked because thunder rumbled around them, followed a split second later by a flash of light and then the heavens opened.

***

"Kitty! It's about time you rang. I've been on edge all day wondering what you're up to and how it's going in France. College was a write off today because I was so busy thinking about you and where you were at. As for you sleeping with Sir Shagalot, I've decided to put you dropping your drawers down to his catching you at a weak moment. So if you promise me you'll have no more to do with him, then I think we'll just notch last night up as a right royal fuck up for old time's sake alright?"

Kitty couldn't help but smile at her friend's not so dulcet, but oh so familiar tones. It was comforting to hear her voice. She was lying starfished on a down-filled eiderdown having been assailed by absolute exhaustion as soon as she'd closed the door of her room and flopped down on the four-poster bed. Everything that had happened, all she'd learned and then Damien showing up the way he had, it had left her drained.

Damien had kept his promise. Once he had given the house a cursory once-over from his hallway vantage point and gotten her to agree to meet him for dinner in the square later, he had left her to settle in. He was probably eager to find a hotel and grab a hot shower after they'd got caught in the rain, Kitty mused as he shut the door behind him. Simone had materialized from somewhere upstairs proffering towels that she and Christian had dried off with as best they could before he had indicated that Kitty should join him in the sitting room leading off to the left. Simone disappeared into a room down the end of the hall that Kitty was guessing from the smell of percolating coffee was probably the kitchen.

Her stomach had fluttered with anticipatory nerves as she followed Christian through to a somewhat chintzy but inviting room where the choice of fabrics in the soft furnishing whispered to her of shopping trips to Paris. A black leather case was sitting on the settee, and he went straight over to it opening it, and after a quick rummage inside he produced a hardback book covered in roses. It was her mother's journal! He handed it to her without pomp or ceremony just a kindly smile. Kitty held it in her hands feeling the weight of it as she stared at the pretty patterned cover that was so evocative of Rosa. She felt the tears that had never been far away throughout the day burn her eyes once more. Flustered; she hadn't known what she should do next. Now that she had the precious book in her hands she was frightened to open it, but Simone had picked that moment to bustle in and offer to show her up to her room. Christian had patted her shoulder and said, "You read it when you are ready, ma chérie."

She had managed a small smile at his understanding, wishing Damien hadn't pushed her so hard to commit to meeting him for dinner later.

"Kitty, are you still there?" Yasmin demanded bringing her back to the present.

"Hi, yes sorry, it's just that my mind's buzzing with everything that's happened since I got here. Oh and to answer your question, considering Damien's here in Uzés I kind of have had no choice but to see him again." She held the phone away from her ear as her friend shrieked as she'd known she would.

"What do you mean he's there?"

"I mean exactly that. He followed me, uninvited by the way, to Uzés because he said it didn't sit well leaving me to go off and meet a group of people who could have been fraudsters with ulterior motives."

"And are they?"

"No of course not."

"Right so he can bugger off back to old Blighty! Tell him his job's done."

Kitty rubbed her temples. "I wish he would. Believe me, Yas, I didn't want him to come. I was happy to put some space between us by getting on that plane this morning."

"I do believe you, but I don't trust him and he knows you're vulnerable at the moment so don't let Mr Shagaround sweet talk you into something you know you'll regret. I don't have to tell you, Kitty, once a cheater, always a cheater." She repeated her familiar mantra.

"I know, I know but I've got way too much on my mind for that. Honestly, you won't believe it when I tell you what I've found out."

"So tell me. I can give you ten minutes because I am working tonight covering your evening shift by the way. Not that I mind because it gets me out the flat and away from Piggy Paula and Slimy Steve. Honestly, Kitty, I think those two fancy themselves as John Lennon and Yoko Ono doing that sixties' bed in thing. They were at it all day."

Kitty pulled a face. "Ugh not a visual I needed, thank you very much and who would have thought Slimy Steve would be a master of tantric sex."

"Tantric what?"

"Don't worry about it, Google Sting and Trudie Styler. You said you were in a rush so listen. Uzés is a gorgeous wee town, and it's well, it's very French." She gave a little laugh. "I suppose you'd expect that, though. To set the scene at this moment in time I am in a beautiful, ridiculously large room, lying on a double four-poster bed. My knickers and jeans are drying out on the rails at the end of the bed."

"Keep it clean thanks very much Kitty, there is enough smutty stuff going on down the hallway."

"Excuse me, but the reason I am currently in nothing but a T-shirt is because I got drenched earlier and I am trying to dry my things off. I packed with the intention of being away for one night, not three remember?"

"Fair enough but get on with it."

Kitty grinned, "Alright. My room's in a three-storey townhouse that the five of us, that's Christian, his assistant Simone, Pierre the chauffeur, Jonny and I are all sharing. It's one in a long row of old houses all with shuttered windows and crumbling plaster exteriors, very shabby chic but inside the house is pretty flash. It has all the mod cons only it's been done in an old fashioned way so it hasn't lost its charm. You want to see the bathroom down the hall, it has one of those claw-foot baths to die for, but the walk-in shower is a proper power shower. It just about knocked me over when I turned it on. It's just me and Simone on this level so at least I won't bump into Jonny on any middle of the night toilet runs."

"Jonny's the nephew of the man in the photo with your mum, right?"

"Yeah, and what an asshole, but I'll get to that. We're not very far from the main town square and all the shops, so I'm going to wander out for dinner later."

"No prizes for guessing who with."

Kitty ignored the comment. "Everything went to plan with my flight over. Until I needed the bathroom on the ride here…"

Yasmin squealed, laughing out loud as Kitty relayed the story of her alfresco toilet stop en route to Uzés. "Oh my God, only you could get stung on the bum, Kitty. I bet it hurts."

"It did and then it itched like buggery. But I got some anti-histamines and they have taken the swelling down, thank goodness. Now that I think about it they're probably why I feel like I have just run a marathon. It's either that or my run in with Jonny. Or maybe it's down to Damien showing up. Nope, actually I think it might be down to the journal on my bedside table. I think Mum might have written down all the things she felt she couldn't tell me about her life in it."

"Your mum has left you like a diary thing?"

"Yes, apparently she wrote it just before she passed away and wanted Christian to be the one to give it to me. That means she wanted me to come to Uzés to do this photograph."

"See? Yassy always knows best. So you have her blessing to be there, that's cool. But you haven't read it yet?"

"No, I wanted to call you first and let you know I was okay."

"And you are okay? I mean I'm worried now because you said

this Jonny guy was an asshole and Damien's sniffing around like a dog on heat."

"I can handle Damien." Even as she said it, Kitty didn't know if it was true. "As for Jonny he pretty much accused my mother of being responsible for his uncle's death that, by the way, was awful."

"Okay spill, but I am walking while you are talking."

Kitty heard the front door slam behind Yasmin, and she pictured her with her nose wrinkled at the smell of curry hovering in the hallway for a moment before she skipped down the stairs. She filled her in on what Christian had shared with her that afternoon and when she'd finished there was silence. "Yasmin, are you still there?"

"Yeah and you'll have to speak up because I'm about to turn onto Ashwin Street and the traffic's bad. I can't wrap my head around everything you just said, Kitty. It's an amazing and sad story that sounds like something I'd go and see at the movies. I can't believe what that ass Jonny said to you either. He was well out of order."

"Christian put him in his place pretty smartly. But I don't think he cared, and you know what, Yas? I think his anger is just a mask for the hurt he's feeling following in his uncle's footsteps."

A horn sounded in the background, and Kitty pressed the phone closer to her ear to hear her friend's reply.

"That or you've been overdosing on self-help books and he's just an asshole."

Kitty felt an overwhelming urge for something sweet then, one of those macaron's she'd spied earlier would help, but there would be no room service knocking on her door here.

"You know the world your mum came from is completely foreign to us. I think knowing you as I do you are going to want to find her people. You're lucky too because you've been given a chance to put things right where she couldn't."

"Yas, you make Mum sound like she came from Mars or something."

"Ooh a Mars bar, I could go one of them right now! Look I might not know much about little green aliens, but from what I have seen on the television the Travellers are a whole different breed. They have their own ways and customs."

"My mother's life growing up was nothing like those horrible shows on TV thank you very much, and they didn't have spray tans back then or money from what Christian told me."

"I suppose not but you do have a family you never knew existed and you've got the opportunity to meet them if you decide you want to."

Kitty knew how much Yas would love a link to her father and her heart went out to her friend. Her tone was gentle as she replied, "I have discovered I have a family I didn't know I had yes, but it is also a family that my mother was too scared to go back and face. I can't say I blame her either because their memories are obviously long if the way Jonny spoke to me this afternoon is anything to go by."

"Well, that's his problem. Tell him from me that I said it's time to move on buddy. It was fifty years ago. My gosh Kitty, yesterday you thought you were all alone in the world except for me of course then twenty-four hours later you find out you have an aunt. For all you know you could have ten or more cousins. I mean she is Irish, and you know what they're like at popping kids out. You have to open that journal and read what your mum has to tell you. Okay, I'm here. Oh crap, I just caught sight of a spot on my chin. How could this appear between the flat and work? Oh, Kitty I hope Mr Amatriciana doesn't decide to do dinner tonight, not with the state of my hair and this growth on my face."

Kitty could picture her friend with the phone crooked between her ear and shoulder as she inspected her chin in the reflection of Bruno's glass door. She felt a sudden yearning to go back in time to before all this had happened and things, although not great, were ticking along.

"I've got to go. Mario just spotted me, and he looks pissed if the way he's glaring at me while tapping at his watch is anything to go by," Yasmin said referring to the restaurant's maître d'. "Shit, I must be late and it's all your fault. Read that journal then ring me okay?"

Kitty's eyes flicked across to the book thinking how innocuous it looked. "I will." She got off the phone with a promise to phone her friend in the morning and a promise that she would not sleep with Damien again. Pulling herself up into a sitting position she plumped the cushions behind her back before reaching over for the book. She stroked its soft cover for a moment before lifting it up to her nose and inhaling deeply in the hope that she might catch a lingering last scent of her mother. She fancied she could almost smell the roses that had made up the dominant base notes of Rosa's favourite perfume, Paris. It was ironic she thought, that a place where her mother had been so sad was also the namesake of her favourite fragrance. Opening the book she began to read.

PART TWO

Chapter 11

Mother's hold their children's hands for just a little while and their hearts forever – Irish Proverb
Rosa's Journal

Kitty, it was never my intention to deceive you, and that was why I kept silent not trusting myself to open up to you. How could I? Not when I had let my family that came before you and Peter down the way I did. There's an Irish saying, the future is not set; there is no fate but what we make for ourselves. It's true Kitty.

Your da knew where I came from but please don't think that I'm passing the blame to him for my decision to keep that lid so firmly shut on my past until now. His reasons for not wanting me to tell you about where I came from were so very different to my own. While I was ashamed of the things that had come to pass, things that I could not rewrite even if I had wanted to, he, I can see now, was frightened. You see the idea of having to share you, his only child, it was too much for him. We waited so long for you. All those years of hoping and heartbreak and finally when we had given up, there you were. Our dreams came true the day you arrived and took your place in the world with us. You, my darling daughter, were quite literally the apple of our eye.

I loved him, your da, so don't think as you read more that I didn't. I loved Peter in a sensible and grown-up way, and we were a happy family the three of us. When he died, another little piece of myself went with him. I felt cast adrift in a world I didn't understand just as I had been once before. I didn't fit into this new version of the life I had built around the two of you without him in it, and I couldn't go back to my old life. Far too many years and too much water had passed under the bridge for that. I felt as though I was hovering in the limbo whispered fearfully about behind the hands of all good Catholic children like the one I once was.

You are probably wondering why I didn't ring you and talk to you about how I was feeling? The thing is though, Kitty, you had your life to lead, which is the way it should be. I didn't want to burden you with woes that you couldn't fix. I once heard it said that your children are only on loan; they are not yours to keep. Those words stayed with me because although it's hard, it is also the natural cycle of life. That's why I sold Rose Cottage when perhaps I should have taken the time to talk to you first.

I know you weren't happy with me about that. In hindsight, I can see that you must have felt like the rug had been pulled out from under your feet. You'd lost your beloved da and then, to top it off, you were losing the home you'd grown up in too. Your childhood home was your safety net in bricks and mortar. A place to come back to when things weren't right in your world but sweetheart try and understand. Things weren't right in my world. I had no choice; I had to move on. There were too many memories snapping at my heels as I roamed the rooms of that house and without you and Peter filling the spaces, the happy memories were seeping out through the cracks.

Peter was there for me when I needed him most. He picked up the pieces, dusted me off and helped me to live again all those years ago. So it was for him as much as it was for myself that I chose not to tell you where I came from until now. I hope you don't think me a coward for not staying around to face the music.

I do have regrets, though. Oh yes, I regret that your da never got to give you away at your wedding. I regret that neither of us got the chance to see you married and happy with a baby of your own. I would have liked to have met my grandchild or grandchildren. I would have been a good granny too, you know Kitty. I would have done all those naughty things like let them eat far too many sweeties and stay up late when they came to visit at my house. I regret too that we only had you for your sake and have often wondered whether we should have tried to adopt. Would you have liked a little brother or sister? Someone to play with, someone to fight with. That was a road we never went down, though, because it would have meant well-meaning people delving into my past, and neither I nor Peter wanted that.

Ah, but I would have liked you to have experienced some parts of the chaotic, rambunctious childhood I had. That's a big word, rambunctious, a big word not learned or understood in my younger years. My love of big and complicated sounding words came later. Do you remember how I drove your da mad with some of the words I'd find to spell out on that scrabble board of ours?

You've grown up knowing no more than that I was raised in Ireland. There was both struggle and simplicity in that upbringing that I have never talked to you about before. Yes, we were expected to work hard, and there was hardship to bear too, but in return, there was the freedom of carefree hours spent roaming fields far and wide with my siblings. Mind you, my girl, I wouldn't have been so keen on you using the language my brothers and sister were prone to tossing about. If our mammy had been bothered by it, she could have taken out shares in the Lux factory with the number of times she should have washed their mouths out. Not mine, though. I always fancied myself to be a bit different from the rest of them even way back then. I proved I was in the end too, but it came at a heavy cost.

Oh, but I am getting ahead of myself and all that's beside the point because nature didn't intend a big family for me and Peter.

I think he liked it that way too because it was what he knew with only your Aunt Maura left on his side. I used to wonder, though, from time to time if my inability to conceive another child was some form of karma for losing my faith, or whether it was divine payback for the pain Michael and I inflicted. It's strange isn't it all these religious connotations from someone who has not stepped foot in a church for so many years? Either way, I think that just having you made Peter and I love you all the more. When there is only one child, it is impossible to imagine it any other way, or that there could ever be another so special whose antics and achievements could delight so. We poured all our energies into you, Peter and I. You were, are, my darling, our greatest achievement. I know too that by the time you read these words that I have taken too long in writing it will be just you left in this world. Know that you were loved, though. Always know that Kitty, my child.

I hope your da and I didn't stifle you with all the love we poured on you our precious daughter. I, of all people, should have respected your need to breathe and to have the freedom to grow up on your terms. You can't know how hard it is to let a child go until you have your own, though, Kitty. That's just another of life's funny little quirks that you find out about along the way.

I always planned to tell you where I came from when you turned eighteen. That date was fixed in my mind as the day you would officially be an adult. Old enough to drink, old enough to go to war. It was an age where I felt you would be able to glean some under-standing for my reasons for keeping silent. You'll realise I'm sure, having spoken with Christian by now, what a hypocrite I was, given what I was up to at sixteen!

That's a mother's right, though, something else you'll realise when you are a mammy yourself. Part of my reason for not telling you where I came from was a mix of shame at my actions so young. Age you see is noble, but youth is honourable. There was also a deep-rooted fear on my part that you would want to find my family. In doing so, the lid on my Pandora's Box could never again be closed. Oh, I wasn't ready for that. The thing is, though; I always thought that the day would come when I was ready to face the past and now that it has, it's too late.

Of course, you know now that your eighteenth birthday came and went with a celebratory and much anticipated long weekend in Prague, and not a word about any of this uttered on my part. Ah, but that was a special holiday, wasn't it? It was so poignant for Peter and myself. We felt like we were saying goodbye to the little girl we'd raised and meeting the woman she'd become for the first time. We were both so very proud of you with your big grown-up plans of moving up to Edinburgh, 'where it was all happening' you said, to begin your chef's apprenticeship. It was to be your first foray towards independence. As hard as the idea of that was to a couple whose child had been their whole world, we also knew it was inevitable. We would have to find a way of muddling along alone together.

It was a sense of pride tinged with sadness at the passing of time, though, and I'll never forget the way Peter gripped my arm that little bit tighter as we strolled across the Charles Bridge. You strode on ahead in your thoroughly impractical outfit. I was amazed that at the pace you were setting you didn't break your neck on the old cobbles. Do you remember those shoes you were wearing? That clunky high heel was all the go that summer and you weren't the only girl tottering about in them, but you were the girl who was drawing all the admiring glances. I think that was when it truly hit Peter that despite all those years of keeping you close, one day soon he was going to have to learn to share you. The alternative should he refuse to do so would be to lose you.

You were so eager to get to the castle on the other side of that bridge. I remember the way the sun caught your hair and made it glow with a Rapunzel-like, spun gold as the gentle wind blew it back from your shoulders. It seemed fitting that we were off to visit a castle with our princess. There was such a sense of joie de vivre about you. Looking at your face alight with all the new and exciting things about to fill your days I knew I wouldn't tell you, not yet. I justified my decision by convincing myself that it was not because I was frightened of losing you to my estranged family. It was because I was frightened of how you'd react to the fact we hadn't had enough faith in you to let you make your own decision where they were concerned.

I didn't trust in my family's ability to forgive either, and I wanted to protect you from a rejection that I was the cause of. Nor, had they been willing to meet you, did I want you to get bogged down in their world and their ways. Not even if I'd known there might have been the possibility of the love of an extended family in return. The world you were destined to occupy needed to be bigger than theirs. At least that's what I thought watching you on the cusp of leading your life independently as you stepped out across the Charles Bridge that day.

You see I know you too well, Kitty. I knew that had I told you, you would have run to them, and you'd have lost yourself and your dreams in doing so. Remember, though, their ways and who they are don't define you as a whole, they only make a half. I was a fool in my choices. I can see that now because as it transpired you left your dreams behind anyway. Now that I have to leave you I want nothing more but for you to fit into a family that you should have been allowed to know.

When your da died it changed everything because I didn't just lose him, it was the beginning of my loss of you. I was so caught up in my grief because Peter had always been my anchor. He was the man who had grabbed hold of me all those years ago and stopped me drifting. Yes, in hindsight I should have spoken to you about selling Rose Cottage. By the time, I had made my mind up to do so, though, you were living in Edinburgh and already making noises about moving to Manchester. You were unsettled and I unsettled you more. But it was me who was the one at home with my memories, and without my lovely Peter. It was too much, Kitty. The silence was unbearable. I craved the sounds of traffic and the sense of being surrounded by others. It is, of course, ironic, given that in my youth I couldn't wait to escape the noise of others; I'd craved the idea of silence. The reality of it though was so very different.

Ah, but sweetheart I wish you hadn't left your apprenticeship in Edinburgh. You'd be a fully qualified chef by now. You could have opened a restaurant or travelled the world making a name for yourself in all the best eating places. You have talent my girl that comes from having a passion. Your passion is your sweet-tooth, and my passion was learning. Oh, and what a sponge I was, soaking everything I could up when I met Peter and at last got the opportunity to do so.

Time as it passes plays tricks on you, and the day I met your da, though over forty years ago, still seems like yesterday when I think of it now. I caught his eye as he swaggered around the fair that had been set up overnight on the outskirts of Preston where I was living, not knowing that was where I would wind up staying too. He was with a group of lads all with hair sitting a tad too long on their collars to mark the end of the sixties, all of them hoping they'd pull. It was those blue eyes of your da's though, that made the sun come out for me from behind the black cloud it had been hiding behind for so long.

A girl, Barbara I think her name was, from the boarding house I was staying in had dragged me along for a day out with her. I'd felt like I was embarking on a game of Russian roulette. My arm was linked through hers as we wandered past the Merry-Go-Round and those hideous clowns with the rotating heads, their mouths agog waiting for a ball to be stuffed in. The smell of popping corn and sickly-sweet candy-floss tickled at my nose as I wondered whether any of my kin were there. It was a possibility you know. Sure my Uncle Davey and his offspring had crossed the water years back and followed the fairs about for work. I never saw them, but the handsome man who had paused to lean nonchalantly against the wall with the Ferris wheel towering behind him became my future kin.

Peter was the first person I confided in that I was illiterate, and *you can close your mouth now sweetheart. It's true I never went to school and neither did my mammy or her auld mammy before her, but that doesn't mean we didn't know things. Those two women, they were wise in ways the written word could never compensate. But I always yearned for more and some would say later that that was my downfall.*

I knew as soon as I met your da that I could unburden an illiteracy I had kept as my secret shame. I had become so very clever at covering the tracks my lack of learning left as I went along my lonely way. I found odd jobs to hide behind and keep the wolf from my door. Your da as you know, was that rare breed of man, both intelligent and kind. He took me in hand, and it was he who I confided my past in. Peter loved me and unleashed my thirst for learning. My quest to drink at the fountain of knowledge became a living breathing thing that was to last me my lifetime. It was my passion and my joy. Please don't lose sight of yours, Kitty.

I try not to blame myself for you taking the apron of your apprenticeship off and tossing it aside after only six months. This little voice has niggled away at me, though, that by selling Rose Cottage in the way I did, I took away your last vestige of security. I gave you more upheaval when your world had already tilted on its axis with your da's passing. The thing is though sweetheart, I've learned as I have gone on something my mammy tried to explain to me when I was a child. A house is just something that keeps you warm and dry. It's the people inside it that make it a home.

That's why I got so angry when you telephoned me that afternoon and told me you were leaving Edinburgh. You had the opportunity to fulfil your dreams and you tossed that chance away. You decided to go and sit in an office like Dolly Parton did in 9 to 5, day in day out typing. Where's the creativity in that, Kitty my girl? I thought to myself as you tried to explain that you were sick of the hours, of being shouted at and the poor pay that was part and parcel of learning your trade. You couldn't see the big picture though, and it frustrated me so.

A few more years of self-sacrifice and then you'd be free to go anywhere and do anything! I'd forgotten that packing things in when the going gets tough is the prerogative of the young because you live in the present and can't imagine a middle-aged or elderly existence. You wanted to be having fun, out in the big wide world. So you set up house with your friends in Manchester and paid your way by starting work as a secretary. Instead of being proud of you for managing your life, I criticised your decisions. I'm sorry for that, my darling; I should have trusted you to take a round about path before finding your way. You are your mother's daughter after all.

If you hadn't taken that job and moved to the city, you'd have never met Damien. I knew you were smitten when you bought him home to meet me. You hadn't done that with any of your other men friends. I will grant you he was handsome, and I know he made you laugh. I sensed he had another side to him, though, so while I could see what you saw in him, I never warmed to him. He'd give you an egg, that one, if you promised not to break the shell.

He made you happy for a while, stilling that restlessness running through your blood as it still does mine, even after all my long, settled years with Peter. I knew he would hurt you one day, though, I had seen it. I have the sight you see, Kitty as did my mammy and her auld mammy. I think you do too. Don't be frightened of it. Some say it is a gift, but I say it just is, no more no less than that.

The day you turned up to show off the beautiful ring he'd presented you with, I hoped I was wrong about him. I wanted to tell you not to mistake a goat's beard for a fine stallion's tail, but you said he was the man you wanted to marry. 'I want to spend the rest of my life with him', you told me, your voice trembling with excitement. The thing was I knew the truth of what would happen but still I tried so very hard to join in on your joy. You were always the kind of child who learned the hard way, Kitty. You were headstrong and wouldn't be told, so I knew if I confided that he was not the man for you it would fall on deaf ears.

Our relationship was already strained once Rose Cottage's sale had gone through. Despite the fractures it had caused between us, my body had twitched to move on like yours did when you left Edinburgh. It's in us you see Kitty, this craving for the distraction of new surroundings. It didn't fix things though, because none of the houses I lived in after your da died ever felt like home without you and him in them.

The problem was that I didn't know how to be alone, and I wanted to be selfish and beg you to come back to me. I wanted to tell you I was lonely, but I had been selfish once before, and it had cost me dearly. I wasn't that person anymore. I knew too that no matter how hard the road you took got, I had to let you take it. Life is a rite of passage and if we don't make mistakes along the way how can we become the people we are destined to be?

You returning to the fold wasn't the answer either because it wasn't you who was responsible for the part of me that had been missing since I was sixteen years old. What I needed, my lovely girl, was forever out of my grasp. I was too frightened of what my family thought of the self-absorbed girl I had once been to try to reach out and touch them again. I wish I had been braver, Kitty. I wish I had the time left to tell them I was sorry for leaving and never going back. I wish I had been able to see that things could have been so very different.

Oh, my beautiful daughter, I know that soon enough there will come a time when you will hurt more than you believed it was possible to hurt. It hurts me just as deeply to know that I won't be there to hold you and tell you that everything will be alright. It will be though Kitty, hold on to that because I've seen that it's so.

I wish my mother had told me that things would work out in the end because she would have seen what was going to happen. At the same time, I have always felt guilt at the knowledge that she knew what I was going to do. Who knows? I have mixed feelings but perhaps the sight is a gift after all because to be able to tell you that you will be happy again my darling girl is my gift to you.

Please, Kitty never forget that you are strong, and you will wake up each day to make your way through the pain of loss. It's a pain that will fade to a dull ache and then it will dissipate, and you will get your second chance to live again like I did mine. Hold on to that with both hands Kitty. You, my girl, will realise that I am always with you in your heart. You will go on to meet someone who will never lie to you. A person who will help you to find your way and not fill you with self-doubt. You will find the man who is worthy of all that love you have to give. He will treat you well and love you well and let you be the person you were always meant to be.

Your da loved me, but he could never accept the girl with the wild blood in her that I once was. So I stopped being her. My life before I met him was as foreign to him and his middle-class upbringing as if I were from a faraway exotic country. The woman that he loved was the mother to you. The woman with the glasses perched on the end of her nose as she lost herself in her books trying to catch up on all those lost years of reading. She was a woman content to no longer walk on the wild side as she lived her days in a rambling cottage, surrounded by roses with her husband and her child.

Oh and it was a good life, Kitty, we were happy. Peter and I cherished one another but once a long time ago I had the kind of love that only comes along once in your life. It was the kind of love that derails you with its passion and trivializes every other aspect of your life. It renders you helpless but makes you fearless, and it blinds you to the things that matter most. It was my first love.

You might think that Damien was yours. That he was your once in a lifetime love, but he wasn't the one. How could he be? Not when he wanted to shape you so that you fit into his world instead of you sharing it with him. Never change who you are because to be untrue to yourself, it eats away at your soul like this damned cancer is doing mine. Your great love, the man who will love you and chase your dreams with you, has yet to come into your life, but he will find you. I know this, sweet child, just as I know that no matter how tough the going gets you have to keep on going, keep pushing and keep going and never give up.

And so now here I am back where I started, and oh my, it all seems such a long time ago now. It's still fresh in my mind, though; all that happened when I was a girl because some memories in life never fade. I have been so adept at keeping that part of who I was separate from you that it feels as though I am going to tell you a story about a girl I once knew, not the girl I once was. Time Kitty, is a good storyteller.

Kitty's vision blurred as her eyes burned, heavy with tears she didn't want to shed. She wanted to know more and so blinking them away she continued to read, and her mother's story began to dance from the pages.

Chapter 12

An old broom knows the dirty corners best – Irish Proverb
1957

Rosa Rourke's fair hair – matted with knots that she refused to let her mammy untangle, not even with the brush that had once been her auld mammy's – fell about her small pixie like face. It puzzled her how something as pretty as that brush with its innocuous white bristles, blue patterned china back and burnished gold handle could inflict so much pain. It did, though, and whenever she saw her mammy wielding it she leapt to her feet and ran! Not like her baby sister, Kitty who loved the fuss. She would sit there with her hands clasped on her lap, an angelic look on her face, without so much as a moan escaping from her lips when she got her hair brushed. Mind you, Rosa thought looking at her sister fondly, Kitty's thick dark hair seemed to behave itself, unlike hers which was forever getting itself into a tangle.

Rosa turned her attention back to the job at hand. Her tongue poked out the corner of her mouth as she pushed her hair back from her face. She frowned in concentration and began to twist the tiny strip of copper wire she held between her thumb and forefingers. Her brothers had salvaged it from the odd bits of disused electric cabling gathered on one of their many jaunts around the villages or towns they camped on the outskirts of. Rosa's task now was to manipulate that wire into a stem for the paper flowers she would sell door to door should the need arise in the ensuing winter months.

She was sitting cross-legged on the sparse grass of the roadside verge; Kitty was sat next to her. Her little sister's legs were splayed out from under her grubby pinafore while her chubby hands clumsily tried to imitate the deft movements of Rosa's fingers. Casting a shadow over them both was the family's fine blue canvas, bow-top wagon. The Rourke's home was a windows and door wagon with pretty lace curtains hanging in the twin glass panelled arches above the door by the stoop. The larder was to the left with cooking utensils hanging on the wall alongside it. A free-standing wardrobe, whose door had to be leaned on in order for it to shut, stood opposite. Two chunky storage chests full to the brim with all their worldly goods were stacked on top of one another next to the wardrobe and always there in the larder was a full pitcher of water. In the middle of the wagon was a small fuel-burning stove. Its flue poked right out through the canvas roof to save them all from getting smoked out. At the far end was their sleeping area.

The family lived their lives outdoors, but at night when they all piled into that wagon of theirs and pulled the covers on top of themselves, they were never cold. Not even when winter threatened them with its worst. Sometimes Rosa found it hard to sleep, like when her mammy and da got up to that grunting, groaning thing she had a fair idea had put the boys and Kitty in her mam's tummy. It was that too that had been responsible for the babies who never got the chance to be born. It was strange, she thought, how something that seemed to make her parents happy could also make them so sad. When she heard their fumbling start up, she liked to listen instead to the rain on that canvas roof or the shushing of the wind as it whipped across the top of it. Those sounds reminded her of the ebb and flow of waves on that pebbly beach near Galway they sometimes camped by.

Nellie their trusty black and white Piebald, who despite her advancing years, had pulled their wagon for many a long year without complaint, was grazing alongside it. The lush green pickings of a few weeks ago were few and far between now, though, thanks to the hens' constant scratching and pecking in their search for grubs. Finola, the goat that Kitty had named so for no particular reason that any of the Rourke's had been able to fathom, hadn't helped matters either.

Finola never seemed to stop eating and once she had escaped causing an uproar by helping herself to some uppity village woman's flowers. Rosa knew it could have been worse; she had witnessed the goat eat washing off a line before. Still, the auld harridan had chased poor Finola back to camp with a yard brush. It wasn't long after that incident all the families in the camp were woken by a din that for once was not of their own making. Rosa had peeped out the net curtains at the back of the wagon to see a posse of men banging their shovels and advancing down the lane toward their camp in a menacing manner. Her eyes had widened as she watched her mammy rally the other women. She'd continued to watch as they all began to holler at the unfairness of it all and her da along with the other men, rounded the animals up in readiness to move on.

Rosa didn't like to think about that incident or the other times they had been forced to pack up their things and get on their way. It frightened her, the animosity she sometimes sensed from the people who lived in the towns and villages they passed through. Sitting there on the ground that morning, she shook those thoughts away oblivious to the damp from the dew that night-time had left behind. It was beginning to seep through her skirt to her undergarments. The crispness of the air she knew was due to the early hour and the day would soon warm up as befitted the latter part of the high summer. For now, though, she was glad of the warmth of the campfire.

Kathleen, her mammy, was keeping an eye on the soda bread she had baked in the skillet pot. The smell of it was making Rosa's nose twitch and her tummy rumble with anticipation.

"That's the best smell in the world, so it is," she murmured to Kitty before shifting ever so slightly closer to the fire that sputtered beneath the pot, smiling at her shadow; Kitty did the same. Their mammy had dressed, despite the season, in her heavy wool cardigan. It seemed to Rosa that she never took it off. A pair of worn brown boots that she'd seen her slide pieces of cardboard inside to patch the soles and keep the cold out, peeked out from beneath the hem of her long plaid skirt.

Occasionally, Kathleen leaned forward to feed the fire a handful of twigs, gathering them up from the stack Rosa's brothers, the twins, had busied themselves collecting from the nearby fields and hedgerows. It was the duty of the younger boys in the camp to rustle the kindling up. It was to the disparagement of the local villagers who, Rosa reckoned from their covert glances as they wandered past their camp, were envious of the stockpile.

To her mind, the settled folk's voices sounded harsh, unlike their tongue that had a musical quality to it. Rosa had asked her mammy once why they spoke and lived differently to the village people. Kathleen had replied, "Sure Rosa we speak Gammon and are we, not the Lucht Siúil, the Walking People? I think it would be a lonely thing to live in a house like them there up the road. No, in a wagon you know what's what and who is who. Don't you think it's nice that when our friends come to visit, we can go off and see what is around the next corner with them?"

Rosa had heard the pride in her mammy's voice, and she had spoken the words Lucht Siúil aloud liking the way they rolled off her tongue.

Kathleen was crooning a song as she stoked the fire. It was the one about the wren even though it wasn't St Stephen's Day. It was called *Lá an Dreoilín,* The Day of the Wren. Rosa knew the tradition stemmed from the little bird supposedly having betrayed St Stephen. She also knew by the small smile her mammy had given her before she began her lament that she knew it was her eldest daughter's favourite.

Rosa loved it when her mammy sang. It was a comforting sound like the wind and the rain on their canvas roof. It meant all was right in their world. Just as their da playing his tin whistle for them of a night or, telling them the stories his auld da had told him under those very same stars that still twinkled down upon them did. When there was silence, Rosa knew hard times were upon them and that her belly would not be warm nor full again until the music and stories started once more.

Now, she tilted her head to one side listening to her mammy's pitch. It was pure and perfect and sure it would send shivers down her spine to hear it. The lines on Kathleen's face always seemed to soften too when she sang. By the time the words, *Mrs O'Gill being a very good woman gave them a penny to bury the Wren* danced from her lips, Rosa could see her mam as she was. What she would have been like before children, loss and hard work had taken their toll. Whether it was because the little bird died at the end or the strange faraway look on her face, Rosa didn't know but either way, she always cried when she heard this last verse sung.

Sniffing loudly she swiped at her nose. "I'd rather listen to mammy than that fandangle radio thing we saw at Ballinasloe last year," she whispered to her brother Joe who had appeared alongside her, referring to the horse fair the family attended annually. All sorts of weird and wonderful things they'd never seen the likes of before would be on display each October. Their job, to tempt the passers-by to part with the contents of their purses at the West Country Fair. Joe, almost hidden under the sticks he had gathered, dropped his haul on top of the pile and patted her shoulder.

Ah, sweet Joe, Rosa thought, quickly wiping her wet cheeks with the backs of her hands as she saw his twin Paddy, approaching. He was the older of the two by a minute or so and never let any of them forget it. She watched him stagger under the load he was carrying. If he spotted her tears, he'd tease her mercilessly despite her having two years on him! He might have been Joe's twin, but that was where the similarity between the brothers ended. Joe with his gentle ways had the ability to make them all smile and laugh while Paddy's antics would have his mammy and da shaking their heads over what to do with him. Still and all, opposites they may be, the two brothers were like yin and yang because together they made a whole. Rosa often found herself watching them, envious of their closeness.

She was the cuckoo in the Rourke's nest, them with their black hair and flashing dark eyes. Her mammy always said she got it from her side when she caught Rosa frowning at her reflection in the mirror that matched the hairbrush. Sure hadn't she been told of her auld mammy's granny having those dark brows and the blue eyes with fair hair too? That was who she got her colouring from, she'd say, but Rosa knew it wasn't just her fairness that set her apart from them. There were times when she looked at her family that she knew the path she was destined to take would be different to theirs. It made her feel sad, but she knew too that she couldn't change it.

This knowledge of how things would be, she did get from her mammy. Rosa had noticed that the only time the villagers would look Kathleen in the eye was when they handed her a coin, in the hope she would tell them what was what, and what would be.

"When will Da be home, Mam?" Paddy demanded having dropped his sticks onto the stack. He strode over to the fire in pants nipping at his shins to inspect the rising contents of the skillet pot.

Rosa looked up; she knew his game. He wasn't bothered in

the slightest about when his da was coming home; he was hungry that was all. Hard work made you hungry; she knew that only too well. There never seemed to be quite enough food to eat their fill but still she knew not to complain, Mammy and Da did their best. Besides, they did better than some in the camp with there not being so many mouths to feed in their family. The Connors were ten altogether, and another one was on the way, any day now too if the size of Nora Connor's belly was anything to go by.

Paddy knew he was wasting his time sniffing around that skillet pot. No bread would be broken until their da appeared wiping his sweaty brow as he took a break from cutting and wheeling the turf. Rosa reckoned they had a few more weeks left around these parts and then when the leaves began to turn yellow it would be time for them to move on for the apple picking.

He was a hard worker, Da, and oh so handsome, Rosa thought. She was fascinated by the strands of silver that streaked their way through his thick dark hair. His brown eyes always seemed disappointed to her, though, and that disappointment never seemed to fade no matter how hard she tried to please him. She wondered at times whether he would have liked a different life. She fancied that if he could change things, then he would trade in the horses. He came alive when they were at Ballinasloe, but the Rourke's were not so far up the hierarchy for the horses. His lot was the turf cutting and fruit picking and when there was none of that to be had he would go door to door selling the rags. When things got bad and there was nothing more than mouldy auld cabbage to put in the skillet pot, Mammy would take Kitty into the town. There she'd sit on the cold hard ground with pretty Kitty on her lap, a tin cup in her hand that passers-by could toss a coin into, "for the baby, like."

"It will be time to eat soon enough lad," Kathleen answered Paddy as she batted him away from the pot. "Go on away with youse both."

Paddy pouted but then took Joe by the arm. "Come on."

Rosa did not miss the glint in her brother's eye and nor did her mammy.

"Don't be getting into bother now," Kathleen warned and Rosa sighed knowing in that way she just did that her mam's words had fallen on deaf ears.

No more than fifteen minutes had passed when an almighty squawking started up. Rosa dropped the bit of wire she was twisting and following her mammy's lead, leapt to her feet. The band of women who had abandoned their chores on hearing the ruckus ran toward Paudy O'Doyle's wagon. A sinking sensation in Rosa's stomach told her Paddy would be at the root of it all. Kitty tried to keep up with her big sister but tripped and sat down on the ground to howl at the unfairness of being small, but Rosa didn't stop.

She saw the feathers first, glorious green and black plumage sailing high above the small circle of cheering boys who'd gathered round the back of the wagon. Joe, white-faced, was hanging back and – shooting him a look that said he should have known better – she pushed past him to see what was going on. As she had suspected, there was Paddy down on one knee cheering Paudy O'Doyle's angry, prize-fighting cock rooster on. She watched in horror as it lunged and pecked at a bird she recognized as Martin Ward's pride and joy. Paddy's arch-rival, Ginger Collins, was crouched opposite him clutching a bag of marbles in his grubby hand. As the two lads spied their mammys bearing down on them, their eyes widened, and they scooted back on the seats of their pants. They both narrowly missed a drenching from the pail of water tossed over the two cocks that seemed to come from out of nowhere. The circle of boys disbanded and scattered quick as a flash, but Paddy wasn't going anywhere. He couldn't, not while his mammy had hold of him by the ear.

Rosa took Joe by the hand. "Come on let's get those birds back in their cages before they start up again. The menfolk will be back any minute, and if they catch wind of this, they'll skin Paddy and Ginger alive."

She shook her head shoving the ruffled bird back in its cage and locking it tight, hearing Paddy plead his case as he was dragged back to the wagon. "But Mam we were only borrowing them and Ginger said he'd give me his bag of marbles if Paudy's cock won."

"Ah, you should have stopped him, Joe. He'll be in for it when Da hears of this," Rosa said as they set about returning the cocks to their rightful homes.

"I couldn't Rosa – you know what Paddy's like when he sets his mind to something."

Rosa sighed, she did indeed know what her brother was like. What made her sad was that when he got his arse kicked by Da, as he undoubtedly would, Joe would walk around clutching the seat of his pants afterwards too. He felt his brother's pain as keenly as if it were his own. It was a strange thing, but it was the way it was between the two brothers, and what was done was done. "I don't understand it, grown men standing around watching birds half kill themselves. It's an ugly, cruel thing."

"Da says it's the sport of kings and that once upon a time every village in England had a cockpit, and everyone from royalty to school boys would join on in. It's been that way for thousands of years."

Rosa knew deep down that her gentle brother agreed with her. "Well, then it's high time they found a new pastime."

"Don't let Da hear you say that!"

She wouldn't. Rosa knew he thought she had far too big a gob on her for a girl as it was. Just the other day she had gotten a cuff round the ear when she had asked him why it was auld man Billy kept himself to himself so. She'd see him sitting, day after day on his own, working his worry beads over and over as he repeated a silent rosary. Da had told her that Billy had been at the Somme and had seen things no man should ever see. That was why he sat so, trying to talk to our Blessed Lady. It was his way of atoning for things that were not his fault, he'd finished. Rosa had asked him why it was our Blessed Lady was taking so long in getting back to him. "Sure," she'd said, "wasn't the war years ago?" Her question had not gone down well.

Chapter 13

Twenty years a child; twenty years running wild; twenty years a
mature man – and after that praying – Irish Proverb
1959

Rosa did not look forward to the onset of winter. Still, she looked
forward to the month of October because it brought with it the
highlight of her year, the Ballinasloe Horse Fair. The colours of
the nine-day annual carnival were to her mind a last ditch hurrah
before the greyness of the ensuing months set in. She promised
herself that this year, she would try to hoard the vibrancy of it
all in the corner of her mind. That way she could pull the images
out to cheer her mood when the drab days dragged on too long.

"Go east for a woman," her da would say as they loaded up
their wagon and joined the throng of travellers heading for the
town of Ballinasloe in the County of Galway, "and west for a
horse."

The weather had turned it on for the start of the fair that year,
and although it was chilly, the sky was a crisp blue. An air of
infectious, high-spirited, good humour filled their camp that
morning too. Rosa's fair hair gleamed with having been freshly
washed. For once, seeing as it was for Ballinasloe, she'd allowed

her mammy to run the brush through it, and her scalp was still stinging from all those strokes. She'd worn her best dress too, although the clean white cotton had taken on a greyish tinge thanks to all its washes. A thick woollen cardigan pulled over the top of it would keep her warm, and her feet were stuffed inside a pair of wellies.

Kitty, overawed by all the noise and people filling the town's street had a firm grip on her sister's hand. She too had dressed in all her finery, not caring about the holes in the elbows of her blue jumper. She had been far too enamoured of the matching blue bow her mammy had tied in her hair in honour of the occasion to notice such a trifling thing as that.

Rosa sniffed the air. She fancied she could smell the frenzied excitement of the young lads riding bareback as they paraded up and down the narrow street. Their antics signalled the start of the fair, and she felt herself get jostled. "Come on, Kitty." Rosa pulled her little sister along behind her as she pushed through the bystanders toward the field. She could see the clusters of stalls set up and ready to do business in there and wanted to see what was on offer this year. She knew too that there would be the usual tug-o-war, singing competitions, music, dancing and horse racing over the next week.

Her mammy had put her in charge of her little sister, but Rosa didn't mind, Kitty was no bother. She knew Mam would enjoy her time whiling away the days as she caught up with women she hadn't seen since last year. They'd talk about things that went right over Rosa's head, things she suspected that you had to be married to understand. Da was already off talking the talk and walking the walk with the other menfolk as he set about inspecting the horses for sale. As for the boys, well no doubt they'd be busy getting under folks' feet and cadging pony rides off the bigger lads. When they tired of that, they'd rile the dogs waiting to compete in their race just as they had done last year and the year before that.

Rosa kept Kitty close to her side as they trawled the stalls. The hard-sell banter of the stallholders didn't intimidate Rosa as she paused to wonder over the latest gadgets and mod-cons. All the while knowing that they would be completely useless additions to their way of life. A stack of colourful plastic hoops hanging on the wall of one stall caught her eye. "How do those work then?" she asked the stallholder, a man with a greedy glint in his eyes and whose grin revealed two missing front teeth.

"Those there are hula hoops imported all the way from America. They're the latest thing over there, so they are, here have a look." He produced a photograph showing a smartly dressed, teenaged girl. Her hair was in a swinging ponytail, and she had a big, happy smile plastered on her face as she twirled one of the coloured hoops around her waist. "The idea's to keep it going, not to let it fall, like. Do you want to try it?"

"Yes, ta." She blinked at the whiteness of the girl's teeth. She had no money to spend and was wasting his time but still and all her curiosity was piqued. He turned his back to unhook a yellow hoop that he handed over to her. She put it over her head and began to rotate her hips in a way that would have seen her get a cuff round her ear were their mammy to spot her. Kitty watched on fascinated as the hoop fell around her ankles in next to no time. Undeterred she had another go and this time managed to keep it circling for a few moments. On her third attempt, she'd gotten the hang of it, and Kitty laughed, clapping her hands with delight. The stallholder, however, had tired of the game and was holding his hand out expectantly. "If you're not going to buy the thing I'll have it back thanks very much."

Rosa reluctantly handed the hoop back, and she and Kitty carried on their way. They passed by a strutting group of teenage girls, their arms linked together. "Look at them Kitty, they're like peacocks, so they are," she whispered out the corner of her mouth not fancying a clout for her smart mouth. "They all think they're the Queen of the Fair." Her attention was diverted from the girls by a sudden shout from over by a cluster of wagons. A scuffle had broken out between two lads who, Rosa decided on closer inspection looked to be about eighteen or so. Both had their shirt sleeves rolled up and their fists clenched tight as they sparred. A beauty of a black and white horse was tethered to the back of one of the wagons, and Rosa wondered if the animal was what had triggered the disagreement.

A fight was not an uncommon sight at Ballinasloe, and she knew one of the older men would be over to sort it out in a moment before it got out of control. In half an hour's time, the two lads would probably be sharing a pint at the pub. She stared with pursed lips at their clean shaven, angry faces. A beard was a foreign sight amongst the Traveller men. They couldn't afford to have anything for their opponent to grab hold of should matters ever have to be settled in the way these two lads were going about it.

She recalled Joe having told her once that he thought he might grow a beard when he was older. "Sure it would keep my face nice and warm in the winter and why would I want to look like everyone else?"

He and Paddy weren't identical twins, so it wasn't that driving his desire to set himself apart from the rest of the lads, Rosa had thought. The worried look that crossed his sister's face didn't escape Joe. "Ah don't be carrying on, Rosa. It won't matter because I won't be fighting any of the other boys. Sure why would I want to do that?" Rosa already knew that things didn't work like that and you couldn't always pick your battles. It was especially true when your twin brother was Paddy Rourke. Just look at Da too, he was a gentle man for the most part, but she had seen him come to blows with Martin Donohue only last winter. Bernie and Martin's grudge ran deep and it ran long. Its roots were firmly embedded in a job cutting and rolling the turf that Bernie Rourke was adamant Martin had cheated him out of.

As the first fist connected with the side of a young face, Rosa startled and pulled her sister away. She steered her toward a donkey to distract her from the spectacle. Its teeth were bared for inspection by a man looking to purchase it. She wandered closer fascinated and peered at it for a few moments before muttering, "Jaysus, would you look at the chompers on that now, Kitty?"

There was no reply and Rosa realized her sister was no longer holding her hand, nor was she by her side. She'd only been distracted for a moment so she couldn't have gone far, she reassured herself. As she swivelled her head this way and that to catch a glimpse of blue jumper there was no sign of her. All she could see in whichever direction she looked were horses whinnying and donkeys braying as throngs of people weaved their way around them. Images of her wee sister getting trampled caused her breath to catch. She turned and headed back the way she had come, the air flooding her lungs with fear. Ducking and diving through the crowd, she passed by the man selling the hula hoops and stopped. She had the strongest feeling that she should check around the back of his stall. Following her instinct, she rounded the corner and nearly cried with relief because there, peering through a piece of green cellophane, was Kitty.

"Rosa, you're all green," she chirruped with a look of wonder on her small face.

"Don't run off on me like that ever again, Kitty Rourke. Do you hear me?" She admonished with her hands on hips. Kitty was oblivious to the stern tone. She was far too fascinated by the world that had suddenly turned green thanks to a piece of cellophane. She had no doubt picked it up off the ground Rosa thought, with a smile at her sister's simple pleasure.

Chapter 14

A word is more enduring than worldly wealth – Irish Proverb
1962

"Mammy, it's beautiful thank you," Rosa breathed running her hand over the crisp white cotton of the dress she would wear to Ballinasloe. Her stomach fluttered with excitement at the knowledge that this year things would be different. This year she would be fourteen and setting her sights on Jerry Connors. That was why her mammy had scrimped on the meat in their stew. She had filled their bellies with potatoes, cabbage and bread so Rosa could have this, her first ever new dress. It would, she knew in her heart of hearts, give her a chance at catching Jerry's eye.

"Ah, but you're beautiful Rosa. You could be Queen of the Fair my girl so you could. Now slip out of it before you get it all dirty like." The praise slipped from Kathleen's tongue awkwardly.

Rosa preened under this rare show of approval from her mammy. She would like to be Queen of the Fair, sure what young girl wouldn't want to be? This year the crown had gone to Bridgette McNally, who in Rosa's opinion, fancied herself something rotten with all those red ringlets of hers. Perhaps she might ask Da to put her forward next year but this year she just wanted to have fun with her friends. Doing as she was told, she carefully hung the dress in the wardrobe. She hoped it wouldn't take on the peaty, smoky smell of Da's jacket as she leaned hard on the door to shut it.

Rosa still couldn't quite believe the dress was hers. As if to reassure herself it was real and not a figment of her wishful imagination, she opened the wardrobe door once more to gaze at for just a moment or two longer.

She'd spotted it in the window of one of the fancy dress shops in the town as she and Mammy went about their business. She had stopped to stare at the window, transfixed by the dress's snowy whiteness and pretty pink edging.

"Do you like it, Rosa love?" Kathleen had asked with a strange twinkle in her eye, the handle of the basket of paper flowers held in the crook of her arm.

"Oh, Mam I love it," Rosa had whispered, her hands subconsciously resting on either side of her waist as she wondered whether its tiny cinched one would fit hers. Gazing at the dress's boat neck and puffed sleeves, she knew she would feel nothing less than a princess in such a dress.

Rosa smiled at the memory as, hearing her mam call out to her, she pushed the wardrobe door shut once more before ducking back outside to begin scraping the potatoes. Oh, she couldn't wait to get to Ballinasloe! It was her turn to be one of the peacocks parading about the place and as she set about the mundane task of prepping the spuds her mind wandered to thoughts of Jerry Connors.

Her mammy and da had made no secret of the fact that they had set their sights set firmly on Willie and Nell Connors' boy for her. Rosa hadn't paid attention when she had heard them talking about their plans for her future. She'd no interest in boys, Paddy's shenanigans were enough to put her off the opposite sex. This year, though something had changed. She felt different inside, and her body had changed. Her mammy had told her when her courses started that she was a woman now, and Rosa did indeed feel like she had left the girl she'd been behind as she looked down at her budding breasts.

As for Jerry Connors, well she knew she could do a lot worse. He was handsome with his wild red hair and flashing blue eyes, and he was an up-and-comer in the world of horses. It was the world Rosa knew Da hankered after being a part of. If his daughter were to marry into the Connors, then this would be his foot in the door. Indeed, Jerry's prowess with the horses was becoming a thing to be talked about with him having come in first in the coveted Horse and Buggy race at Ballinasloe last year. Rosa knew her da planned on talking to Willie Connors about a match between their children over the course of this year's fair.

Joe upon hearing of the purchase of the dress had muttered to his sister in his usual wise beyond his years' manner, "Da might not trade in the horses, but he's trading his daughter."

Rosa had just shrugged. She was too wrapped up in the joy of owning something brand new to care. Besides, her friends were pea green with envy over the prospective matchmaking, and she was enjoying the slightly superior feeling it wrought. Joe was too sensitive by far in her opinion. It worried her because she knew it wouldn't stand him in good stead for a life that would be tough. Such was the lot of the Lucht Siúil.

The big day finally rolled around, and once Rosa had prised a disgruntled Kitty from her waist, she linked arms with her friends, Eileen and Mary Wall. She was glad the two sisters had gotten over their pique at seeing her dressed in her finery. She didn't want anything to spoil this day, especially not her friends being in a sulk. Poor wee Kitty, she thought, looking back over her shoulder to see her mammy with a firm hand resting on her youngest child's shoulder. She was her big sister's shadow there was no doubt about that, but today Rosa didn't want her trailing along behind her. For once, much to Kitty's chagrin, their mammy was in agreement.

The day was clear but cool and full of the promise of exciting things to come her way. She pulled Eileen and Mary closer to her because she had no intention of ruining the look of her dress by pulling an auld jumper on over the top of it. Her mammy had fashioned her hair into a ponytail and trimmed her a blunt fringe. It was in the fashion of the girls she'd seen in the town. Today wearing her beautiful, new dress she knew could give any of those haughty madams who liked to look down their noses at the likes of her a run for their money! She decided she liked the feeling of her swinging ponytail and the way the dress swished about her calves. It made her feel jaunty and grown up as she picked her way over the field's pocked ground with the Wall sisters either side of her.

It was the day when the serious bidding for the horses would begin and the races would be held. The sights, sounds and smells of the fair assailed the three girls as they reached its hub, each of them on the cusp of womanhood. They were all too aware of the looks they were garnering from the groups of loitering lads and the more they put their noses in the air and ignored their catcalls, the more attention they gleaned. Rosa's surreptitious inspection of the talent on offer confirmed what she already suspected. She could do a lot worse than Jerry Connors.

Mary was the first to spot the man himself holding court, a rapt audience of Traveller girls gathered around him.

"That's the horse that won him the Horse and Buggy Race last year," Eileen whispered out the side of her mouth. "It's a beauty, isn't it?"

Rosa shot a cursory glance over to where the gleaming white pony was tethered to the wagon. Its graceful neck was bent low to the ground to graze on the patches of grass. A horse was a horse the same as the next, she thought, her gaze swiftly moving to where Jerry leaned up against the wagon. His freckled workers' fingers raked through his shock of red hair and as his piercing blue eyes met hers she felt her face flush. The self-assurance she'd felt earlier vanished under his knowing stare. She could tell by the way his mouth curved into a half-smile that he liked what he saw. It made her feel strange to think he might know what her da had in mind for them both.

"He's looking at you. You should go and wish him luck with his race." Mary's girlish excitement was evident in her giggle.

"He can look all he likes, I'll not be one of his hangers-on," Rosa replied, her nonchalance a ruse to cover the butterflies fluttering in her belly.

"Ah go on, Rosa, he might be your husband one day soon. It's your wifely duty to wish him well, so it is," Eileen piped up.

"Shush keep your voice down Eileen Wall." At thirteen there was only a year between herself and Mary but sometimes Rosa thought, shooting her a look, Eileen seemed so much younger. Gathering herself, she tugged on both her friends' arms wanting to move them on before Eileen opened her big mouth again. "Come on girls, let's go back over to the other field to watch the tug-o-war. I reckon your man Niall Dunne will be over there Mary."

Mary giggled again. "I don't fancy him."

"Ah, you do, go on admit it. He makes you go all googly-eyed like this." Rosa made her own eyes big and staring.

Mary laughed. "I do not look at him like that, Rosa Rourke."

"Ooh, I hope Jimmy Barry's entered. He's a fine thing, so he is," Eileen added not wanting to be left out.

***

The next time Rosa laid eyes on Jerry was later that day while she waited amidst the crowd for the main event of the racing week to get underway, the Horse and Buggy Race. As the starter gun signalled the race's start and the thunder of hooves filled the air, she squeezed Mary's hand.

"Come on Jerry. You can do it!"

"You'll deafen me with that hollering," Eileen said putting her hands to her ears. Rosa ignored her, swept up in the frenzy of the crowd as she stood on tippy toes and craned her neck to see who was leading. Her cheering made no difference because this year it wasn't Jerry's turn to win. It was Michael Donohue who crossed the finish line first. Jerry Connors had been beaten by her father's enemy, Martin Donohue's eldest son, Michael. The ground that moments earlier had reverberated with horses' hooves shuddered once more with the stamping of boots. A cacophonous mix of cheering and ear-splitting whistles filled the air at this outsider taking first place. Rosa looked up in wonder at the victoriously tossed caps filling the sky. Holding on tight to Eileen and Mary she nearly stumbled but with their help regained her balance knowing were she to fall she might not get up again such was the frenzy of the crowd. The girls felt themselves being propelled forward. As they spilled out onto the track, Rosa's eyes locked for a split second with Michael Donohue's as he sat tall and proud in his Sulky, his strong arms still holding the reins.

It was as though the noise around her dissipated like a fog being warmed by sunlight until it was no more than the distant roar of a faraway sea. For that moment, there was nobody else in the world except her and him.

She felt like she had been branded as she whispered, "Ah Mary that's him, that's the man I am supposed to be with."

"Jaysus Rosa, what are you on about? Your mam and da would go mad if they heard you talking like that. Sure you're marrying Jerry Connors, so you are."

"You only fancy him because he won the race," Eileen said.

But Rosa wasn't listening. Standing on the track that afternoon at Ballinasloe, she knew with an absolute certainty that no matter what trouble it brought to the Rourke family, she would not be marrying Jerry Connors.

Chapter 15

Face the sun but turn your back to the storm – Irish Proverb
1963

"Sure it's just a touch of the flu. Didn't the doctor say so? The medicine will make him better you'll see." Kathleen waved her hand to shoo her daughter away from where she, Kitty and Paddy were huddled outside the family's wagon. Joe, a tangled and sweating bundle, lay on his mattress inside, writhing under a mound of blankets.

He had seemed to rally after his initial doses of the pink medicine Kathleen had gotten from the chemist in the village. It hadn't lasted, though, and they'd barely had a chance to breathe a sigh of relief at his improvement when his cough suddenly worsened. So, now as she herded her brother and sister away, Rosa wasn't appeased by their mammy's words. She could tell things were bad by the way her parents' faces had grown tight over these last few days. Joe's cough, she knew was the kind that struck fear in the heart of Travellers when the air was damp and dense with the smell of burning peat. They'd all heard that kind of rasping bark in the depths of winter before.

"There was blood on his hanky, Rosa, I saw it," Paddy sobbed a day later.

Rosa dropped the sock she was darning and got up to cover Kitty's ears. "Sure it's dark in the wagon with the curtains closed, Paddy. Don't be saying things like that and upsetting yourself so when you can't be sure of what you saw."

Paddy wasn't listening he was already off and running. Rosa sighed with the weight of it all. She watched him sprint down the lane toward the village until his dark hair disappeared from her line of sight. Where he was going, she didn't know. She did know as she carried on with her task, ignoring Kitty's whining for her mammy, that she didn't have the energy to go after him. The rhythm of her chores that afternoon was mechanical as she waited to confront Kathleen. At last her mammy left Joe's side to tend to the dinner and Rosa asked the question that she had a sickening feeling she already knew the answer to.

"Is it the TB, Mammy?"

The despair etched on her mammy's face as she stoked the fire, staring silently at the flickering flames told Rosa all she needed to know. The consumption usually chose to take the older members of the community, mercifully sparing the young, but Joe had never been as strong as the other boys.

Later that night, as she lay in a strange bed quarantined from her brother, Rosa felt burning tears slide down her cheeks. Joe's awful choking sporadically broke the stillness of the night. He was in their wagon across the way with their mammy and da watching over him. The three other Rourke children had been sleeping in the Sheedy's auld wagon these last few nights and Rosa pulled Kitty's warm, slumbering body closer to her. She was grateful for the small comfort of it. She didn't know as she hummed to herself to block the awful sounds out that it was to be her brother's last night with them.

***

"Is he sleeping, Rosa?" Kitty asked looking up at her sister from where she stood by the coffin. Rosa's heart broke at the confused frown on her wee face, and she pulled her close before stroking her brother's cold cheek. At least the terrible convulsions that had wracked his body this past while had stilled, and he was at peace. She tried to hold on to that thought as fresh tears rolled down her cheeks. She had cried so many tears these last few days that she wouldn't have thought it possible for there to be anymore.

It won't do, Rosa my girl, she told herself a moment later, wiping her cheeks with the back of her hands before rummaging in her pocket for a hanky with which to blow her nose. Kitty needed her. They all needed her. It was up to her to be the strong one. "Sort of, my love. It'll be a big long sleep our Joe will be having now because his soul's gone to heaven."

"Are the Angels looking after him now then, Rosa?" Kitty's dark eyes were wide at the thought of it.

"They are, Kitty." She stroked her sister's hair before moving away from the coffin. It was time for the lid to be closed. Their da, Paddy, all of their uncles and cousins were going to raise Joe up onto their shoulders and carry him through the streets of Tuam as he made his final journey.

The news of Joe's passing had spread quickly and within days members of the Travelling community had descended from near and far. They'd come to say their farewells to one of their own who'd been taken from them far too soon. The sky under which the procession set off that afternoon was leaden as befitted the sombre undercurrent of the mourners. Rosa barely noticed the local folk standing in their doorways keeping a respectful distance as they watched the spectacle pass by. She was too intent on keeping her weeping, wailing mammy upright, as she helped her along toward the church.

Sitting down on the hard pew, she listened as the Priest began to intone in his low and solemn voice. Kitty was huddled up to her as close as she could get without sitting on her knee. Her thumb had found a home back into her mouth in a habit she had fallen back on since Joe's passing. Rosa twisted slightly in her seat to rest her hand on Paddy's shoulder. He was rigid beneath her touch, having barely spoken a word to any of them since Joe's illness first took hold. She let her hand fall back to her lap and shivered against the draft the auld building afforded. As the foreign words of the Priest sailed over her head, she glanced down the pew to where her mammy and da sat. They were united in their grief, but their bodies were expressing it in very different ways. Her da sat straight-backed and stony-faced while her mam's body was hunched over as though she were physically wounded.

Rosa was filled with an urge to stand up and shout to the heavens at the unfairness of it all. Just a few short weeks ago her lovely brother had been full of life, and now he was dead. All this palaver on the Priest's part seemed irrelevant to Joe's short life, and she willed him to finish. A stab of guilt shot through her then for thinking such a thing while seated in a place such as this. This service would see Joe safely on his way, and it was the right way to do things, she told herself. Still and all when it was over, she breathed a sigh of relief, getting up from her seat and moving outside to where the grave had been dug. As her brother's body was committed to the cold, hard ground, she whispered a final goodbye before following her mammy and da across the road to the pub.

The pub was warm after the chill air outside but the atmosphere, Rosa thought, huddled inside her cardigan, was heavy with the haunting sound of the uilleann pipes her Uncle Brendon was playing. Soon, she could tell by the way the pints were being sunk, the ballads would begin. They would be maudlin, but she knew that by singing them there would be a sense of togetherness. It was their way. She was perched on a stool at a table with Kitty, who was stuffing crisps in her mouth like there was no tomorrow. Paddy had teamed up with some of his cousins and was making his way around the room clearing the pint glasses.

She pretended not to notice them draining the dregs along the way. Rosa was worried about him; he wasn't grieving like he should be. It was bottled up inside him like a bottle of fizz all shook up and ready to go pop as soon as someone took the lid off.

Her mammy and da were sitting at a table by the window illuminated through the smoky atmosphere by shards of winter sunlight making a last-ditch effort to shine before nightfall. Different friends and family members were taking it in turns to sit down with them and offer up words of comfort. Every time Rosa looked toward them she saw that her da had a fresh pint glass in front of him, and a cold sensation filled her belly. Her mammy's glass remained full and untouched.

The weeks and months that followed Joe's death were hard ones for the Rourke family. Bernie, just as Rosa had fretted he would as she'd watched him knocking back the pints after Joe's funeral, had turned to the drink. These days when her mammy sent her off to find him, she didn't have to look far. He could always be found in the nearest pub lamenting the harshness of life to any willing ears. She would have dearly loved to have taken him by the shoulders and given him a jolly good shake.

"Why can't he see that we need him more than he needs the drink?" she asked Mary Wall as they sat on the stoop of her wagon making the copper wire flowers. The first breath of spring was in the air, and the girls were enjoying the feel of the sunlight warming their pale faces. Mary had shrugged her reply; her da liked a drink too. It was just the way it was sometimes.

"I don't know where he's getting the money from either because he's not turning his hand to anything much other than the raising of his glass."

"Shush Rosa, you're asking for trouble talking like that, so you are." Mary's eyes darted nervously over to where her mam was hunched over a tub scrubbing at a shirt. Her hands, Mary saw were red and chafed.

Rosa was past caring. "Paddy's running wild too." Her friend's guarded expression didn't escape her. "What is it? What have you heard?"

"Ah sure, it's just a rumour that's all." Mary didn't meet Rosa's eyes, concentrating instead on shaping the wire she held between her fingers.

"Tell me, Mary." Rosa's hands were still.

"I heard tell that there was a theft in town and that Paddy was involved. It's probably not true."

Rosa felt a chill run through her. "Sure it's just a rumour that's all. You should know better than to listen to talk like that, Mary Wall." She dropped the flower she had been working on into the basket and flounced off leaving her friend staring after her.

Later, when she cornered Paddy to ask him what he knew about the story going round, he denied knowing a thing about it. He couldn't look her in the eye, though, and so she had not questioned her da when out the blue, he staggered home from the pub and ordered them to pack up. It was time to move on yet again. Rosa had no wish to lose her brother to the Gardaí that came sniffing round the camp that evening and so she had not argued. As Nellie pulled them toward the never-ending horizon, Rosa thought to herself that their mammy, sitting next to her da as he cracked the reins, seemed not to care where they went or what they did. She had withdrawn from them all and went about the day-to-day motions with a lethargy that would not fill their bellies.

They journeyed late into the night, and Rosa had fallen asleep to the rhythmic rolling of the wagon wheels. The next morning as her mam and da slept on, tired from the previous day's travel, she roused herself to make the breakfast. Paddy set about gathering some kindling for the fire while Rosa inspected the slim pickings in the larder. She sighed, knowing it would be a stretch to feed them all on the small amount of oats left in the container.

The three Rourke children ate in silence. Paddy finished his porridge first, and Rosa was tempted to scrape out what was left in the pot to give it to him. She hated knowing he was still hungry and that there was nothing she could do about it because mammy and da had yet to have theirs. They'd all go hungry come dinnertime if she didn't do something, she thought, deciding that there was nothing else for it. She and Kitty would have to take themselves off to the nearest village and do the door-knocking.

It didn't feel good standing on a stranger's doorstep with an upturned palm knowing times were probably tough for them too. Looking at her hollow-eyed sister steeled Rosa's resolve and they worked their way down the street. They walked the mile or so back to the field where their da had decided to camp clutching five potatoes and half a cabbage. It wasn't the makings of a feast, but it would have to do.

***

As the months past, Rosa sensed a waft of change coming like the sheets she'd see snapping in the yards of the village houses. The spring breezes had begun to blow, and she would find herself stopping now and again to look at those sheets. She'd try to imagine what it would be like to sleep in a quiet room by herself with walls and a ceiling. Sometimes too, she found her thoughts turning to Michael Donohue. It was those thoughts that kept her warm at night and spurred her on of a morning to get up and face another day. There had been no mention from either her mammy or da since Joe's passing about her proposed match with Jerry Connors and for that small mercy, Rosa was grateful.

Despite the better living conditions the warmer weather always wrought, there was still a sense of darkness hovering over them. It wasn't just in the distrust on the faces of the people who lived in the towns and the villages they passed through either. Rosa had often heard her da talk of how the Travellers did not believe in the settled folks' system. She was beginning to understand too that sometimes people feared that which they did not understand. The Travellers lived the way they lived. It was outside the conventions of a settled life, but in her da's words that had once been proud she could now hear dissatisfaction. It was there that Rosa thought the darkness was lurking.

"We deserve more, Kathleen." She heard him say to her mammy one evening and the defeat in his voice made Rosa sad. She wrapped her arms around her sister and pulled her to her. She held her tight not caring if she woke her. The darkness was creeping into their daily lives; she could feel it threatening them. Her mammy and da's faith in the old ways had been chipped away at by grief, and Rosa knew then what the darkness was, it was because she too had lost her faith.

Chapter 16

Your feet will bring you where your heart is – Irish Proverb

1964

"It's money for jam," Bernie Rourke said rubbing his hands together, then with a flick of Nellie's reins they were off. For the first time in a long while, Rosa saw a light shining in her mammy's eyes as she sat next to her husband. She recognized it for what it was, hope.

Da had gotten wind that the dole had been made available to Travellers prepared to settle in the permanent camps that were springing up on the outskirts of the big towns. It was a sweetener to appease the farmers who no longer wanted the Travellers on their land. It was also an attempt by the government at solving what they called the itinerant problem, he'd muttered before telling them that they were headed for Ballyfermot. It was a town that straggled Dublin, and if it meant food in their bellies, then Rosa was all for it.

They arrived late one morning, and Rosa looked around at this Promised Land called Cherry Orchard and saw no more than a sprawling field. It seemed to be broken into smaller fields by thickets of bushes like a patchwork quilt and a cherry orchard it was not. To one side of it she spied a high, pebble-dashed wall behind which she would learn later was the Cherry Orchard Fever Hospital for Children. Rosa would think of the poor mites housed in there from time to time with no visits from their mammy or da for months on end. They were quarantined inside its walls until they were deemed non-infectious or cured. She wondered if Joe had gone there when his cough first started whether things might have been different. She knew, though, there was no point in dwelling on this.

The field on which the camp was situated was a flat vista. It was filled with shanty tin sheds, caravans, canvas tents that were held up by wooden poles and carts. Rubbish had been left to pile up and rot where it had been dumped on the hard soil. Rags tethered horses to the trees that hinted at life on the barren field and broken-down cars provided entertainment for the children left to play in all the filth. The air was thick, damp and smoky, and this – Rosa thought, her nose wrinkling – was to be home. The family's infinite horizon that had shifted and moved each time they had packed up and taken to the road was now fixed.

As the Rourkes settled into their new life in the camp, Rosa found that for all the greyness of Cherry Orchard there was also a strange beauty. She would find it in the colours of the rags that would blow in the wind. They were hung from the trees, and their flapping reminded her of a picture she once saw, although she couldn't recall where, of the prayer flags in the Himalayas.

During the day, there was the carefree sound of children laughing. They were left to their own devices to play in the mire and knew of no different way to be so they were happy. Always too, there was the singing, and that same wind would carry the melody across the field along with the whack of tin being hammered. A warming cup of tea was never far from the hand of friendship and loneliness was not to be part of their vocabulary. It was in this environment Rosa noticed her mammy begin to return to them. She knew she wouldn't be the same, though,

153

none of them would be. Still, she would embrace this new version of Mammy gladly.

Things, however, did not improve where Bernie Rourke was concerned because without the need for work his drinking had worsened. This new version of their da was a sloppy and silly drunk. The only blessing in Rosa's opinion being that he was not mean on the drink like the Wall sisters' da was. She had lost respect for him, though, and that too in its way was another kind of death she'd had to endure.

Kitty had gotten the chance for some schooling, and while Rosa was pleased for her, there was a part of her that was envious of the opportunity she had been given. It needled away at her watching her sister skip off across the field each morning. One morning as her mammy went about the daily chore of shaking out the blankets, she got up the courage to say something. "Do you think I could go to the school too, mammy? I'd like the chance of some learning, so I would."

Kathleen laughed. "Sure you're nearly sixteen, so you are. What would be the point Rosa? Now stop standing there like an eejit and give me a hand would you."

It was not the answer she wanted, and Rosa kicked at the soil to vent her frustration at wanting more and being denied it. Her future was already mapped out the way her mammy's had been and her mammy's before her, and so it went. The act, however, achieved no more than hurting her big toe and further scuffing her already worn shoes.

"Aye and you can cut that out, me girl! You're not a child anymore – sure you'll be married soon with babies of your own to take care of. That'll sort you out, so it will." Kathleen picked up the overflowing washing basket and thrust it at her daughter. "Go on, get on with you."

Rosa, lemon-lipped, hoisted the basket onto her hip and stomped off across the field, wanting to escape but not knowing where to. The talk of a union with Jerry Connors had begun in earnest once more. Mammy had told her just a few days ago that it was only a matter of waiting for the Connors to arrive at Cherry Orchard. They'd come at the end of summer when the men of the family's work had dried up. Rosa and Jerry's wedding would take place in the early winter. It was a done deal.

Upon hearing this Rosa had felt the stirrings of rebellion that had been simmering all that long winter through into the spring. She knew that the life she could have with Jerry still roaming free with the Connors was better than the bleak horizon she was faced with living here at Cherry Orchard. Try as she might, though, she could not rid her mind of the image of Michael Donohue. She had set her heart on the young man with the fine black curly hair and eyes dark as a midnight sky. Her mind had been made up that he was the man she would marry when a lighter, freer version of herself had swished around Ballinasloe in her new dress. She couldn't help the way she felt even though she knew it was a foolish fancy that nothing good would come from.

It was as if just by thinking of him that misty morning she conjured him up because when she next looked up, he had somehow materialised through the smoky haze of a nearby camp-fire. She blinked, surely she was dreaming? If so then she did not want to wake up.

As he strode toward her, Rosa's stomach began to flutter with what felt like the beating wings of one thousand butterflies. It was a sensation she had never experienced before as was the sudden weakness in her legs. She was aware of a rush of heat spreading like wildfire up her neck to engulf her face. Her breath was coming in short bursts and so busy was she concentrating on keeping herself moving forward that she never saw the rut in the hard ground, catching her ankle she went down in a heap.

The washing flew everywhere, and she lay sprawled on the ground for the moment it took Michael to jog to her. She didn't care that her family's dirty smalls were laid bare for all to see. All she cared about was the tender concern in the eyes of this young man whom she was sure must be a figment of her imagination such was his beauty.

"Are you alright?" he asked his voice low and melodious as sweet music. It was only when he held his hand out to help her to her feet, and she felt the strength and warmth of it as it closed around her own that Rosa knew he was real. "Are you sure you are alright?" Amusement flickered in his eyes, and Rosa liked the way they'd crinkled around the edges when he smiled. It was then she realized she must seem like a right eejit staring the way she was, and seemingly struck dumb.

"Ah yes, nothing's broken," she answered brushing her skirt down, glad that her voice had not betrayed her nerves. Still and all she wished it wasn't true and that her ankle was broken or at the very least sprained. That way he would have to sweep her up in his arms and carry her back to— She didn't know where she wanted him to carry her back to, certainly not her wagon. Mammy would scold her something awful if she knew she was even talking to a Donohue.

"We've met before I think?"

Rosa was fascinated by the two little lines between his brows that furrowed his olive skin as he tried to retrieve a forgotten memory.

"No, we haven't. Well not really." Her high-pitched, girlish giggle reminded her of Kitty's. "I was at Ballinasloe last year when you won the Horse and Buggy Race." She glanced down and wished she were still in her pretty dress with her hair freshly washed and brushed until it shone. "I was in the crowd. You probably didn't see me."

"Ah yes, I remember now! You were the girl in the white dress. Bernie Rourke's your da, isn't that so?" A strange look crossed his face then as he realized he was still holding her hand. He dropped it like a hot potato, and it flopped down by her side. "Here, I'll help you pick your things up."

Rosa bent to retrieve her da's holey singlet but despite Michael's brusque tone her heart sang with the knowledge he'd remembered her. "The girl in the white dress," he'd said before he made the connection with her da and behaved like he had been burnt. It had not been a figment of her imagination, that moment when their eyes had connected. Her heart was singing. Just then, there was a whoosh as a grubby urchin raced past. Snatching up Kathleen's bloomers and waving them like a lasso, he tore off across the paddock. His cronies sitting on the roof of a wreck cheered him on with delight. For a moment Rosa thought it was Paddy, it was the kind of stunt he would pull, but then she realized with a pang that it couldn't be. The Paddy of old was gone, and besides the lad who was currently in proud possession of their mam's underwear was half his size.

Michael threw his head back and roared with laughter at the sight. Rosa forgot to be angry. She was glad of the distraction if it meant he didn't dwell on their respective family's feud.

"Ah, it's the kind of thing I'd have done myself at that age and thought it hilarious so I would. Wait here; I'll sort out those bold tykes for you."

Rosa saw the funny side of it herself then and smiled. Even so, she knew were she to return to their wagon minus her mammy's knickers she would not be smiling once Kathleen got hold of her. She watched Michael's broad, shirt-clad back as he strode over toward the small gang who, at the sight of him dropped the drawers and scarpered in opposite directions. Rosa wondered how old he was. She guessed he was only a year or two older than herself. That meant he was old enough to be married, but she'd seen no ring on his finger. As he scooped the bloomers up and brought them back, dropping them into the washing basket, Rosa's mouth twitched at the corners. Her mam's undergarments hadn't seen so much action in a long time. It was a pity she would never know a thing about it.

"Thank you."

"Aye, it was nothing." They held each other's eyes for a moment too long, and Rosa felt something unspoken pass between them. The spell was broken by the shrill tones of an irate mammy scolding her kiddies and Michael took his leave. The gruffness of his voice as he said goodbye told her that she was the daughter of Bernie Rourke, his da's arch enemy and no longer simply the girl in the white dress.

As he walked away from her, Rosa was filled with an over-whelming panic that she might not see him again. She couldn't bear that, not when she'd only just found him. She abandoned the basket and followed him toward a cluster of caravans. Women were busy outside them going about their morning tasks and a few small kiddies played nearby. Some lads who looked to be around eight or nine were kicking a ball around and one of them caught her eye. He was a miniature version of Michael and must be his younger brother, she thought. Her eyes strayed over to where a woman sat on a wagon stoop; her head bent over a pile of mending. As she looked up, Rosa recoiled at the sight of her puffy, blackened eye recognizing her as Margaret Donohue, Michael's mam. Her mam called her Mad Margaret, and Rosa imagined she would no doubt have a name as equally uncharitable for Kathleen.

Margaret nodded to her son and pointed to the pot dangling over the smouldering fire to signal there was tea made. Rosa's mammy did the same thing most mornings for her da and Paddy, but of Martin Donohue, there was no sign. Spying Rosa standing there on the edge of their camp, Margaret called out and waved her hand. It was like she was warding her off. Michael turned around to see who his mammy was scowling at and as their gazes met, Rosa saw regret cloud those beautiful eyes of his.

She gave a little cry and ran off, her feet pounding over the rough turf as she wished she'd not followed him. Then she would have been spared the look she had seen so clearly in his eyes. As she collapsed down next to the washing basket, she willed herself not to be sick over the unfairness of it all. Even if she weren't to marry Jerry Connors she would never be allowed to be with Michael. Neither of their families would allow that.

Rosa resolved to put Michael from her mind telling herself he didn't care for her. She was making something out of nothing because she wanted to be his girl in the white dress. No matter how hard she tried, though, her thoughts kept turning to him. She had found her ray of sunshine at Cherry Orchard and almost subconsciously had begun orchestrating ways to catch a glimpse of him. It was this and not her daily chores that gave her a reason to get up each day. Her mammy looked at her with knowing eyes as she set about her tasks humming, the belligerence of a few days prior gone.

"The sooner the Connors arrive, the better, in my opinion, Bernie." Rosa overheard her whisper to her da one night and she cocked an ear to hear what his response would be. There was no sound in the wagon but for his snoring.

As for Michael's da, Martin soon made his presence in the camp known, and Bernie Rourke was just as quick to make his resentment at having the Donohue family at Cherry Orchard common knowledge.

Martin was a natural leader who was not afraid to state his opinion, and on the subject of the inequalities the Travellers faced on a day-to-day basis, he was very opinionated. Some in the camp, Rosa's da for one, were grateful for their dole money. They'd fritter it away in the local pub day after day, singing their songs and talking their big talk. They enjoyed their persecution because it gave them purpose and Martin Donohue, to their way of thinking, was nothing more than a rabble-rouser.

"Aye, I've seen his type before alright. He's all mouth and no trousers." Rosa heard Davey Wall say one afternoon as he hunkered down next to her da over his pint glass. She'd been sent to the pub to fetch her da for dinner.

"Mammy said to tell you your tea's getting cold," she interrupted scowling.

"I don't like your tone, girly. She's getting awful uppity that one."

"Ah well, Bernie, married life will sort her out, so it will."

Rosa walked out of the dim pub her eyes burning with tears that she refused to give them the satisfaction of seeing her shed.

There was an occasion too when she was stirring the skillet pot that Martin Donohue's name was raised by her mammy. Kathleen's arms were crossed over her bosom as she stood in self-righteous conversation with her friend Nora. Nora had one red-cheeked baby hanging off her hip and another tot clutching her skirt, whining. Both women ignored the children carrying on instead with their chat. "Sure Nora," Rosa heard her mammy say. "Martin Donohue has nothing better to do with his time than stir up trouble and his oldest boy's cut from the same cloth. His type, they come, and they go, and they always leave trouble behind them. I don't like the man or his family and not just because of the business with Bernie. I have a bad feeling about him and his lot being here, so I do."

Rosa was undeterred. If anything, knowing how her mammy felt fed her anger, and spurred her on in her determination to somehow cross paths with Michael.

She had taken to walking Kitty to the school the odd time, in the hope she would catch sight of him. She'd lead her sister on a round-about route past the cluster of wagons where she knew the Donohue's to be. One morning, her efforts paid off and there he was, a short distance ahead of her dragging his brother along in the same direction that she and Kitty were headed.

"That's Tyson Donohue; he's always in trouble with Sister Angela," Kitty informed her older sister with the superior attitude of one who paid attention in class.

Rosa barely registered what Kitty had said so intent was she on trying to figure out how she could catch Michael's attention. Her stomach flipped as he looked back over his shoulder to see what it was his brother had stooped to pick up. Seeing her, he waved out.

"Ouch Rosa, you're hurting me!"

"Shut up would you, Kitty, and just get a move on." She loosened her desperate grip on her sister's hand as she picked up her pace, fearful he would carry on before they could catch up.

He waited.

Rosa could feel her face heating up as she reached him, and she hoped he would think it was down to the morning air.

"Morning." There was a quiver in her voice. Her mind went blank, and her insides felt like they had jellified as she gazed up at those handsome, dark features of his. Tiny droplets of dew were clinging to the ends of his hair which was in need of a trim.

"Morning yourself."

He looked pleased to see her, and her heart lifted as she ignored the sulky look on her charge's face. Kitty was not best pleased about the prospect of being seen with Tyson for fear of being tarred with his brush. As she walked alongside her sister, she scuffed her shoes but soon gave it up when it got her no attention. Rosa only had eyes for Michael and her nerves dissipated as he began to chat away easily to her about his love of the horses and how he missed life on the road. He'd check back over his shoulder now and then to make sure his brother was still following him, and Rosa felt herself relax in his company. For once, she was glad of the long walk ahead of them as they reached the Blackditch Road. She began to tell him stories of her own and felt pleased with herself when he laughed at her retelling the tale of the cockfight Paddy had instigated for a bag of marbles.

They saw Kitty and Tyson to the gate and took their time wandering back to Cherry Orchard, neither of them in any rush to get back to the reality of their lives. Rosa felt like she had known Michael forever by the time they returned. Not even the sight of Margaret Donohue with a face on her that looked like a smacked bum as she hollered for her son could dampen her spirits. She felt as if she was walking on air.

Chapter 17

Better be quarrelling than lonesome – Irish Proverb

1964

"Your mammy will find out you've been hanging around outside Martin Donohue's office, so she will," Mary Wall said one morning. They were trudging across the field back from having picked up some flour from the shop down the road. She was referring to the tin hut with its sagging, canvas roof where Martin spouted his political views most afternoons to anyone willing to listen. Rosa had taken to hovering outside of it as part of her never-ending quest to catch sight of Michael. She felt certain he'd be inside listening to his da, he'd told her that's where he sometimes went, and she didn't feel guilty about shirking her chores either. She had done more than her fair share of the work over the years. If her mammy chose to do them herself instead of passing them on to Paddy, who was either bone idle or out getting himself in bother, then that was up to her.

So off she would traipse when her mammy's back was turned. She'd pass by the ever-expanding cluster of tents and huts that seemed to spring up overnight and sidestep the horse poo dropped like brown bombs. She would carry on past the upturned car until she came to Martin's office. She didn't dare peek inside. Instead, she perched on an upturned wash bucket just outside the entrance to eavesdrop. There was an auld sheet tacked over the entrance acting as a curtain that kept her shielded from the men inside.

She'd sit there with her eyes closed imagining Michael, tall and proud inside that hut ready to follow in his da's footsteps. She'd listen spellbound to Martin address the handful of men who had come to hear him talk. He had the makings of a fine politician, and there was a slow-burning fire in his words as he spoke of how Travellers basic human rights were being ignored. Rosa felt like she was being woken up by his words on those afternoons, and she pushed the image of Margaret's blackened eye from her mind. She couldn't equate the passion and honesty she heard in Martin's voice with a man capable of such violence. His musings were music to the ears of a young girl feeling disillusioned by her lot in life since the loss of her brother.

Rosa told herself as she sat with her hands clasped in her lap, head cocked toward that entrance so as not to miss a single word, that she wasn't doing anything wrong. What was wrong with listening to a voice that gave her hope? The things Martin Donohue was saying were the only words that had made sense to her since Joe's death. She knew that Mary was right and were her mam or da to get wind of what she was up to, she would be for it. Thinking of her da and his drinking always made her angry and so she'd dig her heels in, staying put until she sensed the meeting coming to an end. She would scurry away then with a renewed purpose. As to what she thought that purpose might be, though, she didn't know.

Rosa shifted the heavy bag from one arm to the other. "Sure this flour weighs a ton, so it does, and my mam won't find out what I'm up to. Not if you say I'm with you." She glanced over at Mary. "And don't look at me like that." Mary had gone awfully prudish since she'd gotten engaged to Eamon McNally, in Rosa's opinion.

"Mark my words you're playing with fire, Rosa Rourke. You're spoken for, so you are."

"But it's Michael I'm meant to be with."

Mary huffed. "So you keep saying, but it's not right you chasing after him the way you are. People are beginning to talk, and it won't be long until some of that talk reaches your mam or your da's ears and then no amount of me covering for you will help."

"Ah Mary, you don't understand."

"I understand you're mad and that you think you're better than the rest of us."

"What's so wrong with wanting more than just this?" But Mary wasn't listening anymore, and Rosa's lip trembled as she watched her friend walk away.

***

"Martin Donohue doesn't speak for me."

Rosa jumped as, on this particularly cold afternoon, Michael appeared around the side of the hut to stand in front of her.

"I've seen you come to listen to him and I want to know why you do so."

Rosa was flustered. "I-I thought you were in there with him and the others."

"No, I just told you he doesn't speak for me." His face was hard. "Sure why would I want to listen to a man who beats his wife?"

"Oh." She didn't know what to say. She could sense the waves of anger coming off him. She knew what it felt like, that anger, even if her da had never raised his fist to any of them. His boot yes, on more than one occasion had connected with Joe and Paddy's rear ends, but he had never raised his fist to them. His wounds were inflicted by his apathy toward his wife and surviving children.

"So why do you come then? You know you'll get strung up if you get caught listening to what a Donohue has to say don't you?"

Rosa nodded unable to meet his gaze. "I came because I thought you were in there."

Michael shook his head slowly and scuffed at the ground with the toe of his boot. The sound of cheering from inside the hut galvanised him. "Come on, they'll be finishing up soon and it's fecking freezing out here." He offered her his hand, and she took it feeling a surge of something unfamiliar and thrilling course through her at his touch. She let him pull her to her feet and followed after him.

He pointed towards a hut she knew to be abandoned. "It was the Dooleys', but they've packed up and gone back south," he said. "They reckoned their old life was better than this." He threw his arms wide gesturing about them at the littered field. "Sure and I don't blame them either, but my da loves it here because he has a captive audience. He's a hypocrite so he is, going on the way he does about the rights of Travellers when he treats his family worse than you'd treat a dog." His face contorted into a sneer as he pushed open the door of the hut and held it open. Rosa didn't move towards it.

She wanted to go inside with him so badly, but she was frightened of what he might expect from her if she did so.

He read her uncertainty. "I only want to talk that's all, I promise."

She nodded and followed him inside.

That first afternoon to her disappointment, he kept his word. They sat together on the floor of that auld tin hut with the wind rattling against its walls. Both far too aware of the closeness of the other, despite their bodies not touching as they talked.

"He has the gift of the gab, so he does, and nobody sees him for the bully he is underneath all his bluster," Michael confided. "I'll hit the bastard back one day for my mam's sake and my own."

Rosa blinked back the stinging in her eyes at the hurt in his voice. "I'm sorry for your troubles, so I am."

The hard line of Michael's mouth softened and Rosa found herself wanting to tell him of her own family's sadness.

"Joe, my brother, died last year."

"Aye, I heard."

"I miss him so much. He was the best of us all and everything has changed since he left us."

Michael placed his hand on hers and her breath caught in her throat. They sat that way until the late afternoon shadows began to creep into the room. Rosa knew it was time she went and faced the inevitable scolding from her mammy. She would not be happy that she had abandoned her chores yet again. "I've got to get back."

She reluctantly removed her hand from beneath his and got to her feet. She didn't know how she could go back to their wagon and pretend everything was the same as it had been that morning. Not now when she knew from the touch of his hand on hers, that nothing would ever be the same again.

"I'll see you then," she said pushing the door open.

"Rosa?"

She turned and looked at him expectantly.

"Do you remember the day I saw you walking your sister to school?"

"I remember." It was branded on her memory.

"I only walked with Tyson that day because I hoped I'd see you."

Rosa smiled all the way back to their wagon and she was still smiling that evening as Kitty babbled on in between bites of her stew.

"I can do my four times-tables, Mammy. Listen, four times one is four, four times two is eight, four times three is–"

Kitty's mathematic prowess fell on deaf ears because Kathleen was watching Rosa, who could feel her mammy's gaze on her. She could not look up to meet it because she knew her eyes would betray her.

166

***

It became their place, that draft-ridden auld hut in the middle of the field. Some afternoons Michael would struggle to lose his younger brother. Tyson followed him round the same way Kitty had followed Rosa before they came to Cherry Orchard, and she started at school. Unlike Kitty, Tyson had not taken to the schooling and would run off whenever the Teacher turned her back.

"Sure his hand's raw from the sting of the ruler but he doesn't seem to care." Michael shook his head. "He says the settled kids call him a dirty tinker and a pikey and he doesn't want to be there."

They both knew that it didn't matter what Tyson wanted and the consequences for an afternoon's freedom meant he inevitably had to go back to school the next morning and face the Nun's ruler.

"Martin Donohue's youngest son will be educated. It's his basic human right." Michael banged his fist down on the ground upon which they sat in a perfect imitation of his da. Rosa watched as his lip curled up in that way it always did when he spoke his father's name.

The weather that week had turned unseasonably foul. Rosa's limbs felt heavy as she tramped head down against the sleeting rain across the muddy field. As she made her way to the hut, she was reminded of what she had been desperately trying to forget. Come winter she would be married to someone she did not love. She knew she had to tell Michael that she was spoken for. It was unfair the way she had remained silent on the subject. It was just that she could no longer imagine her life without their snatched afternoons together. The thought of him turning away from her when she told him the truth terrified her.

She saw the smoke spiralling out its chimney flue as she drew nearer and was glad Michael had gotten the fire going. The sight of

167

the smoke reminded her of the story that had spread through the camp earlier in the week. A Traveller family camped near a river down Galway way had all perished while they slept in their bell tent when the wind had changed. It had fanned the flames of their dampened campfire toward where they lay sleeping. She paused, her hand hovering in front of the door as a feeling of sorrow overwhelmed her. It was just the news of that poor family she told herself, trying to shake her melancholy off before pushing the door open.

Michael was crouched down feeding the firebox a handful of twigs and his smile when he turned to see her hovering in the doorway was one of delight. At the sight of that smile, Rosa forgot all about her wet and bedraggled appearance but not what she had to tell him. She closed the door but didn't move closer to him, feeling suddenly awkward and fearful of what his reaction would be. If he told her he wouldn't meet her anymore, she knew that she would not be able to bear it.

His eyes darkened as he sensed her uncertainty. "What is it?"

"Ah Michael, I should have told you that first afternoon here, but I didn't want anything to spoil my time with you." She knitted her fingers together as though about to pray. "It's all arranged. I am to marry Jerry Connors come the winter."

Michael closed the fire box and stood up slowly brushing the dust from his pants. He crossed the room in one step and taking her in his arms, pulled her to him. Rosa gasped at the sensation of his hard chest next to hers.

"No, you are not, my beautiful Rosa. I fell in love with you the day I saw you in your white dress at Ballinasloe. It's you and me who are meant to be together, no matter what any of them lot say." As his lips settled over hers, Rosa felt like her body was liquefying, melting into his.

She pulled away just for a moment and reaching up stroked his cheek, feeling the stubble beneath her fingertips. "I love you too." Then his lips reclaimed hers, and she returned his kiss with every ounce of her being.

Neither of them heard the approaching footsteps, and as the door was flung open, they broke apart as if cold water had been flung over them, like the fighting cocks.

"Mam!" Michael cried.

Rosa felt sick at the formidable sight of Margaret Donohue blocking the doorway, her hands self-righteously on her hips while young Tyson peered around her skirt.

"So what do you have to say for yourself, Michael Donohue? Lying to me, your auld mammy? It doesn't look much like you're helping your poor da to me, helping yourself more like and with the likes of her. What were you thinking lad?"

"I'm sorry for lying, mam, that was wrong of me, but I didn't know what else to do. I love Rosa, and I want to be with her."

"Ah, you don't know what you're talking about son. Love? You don't love her, you eejit of a boy. She set her sights on you and she's bewitched you, so she has."

The hysteria was rising in Margaret's voice. She wasn't right in the head; Rosa could see it in the glint in her eyes as she ranted on.

"You'll be marrying a good girl, so you will, not a little whore like this who goes around offering it to anybody who wants it." She spat on the ground at Rosa's feet.

"That's enough mam! We were only kissing – we weren't doing anything wrong."

Margaret took a step inside the hut and Michael moved his body in front of Rosa not trusting what his mam might do next. Tyson cowered in the doorway as the realisation of what he'd done in leading his mammy here sunk in. All he had wanted was for his brother to spend some time with him. Rosa saw his ashen face from over Michael's shoulder, and she tried to look reassuringly at him. To silently communicate to him that it would be okay but as Margaret Donohue lunged forward, shoving her oldest son out the way she knew it would be anything but.

The shame of being dragged across the fields by her hair while

Margaret ranted and raved like the mad woman she was would never leave Rosa. She knew as her hair felt like it was being ripped from her scalp, that it was fear driving Margaret's anger. Fear of Martin's fist and of what he would do to her when he found out their son had been cavorting with a Rourke. It was fear too of losing Michael; it was why at eighteen he wasn't married. Her son was her protector and Margaret knew he was too big to take his da's beatings any longer. He had tried to pull his mammy off her, but she would not loosen her grasp on Rosa's hair. She heard his voice trying to calm her down, but it was to no avail; she was a woman possessed and Rosa was terrified. Of Tyson, there was no sign.

Kathleen was chopping the vegetables for their dinner when she heard the commotion. Like the others who had downed their tools, undeterred by the bad weather, to come and watch the afternoon's entertainment, she appeared around the front of the wagon to see what the din was all about. Her eyes widened, and her blood boiled as she saw that it was her daughter, Mad Margaret Donohue was man handling. She strode over and slapped the larger woman straight across the chops. Startled Margaret let go of Rosa but not before yanking out a handful of her hair. Standing in that muddy field waving a fistful of hair, she screamed to all and sundry that Rosa Rourke was a whore trying to steal her son from her.

Her body sagged suddenly, and she slumped to the ground, spent. Michael hauled his mam to her feet and with an arm around her waist, he steered her away in the direction of their wagon. Rosa rubbed at the tender spot on her head and watched him go; she was sick to her stomach as to what would happen next. Where did they go from here? That blood would be spilled because of a first, forbidden kiss, she was certain.

She watched as her mammy began shooing the small crowd that had encircled them away, flapping her hands at them like they were pigeons scrounging scraps. "What are youse all looking at? Feck off the lot of you!" she yelled at the goggle-eyed, grubby kids, their mammies and the handful of men who had been working on dismantling a car nearby when it had all kicked off. They slowly dispersed and when she turned around to face Rosa all she could see was shame and disappointment in her mam's dark eyes. Her own eyes burned with hot tears. For the first time in a very long while Rosa did as she was told. She did not question or answer her mammy back when she barked at her to get in the wagon and wait there.

Rosa huddled on the pile of bedding, locked away from judgmental eyes as she imagined the worst. The waiting for word of what was happening was a terrible punishment in itself. She learned later that Kathleen had marched straight across the field with a crowd of kids trailing after her. They were keen to watch the next bit of action unfold as she stormed across the road. Pushing open the door to the pub, she had told Bernie Rourke what it was his oldest daughter had been doing to keep herself warm on this wet and wild afternoon while he sat supping his pint. Spurred on by his cronies' indignant cries, Bernie banged his glass down on the table. He pushed his wife aside and swayed out the doors like a cowboy at high noon, calling for Michael Donohue to come and face him like a man.

***

Michael told Rosa that it was her da who swung at him first and that he let him get a few rounds in so as he could save face. "I deserved it; Bernie had every right to be angry." He shrugged. "I should have gone to him and told him how I felt about you. He would have had some respect for me then." He gave her hand a squeeze as they hunched into one another at Busáras, the Dublin bus station. It would be a long night spent waiting for morning.

"It wouldn't have made any difference, you know the way things are done, Michael."

"Aye well, it was hardly a fair fight what with your da having so many pints under his belt. Then my da waded in and pushed me aside as he bellowed that Bernie Rourke wasn't a real man because real men didn't hit children."

Rosa could see the words almost choked Michael to speak them.

"I am eighteen for feck's sake and more of a man than he'll ever be. According to him, real men don't hit other people's children just their own, and it's okay to belt the living daylights out of their wives."

There was nothing she could say, so Rosa simply squeezed his hand back.

It was a one-sided fight on Martin's part; she knew the rest. Her da went down after only a few knocks. Martin, thinking it was over, had shaken his head and spat on the ground where Bernie lay out cold before turning on his heel to stride back to the wagon. He'd indicated in a manner that was not up for discussion that Michael should follow. What Martin planned to come next he did not want an audience for. Neither man saw Paddy with his shirt sleeves rolled up as he bore down on Martin. The first he knew of it was the blows falling on his back. Though young, Paddy was thick set for his age and already a scrapper, he meant business.

Still, Paddy was only thirteen, a boy. Martin held him at bay, laughing at his audacity and letting him get a few punches in for the enjoyment of the crowd. It was when Paddy's balled fist connected with the soft, fleshy part of his solar plexus that he saw red and punched him back. Paddy was staggering around with his hand over his mouth when Kathleen waded in determined that the brute Martin Donohue would not get a second blow in. She threw herself between him and her son wailing at them to stop because she was terrified that she might lose Paddy too if things went any further.

Martin sensed the energy of the gathered crowd had

changed. He had overstepped the mark in hitting Paddy and he knew it. Michael too knew that it took all his father's strength to walk away as Paddy through lips beginning to puff and fatten called after him that he hoped the Donohue's burned in hell.

Rosa thought now of how Paddy had lost two teeth in that fight. Their loss would be a permanent reminder for him of what she had done and how he defended her not knowing she would betray them all by leaving.

Kitty on her way home from school had seen the whole fight unfold, and she'd raced across the turf ahead of her mammy who was helping Paddy along. Kathleen would tend her son first and then go back to fetch Bernie whose pride she knew would be more injured than his body when he came round. Wrenching open the wagon door, she'd clambered inside. "Jaysus Rosa, what have you done?" she'd asked breathlessly flinging herself down on the mattress next to her sister and filling her in on what she had seen.

Rosa wrapped her arms around her middle and bent over with the sickness that assailed her at hearing it all. Taking deep breaths, she straightened, knowing she could not sit there any longer doing nothing.

"What are you going to do?" Kitty had asked staring up at her sister as getting up, she opened the wardrobe door and pulled out the only thing she truly treasured.

"I'm Michael's girl in the white dress, Kitty; I have to go." Clutching the dress to her chest, she closed the wardrobe and leaned down to kiss Kitty on her forehead. "Don't tell Mammy I am after leaving, will you?"

"Ah, don't go, Rosa, please?"

It broke her heart to hear Kitty plead, but she held firm. "Sure what choice do I have, Kitty? I'll not hang around for Da to wake, and I love Michael more than my life."

Rosa and Michael left Cherry Orchard under a veil of misty

173

rain as darkness settled over the field. They had nothing but an auld brown case between them, and the small sum of money Michael had managed to stuff in his pocket.

"Sure, they're only the wages that are my due." He had yelled at his da before Martin threw him out.

"You are no longer a Donohue boy. Run off with your little whore and good luck to you."

Rosa could hear Margaret keening from inside the wagon. Her mammy did not know she was gone yet; she was too busy tending Paddy.

The greatest injury inflicted on Michael that afternoon was not his da's final words to him but the sight of his brother hiding behind a nearby wagon. Tears streamed down his face as he silently begged his brother not to leave him.

They walked from the litter-strewn field with its sounds of children playing, laughter, songs being sung and always the hammering of tin that had for a brief while been home. Rosa thought that her heart should sing knowing that Michael was now hers, but it was too broken by not having the chance to say her goodbyes properly. Her mammy and Kitty, she knew in time would forgive her for her actions. Perhaps they'd even come to understand that she had no choice but to go wherever Michael went. That was what being in love did to you. As for her da and Paddy, male pride would stand in the way of any softening where she was concerned.

"I will do my best by you, Rosa. You won't be sorry you came with me."

"I could never be sorry for being with you." Rosa rested her head on his shoulder and listened as he talked of cousins of his who had set up camp in County Donegal. So it was when the sun had risen to clear away the grey skies and clouds of the day before, she found herself seated on a bus and heading north of Dublin.

Rosa felt buffeted from the strangeness of everything by the warmth of her hand encased in Michael's despite his silence. They sat that way as the bus huffed and puffed its way through the many villages and towns along the way. When it pulled into Donegal's small but bustling station, Michael left her sitting on their case as he asked about as to where they might find his cousins. It didn't take long for him to find out where they were, the locals always knew where it was the Travellers were camped.

It was a long walk they set out on at the end of what had been a long day and a long night before. The bad weather was a memory, even if the bad times weren't and the evening was warm. After all that time spent sitting on the bus, they agreed it was good to be moving. They had barely eaten since the day before, and both were existing on nothing but adrenaline and the need to get to where they had decided to go. Rosa's stomach was in too many knots as to what kind of greeting they would get when they arrived at the camp to be thinking about food. She needn't have worried, though.

Dogs were sniffing around the edges of the cluster of wagons they saw as they rounded a bend in the lane. In the middle of it, small fires burned, and the smell of cooking made both their stomachs growl. It was the dogs that alerted its occupants to their arrival. At first, those strange faces with echoes of Michael in them who swarmed to meet them turned their attentions to Rosa with suspicion. Michael stood there with one arm protectively around her waist and told them their story, and to her relief, they listened without judgment.

They shared a meal that night with his first cousin, Willie and his wife Eileen along with their three littlies before Rosa was shown a wagon recently deserted in favour of work and lodgings in Donegal town. It was hers for so long as she had need of it, Michael could doss in with them, Willie said. Rosa gratefully accepted the armful of bedding that had been put together by Eileen and pushed the waves of unexpected homesickness away.

She had never slept on her own in her whole life, and she felt lonely at the thought of it. This camp was to be hers and Michael's home for the time being, though, and she resolved to make it a happy one for both of them.

Chapter 18

An Irishman is never drunk so long as he can hold onto one
blade of grass and not fall off the face of the earth – Irish Proverb
1965

"You're pretty as a picture, just look at you with all that lovely fair hair. Where on earth did you get those dark eyebrows from?" Eileen, who had taken it upon herself to mother Rosa despite being only a few years older than her, added the finishing touches to the bouquet of daisies and red clover. She had fashioned it for her to carry up the aisle and satisfied she had it just so; she handed it to Rosa.

"My mam said I got my colouring from her mam's auld granny." Rosa admired the white and red wildflowers for a moment before holding the bouquet to her nose and inhaling. It smelled of spring.

"Ah, it's lovely, Eileen, thank you."

Eileen smiled then turned her attention to the wee girl standing beside Rosa. She was a vision in white frills with her mad, red curls held back by a headband. "What's that on your face, Maggie?" She sighed and producing a hanky, rubbed at the smear on her daughter's face.

Rosa watched the scene and forgot her nerves for a moment

as sadness replaced them that it wasn't Kitty accompanying her up the aisle today. Not that she hadn't grown to love Maggie with her cheeky ways. It was just that she was such a poignant reminder of the family she had left behind because it wouldn't be her da giving her away while her mam sat proudly by in the aisle. It would be Willie with his arm linked through hers who would hand her over to Michael when the time came. The thought of Michael waiting at the church for her made her push the unhappiness aside as she resolved to look toward her future, not to her past.

She was wearing her white dress. She hadn't worn it since leaving Cherry Orchard, and Michael had offered to buy her a new one for the occasion, but Rosa knew money was tight. Besides she told him, it was only right that she wore her white dress. Sure wasn't she wearing it the day he fell in love with her? He hadn't argued, putting the money toward matching gold bands for them both instead. Eileen had sewn her the loveliest veil of Irish lace, and as Willie bought the wagon round to take them to church, she let her pull it down over her face. It was time to go and meet her soon-to-be husband.

***

The sky was dotted with cotton wool clouds like fat sheep grazing on a field of blue as Willie helped Rosa down from the wagon outside the church. The building loomed tall and austere, and Rosa's stomach fluttered at the sight of it as Eileen faffed about with the skirt of her dress for a moment. Satisfied she had it just so, she bent down to speak to her daughter.

"Now then, Miss Maggie, don't say a word when you get inside that church." She held up her hand to silence her daughter whose mouth had opened to protest. "I know what you are going to say and if your brother pokes his tongue out at you or something like, ignore him alright? I'll sort him out with a clip round the ear, so I will, if he misbehaves, don't you be worrying about that."

Satisfied justice would be meted out appropriately, Maggie closed her mouth and nodded.

"Just follow Rosa's lead. Do you understand me?"

"Yes, Mammy."

"She'll be grand, Eileen," Rosa said.

"I'd give you a hug, but I don't want to crease your dress." Eileen took her hand instead and gave it a squeeze. "Ah look, I'm already crying and I haven't even got inside the church yet."

"Thank you, Eileen, for everything."

Eileen gave her one last smile before running up the steps of the church to claim her seat.

"Come on then with you. Let's go and get you wed before you change your mind." Willie grinned and held his arm out for her. "Walk behind us, wee Maggie, like Mammy said, that's a good girl."

As Rosa entered those old stone walls and saw Michael through her lacy haze, she wanted to run up the aisle to meet him. She was glad she had Willie setting the correct pace as she glided alongside him doing her best to look demure. At last, they reached the altar, and she was opposite where her lovely man stood with his hands clasped in front of him, his cousin Aidan at his side. The Priest began to intone the service and Rosa thought how very lucky she was. He was so tall and proud in the suit he had borrowed from Willie. Aidan gave the Priest their rings, and he blessed them before Michael took Rosa's ring and placed it on her thumb.

"Take this ring as a sign of my love and fidelity." His voice was strong and certain as he moved the gold band to her index finger. "In the name of the Father." He placed it on her middle finger. "And of the Son." At last he slid it on to where it belonged, her ring finger. "And of the Holy Spirt. Amen."

Rosa repeated the ritual and the prayers were spoken. The rest of the service was a blur as Rosa waited for the Priest to give his final blessing so that Michael could lift her veil and kiss her.

The congregation, made up of the members of their new family clapped as he did just that.

"Ah, but you're beautiful, Mrs Donohue." Michael took his new wife's hand and led her outside into the afternoon sunlight.

Rosa could feel her cheeks glowing as Michael led her by the hand down the lane toward the darkened camp. It wasn't just because of the unaccustomed effects of the alcohol she'd consumed that evening. Glancing back over her shoulder, she could see the lime-washed pub perched on the hill overlooking the bay. An orange moon illuminated it and she knew she owed her flushed cheeks in part to the bawdy send-off they'd just had. Even from this distance, she could hear the strains of music and laughter. It made her smile; the pub had been standing room only as the wedding celebrations had gotten underway late that afternoon. Her voice was hoarse from shouting to be heard over the music, and her feet ached from all the dancing she'd done. It had been a magical day and a magical night, she thought.

Michael was setting a fast pace and by the time they reached the camp she was breathing heavily. His reasons for this made her stomach flutter with anticipatory nerves. The auld wagon Aidan had given them as a wedding gift was set back from the others. Under the moonlight, she could see its flaking paint and sagging bow top. It was furnished with the bare necessities Eileen had helped Rosa scrape together, but it was theirs, and Rosa wouldn't have cared if it were a mud hut.

Michael climbed the stoop and opened the doors with a flourish. "Welcome to your new home, Mrs Donohue." He ducked his head and went inside. It was dark despite the moonlight, and Rosa waited at the entrance while he fumbled around for the moment it took him to light the lamp. As it flared to life and illuminated his face, she saw the hungry look in his eyes. For the first time since they had left Cherry Orchard, she felt self-conscious under his gaze. Sensing her shyness, he took both her hands and pulled her inside toward him kicking the door shut at the same time. "I love you. Don't be frightened." She felt his breath on her hair reassuring her, and as he stepped back from her and unzipped her dress, her eyes met his, wide and trusting. He lifted the dress over her head and helped her out of her undergarments until she stood naked before him. "You're lovely, so you are." She felt beautiful under his gaze.

She watched him take his shirt off and unbuckle his trousers. So often, she had wondered what lay beneath those clothes of his, and now she reached out tentatively to stroke his finely muscled chest with its smattering of dark hair. He groaned and moved toward her, his mouth finding hers. There was a passion in their kissing that they had shied away from in the past for fear of where it might lead. This time they let go, tumbling down on top of the pile of bedding. He stroked and caressed her with a skilled hand learned from where she didn't know until she was desperate for more. Reading her mind, he rolled on top of her and entered her slowly. She gasped.

"Are you alright?" he asked his eyes tender. "Does it hurt?"

"A little but don't stop."

"It will be better next time, I promise." He kissed her and as his rhythm increased Rosa's body relaxed into his as she looked up at his face in wonder.

Afterwards, she lay with her hand resting on her new husband's chest feeling the beat of his heart slow.

"I love you, Michael. Today has been the best day of my life."

Michael snored softly. It was the contented snore of a satiated man. She smiled and kissed him softly on his lips before pressing her body close to his and draping a proprietary arm around him.

In the morning when she woke she felt Michael hard and urgent next to her and he kept his promise because this time it was wonderful.

***

181

"Are you happy?" Rosa asked Michael. He was collapsed on top of her panting, and she smoothed the hair back from his damp forehead. Outside their wagon, she could hear the sounds of the morning, but she did not want to get up and greet them just yet.

"I am the happiest I have ever been Missus," he said raising his head and grinning at her. He rolled off her and onto his back tossing the blankets aside. "Now then, I've got to get up. There's work to be done, and as much as I'd love to, I can't lie in bed with you all day, you wanton woman." As he stood, he frowned. "I hope young Tom's feeling better today."

"Sure it's just a bit of a cold Michael, he'll be fine." Rosa watched him as he dressed. She knew despite his joking words prior to mentioning Tom that his heart still ached for his brother. Though he rarely spoke of Tyson these days, she would catch him from time to time staring at Tom, Willie and Eileen's oldest boy. He was close in age to Tyson, and she could see the pain in his eyes. In her naivety, she wished for a little one of their own for him to dangle from his knee and make silly faces at. Despite the practice they'd been getting in where the baby-making was concerned, her monthly had arrived on time for these past three months they'd been married. It wasn't just Tyson either; she knew he worried about his mammy left to fend off Martin's fists on her own. There was nothing he could do about that – he would tell her she was his family now.

Rosa thought that they would stay as they were. It was a good life they were leading travelling around the North with Michael's kind kinfolk who had welcomed them in so and made them part of their family. The shadows of those they had left behind at Cherry Orchard still stretched long and wide, though, and lately, Michael had begun to make noises about travelling somewhere different by themselves.

"I'll get up and put the tea on," Rosa said getting out of the warm bed with reluctance and setting about her morning routines.

Michael's reasoning, she knew, for wanting to move on was his need to put more distance between them and the memory of the stricken face of his little brother the day they left Cherry Orchard. Rosa didn't have the heart to tell him that it wouldn't change a thing. She knew that no matter how far from Ireland's shores they travelled, Tyson would always be right there with him in his heart just like Kitty, Joe and even Paddy would be in hers. Just the other night he had come home from the pub with a sway in his step and an excited inflection in his voice that she hadn't heard in a long while.

"I met a young couple tonight, Rosa; they were only a few years older than ourselves. They were talking all about the good times they had fruit-picking in the south of France last summer."

Rosa could see that the seed of an idea had been planted and that it was fast germinating as he picked her up and swung her round.

"So Mrs Donohue, how do you fancy going to France? We could pick the grapes during the day and drink wine under the stars by night." His face was aglow at the thought of it.

"Ah, I don't know Michael. It's a long way away, so it is."

He hadn't been put off, and whenever he mentioned this country across the water over the next few days, he would get a dreamy look on his face. Rosa could see that to his mind, France would be the land of milk and honey for them, but she knew no more of France than she'd known of the north of Ireland. Still, she could see the unspoken need on that handsome face of his for her to say yes they would go, she had followed him here after all and look how that had worked out! Yes, she decided, she would happily follow him to the ends of the earth if it meant he would find peace. Pouring him his tea, she waited a moment while he tucked his shirt into his trousers and then passed him the mug.

"Michael, I've been thinking."

He looked up from blowing the steam rising from his mug. "Oh yes?"

"I've been thinking that we should go to France."

***

They said their goodbyes soon after and through her tears, Rosa knew she would be forever grateful to the kind and gentle people of Michael's who had welcomed them into their fold.

For Rosa, her times spent with Michael were a time of firsts. Some were the simple everyday things other people took for granted but that she had never had a need of before, like riding on a bus or a boat. With Michael holding her hand, she had crossed the border of her country and explored the foreign parts of the North. She left the country of her birth with him to go to a land that was even more foreign to her than the settled life. Oh and, of course, there were other firsts too.

With Michael by her side, Rosa was brave and fearless, and so it was they embarked on their fruit-picking adventure. They had enough money to keep them fed and watered until they found the work they had gone to seek. Willie had given them a tent of sorts that could be erected for shelter. Michael was convinced that so balmy would the weather be they would have no need for anything else of a night. Having spent her entire sixteen years in a country where the sun would shine hot one minute, and the heavens would open the next Rosa doubted this. She didn't doubt however that he would keep her warm with his arms wrapped around her even if the tent did not.

They sailed from Belfast and the boat to Liverpool was the worst journey of Rosa's life. The hunk of steel taking them across the sea rocked and rolled across the water with such ferocity that she thought they would all surely drown. She was sick as a dog along with over half the other passengers as she clutched the seat of the toilet to hold herself steady, and willed her tummy to settle. There was to be no respite though until the boat docked.

When she looked back, Rosa couldn't recall much about their short stay in England or the journey from Liverpool to Dover. She did recall however that it took a lot of cajoling and whispered sweet nothings for Michael to convince her to board the boat to France. Thankfully that was a much smoother journey.

With the sun sparkling on a calm sea that day, she put the nightmare sailing from Ireland behind her. She let herself feel alive for the first time since Michael had hatched his plan with the excitement of this grand adventure they were embarking on. They were fortunate on that last leg of their sailing to get chatting to a young couple both with long hair and him with a beard that Rosa thought gave him a look of Jesus.

The woman's name was Joan, and his was Henry. Rosa sat on the open deck area's hard wooden seat next to Michael. The tang of salt from the sea spray was on her lips as she stared fascinated by all the pretty beads Joan had draped around her neck. To her mind, she should have been called Laura, it would have suited her better.

"We're driving to the Rhône Valley where the land's rich and fertile." Henry had a dreamy expression on his face like he was half asleep, Rosa thought, listening to him. "We're going to stay with a group of friends who've pooled their resources and bought an old farmhouse there." He would have been no more than twenty-five, and he said this in a zealous tone that reminded Rosa of the way Martin Donohue sounded when he spoke of the Travellers rights. He carried on talking about how he and Joan were disillusioned by conventional life. They were going to try a new way of living. There would be time to meditate and think about the things that were really important in this world like peace and love. They would achieve this by living communally without all the materialistic trappings and distractions of the modern world. Rosa looked bewildered, and so Joan explained that they would all live together, sharing the workload, toiling the land that would feed them as one extended family. "We'll be self-sufficient and that way the establishment can't tell us who we should be or what we should be doing with our lives."

"We'll make our own rules, man," Henry finished.

Michael had thrown back his head and laughed. "Sure there's nothing new about all of that, that's the way us Travellers have always lived." He told them their story then and it happened that when the boat docked Henry and Joan offered to give them a ride to the Rhône Valley. They told Rosa and Michael they would find grapevines a-plenty there, so long as they didn't mind squashing in the back of their old car.

They clambered gratefully into the back of their Morris Mini-Minor, somehow finding room to perch amongst their bags. After breaking down twice and a night spent sleeping under the stars, they eventually put-putted into a fairy tale village called Gigondas. Michael peered out the car window at the village's mellowed stone buildings. The red tiled roofs settled into the hillside and oversaw the rows and rows of vines below. He leaned forward and tapped Henry on the shoulder. "Can you pull over, Henry? This is where Rosa and I will stay."

It was backbreaking work picking those plump, purple grapes for the Gigondas Rosé each day under an unrelenting, baking sun, but Rosa and Michael worked hard. The kindly winemaker was a romantic sort, and their passion for one another must have reminded him of his youth because he took a liking to the young couple. Their toil was rewarded of an evening with good food the likes of which they had never tasted before. They had basic lodgings and a small wage that would see them through to the next port of call when the season ended. He also gave them an old bicycle that had been rusting almost forgotten in the barn. A quick test run between the vines proved it roadworthy. After their evening meal, Rosa would perch upon the handlebars and Michael would peddle to the top of the hill. They would coast down those gentle slopes in search of a quiet spot away from the prying eyes of the villagers. Somewhere to sit and watch the sunset, among other things that newlyweds do when they're alone together.

It was a magical time spent together in Gigondas and under that hot sun the lines of loss that had settled on Michael's face since they left Cherry Orchard soon softened. Rosa and Michael thrived away from the ghosts of their past but like all good things it had to come to an end. The mornings had a dewiness to them that had not been there when they first arrived. The vines had been stripped bare; their work had come to an end and so it was time for them to move on once more. The winemaker kissed Rosa on both cheeks before turning his attention to Michael. He shook his hand and in that guttural English of his which was far better than any of their pitiful attempts at French he told them to take the old bicycle with them. "There will be work, here again, next season if you come back," he said before waving them on their way. Rosa hoped with all her heart that they would indeed be back but she knew, in that way she sometimes just knew things, that they would not.

They set off on foot from the village. Rosa with a sense of sadness at leaving behind a place where for the first time in her life she had been completely and utterly happy. Michael, she sensed from the spring in his step, was looking forward to what-ever it was that would happen next on this adventure of theirs. He wheeled the bike along, and she carried that auld brown case of theirs as they wandered toward the main road leading south of the village. "Where are we going?" she asked, and he didn't answer her at first.

Eventually, when she had almost forgotten what it was she had asked him he replied, "I think we should just go wherever the road takes us." Rosa smiled, she was happy enough with that.

It was quiet, and there was much to look at in the fields they passed filled with the fading yellow heads of the sunflowers bobbing in the gentle breeze. It was after a bit when their legs had begun to ache that they heard the rumble of an approaching truck, Michael stuck his thumb out.

"If the trucks stops and gives a ride, then we will go wherever it is going."

It stopped.

They pulled into the town of Uzés around mid-afternoon after a bumpy ride on the back of the truck's open trailer loaded up with fruit and vegetables. Somehow they managed to squeeze themselves and the bike in between the boxes. Rosa found herself squashed in beside a carton full of glossy purple and yellow tomatoes. The colours of which were as foreign to her as the taste of the small purple one she was unable, in her curiosity, to stop herself pinching off the top of the pile and scoffing down. Poor Michael got stuck between a box of cabbages and a crate of spuds. Both were foods they were oh so familiar with. Rosa hated to admit it but the sight of those vegetables, that had once been staples of both their diets, gave her a pang for the familiarity of the country she had left behind, despite the beauty of the one they currently found themselves in. She could see by Michael's face that Tyson was once more not far from his thoughts.

"Here," Michael held out his hand to help Rosa clamber down from the truck. "Wait over there I won't be long." He pointed to a fountain as she jumped down. Picking up a crate, he followed the driver into the grocery shop he had pulled up alongside. It was on the corner of a street filled with shops in the market town. Helping to unload the truck was his way of saying thank you and Rosa sat down on the wall of the fountain to wait for him. A cherub stood in the middle of it, busy emptying an urn of water into the pool at its feet. The trickling sound it made was soothing as she kept an eye on the bike and their case. All the while she tried to ignore the dark shadow she had sensed creeping around the edges of her mind's periphery as the day had stretched out. She did not want to think of what that encroaching darkness might mean. The last time she had felt it was when Joe was sick. To distract herself. she glanced around the bustling old town's mellowed gold buildings and tried to convince herself that nothing bad could happen to them now. Sure, she told herself hadn't they been through the worst of times together already?

"What's wrong?" Michael asked wiping his brow with a hanky.

She shook her head. "Nothing, it's just hot that's all." He didn't look convinced, so she kissed him and stroked his cheek trying to inject excitement into her voice. "Come on, let's go and explore." They wandered those pretty cobbled streets with no clue of what they would do when nighttime fell. The weather was still warm enough for them to sleep under the canvas tent if need be. After having had a bed to fall into for the last few months, Rosa wasn't relishing the thought of sleeping on the hard ground again, though. Eventually, their aimless meandering bought them out into the town's main square. Michael was relaying a funny tale from his youth and Rosa laughed. She loved it when he recalled happy times from his childhood because they were few and far between. She had no idea of the pure joy of being in love that shone from her face.

Christian Beauvau did, though. A glimmer out the corner of his eye turned his attention to the old building framing the square. It was the mid-afternoon sunlight and the way in which it was illuminating the century's old stonework turning it umber. He picked up his camera that was never far from reach and had been about to photograph that special Uzés light when a handsome young couple strolled into his lens's line of sight. The look on the young girl in the pretty white dress's face was mesmerizing as she gazed up at her lover, and so he had clicked the shutter. In doing so, he had captured Rosa and Michael forever in the photograph he called *Midsummer Lovers*.

Chapter 19

It is better to be a coward a minute than dead the rest of your life – Irish Proverb
Rosa

You will have seen that photograph by now, Kitty my love. I know that if you have read this far then Christian will have already done what I asked of him by giving you this journal of mine that is now yours. I hope you will see it as a part of me I've left behind for you to open when you feel lonely or sad. Whenever you do so, you will know that you are forever in my thoughts.

Time, my darling girl, is short and it is precious. I have no desire to waste what is left of mine by repeating myself. Nor do I wish to relive the pain of what happened next in mine and Michael's story by putting it down in words because I loved him with every part of my being. I don't know where his body rests. I wish I did so I could have given his family a place to go and grieve had they wanted to. Instead, I fled when I got the news. The only things I took with me were my white dress and the wedding ring he gave me. The ring is yours now to do with it what you want.

The ending to mine and Michael's story is one I can't regret because as hard as it was to bear, I realise now that it was simply our fate. If he hadn't died, I would never have gone on to love Peter and have you. I know too that Mammy and Kitty were strong enough to be alright without me, but my wish is that things could have been different for Tyson. I always hoped that one day he would understand it wasn't his fault that Michael and I left Cherry Orchard. It was inevitable, and his brother never wanted to leave him nor did he ever stop loving him. If I can't tell him in this world, though, I am sure Michael will be there to meet him in the next. I hope too, in reading this Kitty, you understand why I have gone about things the way I have. Joe's death shaped this decision I have made. It was a terrible thing to see someone I loved waste away little by little, day by day. So you see that's why I am grateful you're living your life in London and out from under my roof. It would make this illness of mine so much harder to bear if you were here to witness the ravages of a sickness I won't recover from. I don't want you to go through what we went through watching Joe fade. Know this though Kitty; I never gave up. I fought this cancer of mine each and every day.

I didn't want you to remember me in sickness because a slow death like his leaves its scars forever imprinted on the memories of those left behind and tarnishes the good ones. I went back to Tuam to see where we buried him, our Joe, not long after I first found out about this sickness of mine. I saw my mammy and da's names on the headstones next to his. I didn't know they had gone too. I thought I would have felt it when they went, but I didn't, and I wish I had taken the time to say goodbye when I had the chance. So many years had passed since I'd stood on Irish soil, but I needed to tell Joe how things had gone for us Rourkes after he left. I sat there for an age and talked, filling my mammy and da in on all the gaps until now. Before I left, I told them that I would hold all their hands again soon. I know they heard me, and I know that it will be alright.

I had two great loves in my life Kitty, which makes me a luckier woman than most. That's where I would like you to scatter my ashes, though, next to where my brother Joe's body lies with my *mammy and da in that little cemetery behind that auld stone church in Tuam. I want to go back to the beginning and fly free home in Ireland.*

Kitty, there's an old Irish proverb I want to share with you before I go that says, if you lie down with dogs, you'll rise with fleas. You know who I am talking about my girl, so think on.

I'm done now, sweetheart, and I've said my piece. You, dear child, were all the very best bits of a full life lived. It's time for me to say goodbye now. I love you always.

Your Mammy x

PART THREE

Chapter 20

Men are like bagpipes no sound comes from them until they are full – Irish Proverb
Kitty

Kitty turned the last page of the journal and saw the wedding ring Michael had given her mother. It was taped to the inside of the back cover, and she pulled it free. Holding it up to the light, she looked at the simple gold band. Her eyes blurred making its smooth edges blur. "Oh Mum, I love you too." She let the tears spill over as she said the words out loud feeling for the first time since her mother's death a sense of her with her despite the empty room. The journal lay open on her lap, and she traced her fingers over the words Rosa had, at last, sat down and written. So many words but they'd come so late. With each page and each day that had passed as she'd filled the journal's pages with her life's story, the writing had grown more spidery and faint in its etchings. Until finally with those last words she was gone.

"You could have told me you know, Mum. You should have trusted me because I would have understood." Kitty sniffed, wishing she had a box of tissues handy as she made do with wiping her nose with the back of her hand. The time for recriminations was over, she thought, watching the ineffectual muslin curtains breathe in and out on the evening breeze. It had blown away the remnants of the short-lived storm. Later she would close the shutters, but now it was time for her to move forward. She would look toward the future just as her mother had wanted her to do.

It was clear to Kitty now that Rosa had wanted her to come here. She had orchestrated it with Christian, and it was a pilgrimage of sorts. She wanted her to try to put things right, in the way she had wanted to do with Tyson for Michael's memory's sake. She had been too frightened of the recriminations that might be thrown at her were she to try and so she had left it too long until finally, it was too late. If Kitty could heal those wounds with Jonny then perhaps it would open the way for her to go and meet her aunt and hopefully Paddy too if he were still alive. She understood now why it had been so important to Rosa that Christian be the one to give her the journal. It was here in a way where a part of her mother's life had ended, but it was also here in this little French town where a new part of Kitty's life might just begin.

She slid the wedding band onto the ring finger of her right hand. She knew what she had to do next and, pressing her fingers to her mouth, she blew a kiss to the empty room before closing the journal. She placed it in her case that was still lying open on the bed next to her, knowing as she did so that it wouldn't be the last time she would read through the little book. It would be something she would carry with her always. So she could pick it up often throughout whatever lay ahead to take comfort from the loving words of her mum and to marvel at her life. It was a treasure, and as such, she would treasure it, Kitty hauled herself upright. It was time to put sentimentality aside, she had things she had to go do.

As she swung her legs over the side of the bed, she caught sight of her reflection in the oval shaped mirror angled over the heavy art deco style dresser opposite her. Its bevelled edges caught the light, but she was too perturbed by the face staring back at her to notice how pretty it was. Oh dear, she grimaced, and her hands flew up to her hair to try and smooth it down. It had still been wet from the shower when she'd phoned Yasmin. She had been in too much of a hurry to settle back on those fat, downy pillows and lose herself in Rosa's story to bother blow-drying it when she'd finished the call. Now she wished she had taken the few minutes to do so. Oh well, she sighed, reaching for her handbag and fishing out her makeup purse where she knew a bobble and some hair clips would be, she'd just have to put it up.

A bit of eyeliner and lippy could work wonders, Kitty thought a few minutes later as she snapped the powder compact shut. She was satisfied that with her makeup repairs done, and her hair pulled up in a loose top knot, she was as presentable as she'd ever be. She just hoped her jeans had dried out and pulling them off the rail at the end of the bed she gave them a quick pat down pleased to find they pretty much had. The swelling on her bottom had gone down too, she noticed with relief as she pulled the denim up over her knickers. The antihistamines had worked a treat and the drowsiness she'd felt earlier had worn off. At least the humiliating pharmacy debacle hadn't been in vain, and she would not have to spend the rest of her days carting around three bottom cheeks.

A quick glance at her phone revealed the time to be only just after seven. She had thought it would be later than that but then she'd been in a whole other world for the last few hours and had lost all track of such trivia as time. It was still light outside too, she saw, heading over to close the shutters. She wasn't due to meet Damien until half past eight, but she was sure she could amuse herself by exploring the town until then. Picking up her bag, she slung it over her shoulder and opening her bedroom door stepped out into the darkened, deserted hallway.

The old floorboards creaked as she made her way to the top of the stairs, glad someone had had the foresight to leave the light on in the front entrance below. Otherwise, she'd be taking her life in her hands attempting the stairs not only in a pair of heels but in the dark too.

She found Simone and Christian in the kitchen. The table they were seated at was big and rustic, a centrepiece for the farmhouse styling of the utility room. There was a half-empty bottle of red wine alongside the open laptop over which their heads were bent deep in conversation, and they each had a glass of vino in front of them. Simone, she noted, was dressed in more casual attire than she had been earlier despite the expression on her face that said she meant business as she pointed at something on the screen. Kitty hovered in the doorway for a moment not wanting to interrupt them and had just decided she'd be best to leave them to it when Christian looked up and saw her standing there. He pushed his glasses down his nose before exclaiming with a genuine delight in his voice that made her stand just a little taller in her mock Alexander McQueen's. "Kitty, come join us. You have lots you want to talk about, oui?"

She was tempted to sit down and join them both in a glass of wine, wanting nothing more than to hear Christian speak further of his times spent with her mother. She had so much she wanted to share with him. Simone, however, did not look so pleased with the interruption. Kitty was guessing she quite often had to work hard to keep Christian on focus with the task at hand. She didn't want to be the one who made the other woman's work drag on late into the evening, and so she stopped herself from taking a step toward the table.

"No, I won't, but thank you." She dragged her eyes away from the bottle of wine. "Where's Jonny?" The question popped out of her mouth taking her by surprise because she didn't care where he was.

Simone shrugged. "He went out earlier. Uzés it is a beautiful town, and I think he is probably making the most of his short stay here and why not?"

Kitty thought she caught a slight hint of disapproval in her tone and, feeling reprimanded, she edged backwards out the door. "Hmm, why not indeed, that's what I plan on doing too."

"Christian and I, we have already eaten. I would have asked you to join us, but he said you were busy and that I should not interrupt." She shot him an accusatory look, and it was his turn to shrug. Kitty felt a jolt as she glanced from one to the other realising from the closeness of their chairs and their easy way with each other that theirs was obviously more than just a working relationship.

She wasn't shocked. How could she be after what she had learned about her mother and Michael's relationship? Rosa had only been fifteen when she fell in love with Michael. Okay, so there was only a three year age gap between them nothing like the decades between Simone and Christian. Still, Kitty thought, Simone wasn't the first woman to fall for the charms of an older man nor would she be the last. Besides, Christian was such a gentleman she could see how the young woman would fall in love with him, and who was she to judge? Look at the state of her love life. No, each to their own she told herself, realizing Simone was looking at her expectantly. "I uh, I was reading something Christian gave me of my mother's, and I wasn't very hungry but thank you, Simone. I'm supposed to be meeting my, um, my friend, Damien in town for dinner." She didn't want to, she realized. She wanted to be by herself to wander the town lost in her mother's memories as she digested everything she had learned tonight.

Christian, she thought, taking in his expression, had made it fairly obvious that afternoon that he hadn't been enamoured of Damien. He hadn't said or done anything, but she could tell by the subtleties of his body language. The not so subtle frown on his face, as he looked at her now, confirmed that he hadn't warmed to him. It shouldn't matter what he thought considering the brief time in which she had known him, but for some reason it did, and she felt the need to justify herself. "Like I said earlier, he's an old friend, Christian and it's only dinner. You two enjoy your evening and don't work too hard." She turned and had only taken a few steps when she heard him call out.

"Kitty, don't be late, oui? It is a big day tomorrow."

Simone muttered something at him in French, and Kitty was guessing from the inflection in her voice that she was chastising him for telling a grown woman what time she had to be in by. She smiled, it had been a long time since anybody had worried about her curfew and her thoughts flew to her father. What she'd read this evening hadn't changed how she felt about either of her parents or the choices they'd made. How could it? She reached for the key sitting in the front door lock and turned it, not when their every decision had been made with her in mind. If anything it had helped her understand them better and realise how blessed she'd been to be so loved by them both.

She opened the door and smiled, feeling like a teenager as she shouted back over her shoulder. "I won't be late, I promise." Pulling it shut behind her, she stepped down onto the pavement and stood there for a moment. The students were long gone now, and a few lights were beginning to twinkle in the windows of the surrounding apartments and houses. Inside them, Kitty knew people would be setting about their evening chores and, while her world might have just tipped on its axis, for them, today would have been a day just like any other.

At the bottom of the street despite the early evening dusk beginning to settle in, she could see a circular low-walled, fountain. A cherub's urn tipped water into the stagnant water pooling at its feet. Her mother had sat on that very wall, she realized with a start. It was where she had waited for Michael while he helped unload the fruit and vegetables when they first arrived in Uzés. She remembered it from earlier too, and knew that if she turned right when she reached it, then it would take her back to the main road where the shops were. She could easily find her way about from there. First things first, she was going to follow in her mum's footsteps and perch on that wall for a moment or two listening to the trickling water just as Rosa had done fifty years earlier.

Kitty's heels clacked down the narrow pavement, and she was all too aware of its ankle twistingly high kerbside as she tottered toward the bottom of the hill. She made it in one piece and sat down on the wall seeing that the grocery store, although closed for the day, was still there across the street. Closing her eyes, she tried to conjure up a feeling of her mother as she listened to the tinkling water from the cherub's urn. She frowned, to her ears, it sounded very much like someone doing an illicit wee and her eyes popped open. She did not need to be reminded of her wasp debacle, thank you very much, and casting the cherub a disparaging look she stood up and carried on her way.

Street lights were beginning to come on for the night as she wondered whether Damien had found somewhere to stay, sure that there would be plenty of rooms for rent. As the rows of shops and cafés came into her line of sight, she told herself that it wasn't her problem where he slept. It had been his choice to come here. The deserted buildings that earlier in the day had been bustling with trade were stretched out ahead of her on either side of the tree-lined road. Kitty paused for a moment thinking how very different it looked now that she was picturing the scene through her sixteen-year-old mother's eyes.

The patisserie too was closed, she noticed, and crossing the road she walked toward it. Its frontage pulled her in like a magnet to steel, despite the fact its colourful macaron montage of earlier was gone from the window, and the display cabinets sat disappointingly empty. She stood there at the window her nose almost, but not quite, pressed to the glass as she gazed in at the darkened depths. She could imagine the hustle and bustle that would be going on in a few short hours. While the townsfolk and tourists were still sleeping, the artisan bakers would be getting their wares ready for the day.

That would be her one day soon she thought, feeling a frisson of excitement. She would be out the back of her café whipping up her cupcakes in its kitchen in anticipation of the brisk day's trade to follow.

Kitty inhaled, fancying she could smell the buttery emotive scent of rising cakes. Even though she wasn't inside the shop with her sleeves rolled up folding a mix or spooning it into the tins she would have lined up ready and waiting, she still felt the familiar glow settle over her. It was the glow that came with the sense of wellbeing she always got from the act of making something with her two hands that brought happiness to others and made them smile.

It was a bit like the rush an adrenalin junkie might get from a base jump, only much safer, or sex, she thought, sighing contentedly. When she got home, she would introduce new flavours and expand her repertoire. She pictured herself looking a bit like a mad scientist as she poured a bit of this and a bit of that into the mixing bowl. She was so deeply engrossed as to whether cinnamon would work on its own or if it would need a companion like perhaps coffee that she never saw the man materialize behind her in the reflection of the glass.

"Are you feeling a bit peckish or something? Because you'd be better off heading down to one of the restaurants in the square if you are." He pointed to the sign on the door. "They're shut. in case you hadn't noticed."

Kitty jumped, and her hand flew up to her chest instinctively protecting her heart. She had been so lost in thought she hadn't heard anyone approaching, and swinging round she looked up into Jonny Donohue's amused face.

"Oh God, I was miles away! You gave me a right fright." She saw that those dark eyes of his that had glowered at her earlier were glittering with suppressed mirth, but still she took a step away from him not prepared to trust his sudden shift of mood.

He didn't seem to notice. "Sorry, I couldn't resist. You looked like you were lost in a dream about éclairs or whatever those little biscuit things they had on display in the window today were."

"Macarons, and I am not sure whether I like them or not. They're awfully sweet you know." Kitty hoped she wasn't that obvious, and her hand strayed to her mouth to make sure she hadn't been drooling.

He looked amused by her discomfiture. "So a penny for them then?"

She felt like she should tell him to mind his own business after what he had said to her that afternoon. She should turn on her heel and storm off, leaving him to stare after her with an expression of admiration at her strength of character. That would be better than the current look on his face that said he was doing his best not to laugh at her. Still, she mused, she'd rather that than the surly man she had encountered earlier, and she owed it to her mother to try and soften his stance where she and his uncle were concerned. He appeared to be holding out an olive branch, and after what she had read that evening she knew she had to reach out and take it. "I was fantasizing if you must know."

"Oh yeah," he raised an eyebrow. "Does it involve whipped cream?"

"What? No!" She wished she'd walked off when she had the chance. Where on earth had that choice of word come from? I mean fantasizing for goodness sake! What was she running on? It was his fault; he had her all flustered. "What I meant was I am going to open my own shop in the not too distant future. And I was *thinking* about all the different flavours and colours of the cakes I will have in my front window when I do so. Whenever I feel stressed out, I bake, and if I can't bake then I think about it in some shape or form. It makes me feel better."

"You're a baker then?"

"No, not quite. I mean yes I do bake, I love to bake, but I never qualified as such. I used to work as a secretary, but for now I am waitressing, and on the weekends I sell my cupcakes at the local market in London where I live. I've come into a bit of money recently and what with the money from doing the recreation photo tomorrow I've got nothing stopping me from going into business on my own."

"You're a girl with big plans."

"I guess so, yes, but thinking about how I am going to go about it is as far as I have gotten with those big plans."

"Ah, I see."

Something in his reply annoyed her. "As soon as I get home I will be putting a proper business plan together." How she was going to set about doing that she did not have the foggiest, but it sounded like something that someone who was going to open their own café would do. "So what about you, what do you do?" She could picture him sticking to the old traditions her mother had described so vividly in her journal. He would live in a wagon, no modern caravan in a campground for him, and a sturdy old Piebald would still pull it. Yes, she decided, looking at him in his faded jeans and loosely tucked in shirt. She could see him tugging on a set of reins in the masterful way her mother had described Michael doing. She didn't think he would be married; her eyes strayed down to his hands, but they were thrust into his pockets so no clues there.

"I'm a builder."

Oh, she hadn't expected that. She didn't know what she had expected him to say. Not that he was a Tinker certainly, but she had envisaged him in his angst against the world not working in a steady trade. He'd be far too busy travelling the countryside foraging for his fruit 'n' veg and picking up the odd bit of farm-hand work here and there.

"And I live in an apartment in Dublin."

"Oh, I thought—"

"I know what you thought; I can see it on your face. You thought I'd live in a gypsy wagon, and cook my meals over a campfire while whittling away at a nice piece of tin, singing songs about people dying."

"No, of course I didn't think that." Her cheeks flamed because that's exactly what she had thought.

His mouth curved at the corner in a way that told her he didn't believe her. "It's alright, you're right in a way because I grew up in a Travellers camp in Ballyfermot, but there wasn't much romance about it. It was a hard life. He wasn't a happy man, my da, and he made sure the rest of us suffered for it too. I left as soon as I got my builder's apprenticeship and had money of my own coming in."

Cherry Orchard had been in Ballyfermot, and she wondered if that was where he'd grown up or if it had disbanded and they had set up elsewhere by the time he was born. She wanted to ask after his da and gran, but instead her mouth formed the word. "Oh." She hadn't realized until then how much she was hoping he was still part of the community her mother had once been part of. She'd thought that he might somehow open the way for her to meet the members of her family who were still alive. "Do you still see them, the Travellers then?"

His laugh was throaty. "Oh aye, I still see them, they're part of me, always will be. I just wanted to go a different way for a while." He shifted on his feet, leather boots peeking out of the frayed bottoms of his jeans. "My gran and grandda are long gone and after my mam and da passed on it fell to me to clear their wagon and that was the first I heard of any of this photograph business. I found all the cheques that Da had never cashed. They were in an envelope along with a letter your man Christian had sent to him with the first payment explaining what the money was for. That was the first Da knew of his brother having died."

He shook his head, and Kitty could see the frustration this

memory evoked in the frown lines that appeared between his eyebrows. "If he had cashed those cheques he could have made our lives so much easier, but he didn't. He chose not to because he felt Michael had abandoned him, left him with a da who was too handy with his fists by far. He was only eight when Michael left, and he never let go of that hurt. I reckon it was that what made him sick in the end. Of course not having a grave to visit didn't help him with the grieving process, and that was down to your mam."

"I'm sorry, and I know my mum was sorry." Kitty wanted to reach out and touch him, but something in his posture stopped her.

"Don't be – I cashed those cheques in as soon as I could." He looked down at her then with a challenging expression, but Kitty wasn't about to protest, he had every right to that money, it was what Michael and Rosa would have wanted.

"Do you know I think stubbornness must be a Traveller's trait? I knew nothing about my mother's life before she turned nineteen until today. She refused point-blank to discuss anything that happened in her life before then so I had no idea where she grew up or anything about – well, any of this. I thought when she died that that was it, I would never know."

"I didn't know your mam had passed on until Christian filled me in this afternoon. I wouldn't have said what I said to you earlier if I had." His face seemed to soften as he spoke.

It was as close as she was likely to get to an apology, Kitty decided instinctively, knowing saying sorry would not come easily to this man. "Jonny, I don't blame you for feeling angry with the way things turned out, but my mum told me that Michael never wanted to leave your dad. They had no choice, Rosa and Michael, and he never stopped missing Tyson."

Jonny didn't show any sign of acknowledging what she'd just said as he stared blankly at the empty shelf in the window in front of him, so she carried on. "I'd never heard of the photograph either until Christian contacted me asking me to come to Uzés to do the recreation picture. I couldn't believe my eyes when I saw the original for the first time; it was like looking at a photograph of a person who was part of me but who I had never known."

"You look just like her."

Kitty raised a smile. "That's the pot calling the kettle black because you could be your uncle's double too."

"Aye, he and Da were the spit of each other and I look like Da, so there you go." He rubbed at the stubble on his chin and she wondered what it would be like to feel the roughness of it against the smoothness of her skin. She blinked, where had that come from? She was shocked at her reaction to his physical presence. At the same time, she told herself not to go there. She registered that there was no gold band or tell-tale white mark of there once having been one on his ring finger. She remembered the ring on her finger and held her hand out. "This was the ring Michael gave my mother the day they married. My mum left a journal explaining her story to me with Christian, and this was taped into the back of it."

Jonny gave it a cursory glance, but she could see his mind was elsewhere. "I think that was the problem with my da. Every time he looked at me, he saw his brother and the old hurts could never heal."

It would not help Jonny to know that it was also guilt Tyson had felt each time he looked at his son. Guilt for leading his mammy to the tin hut where Rosa and Michael had met that afternoon, and in doing so setting in motion a chain of events that could not be stopped. "It wasn't your fault, Jonny or your dad's," she said softly. "Michael and Rosa's running away was nothing to do with either of us. I don't think you can blame them either because it was just life. They fell in love and wanted to be together, but those around them weren't prepared to tolerate that."

"Is that so?"

She could see the mix of annoyance and amusement at her declarations of her mother and his uncle's grand love affair, but she needed to make him understand the way it had been. "It is, mum's journal explained it all and I know that Michael never wanted to leave Tyson or your gran. It ate away at him. He was given no choice but to go; they couldn't stay."

She'd overstepped the mark; it was too much too soon. Kitty could see it in the way something in his eyes seemed to shut down, and his body straightened. "And tell me who made you the expert? You know nothing about what Da went through after Michael left. He had a choice alright, and he made it the day he walked away from Cherry Orchard with your mam and left his little brother to fend for himself."

Kitty opened her mouth; she needed to make him understand the way things had played out for Rosa and Michael. He had already turned his back on her, though, and she watched as he strode off in the opposite direction.

Chapter 21

A hen is heavy when carried far – Irish Proverb

Kitty stood there illuminated in the fading light by the patisserie's flickering sign and felt strangely bereft as she watched Jonny get further and further away from her. More than anything she wanted to run after him, stand on tippy-toes and throw her arms around his neck before pressing her lips to his. She pinched her arm hard leaving a red welt behind as she whispered, "Stop it, Kitty Sorenson, just you stop it."

Her mother had written that she was sure Kitty had been born like her maternal grandmother and like Rosa herself, with the sight, and reading those words had been a lightbulb moment for Kitty. It had explained to her why she always knew who was on the phone before she answered it, or who it was standing on the other side of a door before she opened it. She knew, for instance, that Yasmin would go on to become a successful fashion designer. It was more than a belief in her friend's talent; it was something she knew with an absolute certainty. Sometimes too, she'd sense when someone was ill, like her friend Chloe who she had worked with at the architect's firm. Kitty had passed Chloe a tissue one day, and as their fingers touched she had known there was something far more seriously wrong than 'a cold I can't shake' with her friend. She'd suggested she go to see a doctor, but Chloe had looked at her like she was mad, until two months later she was diagnosed with a form of leukaemia. She had pulled through, thank goodness, but for Kitty it had been a terrible thing to know. She'd been unable to do anything about her friend's illness because how could she convince somebody of something she couldn't understand herself?

When it came to what was going on in her own life, she wouldn't have a clue. Okay yes, sometimes there would be that sensation of darkness approaching like spilt paint spreading or a shadowy hand about to clutch at her ankle, but she never knew what it meant. Apart from that, she'd had no inkling that Damien was cheating on her. Then again, perhaps she'd had her blinkers on so tight where he was concerned that she wouldn't have acknowledged it even if she had.

Right now she didn't need the hit-and-miss sight to explain why she had just felt the urge to snog a virtual stranger. A man who had been undeniably unpleasant to her on two occasions now, and to do so while she was stone-cold sober too. It was because Jonny was a tangible part of her mother's past. He was a living and breathing link to what had gone before. He was evoking memories in her that weren't her own, but those that had once belonged to her mum. Together she and Jonny shared the bond not only of an entwined history, but of the ripple effects Rosa and Michael's running away together had created. Tonight, as they had talked she had felt that bond pull and tighten between them, and she only hoped, that in saying what she had said, it had just frayed that bond, not snapped it all together. Jonny had made it pretty clear by walking off the way he had, that he did not like what she represented to him.

Kitty stayed where she was, rooted to the spot until he disappeared from her line of sight. She was guessing from the direction he was headed that he was going back to the house. She had missed her chance to go after him and try to talk further, but perhaps it was for the best. He might need time to think about what she had said. She sighed, and fished her phone out of her bag to check the time, seeing that she better get a move on. If she didn't show up when they'd arranged, Damien would panic and think that something had happened to her. The last thing she wanted was for him to storm round to the house all pumped up and filled with testosterone ready to accuse Christian and Simone of being human traffickers. Despite her earlier misgivings, she realized she was looking forward to seeing someone who knew her well. She needed to tell him about her mum and all that she had learned because it was fizzing up inside her. She didn't think she would tell him what Rosa had had to say where he was concerned, though. He might not like being referred to as a dog with fleas!

**

The square looked magical in the fading evening light. It had been washed clean, and the air was fresh from the rain. Twinkling fairy lights were strewn around the trees lending an enchanted feel to the lively atmosphere. The café tables, where she had sat earlier with Christian, were now filled with candlelight diners, and she didn't have to scan them for long before she spied Damien waving out and gesturing her over.

Her stomach did that thing that she had no control over at the sight of him, and she realized that her mother's words had done nothing to quell the effect he had on her. Kitty wondered how it was that he could still make her knees go weak despite everything that had happened. She hadn't wanted him here in Uzés; she'd needed the space to think, but he had cared enough to follow her here, so that had to count for something surely? She wound her way through the tables toward him.

He stood up to greet her, placing his hands either side of her upper arms before he pulled her close and inclined his head as he made to kiss her. Kitty turned her face at the last moment, so his lips grazed her cheek instead, not wanting him to think that it was a given that they were back together, and all was forgiven. He didn't seem faze by her subtle rejection as he murmured, "You look so lovely Kitty. Thanks for meeting me."

She didn't have a choice with regards to meeting him, she thought, glancing down at her T-shirt and jeans before looking back at him. He had always liked it when she made an effort when they went out. He was much more of a little black dress kind of a guy than the casual look she had donned tonight, so she was surprised by the compliment. Of course with her limited wardrobe, a little black dress had not been an option.

Damien released her arms and went around to the other side of the table to pull her seat out for her. She sat down thinking that he was pulling all the stops out tonight, and as he sat opposite her, she noticed his hair was still damp from having showered. Her eyes travelled down to his chest; he was wearing a cobalt blue shirt with black pinstripes running through it. She'd always loved him in that shade of blue, the colour did something amazing to his eyes, and she wondered if his choice of shirt was deliberate.

She pulled her eyes away and looked at the tabletop between them. It was covered with a white cloth and laid with polished silver cutlery. A stubby candle flickered in a glass, and there was a bottle of wine chilling in an ice bucket in the middle of the table. She wondered what he'd chosen for them; he'd always fancied himself a bit of connoisseur ever since he'd done a wine appreciation course a few years ago. Mind you, she'd never been able to fault his wine choices in the past. It was just that she didn't care if the buttery richness of the Chardonnay was the perfect partner to her fish dish. Or for that matter, whether the tart crispness of the Sauvignon Blanc would set off her choice of chicken to perfection. All she cared about was if it was white then it better be cold, crisp and taste good.

As it turned out it was neither white nor red, Damien had chosen a strong pink rosé for them to share. Kitty knew what it was before he said the words, and her heart skipped a beat at the coincidence of his choice. The wine came from a place where her mother and Michael had discovered the true meaning of happiness.

"It's a Gigondas," he said pulling it from the bucket and inspecting the label. "I'm not familiar with it, but the waiter assured me it was the perfect aperitif drink. I sampled it before deciding on a bottle. It's a generous wine with undertones of almonds and cooked fruit. I thought that since we were here in France, it was only right that we drink a local wine."

Kitty was grateful she had missed the whole wine swishing about the mouth before he spat it out debacle. It was a tasting ritual that always made her cringe. "It's made from grapes that have ripened on the same vines my mother and Michael once picked together," she said softly watching the pink and purple-hued wine fill her glass.

Damien paused mid-pour. "What did you just say?"

"I think we should try it before I tell you."

"Okay." He looked bemused, she noticed, as he finished pouring her glass. "But I propose a toast first."

Kitty did not feel like raising her glass; she wanted to sample the wine and her mouth watered in anticipation of it. She would humour him, so she decided to wait while he filled his glass before raising hers.

"To you, Kitty Sorenson. To finding the answers you have been seeking and," he looked at her hopefully, "to us." He had the grace not to sound quite as self-assured as he waited for her to reiterate his words.

Kitty hesitated; she wasn't ready to say that there was an 'us', and so instead she murmured, "To finding the answers I have been seeking." She clinked her glass to his and avoided his eyes as she closed her own and took a sip of the cool liquid. She let its flavour sit in her mouth for a moment, savouring it before swallowing. It was gorgeous, she decided, picturing her mother and Michael picnicking under a tree by a babbling brook. They would have sipped on the very same wine they were helping to produce and felt oh so avant-guard as they fed each other strong, smelly cheese and crackers.

"So are you going to tell me what you have found out?"

Kitty's eyes flew open at the sound of his voice banishing the image of Rosa and Michael as she looked at Damien's handsome, expectant face opposite her.

"You had better make yourself comfortable," she told him. "It's a long story."

"I've got all night," he said raising his glass to his mouth once more.

She told him of Rosa's earlier life from start to finish only pausing once to glance at the menu as the waiter came with pen and paper at the ready. Kitty noticed he had a much more amenable expression on his face than his earlier counterpart had possessed. She had spied an impressive pasta dish being carried past, and so had ordered the pasta of the day. Damien opted for veal, and after some deliberation and questions as to the suitability of its pairing, ordered another bottle of wine. She hadn't realized he had refilled her glass more than once, and that the bottle of rosé was nearly empty as she relayed Rosa's story.

By the time their plates were deposited with a flourish and a grind of black pepper in front of them, Kitty had finished talking. She watched the waiter disappear to return a moment later with a bottle of white this time and fresh glasses. She drained her glass and handed it to him with a smile of thanks.

"I trust mademoiselle enjoyed the wine, oui?"

It was fairly obvious she had, given the empty bottle. "I did, merci. It was very special."

She smiled, and he gave her a little nod before moving to the next table to add its empty glasses to his tray. Damien poured them both a glass of the white, and she hoped he wouldn't launch into another monologue about the wine he had chosen to accompany their main. All she wanted to know was what he thought about everything she had just told him. Her stomach was in knots as she picked up her fork and toyed with the penne coated in a creamy sauce.

Damien began to slice into his veal scaloppini, and as he held it up to check that it was cooked medium rare the way he had requested it be Kitty felt a spark of irritation. She'd always hated the way in which he could never just sit and enjoy a meal. It was as though he was looking for elements that weren't right. A speck on the plate, or his food not being hot enough so that he could exercise his right to complain as a paying customer. Thankfully his veal must have been just the right shade of pink in the middle because he popped it in his mouth, chewing and looking at her thoughtfully before he finally swallowed and spoke.

"Do you remember our trip to Paris?"

Kitty nodded wondering where he was going with this, and why the change of topic.

"We ate in that charming little bistro with the chequered red and white tablecloths and were served by the waiter that you reckoned looked like George Clooney."

"He looked exactly like him; he could have been his double. I decided that he must be a struggling actor trying to make ends meet by waiting tables." She'd conjured up a romantic tale around him as she'd gotten caught up in the excitement of dining in Paris.

"Yes, you thought he was wonderful until he brought you out a plate of chicken livers instead of the cassoulet you ordered." He laughed, and Kitty shuddered at the memory. "Your face was a picture."

Kitty smiled, it had been too hard to try and get it through to the George lookalike whose English was worse than her French what it was she had actually ordered. She had filled up on the bread accompaniment provided in a basket instead. She was a very hypocritical meat eater she'd had to concede to Damien when she refused point blank to try the chicken livers. "But you eat pâté?" he'd said.

"That's different," she had muttered, breaking off another piece of baguette.

They'd had some good times together, she thought, recalling too how after dinner they had meandered down the banks of the Seine eventually winding up alongside the Eiffel Tower. The sight of the famous monument illuminated at night had taken her breath away. She had felt so happy and contented as they had stood beneath it wrapped in each other's arms kissing. It was Paris, and that's what you should do when you were in the most romantic city in the world.

They'd had a fight on the way back to the hotel; it was over something so trivial that she couldn't even remember what it had been about now. She did remember that it had been her that had backed down in the end. It always was. She blinked that memory away realising that Damien was talking.

"Are you not hungry?"

Kitty stabbed the penne and a mushroom. "I should be. I have hardly eaten all day, and that is not like me at all." She popped it in her mouth, it was delicious, she thought, but her usually voracious appetite was letting her down tonight.

"You have had a big day."

At last he was bringing the conversation around to where she wanted it. "Yes, it's certainly been that alright."

"It's some story you've just told me. Who would have guessed? I mean Rosa always seemed quite refined to me, a little eccentric but she was a clever woman no doubt about that."

"I know, I have thought of so many different scenarios as to where she came from over the years. It never crossed my mind that she might have once been part of the Irish Traveller community. I think I am still in a little bit of shock, to be honest, trying

216

to equate the Rosa in the journal and in *Midsummer Lovers* with the Rosa that was my mum."

"They were two different people, Kitty; that's the thing. Your mother decided she wanted to move on with her life and move forward, and that is what she did. So I don't see how it changes anything for you because she is still the same person you knew, and you are still the same girl you were before you came here and read that journal. Whoever you mother was before she had you is irrelevant to your childhood. She chose to disassociate herself from her family, and the way I see it you are not one of them."

Kitty detected disdain in his voice and looked at him in surprise. "What do you mean I am not one of them? I feel like what Mum told me explained so much about this inability of mine to commit to something and settle down. This need to keep moving, and I often talked to you about those funny little feelings I would get from time to time."

Damien paused, his fork was midway to his mouth with the new potato hanging onto the prongs momentarily forgotten. "Oh, Kitty, that's absolute rubbish, and you know it. You were settled in Manchester with me, but I screwed it up, it's nothing to do with you having Traveller blood in you. You've been a lost soul because of what I did, I mean waiting tables and working on a market stall, come on." He made an inverted commas sign with his finger. "As for 'those feelings' of yours well we all get those from time to time. I always know when it's my bloody mother on the phone. There's something in the way it rings that tells me she's calling to check that I'm eating properly, and have enough clean shirts for work. You have been looking for answers to questions that were never there."

Kitty put her fork down feeling her blood beginning to pass a slow simmer as it began to bubble. "I beg your pardon? I make an honest living out of waitressing, and my market stall is very popular thank you very much. I never realized what a snob you are until now."

Damien opened his mouth, but she held her hand up. "No, let me speak. I am half Traveller, half tinker, a flipping gypsy! And I fully intend to find my family and learn more about them."

"I'm not a snob, Kitty; it's just that you can do so much better than what you have been doing drifting along down in London. All this talk about opening your café, you don't know the first thing about running a business. I am worried about you because you have the chance to do something positive for your future with the money you have just come into from Rosa's house sale. I also think if you go careening off to Ireland to meet these people you might be sorely disappointed. I don't want you to get hurt or fleeced for that matter."

"Pity you didn't think about me getting hurt when you started up with The Bitch then, isn't it?"

He looked chastened, and Kitty regretted her words and the way the conversation had deteriorated so rapidly. The woman was history, and sitting here tonight she had slowly come to realize that she and Damien were history too.

"Look I'm sorry Damien, but I can't go back."

"What do you mean?"

"I mean what we did the other night it was a mistake. I was feeling fragile, and well, we shouldn't have done it."

His hand snaked across the table to rest on hers. "It wasn't a mistake, Kitty! It was right because we fit together. Cheating on you, now that was the mistake."

"No! I mean yes it was, but I've realized that it would always be there between us, what happened," she shrugged. "I am not a big enough person to move forward. I'm sorry, but I'm not, and well the thing is, if I am honest, I don't want to either. I'm just not the same girl I was when we were together anymore, and it's time I started to look forward and not go backwards." Damien's hand still rested on hers, but he refused to meet her gaze seemingly fascinated with the contents of his wine glass. "I'm sorry you had to come all this way just to hear me say this, but it's the way it is. I don't want to try again."

"But what about us? What we had between us. I wanted to marry you one day," Damien said finally looking up, his voice, to her horror, choking.

"Oh, Damien there is no us, there hasn't been since the day I left. You will find the right girl for you, but she isn't me." Kitty pulled her hand out from under his and got up from the table; she slung her bag over her shoulder. "I'm sorry," she reiterated before turning and walking away as fast as her feet would carry her before her resolved weakened.

***

She felt lighter, Kitty realized, and not just because she'd had hardly any dinner. The weight of indecision had lifted from her shoulders. She truly could move on now with no if's or but's lurking in the background. The cherub's urn was still trickling water into the pond at its feet, and she reached down to stroke the stone wall before she turned into the silent street and began the climb toward the house. It struck her then that she had no key to get in if everybody had decided to get an early night. It must be after ten, she thought, as nearing it she saw to her relief that the lights were on in the front room. Good, she had no wish to encounter Simone rudely awakened from a deep sleep. Nor Christian in his pyjamas because she had a sneaking suspicion they'd be red silk, and that she did not need to see!

Stepping up to the front door she tapped on it lightly and didn't have to wait long until it opened. Jonny stood there illuminated by the hallway light; he was still dressed in the same clothes he'd been wearing earlier, but his hair was mussed as though he had been raking his fingers through it. In his hand he was holding a tumbler and eyeing its amber contents, Kitty hazarded a guess that it was whiskey. From the belligerent expression on his face, she would put money on him having had more than one.

Oh, why did it have to be him that opened the door? She ducked past him with a mumbled thanks. She needed to talk to him but now was not the time because she was not up to any more confrontational conversations, especially not if he'd been drinking. She heard the front door close, and as she reached the bottom of the stairs, she froze with one hand on the rail as he cleared his throat. No words followed, and as she took the stairs two at a time she could feel his eyes following her, but she didn't pause to look back over her shoulder.

Closing her bedroom door with a sense of relief, she bent down to undo the straps on her shoes, and kicking them off a moment later she stared at her bed in disbelief. Draped across it was her mother's white dress. She stared at it as questions of how it had come to be here raced through her mind. Her mother must have left it with Christian along with the rest of her history she decided, before picking it up and stroking the soft cotton fabric. It was Rosa's dress. The dress she had been wearing the day she met Michael, the day she married him, and the day Christian took his photograph. She held it to her nose and inhaled, trying to catch the scent of her mother as she had once been. It smelt fresh like summer, and she didn't know she was crying until she put the dress back down on the bed and saw that her tears had turned a patch of the cotton translucent.

Chapter 22

A silent mouth is melodious – Irish Proverb

Kitty sniffed appreciatively as she descended the stairs the next morning and was greeted by the aroma of what could only be freshly-brewed coffee. Following her nose, she headed in the direction of the kitchen. She pushed open the door and found the room empty except for Simone, who was standing at the countertop looking out the window at the courtyard beyond.

She turned upon hearing Kitty enter. "Good morning, you are well rested?"

With a nod, Kitty pulled a chair out to sit down at the table noticing it was laid with a stack of breakfast plates and a bowl filled with croissants. She placed her hands on her tummy as it rumbled at the sight of them, reminding her that she had hardly eaten a thing the day before. "The bed was super comfy, thanks. How about you, did you sleep well?"

"Oui, merci. Café?" She picked up the pot from the stove and Kitty nodded again. "Yes please." She was glad when the other woman busied herself finding a cup and saucer because she wasn't up to much in the way of conversation until she'd had her first cup of the morning, and the caffeine had begun to flow through her bloodstream. Simone, she noticed watching her movements through eyes that still felt heavy with sleep, looked as immaculately coiffed as always, which was no mean feat given the time of morning.

Her gaze travelled to the clock on the wall. It was after nine, so it wasn't that early after all. She couldn't use the time as an excuse for her slovenliness. Her hand had smoothed her crumpled T-shirt before her gaze flicked back to Simone. No woman had the right to look that put together before midday she decided, yawning and accepting the proffered cup a moment later with a grateful smile. She helped herself to the cream in the little jug on the table, and Simone pushed the bowl of croissants toward her before sitting down opposite her.

"Take one, Kitty s´il vous plaît, they are very good. Christian, he is an early riser, he went and bought them for breakfast as soon as the patisserie opened."

Mmm, freshly baked croissants, when in France and all that, Kitty thought reaching for a plate before helping herself to one of the buttery pastries. She had slept solidly, she realized, sipping her coffee, and was beginning to feel more human as it worked its magic. She hadn't expected to after everything that had happened yesterday. Last night, she'd turned the light out and pulled the covers up feeling wired as her mind began to replay all the conversations she'd had. They were muddled in with snippets from her mother's journal and the discovery of her dress. The wedding ring Michael had given Rosa felt foreign on her finger, and she was conscious of it as her thoughts had raced.

Despite all this, exhaustion had won out, and it hadn't taken her long to drop off. She'd only woken once in the night with that befuddled feeling of not knowing where she was, but she had gone back off again pretty smartly.

Kitty placed her cup back in its saucer and picked up her croissant eyeing it for a moment. She knew the French dunked them in their coffee, but she couldn't bring herself to do so.

Preferring the light flaky texture of the pastry just the way it was, she bit into it. It was delicious, and she munched away contentedly, knowing she had crumbs all over her mouth and most probably decorating her chin too but not caring. Simone looked across the table at her in amusement. "I told you they were good."

Kitty mumbled with her mouth full. "Yeah really good, thanks." She helped herself to another one.

The door opened then, and Jonny appeared looking dishevelled as if he'd had a heavy night. Kitty eyed him speculatively as he greeted Simone, wondering just how many whiskeys he had knocked back last night. More than a night cap or two if his bleary eyes were anything to go by. He pulled out a chair and sat down, looking over at her as he ran his fingers through his hair in what was obviously an unconscious habit of his. "Enjoying that are you?"

Kitty's hand flew to her mouth to wipe the crumbs away, and she shot him a look. He must think her a right greedy girl what with her nose having been stuck to the patisserie window last night and sitting here now scoffing croissants. She was grateful to Simone bustling over with a cup of coffee for him. The distraction provided her with the opportunity to size him up, and she could see that he hadn't shaved. His damp hair was curling at the nape of his neck so at least he'd taken the time to shower, she thought.

She wondered what his attitude toward her would be like this morning as she licked her finger before dabbing at the crumbs on her plate. Popping the crumbs into her mouth she made a decision; today was a new day. She would put the things he had said to her yesterday behind her because it was going to be strange enough posing for the photograph without them being at odds too. She would make an effort to get off on the right foot starting with offering him a croissant.

He looked at her over the rim of his cup, and she smiled gesturing to the bowl – he already thought her a bit of a Miss Piggy so what the heck. "Go on, have one before I eat them all because they're delicious." He returned her smile, and Kitty felt a jolt of pleasure from the tips of her toes all the way to the top of her scalp that tingled under his gaze. She felt irrationally proud to be on the receiving end of his nice smile for a change rather than his usual snarl. Simone looked at Kitty and then back at Jonny with a knowing glint in her eyes before clapping her hands and breaking the spell.

"Eat up, you two. Catherine Duvall from *Tres Belle* will be here soon to do your hair and makeup for the photo shoot."

At the mention of hair and makeup Jonny looked aghast but Simone ignored him. "She has caught the express train from Paris and Christian has gone with Pierre to collect her from the station in Nîmes. We are lucky to have her on board because she will work wonders with you both, especially you, Jonny." The look she shot him left little room for doubt that she was unimpressed by his dishevelled appearance.

Kitty hadn't even thought about the practicalities of the photo shoot assuming she would simply tie her hair up like her mother's had been in the original photograph. She'd don a pair of flats for the first time in a long while, and put on that beautiful dress. That done, she'd be good to go and pose in the square with Jonny. After all, she reasoned to herself, the day the original picture had been snapped Rosa and Michael had simply been strolling along minding their own business. She supposed with the magazine commissioning today's shoot they would want what they were paying for, and that was a glossed up reproduction of the original.

At the moment, she thought. glancing over at Jonny, he was looking more than a bit rough and ready. Remembering her own unmade up face, she knew a photograph of her in her current state wouldn't send copies of the magazine flying off the shelves. A thought occurred to her then, and her hand flew up to her bangs hoping that the hair part of hair and makeup did not mean what she had a sneaking suspicion it meant.

"Have you tried your maman's dress on yet, Kitty?"

She forgot about her fringe as she nodded. "It was such a surprise to see it; I never expected you to have Mum's actual dress. How did you get it?" Kitty asked Simone, who had gotten up to begin clearing the dishes on the bench into the dishwasher.

"Rosa, your maman, she gave it to Christian a long time ago I think."

Kitty made a mental note to ask him. She didn't see Jonny's bemused expression as he watched her from across the table.

Her thoughts were interrupted as they heard the front door bang shut followed by the clacking of heels heading down the hallway toward them. The kitchen door was pushed open a moment later by a stylish woman clad head to toe in black, her Gucci glasses holding back smooth, glossy auburn locks from an immaculately made-up face. Both she and Jonny sat up to attention with their respective croissants hovering halfway to their mouths as the glamorous spectre stalked into the room looking like she meant business. Christian followed in her perfumed wake.

She air-kissed Simone first which was just as well otherwise she'd have left great big red lipstick marks on her cheeks, Kitty thought, as the woman then turned her attention to both her and Jonny.

"Kitty, Jonny, this is Catherine Duvall from *Tres Belle* magazine," Simone said looking a tiny bit in awe of the redheaded vision herself.

"Please, you can call me Cat," she said giving them a nod of acknowledgement before tilting her head to one side as she eyed them both uttering a tut-tutting sound as she did so.

Cat suited her, Kitty decided, because there was something feline about her, and she swapped a nervous smile with Jonny as to what they were in for. Cat turned her attention back to Simone and fired something off in French, which Kitty guessed wasn't complimentary given Simone's grave expression. The two women conferred rapidly in their native tongue for a moment before Simone looked at Kitty. "First things first Kitty, Cat says she will need to cut your fringe." She made a snipping motion with her fingers and Kitty slunk down in her seat.

***

Cat had decided after a quick inventory of the house with them all trailing along behind her like a movie star's entourage that the light was best in the kitchen. Once back where they'd started, she shooed the others from the room indicating that Kitty should stay. She pulled a chair out from the table and dragged it closer to the window before patting it. Kitty sat down and watched as she opened her case. She strained forward trying to see what exactly Cat had in her bag of tricks, but the cape she pulled out obscured her view. She gave it a flap to straighten it before draping it around Kitty's shoulders.

Christian popped his head around the door, as Cat lifted her hair out of the way and fastened the Velcro at the back of her neck, eager to see how things were progressing.

"The weather it is *perfectionnement* today for our photograph, as you will be too, Kitty." He put his fingers to his mouth and blew her a kiss.

Kitty smiled nervously and then remembering the question she wanted to ask called after him, "Christian, when did my mother give you her dress?"

"Ah, it is pretty, oui?" He reappeared in the doorway. "She was a vision in it, your belle maman. When she left Paris, she asked if I wanted to keep it. The memories of all that had happened when she wore it were too painful. I have kept it ever since as a memento of her time with me and of *Midsummer Lovers*. It is yours now, Kitty, and that is as it should be."

"Thank you for looking after it. I will treasure it."

"You are welcome, ma belle."

He smiled at her fondly before Cat flapped her hand at him

to leave them to it, and Kitty resisted the urge to beg him to stay and protect her from this scary woman.

True to her word, the first thing Cat decided to do after Christian had closed the door and she had laid out her colourful tools of the trade, was snip at Kitty's fringe. As she produced scissors and a comb from her case, Kitty was reminded of Mary Poppins' magical carpet bag and she was half expecting her to pull out a hat stand next. She closed her eyes and grimaced as Cat began trimming her bangs into the short, blunt style her mother had favoured. It had suited Rosa well enough five decades ago, but she wasn't so sure it would suit her. She clasped her hands together to stop herself from batting the redheaded woman's hand away. Six weeks, she told herself, six weeks and it would be back to her favoured length.

It didn't take long and placing the scissors back on the table Cat combed and pulled her hair back into a high ponytail. She moved swiftly on to tidying up her eyebrows and spent an age coaxing them into the shape she wanted before making up her face. It was strange, Kitty thought, as blusher was rubbed into her cheeks, all this fussing over makeup because her mother wouldn't have been wearing any when *Midsummer Lovers* was taken. Mind you she had been considerably younger than Kitty was now so she was probably going to need all the help she could get to pass as a girl of sixteen.

The process seemed to take forever, and she silently asked all the models she had ever thought earned shed loads of money for doing pretty much nothing for their forgiveness. She could not be doing with all this primping on a regular basis – it would drive her potty. It wasn't as if she and Cat could pass the time by exchanging sparkling conversation either, thanks to the language barrier. She'd given up after a few attempts of asking her how her trip down from Paris had been or who the last famous person she worked with was. All she had gotten for her efforts was a frown followed by a bewildered. "Pardon?"

Kitty was just beginning to squirm at the uncomfortable reminder of yesterday's sting that thanks to all the sitting was beginning to ache when Cat, at last, undid the cape. Pulling a mirror from her bag, she held it up in front of Kitty with a satisfied, "Voila!"

Peering into the mirror, Kitty's eyes widened, and she gasped because the girl who was looking back at her was just that, a girl, she looked so young with her chopped bangs and dewy makeup. She looked, she realized, just like Rosa. "Oh my gosh – wow!" she breathed and Cat, who understood the sentiment if not the phrase, looked pleased as she shook out the cape. Kitty stood up and stretched before thanking her.

"Oui, oui no problem. You ask Jonny to come in pronto, s´il vous plaît."

Kitty nodded and felt suddenly shy at showing the others Cat's handiwork as she left the room. There was no sign of Simone and Christian, but she found Jonny sitting in the front room. His foot casually rested on his opposite knee as he flicked through a magazine looking like he was sitting at the Barbers waiting his turn. He didn't see her and she took the opportunity to observe him for a moment. When he wasn't glowering, he was rather handsome in a swashbuckling sort of way. Visions of him wielding a sword on the decks of a pirate ship assailed her as she decided that, on closer inspection, while he had the look of his uncle there were subtle differences. The hint of a cleft in his chin, for instance, that must belong to his mother's side. He looked like a man who worked with his hands too, she decided, annoyed that the very thought of those hands had made little goose bumps stand up on her arms.

She shook her head, telling herself not to go there as clearing her throat she was pleased to see him jump. It was payback for his sneaking up on her the way he had outside the patisserie. It was nice, she thought, as he nearly dropped the magazine at the sight of her, to see him flustered for a change.

"Jaysus, you're the spit of her! That's spooky, so it is."

Kitty felt herself flush under his gaze and was filled with the need to get away from him. "Well, that's the whole idea. Cat asked me to send you in. It's your turn now."

"If she did that to you what in God's name is she going to do to me?" he muttered getting to his feet, but she was already halfway down the hall and didn't hear him.

***

Kitty sat down on the bed; the dress was lying over the rails at the bottom of it. She'd change into it in a moment but first she needed to talk to Yasmin and fill her in on what had happened with Damien last night. She needed some firm words where Jonny was concerned too because the way he was making her feel like a silly schoolgirl every time she was around him was just not on. Yas would put things into perspective for her, and with a glance at the time she saw that she wouldn't have gone to work yet. She hit the call button and after a few rings her friend picked up.

"Kitty! I wanted to call you last night, but Mario had his beady eye on me all night, and we were flat out, so I didn't dare slip away and ring you. Then by the time I got home, it was too late, but I seriously contemplated phoning because the headboard banging against the wall kept me awake until at least two a.m. Honestly, Piggy and Slimy can go at it for hours on end. I know I have said it before, but I reckon he must take a supplement because I am telling you it is just not natural. That girl should be bow-legged with all the action she gets."

"Slow down, Yas, what happened last night then?" Kitty smiled at her friend's one hundred miles an hour gush; refusing to think about Paula and Steve's bedroom antics.

"Mr Amatriciana came in again last night, and this time he was by himself."

"Oooh," Kitty said. "Love is in the air!"

"Kitty, I am telling you he is gorgeous. To die for, gorgeous. I think when I asked him if his meal was to his liking he was on the verge of asking me on a date. Then this man with a stomach that looked nine months gone, and who should not have ordered spaghetti carbonara – I mean come on, all that cream, ugh – interrupted us wanting more parmesan. I was so pissed, I wanted to pick up one of his noodles and flick him in the face with it before marching him off to an Overeaters Anonymous meeting."

Kitty laughed. "I don't know how you get all those words out in one breath. It's a good job you didn't assault a customer with a noodle or Mario really would have just cause to say something!"

"Mario can get stuffed, just because he is Bruno's cousin he thinks he can lord it over me. He's the maître d', not the boss. Ugh, so annoying."

"Um, Yas, it's because he is Bruno's cousin that he can lord it over us."

"Yeah, whatever. Anyway, what with Piggy and Slimy at it, I couldn't help fantasizing about Mr Amatriciana and I doing some headboard banging of our own. In between all of that, I was busy worrying about you swanning about the town with the Shag Beast. Please tell me you did not sleep with him?"

Kitty couldn't help but smile at her friend's terminology. "I did not sleep with him, in fact, you will be proud of me because I gave him the push, for good this time." She filled her in on what had transpired over their meal last night. When she had finished, she heard a clunk followed by clapping. Yas must have put the phone down to give her a round of applause, she realized, grinning and sitting up a bit straighter. She'd earned that show of appreciation, and she was proud of herself. Sitting here now having resolved things with Damien once and for all she felt a lot better than she had in a long time. It had been a rocky road to get this far, but she had made it.

Yasmin came back on the line. "Yay, you've done it, girl! You've officially moved on."

"Mmm."

"Uh-oh, I don't like the sound of that. What's going on?"

Kitty took a breath and began to tell her about Jonny and her suspicion as to why her knees seemed to go weak whenever she was around him. It happened despite his apparent ability to be a right arse when it suited him, and she thought it might be something to do with her getting swept up in the drama of her mother's old romance.

"Tread carefully, Kitty. You can recreate the photo, but you can't recreate the past."

"I know but speaking of recreating the past, you want to see what Cat's done to me."

"What are you on about, what cat?"

"Cat's the makeup artist *Tres Belle* sent; she arrived this morning to do hair and makeup, and she has turned me into a clone of my mother as a sixteen-year-old."

"Ooh, lucky you. I wish some expert would come and knock fifteen years off my age with a wave of her magic brushes. I want to see, take a selfie and flick it through."

"No."

"Oh come on," Yasmin wheedled. "You can't tease me like that; it's not fair."

"I am not sending you a pic because you will only laugh at it."

"I won't."

"Oh yes, you would, especially when you saw the state of my fringe."

"Oh dear, is it above the eyebrows?"

"It is so far up my flipping forehead that it might as well not be there."

There was a snorting sound down the phone.

"Told you you would laugh and you haven't even seen a picture."

"No, but I will soon when it's featured in *Tres Belle*. Hey, who knows you might even make the cover. I can see it now, all those bored people in the supermarket queues gazing at your face wondering who did your hair."

"Don't!"

"Sorry. Just grit your teeth and think of the money. It's a small fortune. If it makes you feel better, I'd get a perm, a bloody blue-rinse and pose naked for the cover of *Marie Claire* for the sake of five grand."

"I suppose," Kitty muttered grimly. She was not sure how she would handle posing with a look of adoration on her face as she gazed up at Jonny in the square in just a few short hours. Not when she was already feeling so confused. She didn't need to muddy the waters, what she needed to do was bring him round just enough to take her back to Ireland with him.

"I can hear the cogs turning from here, what are you plotting?"

"I'm thinking of changing my flight home and going to Dublin."

Chapter 23

An empty sack does not stand – Irish Proverb

The little group was clustered around the spot in the square where the original *Midsummer Lovers* had been snapped fifty years ago. A print of the photograph was propped up on an easel over by where Christian was standing. It was for him to reference, having announced he had no time for those handheld devices like the iPad Simone was currently toting about importantly. The leafy tree nearby was creating the dappled light that he had exclaimed '*perfectionnement*' over; it was his word of the day. He had used it when he'd first caught sight of Kitty wearing Rosa's dress too. Now, his head was bowed as he fiddled with his camera in between signing autographs with a flourish that suited him. It was much to Simone's consternation as she tried to keep the crowd of spectators who had gathered around them at bay.

Standing there with Jonny, both of them dressed in their 1960's garb, Kitty was feeling vaguely ridiculous as she waited to be told what to do next. She could tell by Jonny's bowed head that he did too. He stood with his hands resting on the bicycle that had materialized seemingly from thin air just in time for them to walk the short distance down to the square. The bike looked like it had been salvaged from a local museum. Gazing at it now, she felt sad knowing what Michael's fate had been as he'd cycled along on a bicycle just like the one his nephew was now holding onto.

She couldn't help but wonder how seeing that bike leaning against the wall in the hallway for the first time this morning must have made Jonny feel. How recreating this image he loathed because of what it had represented to him must be making him feel now. She guessed he was probably doing what Yasmin had suggested she do, and that was grit her teeth and think of the money.

He wasn't giving anything away. There was no sign of emotion on his face other than embarrassment, Kitty thought, eyeing him surreptitiously. He looked the rakishly handsome part too, dressed as he was in a shirt and black trousers with worn workboots on his feet. It was just like the get-up his uncle had been wearing all those years ago. Cat had worked her magic on him too, and his eyes were no longer bleary nor was there any sign of the six o'clock shadow he had been sporting earlier.

Glancing around at the spectators who had gathered to watch the photo shoot, Kitty felt her insides flutter because she had not factored in an audience when she'd envisaged this current scenario. A tourist jostled past her to get to Christian, and she pulled a face. Simone leant over and whispered in her ear that it was to be expected because he was one of the photography world's greats, and *Midsummer Lovers* was the photographic icon of its decade.

Kitty raised a well-shaped eyebrow hearing that because she suspected a lot of the people crowding around them would never have even heard of it, given their age. They just wanted to be part of whatever it was that was obviously about to happen as they took sneaky snaps of them with their phones to download on social media later. The thought of being splashed all over strangers' Facebook pages didn't help settle her nerves, and she wished they could just get on with it instead of all this faffing about.

At last, Christian looked up and announced he was satisfied his equipment was ready before signing his name to one last scrap of paper being thrust at him. Simone clapped her hands and barked in a tone that brooked no argument first in French, and then in English for everybody to please stand back while they began shooting. "Monsieur Beauvau will be happy to sign any further autographs when we have finished," she added.

Kitty's mouth twitched as she watched Christian preen, he loved the attention, she realized. He did not fall into the category of a photographer who preferred to live his life behind a lens rather than in front of it.

As the crowd fanned out, Simone began directing Kitty and Jonny with all the skill of a seasoned film director as to where they should stand. Satisfied she had them in the right spot so that the light seeping through the nearby foliage was hitting them just so, she demonstrated to Kitty how she should angle her body. Kitty tried to emulate her, and Simone eyed her critically for a moment. Taking hold of her arm, she moved it, so it was angled slightly behind her skirt as befitted the motion of walking. Glancing at her iPad and then back at Kitty she ordered her not to move as she turned her attention to Jonny, and began manipulating him into position until she was certain she had his pose right. She looked toward Christian and seeing him give the thumbs up she moved away from them both to go and stand by his side.

Kitty had been worried about the emotion of the moment when she finally had to look up at Jonny just as her mother had done that day with Michael. She was so tense with the unnaturalness of the situation that there was no room for emotion. It all felt so impersonal and forced. She had a feeling Christian was going to earn his money this afternoon. It was like what she'd read movie stars say about filming intimate scenes; there was nothing in the least bit intimate about it when you had a roomful of people directing your every move.

Christian peered into his camera and told Simone that she should move the bicycle just so. She dutifully did so and when he was satisfied it was now where it should be he called out, "Okay, so we count to three and then Kitty I want you to smile as you look up at Jonny, oui?"

"Oui," Kitty called back to him feeling like a talking statue.

"Smile like he is the only man in the world, and you are brimming over with happiness. Jonny, you are a witty man who has made this woman that you love with all your heart and soul laugh."

Kitty squirmed; Jonny must be hating every second of this. He held such a skewed memory of the events surrounding this picture. As for Jonny being witty and her brimming over with happiness, well that was a big bloody ask. Christian held his fingers up as he began counting and on the cue of three, she forced her mouth into a smile. She turned her head to look up at Jonny, who in turn was looking down at her with a smile playing at the corners of his mouth. She hoped as she met his gaze, she was managing to convey a look of longing. Apparently not, because in a show of artistic temperament, Christian stamped his foot.

"Non, non, non! You look like you need the toilette, Kitty. You are in love! So I want you to smile, oui? Not this terrible grimace like you have the stomach ache, understand?"

Kitty felt her face flush as she heard tittering from the crowd. The next attempt didn't go much better. She felt like playing the temperamental diva, and flouncing off as the sweet, kind Christian she had grown accustomed to over the last twenty-four hours was replaced by a steely-eyed professional she did not recognize.

"I'm sorry, Christian," she mumbled taking a deep breath and telling herself to try and zone everyone out except Jonny.

"Okay, we try again, and maybe this time we will be, how you say? Third time lucky. One, two, three and turn your head."

Kitty did so, only this time when she looked up at Jonny she saw a warmth in his eyes that reassured her. He looked down at her with a smile and out the corner of his mouth whispered, "Get this fecking shot in the bag so that we can stop feeling like a right pair of eejits and get the hell out of here. I promise I will buy you one of those éclairs you were fantasizing about last night if you nail it."

Her face broke into a grin at his words, and she couldn't help but laugh. That was the moment Christian got his shot and declared with all the finesse of a Hollywood director that it was a wrap. Kitty was sure he only said it as a crowd-pleaser, and he got his round of applause but either way she was pleased the ordeal was over and planned on holding Jonny to his word. She wanted desperately to get out of here, and there was no way she was going to leave France without sampling at least one delight from the patisserie.

Christian and Simone were otherwise occupied talking to curious spectators about what the photo shoot was in aid of and Kitty saw an opportunity to slip away before anyone decided to accost her.

"You owe me an éclair," she said to Jonny.

He grinned at her. "I'm a man of my word, follow me." He leaned the bike up against a wall and leaving it there strode off toward the main road.

***

"You've got something green on the end of your nose."

Kitty's hand flew up to wipe it off. "It's pistachio infused pastry cream, thank you very much, and this éclair is quite possibly the most divine thing ever to pass my lips."

Jonny looked at her as she bit into the choux pastry with its light green icing. The matching filling oozed out the sides as she did so, and his mouth twitched with amusement. "I can tell that by the daft look on your face."

"Alright then," she challenged. "Tell me that isn't one of the best tarts you have ever had."

"You have a real way with words, do you know that?"

It took Kitty a moment to twig. "And you've a filthy mind. I meant tell me that isn't one of the best fruit tartlets you have ever eaten." She pointed to the half-eaten cup of short, sweet pastry filled with brilliant red raspberries encased in a shiny glaze he was holding in his hand. "And you've got crumbs all over your chin."

He brushed them away with a grin. "Well I can't say I am a connoisseur of the fruit tartlet, but yes okay I'll admit it is pretty good."

"The French make baking into an art form. They take it to the next level." They were sitting on the bench where Christian and Jonny had sat yesterday. Kitty's gaze fixed on the window of the patisserie; she was desperate to try one of the macarons on display in it, but she didn't want to look like too much of a glutton.

Jonny read her expression. "Ah go on and get one. You know you want to, you've a sweet tooth on you alright, woman."

Kitty shivered at the way he said woman, there was something primal about it. Telling herself to cut it out, she popped the rest of the éclair into her mouth and sat there for a moment concentrating on savouring the last morsel of it instead as she continued to eye the macarons. The pull was too strong, she knew she wouldn't be able to resist and so what if she felt sick afterwards? It was a form of market research for her impending business venture. "Alright, I will but only because I want to see why people go so mad for them and only if you have one too."

"Go on then twist my arm, you pick a colour, any colour except those pink ones; they're far too girly."

"Oh darn, I just remembered I haven't got any Euros on me."

Jonny dug into his pocket and produced a note. "That should cover it, but if I'm ever in London, you owe me a cupcake on the house."

"Deal." She took the money with a grin and found herself liking this affable version of Jonny a lot as she stood up and swept the crumbs off her lap. Heading back inside the patisserie she was so focused on the treat nearly at hand that she was oblivious to the strange looks her appearance was garnering. Rather than waste time trying to speak to the girl serving behind the counter in her pigeon French she decided she'd get further by showing her what she wanted. She held up two fingers in the universal peace sign. Then she pointed to a gold macaron she hoped would be caramel for Jonny, and a green one she was guessing was mint flavoured with dark chocolate filling for herself.

Clutching the bag the girl had placed the little biscuits in she pushed her way out of the shop that was beginning to fill up, it must be lunchtime, she thought, sitting back down next to Jonny. "Here you go." She handed him his biscuit before taking her own from the bag.

"Is that one mint and chocolate?"

"Mmm yes, I think so." She opened her mouth to take a bite.

"Mint's my favourite."

She paused the macaron hovering in front of her mouth. "You said you didn't care what colour I got you so long as it wasn't pink."

"Ah go on, give me the mint one."

Kitty handed it over grudgingly but got over herself as soon as she bit into the caramel flavoured one, and the salted filling cut into the overtly sweet biscuit. Two bites and it was gone.

"That was very sweet."

"But delicious."

"Aye, it was that."

"I have a newfound respect for the macaron."

They sat in silence watching as a woman dressed to the nines in couture sashayed past, a clichéd white poodle trotting on its lead beside her.

"That whole photo thing was pretty weird, wasn't it?" Jonny ventured.

"It was but not in the way I expected it to be. I thought that I might get upset. You know at reliving a moment that was so poignant in my mum's life like that? With all those people standing around, it was hard to feel anything except a bit silly. What about you, it must have been hard for you with everything that happened?"

"Not hard, surreal maybe but coming here you know it was never about the money."

Kitty must have looked surprised because she had thought that for him it would have been all about the money.

"Alright five grand for looking like an eejit in a small French town that I will probably never set foot in again in my life was tempting I admit, but there was more to it than that. I wanted to see this place for myself, and I wanted to see you too. I thought you would probably look like her, and I was curious as to how she captivated Michael to leave our family the way he did."

Kitty was too aghast to think about his choice of words. "Oh, but it wasn't like that! They loved each other, and they had no choice but to walk away from Cherry Orchard. Your grandfather disowned Michael when he found out about him and Rosa thanks to the feud between our families. God knows what would have happened to Rosa when her father, my grandfather, sobered up if they'd stayed. From what I read in my mother's journal last night, Michael never got over leaving your dad and your gran to fend for themselves. It haunted him."

He looked angry. "He was a cruel bastard, my grandda, Martin, and there were no tears shed in our family when he died. He did a lot of damage, not just with his fists but up here, you know." He tapped the side of his head. "Da turned to the bottle."

"Like Paddy did because he never got over losing Joe," Kitty murmured.

"Paddy was Rosa's younger brother?"

She nodded. "Do you know him?" Her voice was hopeful at the tangible link to the family she had never known.

"Aye I know of him, he's a Rourke isn't he."

Kitty frowned at the inflection in his voice. "You are not telling me that the feud between the Rourke's and the Donohue's still exists?"

"The Travellers have long memories."

Kitty shook her head. "So I'm learning, but it was so long ago surely it's time to put the past to bed?"

He raised an eyebrow. "It's the way it is."

Kitty could see by the set of his jaw she wouldn't get very far following this line of enquiry, so she decided to change the subject. "Do you come from a big family?"

"Not by Traveller standards, there's only me and my four older sisters left now. They all married young so as to leave home and are off doing their own thing with their families now. Ours was not a happy home; Da was there when we were growing up, but he wasn't, if you know what I mean. It was our mam that reared us, but a boy needs a father, and I used to think when I was a young fella that maybe things would have been different if Michael had stayed around," he shrugged. "Now, I'm not so sure, maybe there would have been a weakness in my da anyway. It's a sickness, the alcoholism."

He was holding onto bitterness all of his own, Kitty realized. She could tell that being here in a town where his uncle, unlike his father, had so briefly been happy was taking its toll.

"The decision Rosa and Michael made to leave that day ate away at my mother for the rest of her life too. She left people she loved behind too."

"What about your father? Where does he fit in then?" he asked, his turn to change the subject.

"Mum met Dad when she was nineteen, and they were happy together, but he died a few years ago now, and she was never really the same afterwards."

"Then she got cancer?"

"Yes, I think she blamed all the secrets she carried around inside her for her getting sick."

241

He nodded slowly. "It will make you sick holding onto things; I think that's what got my mother in the end too. All that anger at my da's drinking and the miserable existence she led as a result of it. She let it fester instead of doing something about it. I don't want to be like that. I want to move forward with my life and put the past to bed, as you so eloquently put it. That's why I came."

Kitty reached out and touched his arm. "I think you're brave."

"Not brave, selfish."

Kitty shook her head in contradiction. She felt a bit like Sandra Dee from Grease as her ponytail swung back and forth waiting for him to elaborate, but he didn't.

"So you've no parents left either? What about a brother or a sister?"

"No, Mum and Dad could only have me, lucky them." She gave a sardonic little laugh.

"I'd say they were very lucky." It was said so softly that Kitty wasn't sure if she'd imagined hearing the words and his tone was brusque as he asked, "You've a boyfriend, though?"

"He's not my boyfriend, not anymore, so I'm officially alone. All by myself." Not wanting to sound like Bridget Jones she quickly added, "I've got friends obviously but not having either of my parents it's the strangest feeling and the realisation keeps taking me by surprise. You'd know what that's like." A lump formed in her throat. "The thing is, even though I've been caught up in my life these past few years I always knew that I had a safety net in my mother. Now it's gone." She swallowed hard. "It's scary."

"Aye, but you're a big girl." The gruff Jonny was back, and he got to his feet. "We should head back and get changed; it will be time to head to the airport soon."

Kitty stood up too. She didn't have time to wonder over his mood change, it was now or never, she realized. running after him. "Jonny I was uh, well I was – you see the thing is, what you were saying about putting the past to bed, well—"

242

"Those were your words and for feck's sake would you spit it out, whatever it is you're trying to say." He stopped and looked at her. "I want to get back and change out of this shite." He tugged at his shirt and as he waited for her to speak she was filled with a sudden terror that he would say no and that would be that.

"Right I will. What it is, well, what I was wondering is whether I could fly back to Dublin with you today."

"What the feck for?"

She would have been affronted by anyone else's continual use of the 'f' word but somehow his Irish version of it didn't sound so offensive.

"I want you to take me to Cherry Orchard."

Chapter 24

Bad as I like ye, it's worse without ye – Irish Proverb

Jonny stared at her. "What the feck do you want to go there for?" He began to stride off, and Kitty had to trot to keep up with him.

"I want to see where my mother lived and to find her brother and sister."

"I thought I told you to get that idealistic shite about the way Travellers live out of your head. You'll not find your aunt or your uncle at Cherry Orchard; you'll find nothing there but ghosts. They're long gone. Go back to London and open your little café like you planned."

His condescending tone rankled, but she couldn't afford to bite back. "But I can't go back to London, not now, you of all people should understand why. I thought it was just me, but now I know I have this other family. You were just saying you need to move forward, well I can't do that until I can close this final chapter for my mother's sake."

"What if they don't want to meet you? How will you feel then, have you thought about that?"

She wasn't going to be put off. "I have spent thirty-one years without them in my life, so I'll survive, but I've got too much to lose if I don't at least try to meet them."

The cherub's urn had run dry today, Kitty saw out the corner of her eye. She scurried across the road unused to flat shoes as she tried to keep step with Jonny, who remained frustratingly silent.

"Please, Jonny, I know what I am asking of you but I wouldn't if I knew of any other way."

"Ah alright." His voice was so low she hardly heard it.

"Does that mean you'll let me come? I won't rake up trouble for you I promise, but I need your help to find them."

"I said alright but I'm not responsible for you if the shite hits the fan and you don't get your big family reunion. Your mam left on bad terms and like I said, the Travellers have long memories."

She noticed he used 'the' instead of 'we' and she wondered if he had closed himself off to that part of his life too. "I'm aware of that, just like my mother was. I promise if we can find them, and they don't want anything to do with me then I will leave it be and go back to London to open my *little* café."

Her sarcasm wasn't lost on him, and he shot her a sideways glance. "They won't be hard to find."

"What do you mean?"

"That I know where they are living."

"But why didn't you say something earlier?" Kitty was gobsmacked.

"Because I wasn't sure about you, that's why. You can't just go barrelling in wanting to be all friendly like until you decide their lifestyle's not to your liking."

Kitty saw red then. "You don't know the first thing about me! I am not responsible for something that happened over fifty bloody years ago so stop acting as if I am my mother."

They'd reached the house, she realized, breathing heavily. He stopped in front of the door his hand resting on the handle as he gave her the once-over. "Hard not to when you are dressed like that." He opened the door, and Kitty felt like kicking him in his obnoxious backside as he strode toward the stairs, but she reined her temper in. "She was a good woman you know, my mum." She called after him unable to stop herself from adding, "Your uncle thought so too."

She closed the front door behind her with a bit more force than was necessary and turning spotted Pierre, the chauffeur. He'd obviously been enjoying the peace as he sat in the front room with a newspaper open in front of him. Now he lowered it and looked at her with a startled expression at all the noise. Kitty blushed and apologised, sure that even if he didn't understand her words he got the sentiment behind them.

He shrugged in the international language of it's no big deal and pointed to his watch before muttering something that went right over the top of her head. Seeing her bewilderment, he put the paper down and twisted around to point out the window to where the car was parked before holding up four fingers.

"Oh, I see! We are leaving for the airport at four o'clock, merci," she said and not giving him the chance to look blankly back at her she turned and took herself off up the stairs.

Packed and ready to go, Kitty's phoned beeped a message. Her face broke into a grin as she scrolled through it, Yasmin texted like she talked, one hundred miles an hour:

Big news, the hot Mr A asked me out for dinner tomorrow nite! So xcited. Wot r u doing bcos I need you here to hlp me choose outfit, it is emergency, will NOT be asking Paula's advice. How did photo shoot go? x

Kitty sat there for a moment, she could imagine Yasmin's excitement. She deserved to meet someone fantastic and who knew, maybe Mr Amatriciana would turn out to be Mr Right. She hoped so. Poor Yas, the next twenty-fours would drag by, and she hoped she wouldn't get herself in too much of a state about her date with him in that time. She began to text back:

Fantastic news! Go girl!!! Wear ur fitted black dress, its vry classy and u look gorgeous in that. Don't b nervous, he will luv u. Photo

246

done, ordeal over and it's happening, at least I think it is happening
– off to Ireland tonight. Phone you when I know what's what. XXX

She hit send aware of noises downstairs, Christian and Simone must be back, Christian having soaked up every second of his latest moment in the sun. She wanted to talk to him before they left. To thank him for the part he had played in getting her this close to meeting her family. She finally understood the events that had made her mother act the way she had for all those years. Casting her eyes around the room to make sure she'd packed all of her meagre belongings including the precious dress, she was satisfied nothing had been forgotten. She stroked the cover of the journal for a moment as if to reassure herself it was still there and zipped her case up.

The little wheels bounced over the stairs behind her, and as she reached the hallway she poked her head into the kitchen first – it was empty. She found Christian and Simone relaxing in the front room both with a drink in hand. Christian was reclining on the sofa and Simone was perched on the edge of the one-seater in what must be her version of kicking back. There was no sign of Pierre. Christian spotted her first standing uncertainly in the doorway unsure as to whether she should interrupt them, his face lit up as he exclaimed, "Ah, Rosa, she is gone and ma belle, Kitty is back!"

"She is," Kitty said with a smile as she sat down where he was patting the seat next to him.

"When I work I think of nothing but the picture I am trying to capture and I was harsh on you today. I apologize, but sometimes it is the only way."

"It's fine, and I think maybe you needed to be a bit hard on me."

"Oui, I think maybe I did." His eyes danced. "Kitty, the photo it is going to be special, very special. I think you will be surprised when you see it."

Kitty smiled, she wasn't sure what she should say.

Simone drained her glass and popped it down on the coffee table. "I will go and tell Jonny that you will both be leaving for Marseille Airport in twenty minutes." As she stood to leave the room, Kitty flashed her a grateful smile for leaving them to talk, finding herself liking this woman despite her uber professional demeanour. She wondered whether they would ever meet again and hoped that they would.

"Do you go back to Paris this evening too?" She turned her attention back to Christian.

"Non, I am an old man, and I like a slow pace these days. Sadly, I am an old man in love with a young woman, and she is busy, busy always trying to get me to work. She is one of these, erm 'ow you say?"

"Workaholics?" Kitty offered up.

"Oui, workaholic." His grin was wolfishly charming. "But this time I have got my way and we will be staying on in Uzés for a few days to enjoy the charms this beautiful town has on offer."

Kitty sensed it was his work that kept him young and Simone was a smart enough woman to know that.

"I think things, they are different for you now you know what it is Rosa wanted to tell you. So what will you do next, ma chérie?"

Kitty fiddled with the hem of her T-shirt twisting it and knowing that she shouldn't because it would lose its shape. She needed something to do with her hands and since she didn't smoke the T-shirt had to suffice. "I want to go back to Ireland with Jonny this evening, and I was wondering if the flights could be changed at such short notice."

Christian did not seem surprised by what she'd said, in fact if anything, he looked like this was what he had expected her to do. She wondered what he and Rosa had cooked up between them on that final visit. "And tell me, what will you do when you get there?"

"I am hoping Jonny will take me to meet mum's family; he knows them apparently." She couldn't keep the edge out of her voice.

"You sound unhappy about this?"

"I am, but it's not about him knowing who they are. It's about the way he's made his mind up about them and me, thanks to an ancient feud between our two families. He doesn't seem prepared to let it go."

Christian nodded. "Oui, I understand. But you … but Kitty you need to understand that Jonny is a man whose life perhaps has not always been a happy one and he is looking for people to blame for this. By going back to Ireland with him, he will get to know you better. Then maybe he will see that holding on to all this anger of his, it is not the answer. He is a man who needs to let go of his pain and I think you might be the one to help him do this."

Kitty's eyes narrowed as she looked at the wise old man sitting next to her. "Did you discuss this with my mother when you came to see her? Was this what she planned all along by my coming to Uzés and you giving me the journal here?"

Christian's smile was wistful. "Jonny contacted me when his father died and told me to stop sending the royalty payments from *Midsummer Lovers*. He said that his father hadn't wanted them and neither did he. I told Rosa this."

"That's not what he told me!"

"He is a proud man, like Michael, was. Your maman, she was a good woman. She wanted to put things she believed she was, erm, responsible for right, you understand?"

She nodded as he patted her hand before giving it a squeeze.

"Rosa I think knew in that peculiar way of hers that you would be the one to help Jonny to heal. He, in turn, would help you to find a side of yourself she never shared with you. She was also a clever woman, your maman, and you need to trust in her and yourself. Go to Ireland with an open heart and an open mind, Kitty."

Any doubts she had been having about what she was about to do being mad vanished, and she would think about the practicalities of her shifts at Bruno's later. Depending on how things went she might be back in time for her stall on Saturday and if not, well she would cross that bridge when she came to it. It was only Monday but so much had happened in these last few days that it felt like weeks had gone by. It was then she looked up and saw Jonny in the doorway; her face felt like she had just bitten into a particularly strong chilli as she wondered how much of the conversation he had overheard. His nonchalant expression was giving away nothing, but then she thought, that was hardly a surprise because it never did.

He cleared his throat. "Simone said we'd be leaving soon."

"Jonny *entrer*, come, come." He gestured to the seat Simone had vacated a few moments ago. "Sit down and join us."

Jonny looked at Kitty for a moment and hesitated but then leaning his backpack against the wall he did as Christian bidded. He was clad in jeans and a T-shirt that announced he had been to a Foo Fighters concert in 2005. Either he hardly ever washed it, or he used a particularly gentle washing powder, Kitty thought, noting its good condition. She was more of an Ed Sheeran girl herself.

"I have just been telling Kitty how pleased I am with the photograph I have taken today. It will be wonderful I think."

Jonny looked as if he'd like to say, 'whatever' but he bit back the reply and nodded instead.

"Kitty has just been telling me that she wants to change her flight and return with you to Dublin?"

"Aye, she does." He was not giving anything away, Kitty thought, looking at him and feeling a surge of frustration.

"Simone can organize this; it will not be a problem."

He nodded again and to break the ensuing silence Kitty stood up. "Well, I suppose it's time we said our goodbyes."

Christian got to his feet and held his arms out to her; she stepped into his embrace. He smelt of red wine, olives, garlic and a spicy aftershave. She knew it was a scent she would always remember fondly. "Thank you for everything, Christian."

"You are welcome, ma belle Kitty. Please keep in touch with an old man who would like to know how you are from time to time."

Kitty felt her eyes smart, but she was determined that she would not cry, and she blinked them away. "I will, Christian, I promise."

"We will find Simone in a moment. She will want to say goodbye too."

He turned his attention to Jonny then, holding out his hand and shaking the younger man's with a vigour that belied his years. "Thank you for helping to make this photograph I have taken today a reality."

Jonny nodded, and Kitty felt like kicking him, it wouldn't kill him to speak.

"Bonne chance, good luck with the future, Jonny."

"Thanks," he muttered grudgingly not looking at Kitty as he released the old man's hand and picking up his pack swung it over his shoulder.

Chapter 25

Instinct is stronger than upbringing – Irish Proverb

The plane bounced as its tyres hit the tarmac. Kitty looked out the window at the uninspiring evening waiting to greet them outside. Jonny peered past her into the gloom and muttered, "Welcome to Dublin."

His sarcasm wasn't missed on her because the drizzle coating everything with its grey droplets looked a world away from the balmy, blue skies they had left behind in Uzés. Kitty's stomach turned over as the plane began to slow, finally coming to a stop. The sudden churning in her belly wasn't down to the glutinous pasta dish she had chosen for her evening meal on the short flight either. She'd got it down her regardless of its gloopy lack of flavour doubting much else would be on offer once they landed in Ireland. Nor was it down to having been sat so elbow bumpingly, leg brushingly close to Jonny for the last two hours. It was the realization that she was here. There was no going back and the certainty she had felt announcing to Yasmin earlier that afternoon that coming to Ireland was something she had to do was fast being replaced by doubt.

She had no idea what the next day or two would bring and

to quell her queasiness she told herself she would phone her friend as she had promised when she got to Jonny's apartment. Yas's black and white viewpoint would help put things in perspective for her. That was assuming Jonny was going to let her crash the night at his place and not drop her off outside some cruddy hostel leaving her to her own devices. That was another thing, she fancied him, she wasn't sure that she liked him, but she fancied him. She had admitted it to herself somewhere over the English Channel when her leg had brushed against his and she had felt a shock ricochet through her. So with that being the case, was staying at his place the best move on her part?

She closed her eyes thinking back on the last couple of hours as she waited for the seatbelt light to go off and the exodus to begin.

After they'd boarded the plane, she'd opened the women's magazine she had just bought to entertain herself for this last leg of her journey. As the plane began to taxi down the runway, she found herself reading with morbid curiosity about Kim's life changing decision, shaking her head as she did so. It was ludicrous with all the big stuff going on in the world that this kind of trivial crap sold magazines, she thought, feeling Jonny's gaze on her. Turning to look at him she saw that he was grinning.

"What's so funny?'

"You are. Did you know that you mouth the words you are reading?"

"No, I don't."

"Ah yeah, you do. I could tell you exactly what you were reading just now."

She frowned. "Alright, Mr Lip Reader go on then."

"Okay, Kim Kardashian has opted to have her bottom reduced in a radical surgical procedure that she is hoping will change her life."

Kitty couldn't help herself; she started laughing. "You cheated. You looked at the headline and made the rest up."

"Maybe, but you still mouth the words when you read."

They'd sat in silence until they were airborne and then to her surprise, Jonny began to talk. "You wanted to know a bit about your family."

"I did." Kitty held her breath.

"Okay, well I don't know all that much so don't get too excited," he said gazing back at her expectant face. "But with the Rourke's and the Donohue's history I knew who your Aunt Kitty was. By the time I arrived, my family had moved onto another site in Ballyfermot. Kitty was there too, married to Davey O'Connor. Neither of them had any beef with my mam and da although they kept their distance. From what I remember of her she was always surrounded by a load of kids. They'd all be nearly grown up now. The Travellers world is small, and I heard a few years back that they set themselves up in a permanent site in Wicklow. I don't know what happened to her brother Paddy, he was always a wild one, handy with his fists, and he never married so far as I know. To be honest, I'd be surprised if he's still alive given his love of the bottle. It was that what pickled Da's liver in the end."

Kitty nodded, so Paddy was like his father then, she wasn't surprised, her mother had alluded to this in her journal. She hadn't expected to learn she had cousins and lots of them! Jonny had obviously decided he'd said enough, and he'd put his headphones in and settled back in his seat leaving her to wonder as to what they were all like.

Now as she felt him get up from his seat, she opened her eyes and thanked him as he passed her wheelie-case down to her, before pulling his pack down. At least they wouldn't have to wait around for their bags, she thought, edging across to wait for the line of people to start moving. She hated this bit of the whole air travel process.

"I guess you'll be staying at my place tonight, so I'll drive you up to Wicklow tomorrow morning. I have a fair idea where the camp Kitty is living at is," Jonny said as they began to push their way forward toward the exit, and she wished he'd sounded a bit more enthusiastic about it.

***

"I'll get this," Kitty said leaning forward in her seat but Jonny already had his wallet out and, fishing out a note, he told the taxi driver to keep the change. It had been a relatively short ride from the airport so it shouldn't have been too expensive, she thought, still feeling guilty. She was staying at his place after all. Thanking the driver, she climbed out of the cab to find herself looking up at a high-rise apartment block. So this was where he called home, she thought as she heard the car boot pop. It was not what she'd expected. Jonny grabbed their bags out and slammed the boot shut before giving the driver a wave. "Cheers mate."

"So where are we then?" Kitty asked waiting on the step as he punched a code into the front entrance security pad.

"Swords. It's not a bad spot, pretty handy for most things."

The name didn't mean much to her, but then Kitty had never visited Dublin before. She only knew the tourist basics about the city such as the River Liffey, Grafton Street, Trinity College, the Great Post Office and the Guinness Factory. Oh, and she recalled a boozy weekend her old flatmate Gemma had spent in a place called Temple Bar on some hen night. She'd had a great time along with all the other Brits trawling the bars.

Jonny pushed the door open, and she followed him into a well-lit foyer to wait for the lift. "Quicker to take the fecking stairs," he muttered as they stood waiting but at last it arrived disgorging a young man in a cap, hands thrust deep into his jeans pockets. He nodded in Jonny's direction. "Alright mate," Jonny said stepping into the lift not waiting for a reply as Kitty followed him in. They got out at the sixth floor.

"This is me," he said stopping outside number twenty-two.

There were three other doors on this floor, Kitty saw, glancing around as she waited for him to fish his keys out and unlock the door. A moment later he pushed it open and flicked the light on. Kitty followed him inside his apartment.

It was a one bed, she noted as she trailed behind him passing by a bedroom on the left and a bathroom on the right before coming out into a kitchen and living room area. Spacious it was not, but then he only had himself to think about.

"Make yourself at home." Jonny indicated the couch and Kitty saw that with its sagging middle it had seen better days. She went and perched on the edge of it with her case at her feet feeling anything but at home.

He disappeared back down the hall to put his pack away, Kitty guessed, using the opportunity to glance around the room. It would have been a reasonable size if it didn't have such a ridiculously large flatscreen TV taking up over half of the wall facing her. From where she was sitting she could see out the windows to a vista of twinkling lights spread over the suburb of Swords. Cities always looked far more magical at night than they did in the harsh light of day, she thought, her eyes taking in the fact the walls were bare. It was certainly a utilitarian room in its furnishings, but there was something bothering her about it – she couldn't put her finger on what it was.

"Drink?" Jonny said startling her as he came back in the room.

"Yes please."

He opened the fridge. "I've only got a beer or whisky other than that it's tea or coffee?"

"I'll have a tea, please."

He pulled himself a can out of the fridge before filling the kettle. Kitty got up to give him a hand. As he opened an overhead cupboard to get a mug, she saw that there were only two others in there alongside two plates upon which was stacked a couple of bowls. That was when it dawned on her as to what was niggling at her about his apartment. It felt temporary, like a motel room;

there were no photos or trinkets about the place, nothing to indicate the kind of life he led or person he was at all.

Perhaps he'd not long moved in, Kitty thought, pouring the boiling water on the teabag he'd found for her as he pulled the tab on his can. "How long have you lived here then?'

"A year or so, I rented it furnished and it's close to everything. It came with a parking space too; that's a bonus."

That put paid to her just moved in theory, then. "Oh right, it's nice."

He raised an eyebrow at that. "It's a roof over my head and a bed to sleep in is what it is." Opening the fridge, he got a carton of milk out and sniffing at it declared it off. "Sorry, hope you don't mind your tea black."

"It's fine, thanks." She hated black tea but carrying it through to the living room she sat back down. Jonny sat down the opposite end of the couch, and she was grateful it was a three-seater because this situation felt strange enough as it was without being squashed up next to him again. If she had to suffer through any more inadvertent leg brushing, she'd probably do something daft like spill her tea all over herself.

He picked up the remote and turned the telly on. "I hate that shite," he muttered referring to the programme filling the screen. "Why anyone would want to put themselves forward for any of those reality shows is beyond me."

It looked like a survivalist show given the lack of clothing on its stars and the jungle backdrop. "I know. they're pretty awful," Kitty agreed as he flicked through a couple of channels pausing on a rugby game before turning to her.

"Anything you want to watch?"

"No thanks, you go ahead watch what you want. I wouldn't mind making a phone call, though."

"You can use my room if you want some privacy. It's not hard to find."

She smiled. "Thanks. I'll yell out if I get lost."

He didn't smile at her little joke.

Stepping inside his room and pulling the door shut behind her, she exhaled slowly glad of the opportunity to be on her own for a few minutes to try and make sense of the way she was feeling. What she was half hoping would happen, couldn't happen. It would ruin everything, she told herself. She didn't want to admit to herself that Jonny hadn't given her any indication that he was feeling those same jolts of attraction she was every time she looked at him.

His room was small, she saw, glancing round it. His double bed was neatly made and it took up the bulk of space in the room. There was a built-in wardrobe, and a small chest of drawers pushed into the corner, but it was what was sitting atop those drawers that grabbed her attention. It was a framed photograph and from where she was standing she could see it was a picture of Jonny and an older woman, his mother she guessed. Feeling ever so slightly stalkerish she picked it up noticing a piece of crumpled paper next to it as she did. 'Pick Tess up at five' was scrawled on it. She frowned, he had a girlfriend. For some reason, she had just assumed he was single, and her heart sank at the realisation that the attraction she had been feeling toward him was obviously one sided.

Peering at the photograph, she could see it had been taken a good few years ago. Jonny only looked to be about fifteen or so in it, she thought, but he was already showing signs of the handsome man he would become. His mother's face was pinched as befitting the life she had probably led married to an alcoholic. Her lips were pressed together tightly in a line that alluded to dissatisfaction, and there was not much softness about her. Behind them was a caravan that had seen better days and tracing her finger over the photo she tried to imagine what it would be like to live in such close quarters with another person, with Jonny.

Hearing a noise, she put the photograph back down guiltily then realising Jonny must have gone to the bathroom decided it was time to stop her sneaky inventory and do what she'd come into the room to do. Sitting down on the bed, she ran her hands over his duvet and imagined herself stretched out alongside Jonny in it. Oh for goodness sake get a grip girl, you are in danger of turning into a bunny boiler! She hit the call button and waited for Yasmin to pick up.

Chapter 26

Three diseases without shame: love, itch and thirst – Irish Proverb

Later that night, Kitty lay on her back in Jonny's bed staring at the ceiling. In one breath she willed morning to hurry up and get a move on, and in the other, she wished the night would never end. Every time she thought about the day ahead her insides began doing an Irish jig.

Jonny had gallantly insisted she take his bed, and he was currently snoring on the couch in the lounge. It was pitch black outside, and there was no sound except for the snoring that she could hear even with the bedroom door shut. It had taken her an age to get off to sleep, but she had finally drifted off only to be woken by some mid-week revellers making a ruckus as they crossed the courtyard area below her window. She'd woken with a start not knowing where she was as she lay there in the darkness with her heart pounding. By the time she remembered she was in Jonny's apartment in Dublin she was wide awake, and she'd begun mulling over her conversation with Yasmin earlier.

Yas had been buzzing with anticipation for her date with Mr Amatriciana who, she'd informed Kitty, was called Carlos. "Yasmin and Carlos, it has a great ring to it don't you think? I wonder if he's of Spanish descent with a name like that."

"It sounds very exotic, yes," Kitty had replied with a smile before filling her friend in on where she was and what she was planning on doing tomorrow.

"Kitty," Yasmin's tone had taken on a warning note. "I know you're worried about how your aunt's going to react to you showing up out the blue tomorrow but don't go doing anything tonight that you might regret in the morning."

"What do you mean?"

"I mean trying to find an outlet for all that tension with the gypsy boy."

"Yas!"

"Well, I am just saying and it wouldn't work even if you did throw a leg over because afterwards you'd still be uptight about going to Wicklow. I mean all that sex hasn't done a thing to mellow Paula, she is still piggy, you want to see the state she left the kitchen in this morning."

Kitty had to laugh. "Okay, you've just managed to put me right off any amorous activity for at least a year."

"That was my cunning plan."

"Chance would be a fine thing, he's not interested in me; he has a girlfriend called *Tess*." She couldn't help the sarcastic tone in her voice. "All he sees when he looks at me is the daughter of the woman whose family has been feuding with his for decades," she'd whispered down the phone adding, "Actually, state of my fringe at the moment, all I see when I look in the mirror is my mum too." Then not wanting to dampen Yasmin's excitement she'd told her she would ring tomorrow to wish her luck on her date and to tell her how she got on in Wicklow.

"It will be okay Kitty, whatever happens tomorrow, it will be okay," Yasmin told her before hanging up.

Kitty must have drifted off again as this time when she opened her eyes the room was lighter. Her eyes felt gritty, and she rubbed at them. Across the hall, she could hear the shower running, and reaching over to grab her phone she saw that it was just after seven. She let herself lie there for a few minutes longer, wishing she didn't feel so wound up.

Normally when she felt worried or stressed like this, she would get up wander into her kitchen and begin making a batch of something yummy. It was her version of having a drink or a cigarette and was the perfect antidote to taking her mind off whatever it was that was bothering her. By the time she pulled her sweet treats from the oven she'd be feeling positively Zen-like, and it required a lot less energy than a yoga session. Just thinking about the process of mixing and measuring wouldn't work this morning, she was way too wound up to concentrate on visualising anything else other than how today would pan out.

Nope, coffee would have to suffice this morning, she thought, yawning as she sat up and stretched. Not willing to parade around in front of Jonny in her PJ's she threw on her jeans and T-shirt before padding through to the kitchen. She'd just flicked the switch on the kettle when she remembered there was no milk. Bugger it, she thought, standing there for a moment, she needed a coffee this morning of all mornings. There must be a convenience store nearby. She frowned. Jonny was still in the shower; she'd have to go out and grab a carton.

***

Returning from the supermarket with cupcake ingredients as well as milk, Kitty let herself in and found Jonny munching a piece of toast sitting on the couch watching the television. He looked bright for someone who had slept on the sofa. He looked up as Kitty walked into the room and placed her bags down on the kitchen floor. He muted the TV. "I thought you'd gotten cold feet and headed off home, not gone and done the fecking groceries," he said checking out the bags.

"I did get cold feet, well kind of because I woke up feeling pretty stressed about how today is going to go." Kitty flicked the switch on the kettle and gave her mug from the night before, that was still sitting in the sink, a quick rinse before spooning coffee into it. "I remembered there was no milk so I decided to pop out and buy a carton because I can't drink my coffee black and this morning I am in need of caffeine. Do you want one?" She gestured to the jar of coffee and Jonny shook his head.

"No ta."

"Anyway, I found the Tesco and when I saw the baking aisle I had this brilliant idea." She began pulling items from the bags and setting them out on the bench. "If it is okay with you I am going to make some cupcakes to take with us to Wicklow."

Jonny looked at her like she was slightly mad.

She shrugged. "Baking is my drug of choice. It soothes me, calms my nerves and believe me, I am very nervous about going to meet my aunt this morning. First things first, though, I could do with a shower."

He looked her up and down, and she could tell he was trying to hide his amusement. "Do you always go out and about looking like you just got out of bed?"

She didn't think a rude gesture was an appropriate reply given that he was her host. Instead, she kept her hand signals to herself and headed down the hall hearing him call out after her. "There's a clean towel on the vanity."

***

Feeling a lot better after sluicing off the previous day's travel under the hot water, she'd cast a rueful eye at the pile of clothes she was going to have to get dressed in yet again. Never again would she pack lightly, she vowed, drying off. The next time she travelled anywhere she would be prepared for any eventuality, and pack at least three of everything. She sorted her hair out so that her Aunt Kitty didn't think she was a mad woman escaped from somewhere. By the time, she finished putting on her makeup, she felt ready if not to face the day then at least to bake cupcakes.

Donning the cheap pinny she'd bought because she was not willing to risk any more stains on her top, she missed the amused glance Jonny shot her from the couch. He'd spotted the apron's 'I'm a Bacon Girl' logo.

"Are you now?" he asked eyebrow raised.

"What?" She followed his gaze. "Oh right, it was this or 'Bacon gives me a Lard On.' There was a bacon promotion going on."

"Right. Good choice then."

Fastening it at the back, she looked toward the oven. First things first, check if it's empty, then pop it on to preheat, she told herself. Closing the door a moment later, she wondered if Jonny had ever even used it, the inside was spotless. To her surprise, he switched the television off and came over to stand beside her.

"So where do you start, then?" he said waiting for instructions. Kitty felt a tiny thrill course through her at his proximity. Chewing her bottom lip she told herself to focus. "Well, um, it's a pretty basic vanilla recipe, so the first thing to do is wash your hands." Oh dear, she sounded like a mother instructing her pre-schooler. "If you haven't already this morning that is."

He smirked and held his hands up. "They're clean – I promise."

"Okay, right, well measure two hundred grams of flour into the bowl then and while you are doing that I am going to melt the butter." She handed Jonny the measuring cup she'd bought. He set about doing what she'd asked while she sliced off a wedge of butter, and putting it in his one and only pot, waited for it to melt. She felt Jonny's eyes on her waiting expectantly for further instructions. "Okay, so now you're going to add sugar and mix it in with the wooden spoon." She couldn't help but smile at the look of concentration on his face as he carefully poured the sugar into the cup before tipping it into the bowl. Once he'd mixed the two ingredients she told him to make a well in the middle of them. She moved to show him what she meant and felt a tingling shock run through her as their fingers brushed each other in the floury mix.

Kitty was filled with the strongest feeling that were she to look up at him right at that moment then he would kiss her. Knowing now wasn't a good time to get involved, especially if he did have a girlfriend, she forced herself to keep her eyes on the mix in the bowl and began to demonstrate how to scoop it to the sides. "Okay, so you need to crack two eggs into the middle now." She hoped he couldn't hear the huskiness that had crept into her voice as she added a few drops of vanilla essence. Picking up the wooden spoon, she showed him how to combine all the ingredients gently. Handing the spoon over to him, she poured in the hot liquid butter and milk, getting him to continue mixing until she was satisfied they had a smooth cake batter.

She filled the tin with the prettily patterned papers she'd bought, and Jonny began to spoon the mixture in. "Oops, that's a bit too much," Kitty said picking up a teaspoon and scraping some out. "Just fill them to about three-quarters."

"Uh-huh, so how long will they take to cook?"

"Depending on how hot your oven is around ten to fifteen minutes. I bought vanilla flavoured icing sugar to sprinkle over the tops of them, so we don't have to hang around waiting for them to cool before I ice them."

He looked disappointed at hearing she wasn't going to ice them as such, and she felt sorry she hadn't bought a piping bag. She would have liked to have seen his face were she to pile the little cakes high with swirls of her secret vanilla buttercream icing. She imagined his awe were she to demonstrate the full extent of her prowess in the cake icing department. Feeling his eyes upon her, she realized he was looking at her with a smile playing at the corners of his mouth again. "You were miles away, what were you thinking about?"

She blinked, feeling a flush spread up her neck. "Um, oh nothing. Are they ready to go in?" She needed to stop acting like a schoolgirl with a crush.

He nodded, and she picked up the tin sliding it into the oven before setting the timer for ten minutes. When she turned back to the bench, she caught Jonny licking the spoon and laughed. "That was always my favourite part; I bags the bowl."

"I think you got it all." Jonny indicated the bowl she'd wiped clean with her index finger. The taste of the batter, when she popped her finger into her mouth, had conjured up the memory of those happy times spent baking with her mother the way it always did. Jonny had filled the sink with hot soapy water to begin washing up. She passed the bowl to him and had to stop herself from reaching up and brushing the smudge of flour from his cheek.

"What are you going to do with this stuff, take it home?"

"No, you keep it. You never know next time you're feeling wound up about something you might decide to do a spot of baking." She nearly added, or your girlfriend might feel like making you a cake sometime, but stopped herself, it was none of her business. She cast a sideways glance at the living area. Maybe they were only dating casually as there was not so much as a hint of a feminine presence other than her own having ever stepped foot over the threshold.

"You never know. I reckon I could just about manage to make another batch of that one day," he said, and their eyes locked as they exchanged a smile.

Kitty checked on the cakes and saw they were rising nicely before going to sit down on the couch while they browned off.

"There's something about the smell alright," Jonny said sitting down next to her and she wished he hadn't sat quite so close to her. "It makes a place feel like home knowing there's something nice being cooked in the oven, and this is the first time this place has felt like that."

"It does have a rather temporary feel about it." The words popped out of her mouth and, she hoped he didn't take them the wrong way. "Not that it isn't nice or anything."

He shrugged. "It's got a roof, walls, and a bed to sleep in. I get itchy feet, and Tess and I have to keep moving on. It's in me."

Tess! Kitty felt a spike of jealousy. They must be serious then she surmised, guessing she was a Traveller girl.

"That's why I went into the building trade; I love it, but it also means I can find work in most places we decide to pitch up at."

"But you obviously had to take a lease out to get this place?"

"I did, six months fully furnished. I've a Georgian manor house restoration on the go not far from here. It's a big job, too long just to park up somewhere. It's the longest I've been in one place since I lived with my mam and da. I suppose part of me wanted to see what it was like to put down roots for a while."

Kitty wondered where this Tess of such poor homemaking skills was. "But it's not for you, putting down roots."

"No, it's not for me. I'll be moving on once the job's done."

"In my mum's journal she mentioned that her mother once said to her that she thought it would be a lonely thing to live in a house."

He nodded slowly. "Did she settle down then, your mother?"

"She did, yes, when she married my dad. We had a lovely home too; it was called Rose Cottage, and it always smelt warm and welcoming like this does now." Kitty gesticulated to the aroma wafting from the kitchen. "It was my mum who instilled my love of baking in me because I associate the smell of something wonderful cooking in the oven with the happy times I spent with her growing up." Her eyes welled up, and she felt Jonny touch her arm fleetingly, and she blinked the tears back, wanting to finish what she was trying to say. "Having read her story I under-

267

stand her better now and I can see that when my dad died she hankered to return to the travelling life but she didn't know how to. That was when we grew apart because I didn't get what she was she feeling and how it was driving her actions. I mean how could I? When I never had a clue about where she'd come from."

"She never breathed a word of it?"

"Not a word and I know from reading her journal that she had her regrets but that she wouldn't change anything either. She never saw her family again, and it hurt her leaving Kitty, Paddy, her mum, and even her dad. He was different before they lost Paddy's twin, Joe. He didn't cope with losing his son and turned to the drink. She loved who he was before. I think that cutting herself off from the people she loved was her way of trying to atone for Michael's death and the way she handled things afterwards."

"Jaysus." He ran his fingers through his hair in that now familiar gesture of his.

"I feel closer to her now than I have done in years with all that's happened since Christian asked me to come to France. How sad is that?"

He didn't reply, and they sat in silence for a moment until Kitty broke it. "You know she thought it was in me too, this need to keep moving, and that's why I haven't been able to stay put in any one place too long." She gave a sardonic little laugh. "Mind you if my fiancé hadn't cheated on me when we were living together in Manchester I'd probably still be happily playing house there now."

"Was that your man who came to Uzés?"

"Yes, he'd seen the error of his ways or so he said. My friend Yasmin says once a cheater always a cheater. She's probably right, but I realized seeing him again in Uzés that no matter how many times he said he was sorry, and that it wouldn't happen again, I couldn't go back."

"Sounds to me like you made the right choice; besides you are soon to be a woman of independent means with your own business. You'll have to settle down for a bit then."

Kitty frowned, picking a bit of what looked like dried pasta off her jeans. She didn't know why but the idea of her long-held dream becoming a reality wasn't filling her with the same sense of excitement it had done when it was out of her grasp. It wasn't the baking and selling of her cakes; she loved that part of it. There was nothing better than the look of anticipatory pleasure on a customer's face when she boxed up their treat. It was what Jonny had just said, she realized.

"You don't look too enthusiastic."

"It's the settling down side of it that's been bothering me about the whole thing. I don't know if I want to commit to a lease that will tie me to one place for any length of time at the moment. I thought I was ready to do that. Now I don't know because with everything that's happened since I got that first text from Christian, I just feel unsettled as to what's next."

She was saved from having to ponder this any longer by the pinger announcing that the cakes should be ready.

"Do you want to do the honours or should I?"

"I will," Jonny said, getting to his feet.

Kitty smiled watching his face light up as he opened the oven door and spied the plump golden cakes inside. Grabbing a tea towel, he pulled the tin out holding it up to his nose and breathing in deeply before putting it down on top of the stove. He blew on his fingers. "Feck, that was hot." It didn't deter him from taking a cake and juggling it from hand to hand for a moment, though, before taking a big bite out of the top of it.

"Ten out of ten. I'd say," he mumbled sending a mouthful of crumbs flying.

"See I told you, baking is good for your soul," Kitty said smiling at him as she got up and wandered over to help herself to one.

Chapter 27

Every tide has an ebb save the tide of graces – Irish Proverb

Jonny jangled his keys in the hallway while Kitty wrapped the baking tin in a clean tea towel. "Right I'm ready," she said. As she picked up her handbag a thought occurred to her, she should bring Rosa's dress with her. Not the journal, that was meant for her eyes only, but her aunt might like to see the dress that had been so special to her older sister again. She picked it up out of her case, and placed it carefully in one of the empty shopping bags, before following Jonny out the door. They rode the lift down to the basement and crossing the parking lot, she saw it was virtually empty apart from one of those cute vans that she always associated with hippies. It was not at all what she would have picked as Jonny's choice of wheels. What were they called again? That was it, Kombies, and at least this one wasn't painted in psychedelic colours.

In the dim light it looked to be a light bluish colour with white trim, and on closer inspection, she saw that it was in really good condition despite its obvious age. There were curtains drawn on the windows so she couldn't see in the back, but she guessed it was probably chock-a-block with builder's gear.

"Kitty meet Tess; Tess meet Kitty," Jonny said before unlocking the driver's door and reaching over to unlock the passenger side for Kitty. A stupid grin spread itself across her face as she climbed in – this was Tess? Ha! That would teach her for being a nosy rosy and jumping to conclusions. Her mood lifted instantly at this news. She didn't have Jonny down as a man who would name his van but then she hadn't had him down as a man who would bake cupcakes with her either.

Glancing back over her shoulder, she gasped twisting around in her seat so she could get a better view. "Oh wow I didn't expect that!" Her eyes swept over the cleverly fitted timber overhead cupboards and down to the back of the van where a blue and white surfboard was attached to the wall next to a bench seat.

Jonny followed her gaze "That folds out to act as a table."

"What a great idea." The walls were decorated with driftwood and shells in keeping with the obvious nautical theme. A brightly-coloured towel hung from a hook with another surfboard strapped to the wall next to it, should he decide to go for an impromptu ride on the waves. The only sign that Jonny used the van for work purposes too was in the fisherman's basket under the bench seat in which she could see various tools of the trade. She looked around for a bed. "Where do you sleep?"

He pointed up. "It has a pop top. If you lift the lid on that chest just behind your seat there, you'll find a two ring gas hob tucked away inside it." She could hear the pride in his voice and could tell Tess had been a labour of love. She handed him the tray of cakes and turning around got on her knees so she could lean over the seat. She did what he'd suggested, and saw there was indeed a two ring hob housed inside the chest.

"It's amazing, did you do her up yourself?"

"I did yeah, she was a bit of a project, and she's not exactly a Piebald, but she does me proud."

His tongue-in-cheek mention of her romanticism of the Travellers choice of transport did not escape her, and she gave him a gentle thump on the arm.

271

"She's not always all that reliable either but we get there in the end. We've spent many a happy night together, me and Tess."

"Well she's gorgeous, I'm impressed."

"You won't be if she doesn't start, here—" He handed back the tray before turning the key in the ignition, grinning when the engine roared into life. "Good girl." Patting the steering wheel, he put the gearstick into reverse. Pulling out of the park and driving toward the exit, he pressed a button on his sun visor. As the basement door slid open, Kitty blinked at the sudden shards of daylight.

"How long do you think it will take us to get there?"

"This time of morning most of the commuters are long gone so it shouldn't take us long, about half an hour or so." Jonny navigated the streets with ease obviously familiar with the route he was taking, telling her how he often took off in Tess when the need to just get away grabbed him.

"You surf, then?"

"Oh yeah, I love it, when I am out there on the water it's the best feeling, you know?"

"Not really, I don't even like putting my head under water. What's it like?"

"Oh I don't know, I guess it's like being alone with something so much bigger than yourself that it puts all the trivial shite into perspective. I read a quote somewhere that said the gods seem to be around in the best waves of your life, and that stuck with me."

"Well, I just hope you've got a good wetsuit because I imagine the waters around these parts can be a tad fresh."

"Fecking freezing." He grinned.

They garnered lots of looks as they putted along with the gears grinding to remind them of the van's age, but Jonny was oblivious, concentrating on what was in front of him. It didn't take long before the urban scenery gave way to the green belt. Kitty was leaning back in her seat admiring the view of the passing golds and browns of the countryside when he jerked the steering wheel right. "Feck, nearly missed the turn-off." Her shoulder smacked into his. "Sorry about that, are you alright?"

She nodded rubbing her shoulder with one hand and grasping hold of her seat with the other. They bumped their way up a gravel road until he veered off down another side road, and they reached a clearing. A cluster of not so much caravans as mobile homes, like the kind found in holiday parks, were all parked up. It looked quite civilised, she mused, and there was obviously power to each of the sites.

"We're here," he said pulling the handbrake.

Kitty looked over, and as she wondered which one of those caravans belonged to her aunt, she felt her stomach lurch.

"Okay?"

"Actually no I'm not, I feel sick, I don't think I can do this." She sat there looking fearfully at the mobile homes hoping they could turn around and go back before anyone looked outside to see who the interlopers were.

"Yes, you can," Jonny said firmly unbuckling his seat belt. "Come on, I didn't take the day off work just to take you for a nice country drive in the Wicklow Mountains."

That did it; she hadn't thought about him losing a day's pay to bring her here. She did owe it to him to follow through, and she knew she would be so angry at herself later on if she let this opportunity go by just because she was scared. She was made of stronger stuff than that. "Okay, just give me a sec." Kitty peered into the mirror on the inside of her visor and was relieved to see her face wasn't reflecting the sudden terror she had been filled with. That was so long as you didn't look too closely and see the tell-tale beads of sweat that had popped out on her upper lip, she thought, wiping them off.

"You can do this, Kitty Sorenson, for yourself and mum," she muttered not caring that she was talking to herself as she unbuckled and opened the door. Stepping down, she felt her foot squelch into something warm and moist. Glancing at her shoe saw that it was also brown, and she didn't have to inhale to know it would be smelly. "Shit-Shit-Shit!" she yelped, putting the tray down on her seat before pulling her foot out of the muck.

Jonny came round to see what she was making a fuss about and seeing her predicament laughed. "Yeah, literally."

She scowled at him. "Ha, bloody ha!" Scraping the heel of her shoe against a dry mound of grass she began wiping the worst of it off.

"That'll teach you for choosing inappropriate footwear for a day in the country."

"I wasn't exactly spoiled for choice." Having cleaned her shoe up the best she could, she picked up her tea towel wrapped offering from the van seat and set forth across the rough paddock. It was hard to muster much dignity considering she was wearing stilettos and had just trod in a cow pat.

"We'll try that one first." Jonny pointed at a large mobile home up on blocks that reminded Kitty of the luxury caravan she'd once rented for a week's holiday down in Cornwall with Damien. It had been able to sleep six comfortably, and been completely beyond their needs but still she recalled Damien complaining, and saying they'd have been better off in a hotel. She wondered what he would make of this place here and realized she didn't care what he thought anymore. It was quite satisfying.

The whole place was quiet, eerily so, Kitty thought, spying a few shirts flapping on the line strung up alongside the caravan. Its curtains were open but still maybe nobody would be in, and she could take that as a sign that this meeting wasn't meant to be and head back to London pretending none of this had ever happened. She crossed her fingers behind her back.

Jonny reached the door first and knocked. Kitty stood behind him shifting anxiously from foot to foot. "I don't think there's anyone home," she said after a moment, tugging on his sleeve for him to go just as the door opened.

Kitty peered round Jonny to see a petite woman clad in jeans and a tight, sparkly singlet top from which her bust threatened to burst forth. On her feet, she wore high heel slingbacks decorated with diamantes. She must be frozen, Kitty thought, knowing her arms had goose bumps from the dewy freshness of the morning air. Her dark hair showed not one streak of grey, and her face was made up, conspicuously so, with an orange-tinged powder cake. Her hand, Kitty noticed, holding the door open had chunky gemstones on each finger, and her nails were painted a bright pink with little jewels in them. This woman couldn't be Rosa's sister, surely? She was the polar opposite of her demure mother, who thought she was pushing the boat out when she'd applied both lipstick and mascara? Kitty shifted nervously from foot to foot. The woman stared at Jonny for a moment frowning as she tried to place him.

"Well feck me if it isn't a Donohue. You'd have to be Tyson's boy, by the looks of you?"

He held his hands up. "Yes, Jonny Donohue and I come in peace."

Her heavily mascaraed eyes grew wide. "Feck me! Jonny bloody Donohue, it's been years, so it has. You were a lad in short pants last time I saw you. So what is it that brings you here?"

Kitty stepped around to introduce herself then, and the woman looked at her for a moment her face paling beneath her tangerine makeup as she crossed herself. "Holy Mary Mother of God! Rosa, is it you come back after all this time?"

Jonny reached out and offered her a steadying hand. "No not Rosa, this is her daughter. She's named after you. Kitty Rourke, er O'Connor, this is your niece, Kitty Sorenson. Do you want to sit down, Kitty? You're awful white. I think maybe you've had a bit of a shock."

She waved his hand away still staring at her niece, gobsmacked.

"Er, hello. I'm sorry just to show up like this, and I didn't mean to upset you." Kitty's voice was tremulous, and her hand holding the tray shook as she waited to see how this woman, her aunt. would greet her.

She blinked a couple of times and then taking a step down from the caravan she pointed at the tray. "Are you here about the money? It's too fecking late if you are because it's gone so it is." Her hand moved to the door, once more poised to slam it shut.

Kitty's mouth fell open at the realisation that she thought Kitty was here to ask for the royalties her mother had bequeathed to her little sister.

"No! Wait, that's not why I am here. That money's yours as far as I am concerned. It's what my mum wanted. I just wanted to meet you that's all."

Kitty O'Conner's body relaxed, and she glanced at the tea towel wrapped offering. "What have you got there. then?"

"Jonny and I, we, um baked you some cakes."

She raised an eyebrow and glanced over at Jonny. "I see; like that is it? Well, the pair of you had best be coming in for a cup of tea then." She disappeared back inside the caravan trailing a waft of Paris perfume behind her. It had been Rosa's favourite perfume, Kitty thought, breathing it in as she followed her inside.

Chapter 28

Listen to the sound of the river and you will get a trout – Irish Proverb

Kit, as Kitty had said she should call her because that's what everybody called her these days, busied herself putting the kettle on to make tea while Kitty and Jonny sat down at the table. It was laid with a white linen cloth. Irish linen, Kitty noted, spying the label on the hemmed edge. The whole set up was all very civilized, she thought with a glance round at the caravan's interior. The space was immaculate and surprisingly roomy with a lovely homely feel to it thanks to all the knick-knacks dotted about the place. She spied a neatly made double bed down the end piled high with plump cushions. Trinkets lined a shelf along with framed photos, and she itched to get up and have a look at them, to see the rest of the family but didn't want to appear too forward.

"How do you have your tea?"

"White please, no sugar."

"Me too ta." Jonny chimed. "I'll have a cuppa and make myself scarce, leave you two ladies to your catching up."

"You don't have to go." Kitty shot him a pleading look that he ignored.

Kit was like a busy, colourful little bird as she flitted around her kitchen and Kitty realized, as she watched her actions that she was nervous too. The thought comforted her because nervous was better than bitter and angry.

At last, she poured the pot and placed a china cup and saucer down in front of them both before piling the cakes high onto a plate in the middle of the table. "Mmm, these look good. I can't wait to try one." Getting her tea, she took one and peeled the paper off before biting into it.

"They're good," she muttered her mouth full. "And you say you helped make these little gems?"

Jonny grinned. "I did, yeah."

"You could show my Davey a thing or two in the kitchen so you could. All the men are in Wicklow today working on a big job site there, but I think auld man Tommy is in. His is the light green caravan closest to the road. He'd welcome a bit of male company so why don't you take a couple of your cakes over to him. I'm sure it's been awhile since he's had a taste of the home baking."

Jonny nodded and picking his tea cup up, balanced two cakes on the side of the saucer. "I'll pop over now and take this with me." Kitty felt like kicking him under the table for abandoning her this early. She took a tentative sip of the hot tea watching him go and hoping he could feel her eyes boring holes into his traitorous back.

"Right now then my girl," Kit said laying her hands down flat on the table once he'd shut the door behind him. "Where the feck do we start?"

Kitty nearly spurted her tea everywhere. But it did the trick by breaking the tension, and they began to talk.

She told her aunt that her mother had passed away earlier that year. She didn't seem surprised, nodding as she said. "I felt it when she went. I knew she was no longer with us." Kitty reached over and placed her hand on top of hers, and Kit smiled. "You're the spit of her you know."

"It's the haircut. I had it done for the photograph that started all this, *Midsummer Lovers*." Kitty explained the story. When she finished, Kit stood up and indicated that she should follow her. She did and found herself in the bedroom part of the caravan standing in front of the familiar print in pride of place on the wall.

"We knew Michael had died, his mam Margaret made sure of that. My mam used to call her Mad Margaret, and she was that alright. We weren't sure how she knew, though, because we never heard a word from Rosa. There was a lot of bitterness over the Donohue's not knowing where he'd been laid to rest. As I recall it his da, Martin had told all and sundry he only had the one son left, and that was Tyson after Michael and Rosa left. The only news I've had of Rosa in all these years was from your man Christian. He sent me that print when the money began coming to me along with a note to say Rosa was to remarry. There was no further explanation and no return address. I looked him up and wrote to him asking where she was. He never replied, so I assumed she didn't want any further contact with any of us, and I let it be."

"Oh Kit, Mum never stopped missing you. But she never stopped punishing herself for running off with Michael either, or for leaving him to be buried in an unknown grave in France. She was so stubborn, my mum, but then you'd know that."

Kit nodded sagely. "Aye, she was that alright."

"The longer she left it, the harder the idea of going back became and then it was too late. But I know she wanted me to come here and put things right."

Kit blinked back the tears sparkling in her eyes. "Ah well all that business, it's all in the past now, so it is. Come on, your tea will be getting cold."

The two women took their places back at the table, and Kitty studied her aunt for a moment. "I knew your colouring was darker than hers, but you don't look like Mum at all apart from around your eyes. I can see a bit of a resemblance there."

Kit gave a little laugh. "I was always envious of that blonde hair of hers. She was one out of the box, your mam, both in her looks and her ways. I bleached my mop once wanting to look like her." Her hand strayed up to pat her dark curly hair worn a tad too long for a woman her age. "Mammy tore pieces off me when she saw it. I looked like a sheep, so I did. It was awful, and it took forever to grow out. Enough about me and my hair, though, tell me how you came to find me, and I am glad that you did by the way." Kitty glowed with the genuine warmth of her gaze. "Who did she marry?"

"My dad, Peter. when she was twenty. But I didn't come along until later. A much longed for surprise, Mum used to say."

"So you were her only child?"

"Yes, it was just me."

"And was she happy? Because I know how much she loved Michael, and it must have nearly killed her when she lost him."

"It did, but of course I didn't know any of that until I read her journal. She wrote that she drifted for a few years after he died but yes, she was happy again. She loved Dad; he was a good man." Kitty went on to tell her about growing up with no knowledge of where her mother had come from. She told her how hard that had been, the not knowing. Eventually, she got round to where she had begun with the story of the photograph, and how she had come to be in France where she'd met Jonny. She realized, she told Kit over her cooling tea, that her mother had engineered everything with Christian. Together they had conspired to give her the journal and the dress in France. She finished by telling her that she was now beginning to suspect it had been Rosa's plan all along that she would come back to Ireland with Jonny too. "I brought her dress with me if you'd like to see it."

Kit nodded, her dark hair bobbing. "Oh, I would. Yes please."

Kitty produced it from her bag and passed it over the table to the older woman who shook it out and pressed her lips together as she fought back fresh tears. "Ah God, I remember her wearing this as though it was only yesterday. Our Rosa thought she was the Queen of the Fair strutting around Ballinasloe, so she did. And she married Michael in it too, you say?" Kitty nodded, watching as a solitary tear escaped and streaked down her cheek carving a path through her foundation.

"She wrote in her journal that it broke her heart to leave you, you know."

"Did she? Well, it broke mine her leaving. I know Rosa felt we were growing apart, what with me getting the learning, and that she felt trapped, but my schooling was a farce I tell you. I wasn't cut out for all of that, not really. It should have been our Rosa who went, but it wasn't the way things were done. The day she left us is a day I'll never forget. The sight of her running off, it's haunted me all these years."

"So much misunderstanding," Kitty murmured.

"Too much. I would have given my right arm for her to come back. But she was always a one, your mother, too fecking head-strong for her own good. Mammy regretted not going after her when she heard she had left Cherry Orchard with Michael, and she never stopped regretting losing two of her children. Da lost himself for good in the bottle, and he found a reliable drinking partner in our Paddy." She shook her head. "Ah, so many wrong turns made along the way, and grudges held for too long. Did you know you've an uncle too?"

"I did yes. Mum said he was a twin; she told me about Joe in her journal."

"I was only little when Joe died. I don't remember much about him. But I do remember that it was hard on us all, and that's why Paddy is the way he is."

"He likes a drink."

She made a snorting sound. "That's a polite way of putting it. He's a drunk, my girl. It took me a long time to accept him for what he is, and to know that I can't change him, just like I couldn't change Da. Joe's death was very hard on Rosa too you know with the way our mam put the care of us all on to her afterwards. She was like a second mother to me when our Mammy wasn't up to the job, and I don't think she ever got time to grieve properly for him. She was too busy trying to keep the rest of us clothed and fed. He's buried down in Tuam alongside your granny and grandda."

"I know Mum visited their graves shortly before she died, and I wanted to ask you if you would come with me to scatter her ashes there. It's what she wanted – to be close to them both again. She wrote in her journal that she wanted to fly free back in Ireland."

"Ah what poetic shite, that's your mam alright." Kit laughed, but Kitty could see the tell-tale glistening in her eyes once more. "And yes, Kitty my girl, I would be honoured to go with you to Tuam."

"Thank you."

"Thank you for coming here. It can't have been easy for you."

"It wasn't because I didn't know the reception I would get. I wasn't sure how you'd feel about seeing me, but I had to come for my sake as much as for hers."

"I've thought about Rosa every day that's passed since she left. That girl was a mother to me when our Mam couldn't be. I loved her you know?"

Kitty nodded her own eyes tearing up.

"She was more than just my sister, and I never stopped missing her. You coming here today, well, I feel like I have got a part of her back." Kit reached out and laid her hand on Kitty's.

Kitty's smile was tremulous as she placed her other hand on top of Kit's. "I feel the same way looking at you. It's amazing I thought it was just me, that I was on my own. You know it ate away at Michael too, leaving Jonny's da, Tyson and his mam. Their da was a brute, by all accounts. Mum bore a lot of that guilt too. She wanted me to put things right with the Rourkes and the Donohues so she could rest peacefully."

"Martin Donohue was that alright. Excuse me."

Kit had got up and gone to the toilet then, unable to hold back the flood of tears any longer. She returned with a wad of toilet paper to wipe her eyes and blow her nose. When she'd done so, she sniffed. "Do you know, Kitty my girl, I think from what I have seen today that where Jonny Donohue's concerned you are putting things right."

The photographs came out then, and Kitty pored over them hungrily looking for traces of herself in the faces of her five cousins. Kit brightened as soon as she began to talk about her children, two boys and three girls. The girls had given her much bigger headaches than the boys had, but they were all married now and behaved themselves these days, she said. Ciara, the oldest was having her third baby and was due any day now. She lived in a caravan near Galway with her man Aidan, and their two babies, Finola and Finbar. They weren't Kit's first choice for names, she muttered through pursed lips. She had her fingers crossed they weren't going to go for the trifecta and call the new baby Fidelma, or, God help them all, Fergus.

A moment later, Kitty knew where Kit's eldest daughter's fascination with calling her children by matching lettered names came from as she told her that Christy was married to Brendan. They lived by Ciara in Galway, and only had the one baby who they'd blessed with the nice normal name of Lily. Then there was Caitlin, she had the look of Kitty about her, Kit reckoned, pointing her out. Kitty peered closely at the picture. Caitlin's brown hair was waist length and her eyes Bambi brown, but she could see a resemblance between them. It was in the shape of their mouths, and a slight tilt of their noses. "Were you a bold one like her, because I tell you of the five she was the one who turned me grey?"

Kitty laughed. "No, I was more of a handful when I got older and picked the wrong man."

Kit nodded knowingly. "Ah yes, we never stop worrying, us

mammies, no matter what age our babies are. Caitlyn turned out alright in the end, and she is a great little mam to her Devany and Beyoncé." Kitty glanced at Kit to make sure she wasn't pulling her leg with the latter child's name; she wasn't. "So do you have a fellow on the go because you must be in your thirties?"

Kit, Kitty realized, was not shy about coming forward. She supposed too, that in the Traveller's world she was over the hill. "Thirty-one, and I did. We were engaged. I'd even got so far as subscribing to Blushing Bride magazine but then he cheated on me, and that was the end of that. Mum never liked him. Now I think it was because she knew what would happen."

"She would have yes, all of us Rourke women have the sight."

Kitty liked the way she had been included in the equation.

"But I think she would have known you'd meet the man who's meant for you too."

"She did seem pretty certain in her journal that I would meet the right man, yes. He just hasn't come along yet." She gave a little laugh.

"Oh, I think perhaps he has. The pair of you just haven't realized it yet."

Kitty felt her face heat up; she knew who Kit was referring to, just as she wondered if the attraction she had been feeling for him was a one-sided affair. She decided it was time to change the subject. "And the boys, are they married? They're a handsome pair aren't they, do they look like their dad?"

Kit sat up a bit straighter. "They've got Davey's looks those two alright, and they're good boys. That's Ryan – he's a mammy's boy that one. He's married to Tegan, and they live by her family in Sligo. I worry about that boy with her, though; she's a slovenly housekeeper. They're trying for a baby but not hard enough in my opinion." Her expression grew sage. "I think if she made a bit more effort in keeping her caravan clean they'd stand a much better chance of conceiving. It's the stress of coming home to a midden. I think it's affecting the—" she pointed at her lap. "You know."

Kitty nodded, she got the idea. Next, she stabbed at the picture of the smaller of the two lads with a shock of black hair and the cutest set of dimples. Kitty liked him immediately "That's my baby Regan, he lives over yonder in the small caravan, and he's stepping out with a lass from Wicklow. She's not a Traveller." Kitty smiled at the dismissive tone of Kit's voice.

Kit mentioned organizing a big family get-together in a couple of months when Ciara had had the baby so that Kitty could meet them all. "They'll love you their English cousin, so they will. They all have this idea that everything's exciting and glamorous over the water, but none of them has ever been."

When the caravan door opened, Jonny reappeared looking weary. "I've been hearing all about Tommy's days of fixing tractors in County Clare."

"Ah yes," Kit said. "You don't want to get him going on that. He can talk for hours about how they don't make them like they used to."

Kitty glanced up at the clock on the kitchen wall and saw with a shock that two whole hours had indeed slipped by.

Jonny looked from one to the other. "So have you two gotten to know one another a bit?"

"We have haven't we, Kitty my girl?"

Kitty smiled. "Yes, we have."

They left with the promise of Kitty coming back over to Ireland in a few weeks' time. They would say a proper farewell to Rosa then, and this time she would be armed with photographs from her childhood.

The sun was high in the sky as Jonny drove back down the unmade road. It was casting the surrounding fields in its golden glow. They had bumped along in silence for a few minutes before he broke it. "Well, I don't fancy your chances of getting on a flight this late in the day. I reckon you'd be best to ring up and book yourself on one for tomorrow when we get back to mine. You can stay again tonight if you want, and I'll drop you at the airport in the morning."

"Thanks, that would be great." Kitty rubbed her temples. "I can't believe it's only been three days since I left England, so much has happened my head's spinning with it all."

He cast a sidelong glance at her. "It went well today, didn't it?"

"It did, thank you for taking me. I don't think I could have done it if you hadn't been with me."

"Ah, you'd have got there one way or another."

"I don't know about that – I was pretty bloody scared about meeting her."

"I do. You're stronger than you give yourself credit for." He looked at her with an expression she couldn't read and missed the large pothole in the middle of the road. They both bounced hard in their seats. "Shite! Sorry about that."

Kitty rubbed her head and gave him a rueful grin. "I'll let you off. If I head back tomorrow, I'll still be back in time to open my stall on Saturday and to give Yasmin a break. She's been a really good pal covering my shifts at Bruno's for me."

They drifted into silence again with Jonny keeping his eyes firmly on the road. As Tess idled at the lights, they headed back into the hustle and bustle of Dublin's suburbia, joining in with the throng of harried mums doing the school run. Kitty smiled to herself. Leaving her aunt hadn't been hard because it wasn't goodbye, it was just the beginning.

Kit had promised too that she would begin organizing the family reunion. Kitty couldn't wait; she already felt like she knew all her mad, crazy cousins after spending the afternoon in their mad, crazy mother's company. She'd felt, she realized as the light turned from orange to green and Tess juddered forth, like she'd finally come home.

Chapter 29

Mere words do not feed the friars - Irish Proverb

"I'm booked on the ten o'clock flight tomorrow morning. Thanks for letting me stay again and thanks, you know, for today." Kitty was hovering in the living room doorway her phone in hand, not sure where to put herself. Jonny muttered something that sounded like 'it's alright' from where he was sprawled on the couch holding a takeaway menu.

"Indian or Chinese? I've not much in, so I thought I'd get a takeaway. I'm fecking starving."

"Um, Indian, please. We forgot about lunch today, Kit and I had so much to talk about." She was hungry too, she realized, but if there were anything else on offer she'd rather a bit of that than a curry. He was a handsome man, Jonny, with that dark hair flopping down into his eyes. The white shirt he was wearing set off the olive tones of his skin to perfection. Oh, and the way his long, leanly-muscled legs filled out his jeans. She pulled her mind back out of the gutter as she realized he was waving something at her.

"Here, have a look and pick a dish." He sat up making room for her, and she took the menu from him sitting down as she scanned the dishes, but her eyes blurred. She couldn't concentrate with him sitting so close to her. It was crazy; she'd been sitting next to him in Tess all the way back from Wicklow and managed to contain herself. It felt different now that they were back in his apartment with the proximity of a bedroom. The atmosphere had grown tenser – something had shifted between them, she could feel it. The easy rapport of earlier was gone, and she felt awkward as her senses went into overdrive. She was acutely aware of everything about him from the musky scent of his aftershave to the soft dark hairs peeking out from where his shirtsleeves ended. What she wanted to say as he looked at her expectantly with those coal coloured eyes was. "Feck the Indian, just get on with it and kiss me."

What came out of her mouth, though, was; "Um, can't go wrong with Butter Chicken and a plain naan, please." Her voice sounded squeaky, Minnie Mouseish, and she cringed.

"Right, Butter Chicken it is."

He dialled the number and ordered her dish, and a Lamb Tikka Masala for himself. "It'll be half an hour," he said to Kitty, hanging up.

Her tummy growled reminding her that yes actually she was hungry, and she hoped she didn't begin nibbling on the furniture between now and then. "Great, thanks."

"Beer?"

She'd rather a nice crisp glass of white, but beggars couldn't be choosers. "Yes, ta."

Jonny got up to get a couple of cans, and Kitty turned her attention to tapping Yas out a message to distract herself.

Today was wonderful. Will tell you all about it tomorrow night, on 10 am flight home in the morning and do not expect to walk in on you doing the wild thing with your Carlos chap, remember the golden rule of first dates – keep your knickers on and have the best time ever LOL me xxx

"Here you go."

Kitty pushed send and reached for the can. "Cheers." As she

took it from him, her fingers brushed his, and they lingered there just touching his as an electric frisson of excitement coursed through her body. He felt it too, she could tell by the hungry, searching look in his eyes just before he took the can from her hand. He placed it down and took her hand, pulling her up from the sofa and into his arms, moving his lips to where she'd longed to feel them, on top of hers. They kissed each other long and crashed onto the couch, hard rolling about like frisky teenagers whose parents were out for the night. He pulled her T-shirt up over her head and Kitty began to wrestle with his shirt. They staggered half-naked in a lip-locked dance into the bedroom.

***

Afterwards, they lay in each other's arm waiting for their breathing to slow as they felt their bodies' sweat cool on each other's bare skin. The sheets were a tangle at the foot of the bed. Kitty kept her eyes tightly closed as she tried to capture the essence of this moment. Her finger traced an unconscious heart shape, and she could feel the light tickle of the smattering of dark hairs on his chest beneath it. It was pure contentment, happiness in its raw state. It was how her mother must have been feeling as she looked at Michael at that moment Christian's camera clicked.

She wanted to photograph her moment now with her mind's eye. She wanted to be able to bring back the feeling of lying here entwined with this beautiful man with his messed up past and whose strong arms were wrapped around her, at will. That somehow she had fallen completely in love with his ever so slightly arrogant ways in the last three days, she knew without a doubt. They were ways that masked a marred upbringing thanks to a past he couldn't change. She started as he disentangled himself from her, and sat up.

"I'm going to go and pick up the food."

Kitty had forgotten she was hungry, but she supposed after the performance Jonny had just put in he deserved sustenance. "Okay." She pulled herself up on one elbow.

"I'll be ten minutes or so." He looked at her for a moment. She waited for him to lean down and kiss her, but he didn't. Instead, he got up and pulled his jeans and shirt back on before walking from the room. She heard the front door slam and tried to quell the uneasy sensation beginning to build as she got up and put her clothes back on to wait for him in the living room.

***

He returned toting a plastic bag, and she got both of his plates down spooning the contents of the different plastic containers onto them. There was an awkwardness between them now, and she could see him distancing himself from her in his body language. Her appetite dissipated as soon as she'd dished the meals up. She sat next to him, toying with her food, managing to nibble down a bit of naan as he wolfed down what was on his plate in silence.

"Do you not like it?"

"It's not that."

He raised an eyebrow waiting for her to elaborate.

"Are you regretting what we just did?"

He coughed – taken aback by her directness. "No, not regretting it. It was great. It's just that I don't want to take it any further."

Kitty felt as if she'd been punched.

"I don't want to get involved with you, Kitty, or with anyone for that matter. I am happy the way I am, on my own, and there isn't room in my life for another person. I'm sorry that's just the way it is."

She got up and tipped her meal in the bin. "Nice of you to

tell me beforehand and don't be sorry. I'll be fine." She stalked out of the room and shut the door on the bedroom before he could see her cry.

***

Kitty sat in the near-empty Starbucks thanks to the ungodly hour of the morning, huddled inside her jacket. She blew on her coffee and stared at the half-eaten scone on the plate in front of her. She hadn't felt like eating but knew she had to put something in her stomach or risk feeling nauseous, and she felt bad enough without that thrown into the mix. She'd slipped out of Jonny's apartment before the birds had begun to sing, unable to sleep and not wanting to be there when he got up. He had set up camp in the lounge, knocking once on the bedroom door later that night to ask if she was okay. When she hadn't answered him, he had opened the door a crack to check on her, but she'd pretended to be asleep. The pillow was wet beneath her cheek as he closed the door again. She wished she felt angry at his treatment of her. It would be easier to handle than this awful flatness at the knowledge that something that had felt so very right to her was over before it had even had a chance to begin.

Kitty thanked God for technology as she'd looked up the number for a local taxi company on her phone. She'd sat on the step of Jonny's building in the grey morning light with her wheelie-case at her feet, waiting for the operator to answer. Trundling it into the airport a short while later where a skeleton staff was on duty at the check-in desks, she was relieved to smell the freshly brewed coffee. At least she'd be able to get a couple of cups into her while she waited.

Taking another bite of the scone she saw the WH Smith's bookstore was opening. Good, she could go and buy a book to read. She'd need something to fill the next five hours. But she knew it wouldn't matter how good a tale it was because nothing would help her forget.

Chapter 30

You can't make a silk purse out of a sow's ear – Irish Proverb

Kitty unlocked the door to her flat nearly dead on her feet. It had been such a long day already, and it was only just after lunchtime. She'd dozed off briefly on the flight back to London but had been jolted awake by the Captain's cheery voice. It had boomed over the speakers as he told them to expect a little bit of turbulence due to a storm over the Irish Sea. Surprise, surprise, she'd thought, opening one weary eye. She'd had to fight the urge to fling her shoe up at the speaker before telling him to shut-up so that she could get a bit sleep.

The flat was blessedly empty with Yasmin and Paula both at work. She didn't feel like talking to anyone, not even Yasmin until she'd gotten a couple of hours sleep. Her plan was to have a hot shower and then she would climb between her familiar sheets and try to stop thinking about everything for a little while.

***

Her plan must have worked, she thought, as the slamming of the front door woke her up. One of the girls must be home from work. She sat up rubbing at her eyes before picking her phone up. She'd slept for three hours! It was after five, she realized, hearing a knock on her door.

"Kitty?"

"Yeah come in, Yas," she croaked.

Yasmin opened the door and flicked the light on. Kitty blinked against its brightness.

"Geez you look rough, but I'm glad you're home. I've had such a crappy day," she said entering the room, and flopping down at the end of the bed.

Kitty looked at her friend properly. "Actually, Yas, for someone who is all loved up with a potential new man I have to say you're not looking too darn hot yourself." She hadn't bothered to do her hair, and it hung limply from her head, her face was bare too with dark circles beneath her eyes. "Hey, are you okay?" Reaching out she took her hand. "Did something happen?" She frowned; you heard about things going badly wrong on first dates.

"No, yes, kind of." Seeing the look of panic on Kitty's face, she quickly added, "I am okay. He didn't hurt me or anything. Just my pride that's all."

Kitty pulled herself upright. "So what happened?"

"Well, I got all dressed up. I toned down the rockabilly look, and wore the black dress like you suggested because I had the feeling he was the kind of guy who would take me somewhere classy, you know?"

Kitty nodded. "I bet you looked great."

Yasmin gave her a wan smile. "We went to The Cantina. The food was gorgeous, it lived up to all its rave reviews, and he was good company too. We were having a right laugh. It turned out we both love Elvis, and neither of us can stand those cheesy impersonator shows. Oh, and his favourite chocolate bar is a

Mars too, or so he said. I thought it was going well. Honestly, Kitty, I thought I had hit the jackpot this time. It went pear-shaped after dinner when we moved onto the tequila shots. He put his hand on mine and asked me if I was keen to try something a bit different."

"Uh-oh, fifty shades different?"

"No, two plus one different. The woman I saw him dining with is his girlfriend, and they're into ménage á trois's. When I said that wasn't my thing he got quite nasty. He said that after the amount he'd spent on me with drinks and dinner, it was the least I could do."

"You're joking! So this guy goes out trying to groom women he fancies to take home to share with his girlfriend."

"I wish I were joking and yeah that's obviously how it works. Sick, I know." Her bottom lip trembled. "An asshole like that could only happen to me. It's in my DNA."

"Rubbish and I hope those are angry tears because the guy is not worth wasting your energy on. If it helps, my track record's not exactly outstanding either when it comes to the male species, you know. So what did you do then?"

A small smile played at the corners of Yas' mouth as she blinked the tears away. "I picked up the glass of water on the table and dunked it in his lap. I said that should help to cool the old boy down then I got my bag and tossed down some cash on the table. I told him that was my share of the meal because I like to pay my way. Oh and before I walked out, I said I would appreciate it if he didn't dine in Bruno's again. I told him if he did I would ask my cousin Mario, the maître d' who is in the Ashwin Street Mafia, to deal with him."

Kitty clapped her hands together. "Is there such a thing as the Ashwin Street Mafia?"

"I don't know, but Mario looks the part."

"Well good for you! Well done. He'll think twice before prop-ositioning anyone else like that."

"It's not so much the propositioning, it was the way he tried to make me feel cheap afterwards. He was a right nasty bugger."

"Yes, but you didn't let him succeed."

"No, I was shaking afterwards, but I was glad I said my piece."

"Well, I for one think you are fab. Give me a hug." Kitty held her arms out and wrapped them around her friend who leaned her head on her shoulder. "I guess I am going to have to meet a few toads before I find my Prince," Yasmin mumbled.

"You and me both. Now I suggest we go and open a bottle of wine. Let's get good and tipsy while I tell you all about how I slept with Jonny, and got short shrift afterwards. Kitty Sorenson once again meets a commitment-phobe."

Yas pulled out of the embrace and looked at Kitty with her eyes widened. "Right, my friend you've got some explaining to do. Best you throw some clothes on, and I'll crack open the vino." She got up and paused as she got to the doorway. "Have you told Mario you're back yet? He was muttering on about shifts tomorrow and asking me when you'll be back. He's been such a grump lately. Honestly, I don't know what's up with him."

"Sorry, I can't face it today. Actually, I don't think I can face it tomorrow either. I am going to be so busy getting everything ready for Saturday's stall."

Yasmin shot her a look. "You might be loaded, but you still need to let them know your plans and work your notice out."

"I know. I will, I promise. I'll phone him tomorrow and sort some shifts out, so he doesn't put them all on to you, okay? It's just my head is all over the place, and I don't know what I am going to do next."

Appeased, Yasmin left her to get dressed.

Kitty mooched out a few minutes later in her pyjamas and Ugg boots. Yasmin, as promised, had opened a bottle of wine and was throwing together whatever bits she could find in the fridge suitable for a platter. From what Kitty could see it didn't look very exciting. So far she had produced a jar of pimento stuffed olives, a block of cheddar and a packet of half eaten crackers that she had begun to arrange on a plate.

Catching her friend's frown Yasmin waved her over to the couch. "Go sit down. It is the best I can do on short notice. Besides eating is cheating when you are having a Bridget Jones girls' night in. This here food is just a token gesture." She put the meagre offerings down on the coffee table before heading back to the kitchen to pour two very generous glasses of the wine she'd opened.

Carrying them over, she sat down next to her friend and handed her a glass. "Right, come on then. spill. What happened? And from the start. please. I want the uncensored I am your BFF version."

Kitty took a large gulp of her drink before filling Yas in on everything that had transpired in Dublin.

Yasmin listened goggle-eyed on the couch sipping away on her wine. She put her glass down to reach over and hug her friend when she heard how well her meeting with Kit had gone. And how she planned to head back over to Ireland in a fortnight. Where she would finally sprinkle her mother's ashes in Tuam at the site her parents and brother were buried, with her aunt in tow.

"I am so happy that you finally have the answers you wanted. It's an amazing story. I could see it being made into a movie with uh, hmm let's see. Maybe Reese Witherspoon playing Rosa, and I am visualising an Orlando Bloom or maybe Jonny Depp type for Michael." She got up to refill their glasses, and then sat cross-legged opposite Kitty as she told her what had happened with Jonny when she got back to the apartment later that day.

"So it was good, then?"

"Unbelievable."

They both sat silently contemplating that until Kitty said, "But then he told me he wasn't interested in taking things any further."

"What, while you were lying there, post-shag?" Yasmin was outraged.

"No, he'd gotten dressed, and gone and gotten the takeaway by then. It was while he was scoffing a Tikka Masala."

"Oh, that would put you off Indian. It still sucks big time."

"I know," Kitty mumbled into the dregs of her glass.

"Right drink up, there is nothing else for it. With love lives or lack of them like ours, we have a God-given right to get utterly shitfaced while singing along to my 80s and 90s power ballads compilation. I need to scream my lungs out to Guns N' Roses' *November Rain*. It always helps when I have moved on from the depression stage of playing Elvis's *Love Me Tender* over and over, and headed into the 'I am so angry because everything has gone to shit phase'."

"Have you got REM's *Everybody Hurts*? That's my ultimate self-pity song."

"But of course."

Kitty held out her glass for a refill.

***

Paula walked in dragging Steve behind her who, Kitty thought from where she was doing some impressively high kicks on her couch stage with a rolling pin microphone in her hand, looked utterly exhausted. Oh well, served him right, she opened her mouth but realized they'd made her lose her place in the song. There was nothing else for it; she'd just have to improvise.

Paula stood hands on hips; nose curled up as she stared at the two apparitions that were her flatmates, and who had taken over the living room. She shook her head disgustedly as she observed Yasmin, unaware she had an audience. She was lying on the floor writhing as if in pain with an egg beater that she was currently singing into, and twirling round simultaneously. *Always* by Bon Jovi blared out loud enough to rattle the empty bottles of wine lined up on the coffee table.

Paula, realising neither girl was going to stop their one-woman show mid-song marched over and hit the power button on the

298

stereo. Yasmin sat up looking around to see what had happened. "Don't do that to lovely Jon when he's singing, Paula. That's sacrilege, and why are there two of you and two of him." She pointed past Paula to Steve.

"Yeah, sacrilege," Kitty added feeling she should say something.

Paula's lips pursed, and for someone both girls knew had nymphomaniac tendencies, she was managing to look quite prudish. "I don't know what you think you are doing. But I have to say it is sad to see women of your age carrying on like this isn't it, Steve?"

Steve looked like a rabbit caught in headlights as he nodded to appease his girlfriend. "I mean, come on you two, it is totally inconsiderate. How do you think Steve and I feel walking into this mess and noise?"

Yasmin snorted and took a swig of wine. She'd given up on the civility of pouring a glass and just glugged from the bottle. "Um, first off I wasn't aware Steve lived here. I thought we rented the room to you. And, Paula, you probably feel how I have felt for the last week listening to you two do the wild thing day and night," she slurred. Kitty bit her lip but was unable to stop a giggle from bubbling forth. She couldn't help herself, tense situations like this always made her start to laugh.

Paula turned a beetroot colour and turned on her heel. "Come on Steve, let's go to your place. We don't have to listen to their crap." Steve scurried after her.

Yasmin yelled after them, "Yeah, and we don't have to listen to you two shag. Oh and Steve, what's your secret? Come on what's the magic potion? Share the love!" Kitty and Yasmin collapsed in a heap of giggles on the floor as they heard the front door slam shut.

***

There was not much giggling the next day when Kitty awoke feeling as if her brain had shrunk to the size of a pea. She was certain that instead of lying prone in her bed, she must be sailing on especially stormy seas for all the lurching her stomach was doing. She ventured forth from her room around ten o'clock in search of water and pain relief. She found Yasmin curled up on the couch with a bowl to hand. Spying her partner in crime she groaned. "I reckon the cheese was off. It's food poisoning; it has to be."

"Aren't you supposed to be at college?" Kitty asked, wincing as a sharp pain zig-zagged its way across her forehead. She opened a cupboard in search of the first-aid kit. She knew she had thought about putting one together but wasn't sure whether it was one of those things she'd meant to do but hadn't gotten around to doing.

"Stop banging the cupboards, my head hurts. I'm too sick to go in today. I phoned Bruno's as well and left a message to say that I have food poisoning. I said I would be a liability."

Kitty's hand closed around a box of paracetamol. Thank goodness, she thought, opening it and popping a couple of tablets out before knocking them back with a glass of water. "Self-inflicted alcohol poisoning more like."

"Don't say that word."

"What word?"

"Alcohol. I never want to hear that word again."

Kitty mooched through to the lounge and sat down next to Yasmin. "Come on, give me some of that blanket." Curling up under it, she flicked the television on and settled back to watch Dr Phil before quickly changing the channel upon hearing him announce that today they were addressing the serious topic of alcohol abuse. "I wish I could phone the Minimarket on the corner and get them to deliver us an icy pole each."

"Oh yeah, lemonade flavoured!"

The two girls lay on the couch for the rest of the morning each intermittently dozing, and dreaming of lemonade ice blocks.

It was the knock on the door that stirred them into life as their puffy eyes met across the couch, silently asking each other. "Who on earth could that be?"

The knock sounded again. Yasmin was the first to rally herself, getting up off the couch, and tightening the belt of her dressing gown before staggering down the hall to open the door. Kitty got up too. She was hungry, which was a good sign, and she thought some toast might help settle her stomach. It was only when the toaster popped that she remembered Yasmin, and realized she'd been gone awhile. She could hear the murmur of voices down the hall and wondered if she had been cornered by some zealous member of a religious organization. She was debating poking her head round the kitchen door to see who it was her friend was talking to when she heard the door close. A moment later Yas reappeared clutching a big bouquet of red roses and looking decidedly perkier than she had done earlier.

"Oh wow! They're gorgeous. Who are they for?" Kitty asked before chomping into her toast.

"Me! Mario just delivered them and guess what?"

"What?" Kitty asked spitting toast crumbs everywhere.

"He asked me out."

"What, Mario? As in grumpy, ideas above his station Mario from Bruno's?"

"He's not grumpy, and he is the boss's cousin, so he's entitled to think big. It shows he is ambitious, and actually he's rather cute. We are going to go to the movies on his next day off."

"Go you!" Kitty smiled at her friend's abrupt change of heart where Bruno's maître d' was concerned.

"He apologised for being short with me lately. He said it was because he didn't like the look of Carlos but felt that it wasn't his place to say anything. Then he realized the reason he didn't like the look of him was because he was jealous."

"Oh, Yas, I'd say let's have a celebratory drink but—"

"Don't even go there!"

Chapter 31

Neither give cherries to a pig nor advice to a fool – Irish Proverb

Kitty shivered despite being wrapped up in her coat. The weather had cooled noticeably in the two weeks since she had last stood on Irish soil, and although the sky was ominously grey it didn't match her mood. She was standing in the churchyard in Tuam beside the graves of her family members. Kit was arranging flowers, sharing them out on the three graves marked with their Celtic Crosses while murmuring away softly to each of them. Paddy was pulling the odd weed that had sprouted around the mossy headstones.

At Kitty's feet was Rosa's urn. When her aunt and uncle were ready, they would do what they had come here to do. That was to scatter Rosa's ashes so that she could, as she had requested in her journal, fly free in Ireland once more.

So much had happened in those last two weeks too, Kitty thought, rubbing her hands together to warm them up. Once she had shaken off the hangover from hell, she had decided that life was too short to procrastinate or to wallow. Yes, she had cold feet when it came to taking that final step and signing on the dotted line for a premises in which to open her café, but she decided, that was only natural. It was a big step, and as Jonny had said to her, she was a big girl. It was time she moved forward with her life. She wanted to make her mother proud, and so pushing all thoughts of Jonny aside she had gotten busy. It had been just the ticket.

In between her shifts at Bruno's, and baking up a storm for her market stall she had been checking out possible sites for her café. So far the only one that was a contender was currently being used as a burger bar. It had potential, though. That's if you used a bit of forward vision when looking at the greasy walls, and managed to get past the smell of onions! She was going to go back for a second viewing next Saturday when she finished up at the market and was determined to make up her mind one way or the other then.

Kitty knew she would be sad to shut up shop on her market stall but who knew? Maybe her faithful regulars would come and see her in her café when she got it up and running. If she went with the burger bar location, though, it would mean a journey on the Underground, and that might be too much to expect from even the most loyal customer for the sake of a cupcake.

It had been so lovely to see the familiar faces on Saturday, and she had been pleased to hear that her little old Chocolate Dream lady's sister was doing much better. She was on a new medication, and it was helping her arthritis no end, she'd said. Kitty had put the two cakes in a box and told her that they were on the house.

She smiled to herself recalling too how the young Justin Bieber lookalike had appeared looking down in the mouth as he requested a Pink Lady cupcake. She'd raised an eyebrow asking. "What? No Vanilla Kisses today?" To which he'd shaken his head and said no, his girlfriend had broken up with him in the week. She'd handed him his box, and told him his cake was on the house too. She would have felt quite sad for him if she hadn't seen his eyes light up as a young girl swayed past in tight jeans and a puffa jacket. Ah, the fickleness of young love, she'd thought, watching him wander after the girl, tap her on the shoulder and hand her the box in which she had just put his free cupcake!

Perhaps the nicest thing that had happened over the fortnight was Paula announcing she was moving in with Steve. She had stated that they felt that they needed their space. No scratch that, she thought, the nicest thing was the way in which life seemed to be working out for Yasmin. She had been on four dates all in quick succession with Mario, which was a record for her. She was smitten, and it was lovely to see. Kitty was happy for her friend; she was. But being back in Ireland was a harsh reminder that the man she wanted more than she'd ever wanted any man, didn't want her. She wouldn't go there, though, not today because today was about Rosa.

Kit had picked her up at Dublin Airport earlier that morning as arranged. She'd enveloped her in a bosomy, perfumed hug before exclaiming how happy she was to see her again. The rest of the family couldn't wait to meet her too, she'd added. Kitty was to stay with them tonight in Wicklow, and where she'd sleep she had no idea. She was sure it was all in hand, though. She had brought a stack of family photo albums with her as she'd promised Kit she would. They would pore over them together later. Her aunt had kept up a fast pace of chatter for the two and a half hours it had taken them to drive down to Tuam, and Kitty had sat back in her seat soaking it all up. She loved the feeling of being part of Kit's family with all their trivial dramas, and although she had yet to meet them in the flesh, she already felt she knew them all.

To her surprise, Kit had arranged for them to meet Paddy in the warmth of the pub. It was the same pub where she had sat with him and Rosa all those years ago while their parents had mourned Joe. Her brother was living, she informed Kitty parking the car out the front of the pub, not far away in a camp on the outskirts of Galway. It had been awhile since brother and sister had caught up she stated, and this today was timely, and it was proper.

Paddy had been nursing a pint when Kitty walked into the quaint room behind his little sister. Its beamed ceiling was low, and its walls were soaked with beer and memories. She'd have known him even without Kit tottering straight over to his table in a pair of heels that made hers look positively sensible by comparison. Now she knew where she got her penchant for high-heeled shoes from! Kitty listened as his sister told him off for being on the ale this time of day before embracing him. He looked, Kitty thought, just like Kit but without the fake tan and bling. Instead, he had stubble and a pot belly not to mention two missing front teeth – a legacy from his fight with Martin Donohue all those years ago, she realized. When he spied Kitty hanging back shyly, his ruddy features had paled, and he'd blinked a couple of times before looking down at his pint as though that were responsible for her standing there.

Kit rested her hand on his heavily tattooed forearm. "It's alright, Paddy. This is our Rosa's Kitty."

"Aye, I can see that now. Sit down, lass. I've waited a long time to meet you, so I have."

They'd shared a drink together in the pub, and Kitty had listened to the stories Paddy told them. They were stories about when they were younger, happy times together when Joe and Rosa were still with them both.

"You're just like her, you know?" Paddy said fixing his blood-shot eyes on her.

Kitty smiled. "Yes."

"I miss them all, you know?"

"I can see that, Paddy."

Kit had got up then and pulled her top down. It had managed to inch its way halfway up her midriff. She'd shrugged back into her faux fur jacket with a brusque, "right we're not here to get all maudlin. That's not what our Rosa would have wanted. Come on, Paddy, up and at it. Let's go and do what we came here to do."

They'd linked arms, the three of them. As they made the short walk down a well-worn path to the churchyard, Kitty had known in that way she sometimes did, that no matter what the future held for her these two people would be in her life from now on. They weren't perfect but then neither was she, and that was what being part of a family was all about. You didn't get to pick them, they just were, and the mistakes of the past would not be revisited in the future. They would be there for her, and she would always be a part of this big rambunctious family her mother had always loved so dearly. She smiled at her unwitting usage of the word her mother had so loved to drop.

Kit had pushed open the rusty churchyard gate, and it squeaked its protest at letting them into the small cemetery. The graves were laid out behind the old stone building, and she led them over to where Kathleen, Bernie and Joe had all been laid to rest.

Kitty had crouched down, and run her fingers over the inscriptions of the names of her family members. She would never meet them but thanks to the legacy her mother had left her by writing her journal, she felt she had known them. Through Rosa's written words bringing her story to life, it was as if Kathleen, Bernie and Joe had been a part of Kitty's life too. It was a wonderful gift to have been left.

She felt Paddy's strong arm encircle her shoulders. "They would have loved you, so they would." She'd blinked back tears as she heard him mutter. "I'll try to do better, Mammy, for you, Joe, Rosa and Da. I promise."

Kit stood up then, and spying Kitty huddled in her coat lost in her memories startled her back to the present. "It's time to send Rosa on her way, my girl, before we all fecking freeze to death ourselves, and join her."

"I think Mum would like it if we all did it together," Kitty said picking up the urn. She removed its seal as her uncle and aunt came to stand on either side of her. The three of them wrapped their hands around it, and on the count of three shook it hard.

They stood huddled together; Rosa was floating free back in Ireland just as she had wanted to.

"Bye, Mum. I love you," Kitty said letting herself cry then. She felt the comforting solidity of her family standing on either side of her as they murmured their final goodbyes to a sister they'd both lost a long time ago.

"Come on then; it's time we got ourselves back to the pub to warm up," Kit said after a bit, brooking no protest from Paddy. Kitty too would be glad to go and sit by the roaring fire.

It was as they made to leave the cemetery that Kitty was aware of a clip-clop sound echoing on the breeze. It sounded like a horse, she thought, but surely not in a residential street like this? She turned to look and found herself wiping her eyes with a soggy tissue not quite believing what it was she was seeing. There, leading a beautiful brown and white Piebald horse who was pulling a barrel top wagon behind him, down the middle of the deserted village street, was Jonny.

Her gaze swung first to Kit and then to Paddy to make sure it wasn't just her having some sort of mad hallucination. They were both smiling, though, and didn't look in the least bit surprised. Kit squeezed her arm. "Mark my words lovely girl, yours and Jonny's story is going to have a happy ending. It's what Rosa would have wanted."

"Aye," Paddy muttered gruffly. "It's time to let bygones be bygones."

Kitty was rooted to the spot unable to move, and she felt Paddy push her gently in the small of her back. "Go on with you lass, and hear the lad out. Kit and I will wait for you back in the pub."

She did as she was told, and opened the gate, walking up the cobbled street to where Jonny had stopped to wait for her. Her legs felt unsteady and were moving on automatic pilot as they carried her toward him. She was unsure of the greeting she would get, or what it meant, him turning up here like this with a horse and a wagon. Oh, and he looked so achingly handsome in his white shirt and black jeans, she thought, as at last, she reached him. "Jonny, what are you doing here?"

"Hello, Kitty, this here is Toby," he said ignoring her question as he gestured to the horse.

"Er, hello, Toby." She dragged her eyes away and began to pat the docile old horse glad of something else to focus her attention on rather than him, and whatever it was he had come here to say to her.

"I, er— I rang your aunt a few days after you left, and told her I had been a fool for letting you go off the way I did. She agreed with me. She doesn't mince her words, your Auntie Kit."

Kitty raised a smile at that, but she couldn't meet his gaze.

"She told me you were coming back to sprinkle your mammy's ashes with her and Paddy. So I had to come here today. Ah, Kitty, I knew the moment I saw you in Uzés I wanted you in my life. I've fallen in love with you. I mean, how could I not? You bake the best fecking vanilla cupcakes I've ever eaten."

Kitty looked up at him, and she melted into those dark eyes of his. She wanted nothing more than to feel his mouth on top of hers again. Toby had other ideas, though, snorting through his nostrils. As Jonny stroked his neck and murmured to him, he caught her quizzical gaze.

"You deserve to have those romantic ideas of yours made a reality and—" he gestured to the wagon, "I wondered how you might feel about me converting this wagon here into a mobile cupcake café? There's big business to be had in going around the fairs and the festivals, so I've heard, and I could have it fitted out in time for Ballinasloe this year." His expression was hopeful as Kitty looked from him to the wagon before wandering around it. Peering into the back, she pictured a counter with a hissing coffee machine on it. Next to it was a colourful display cabinet filled with her cakes, Pink Lady's, Chocolate Dreams, Vanilla Kisses and whatever other flavours she conjured up. On the wall behind the counter, there would be two framed black and white prints of *Midsummer Lovers*. One featuring Rosa and Michael, and the one she had yet to see of her and Jonny.

She twisted the wedding band Michael had given her mother on her finger, and an image of a little girl appeared in her mind's eye. She looked a lot like her, but her hair was dark and curly. She was playing dress-ups in her gran's auld wedding dress. It was Rosa's dress, Kitty realized. She blinked, and the little girl disappeared as Jonny came round to join her.

"Rosa and Michael weren't responsible for the choices my Da made. He was his own man, and I don't want to be bitter like him. The past wasn't our making, and it isn't our future either. We need to build our own, and it could be wonderful you know."

Her eyes glistened, and he held his arms open. Stepping into his embrace, she raised her head so her lips could meet his. As his mouth closed over hers, she knew in that certain way she just knew things from time to time, that things were indeed going to be wonderful.

Acknowledgements

I'd like to thank Alen MacWeeney and his beautiful book *Tinker's No More* for providing such a visual insight into the 1960's world of the Irish Traveller. His referral of Mervyn Ennis meant I was privileged to read his delightful memoir, *Once Upon a Time in Tallaght* which inspired some of the stories told in this book. I'd also like to thank my agent Vicki Marsdon of Wordlink literary agency for her invaluable editing pointers that shaped this story into a book I am proud of. The wonderful Irish proverbs I've have included throughout this book were sourced from Mark's Quotes.com. Thanks too, to the fabulous team at HarperImpulse for making my dream a reality. Lastly to my family and friends and of course lovely Paul and our boys, Josh and Daniel, my writing wouldn't happen without your ongoing support. Love you guys.